ROAR OF THE WEST

ROBERT H. LANGE

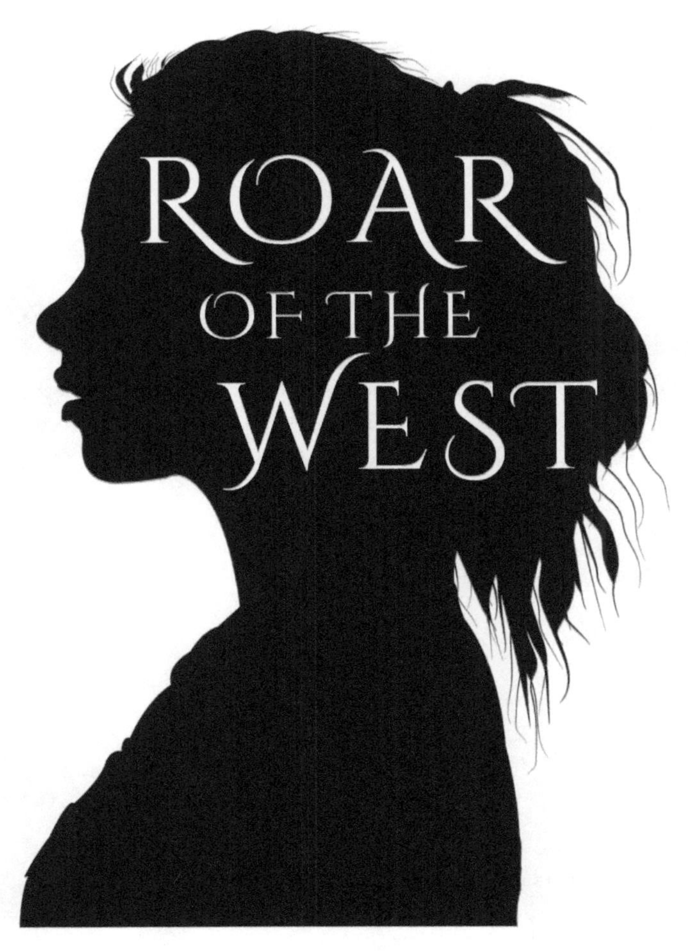

ROAR OF THE WEST

This book is a work of fiction. Names, characters, places, and incidents are the product of the author's imagination or are used fictitiously. Any resemblance to actual events, locales, or persons, living or dead, is coincidental.

Cover Design | Rose & Lavender Press, LLC

Formatting | Rose & Lavender Press, LLC

Map | @mnash884 (Fiverr)

Editing | Hannah @ Double Check Editing

Thank you for your support of the author's rights.

Printed in the United States of America

To Nina

Without whose strength, I would not have arrived

N
W
E
S
Vaalan Gut
Bowl of Mirrors
MAHNBUSA
Maasin Luut
Hand of Mahnbusa
Dragoncrest Mountains
Collis
Rivead
Lake Still
Avorren
REGINAAN
ALDE-BRAAN
Blackcrest
Silent Coast
Nelbren
Elaan
River Auor
The Seawastes
Darhaba
HEMOR
Brightwater
Shallow Sea
World Tree
Blunha Isles
Sternan Ocean
DEYDALUS
Forhault
Echar
ARKYA

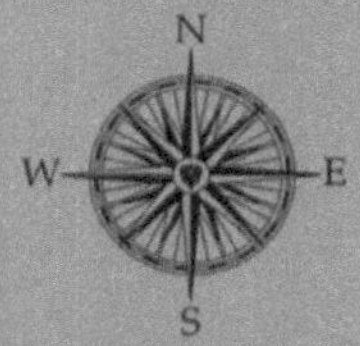

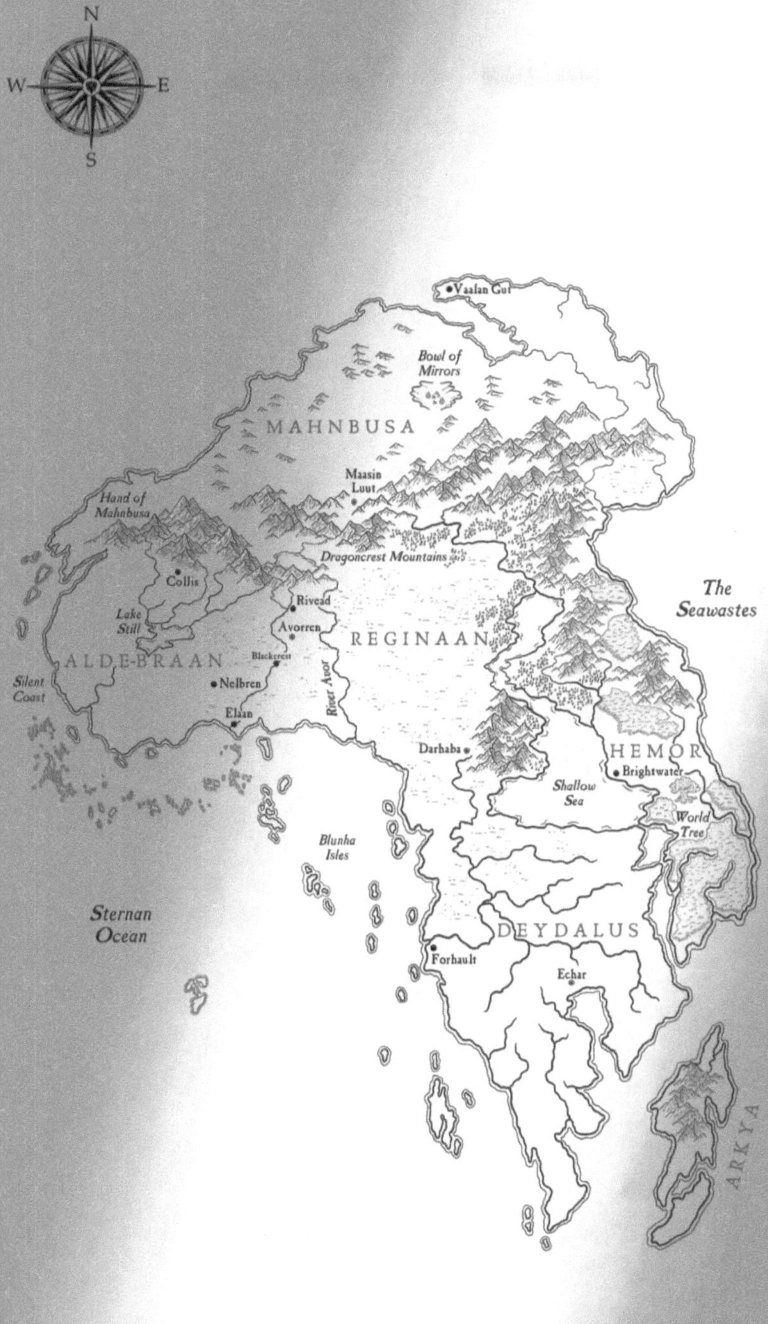

IREA

Chapter One

The newcomers arrived in the middle of the night and cut the darkness like a knife. No one knew why they came, except to entertain, but nobody came all the way into the Blackness without a very good reason, and anything less than necessity could hardly be called a good reason.

The roads were long, often overgrown with moss and water, and of course, if one didn't know the stars, they would be lost without the guidance of the sun. So when travelers came as far as Nelbren with no real intention, setting up their camp with lamps and posts that shone like a beacon, even the bugs took notice.

Linara almost thought it to be a dream, a remnant of deep sleep crossing her eyes on their morning walk into the village. But the bright light that broke through the shadows, of tent cloth and stakes painted with vibrant luma paste was very real. Poles made of actual wood, and canvas of enormous swaths of fabric. It must have cost a fortune.

Linara had only heard stories of traveling troupers—performers and poets who graced the land with such fantastical events. She had been just a child when they came through Nelbren last, too young to remember anything but a few flashes of sights and sounds.

She forced herself to stay calm, keeping her feet from rushing off toward the camp herself. The moon hadn't quite risen for the morning yet, but stars bloomed upon the sky like a canvas of light. She spotted her star sign, Elthraal the Dragonmother, breaching the horizon. Fordring, her father's sign, the mark of his birth, lay just above them, at the peak of its rise.

Another day and it would be at its apex. Her father's birthday would be tomorrow, and what better way to celebrate than the trouper's performance? Her usual plans were getting stale now. Year after year, the same bland cake, barely paid for, and an extra egg for breakfast.

No, this year would be different. This year would be defined by the troupers' arrival, a boring existence separated by some new glorious memories. Sure, they would be going for *his* birthday, but that didn't change the fact that Linara's life would surely be different after it.

"Don't lag too far behind," her father called back. He hadn't even slowed when he saw the trouper tents. He was tense, though. He must've known they arrived during the night, but he made no mention of it. Strangers had him nervous at all times of the year. Even when the peddlers arrived.

It would take some doing to convince him, but that would have to wait. The answer was surely no if she didn't finish her chores for the morning. It would give her some time to think of the proper angle, anyhow.

"I'm heading to the grove; I'll meet you at Mr. Pen's?" Linara said, breaking off from the dirt path into the mossy countryside. She usually procrastinated far more on a normal day, so she hoped she wasn't *too* suspicious. Her father frowned at her in response, but otherwise gave his approval.

Linara kept her pace to a brisk walk. Running would certainly catch his eye, and as it was, her eyes could barely keep up with the hunting mosskimmers, gliding across the moss. Stepping on them wouldn't be ideal for either involved.

In the Blackness, they needed all the light they could get, without the sun to guide their way. Close to the paths, tiny pinpricks of wild luma dotted the edges, lighting the road enough to see by. The spores of the fungus were a remarkably sticky thing, and the mushrooms sprouted wherever people walked. Out in the hills and wilderness, this was not the case.

Even a few dozen steps out, the darkness was thick enough she could hardly see her destination. The distant glow from Fairgrave farm was enough of a marker, but if she didn't spot the silhouette of gangly trees on the hillock, she'd get lost in no time.

Thankfully the stars were bright enough that morning that she spotted the grove a few moments later as she crested the top of the hill and walked into a small cluster of trees, barely taller than her, but twice as wide. Their stretchy limbs twisted out and around each other in knots. Linara breathed in the sweetness of the air. A pleasant smell, if one didn't know just how toxic the sap could be.

Linara fished out an old strand of dried tanglegum from her pocket and pulled her long, dark hair away from her eyes. She pulled the knife from her belt and balanced it in her hand as she studied the mess of branches.

She reached for the thickest branch, sap squishing out between her fingers. She wrestled the limb down and cut it clean at the base. Avoiding her clothing, she tossed the branch onto the moss, moving on to the next.

What sort of performance would the troupers be putting on? Fire-breathers maybe? But there wasn't much to burn in the Blackness. Plays and storytelling was apparently a staple, though. Mr. Trel could tell a good story, but surely it would be even greater in costume.

Linara had heard all of Mr. Trel's stories twelve times over by now, but hopefully she would hear something new. Of oceans and deserts, all lit by a sun she'd never see. To live in the Blackness was to work the land, and there were no breaks given. A boring life, but one that could be made bearable by the troupers.

Once the pile of tanglegum grew large enough, Linara knelt upon the moss and steamed the branches over a naturally occurring vent in the ground.

No one else could work the sap in the same way. The steam vents were way too hot for most people. For whatever reason, heat never seemed to bother Linara, however. Fire passed straight through her, leaving no scar or burn, while others would cry in pain. When the village would walk in thick coats through the cold mist, Linara could walk with a simple shirt, barely noticing the fall of rain. And most importantly of all, she could use the steam vents when others could not.

All she could feel from any source of heat was a faint tingle within her birthmark, a splotch of red that webbed out across her shoulder. A mark she'd never shown to anybody, except her father. A mark he had told her never to tell a soul about. It was why she wore coats into the mist, and why she pretended to cry out in pain if she got a little too close to a steam vent when others were nearby.

The branches over the vent dripped sap, sizzling upon the hot stones beneath. Linara pulled them away and slicked the sap into a small pile, forming a folding lump of sweet syrup. It was almost a tradition among the children to eat it. It tasted delicious enough, but it always left you heaving up your last meal.

In a matter of minutes, one bundle of branches was free of sap. Without the steam vents, Linara would be up on the hill for hours, scraping the sap with bits of stone. She reached over for another bundle, but her eyes caught on a rustle in the moss.

A small umbrin, barely the size of her palm, scurried from underneath the thick moss and sniffed at her legs, front paws batting at her trousers. Linara lowered her hand, allowing the tiny creature to scamper up her arm and onto her shoulder as she continued to work.

Its leathery hide felt smooth, but still damp from the morning dew. Most hated the pests, but Linara always enjoyed their company. They ate the bugs in their mound, and those were much worse.

The curious umbrin skittered around her shoulders and up into her hair as she held the next set of branches over the steam vent. She let the umbrin do as it pleased for the time being, her hands too covered in sap to stop him. It didn't take long for the little creature to settle itself. Perched upon her shoulder, it simply watched.

Once she finished the last of the branches, Linara stuck her hands into the steam vent, letting the sap drip and ooze from her fingers before she wiped them clean upon the moss beside her. That was another benefit of her secret mark, an easy cleanup.

Linara plucked the umbrin from her shoulder and inspected it in the light of the rising moon. A small pattern of stripes ran across its back. Even held firmly in her hands, it still tried to scramble around her palm, looking for new things to explore. Linara placed it back on her shoulder, and it scampered across from one side to the other, even as she bent to pick up the cords of tanglegum branches.

"You're certainly a skittering fellow," Linara said. "All creatures deserve a name. Maybe Skitter?" The umbrin darted down and explored the knots of tanglegum before sticking its head out and staring at her with tiny black eyes. "Skitter it is, then."

The downhill slope made the journey half as long and just as easy. By the time Linara crossed the first line of mounds into Nelbren, the moon had finished its rise, casting a pale light across the Blackness.

On the other side of the village, she could see another tent rising in the trouper camp, shadows of people busy at work. Linara was no closer to a plan on how to convince her father to even go. She could appeal to his primal curiosity, that inner sense within everyone to explore and expand their horizons. Except, the more Linara thought about it, the more she wondered if he possessed any of that. She must have inherited that from her mother . . .

Two rings of mounds lay around the center of the village—houses, shops and barns. Most of the village lived in the expanse beyond, in the midst of farmland or the like. Only a handful had the luxury of living so close.

"Ho, Miss Farrow," Mr. Trel called out, wedging a lump of wet clay upon a table just outside the door to his mound. A single luma lantern barely provided enough light to see by, and smudges of dried clay were already smeared across his wrinkled scalp. He paused to clap his hands across his arms in greeting.

"Ho, Mr. Trel," Linara said, awkwardly adjusting the tanglegum branches around to clap her arms in return.

"How are those new planters holding up?" he asked.

"Well enough, I think," Linara said. "You know my father. He always prefers his old stuff, even if they break." She hefted the bundle up. "I brought the last of the tanglegum."

"Oh my, has it been a week already?" he asked, looking up at the stars. He whistled softly between his teeth and shook his head. "Time just tumbles from my old bones these days."

"It can't be *that* bad," Linara said, shifting as Skitter ran down her arm to catch a better look at the old potter.

"You're only, what, nineteen? Tell me that again when you're my age." Mr. Trel adjusted his eyeglasses to catch a better view of Linara's hand. "Ahh, a little umbrin? A second gift for Frennik, or another addition for your barn?"

"You know my father, he won't even *eat* an umbrin if he had a chance," she said, watching Skitter balance upon her hand as she turned it over and over in an endless rhythm. "Skitter seems pretty attached. I don't think he'll be content just catching spiders and fogbiters, either."

Trel reached into his pocket for a small scrap of dried jerky. He held it out to Skitter with old shaking hands. The little umbrin scurried down and took it hesitantly before crawling back into Linara's hair to eat it.

Trel laughed and wiped his fingers upon the rag at his belt. "Perhaps not a simple barn umbrin, then. But will your father allow such a thing inside your home?"

Linara shrugged. "It's his birthday, there's no better time to ask for a favor."

"Nothing truer," Mr. Trel said, disappearing through the curtain of his mound. He returned a moment later with a long, cloth-wrapped bundle. "Though Frennik does hate all things new and different."

Linara grimaced. "The troupers' arrival is already a shock. I was hoping we would go to their performance."

"Well, your father is also pragmatic. He knows the value of a scarce event."

"Do you know why they're here?" she asked, taking the package from him. It was deceptively heavy in her arms.

"I've heard rumors of trouble on the roads. According to Vahn, they wanted to avoid some of the major routes on the way to Avorren."

"What sort of trouble?" Linara asked absently, lifting the edge of the cloth, revealing a sharpened axe-head, bound neatly by thin strands of dried tanglegum. Despite Mr. Trel being a potter, he knew how to work tanglegum better than anyone in the village.

He scowled, "Their lips are locked tight. I only hear whispers of wars and dragons."

Linara brightened. "Dragons?"

"The real travesty here is that these newcomers arrive with such suddenness to cause the biggest stir in this tiny village in a decade, and have not the decency to even talk about why!"

Linara rolled her eyes. "I'm sure they'll agree that their silence on the matter is far worse than the dragons on the road."

Trel waved a dismissive hand and lowered himself back into his chair. "There's always something travelers complain about. I doubt any of it is true, anyway."

That *was* a curious thing. If anybody knew the true purpose of the troupers here, Mr. Trel would know about it. Maybe they *were* just here to perform for a night. It wasn't completely out of the question.

Still, it wasn't a complete loss asking about it—any travelers' complaints made for a good story. It wasn't often that news reached their doorsteps, good or bad.

"Whenever you do find out, you know where to find me," Linara said, fishing Skitter from her hair as she moved off, further into the village.

Linara found her father wrapping up with Mr. Pen. He held a basket of seed loaves under one arm, talking through the doorway at the baker still kneading a pile of dough at the counter inside. He was probably convincing Mr. Pen to forget about the cake for tomorrow. Linara would have to swing by later to let him know otherwise.

Her father let the curtain drift closed, his eyes finding Skitter imme-diately. "You found another one."

"His name is Skitter," Linara said, letting the umbrin run along her arm to sniff at her father's beard.

"He'll go unnamed, within the barn."

"I expected nothing more," Linara lied. It wouldn't be worth the trouble arguing about it now. She had a bigger issue to push anyway, and that was far more pressing.

"You have the axe?" her father asked, swapping the basket of loaves for the cloth bundle. He unwrapped the end and flicked his finger along the edge, nodding with satisfaction. "He works fast. Just in time for the harvest."

"You're harvesting on your birthday?"

He started off back toward the house. Coincidentally, also toward the trouper tents. "I always harvest on my birthday. It's the best day of the month."

"Yeah, yeah, the culmination of all your effort, the results, the fruit of your labor. But what if we could do something better for once?"

"You want to see the troupers," he said without missing a beat.

Linara sniffed. So she *was* being far too suspicious. Well, having no plan always worked for her in the past.

"No," Linara said, steeling herself, "*You* want to see the troupers. To reward yourself for a job well done."

Her father laughed. "Is that right? For surviving another year without serious injury? What I'm going to do is reward myself with another harvest."

"But there's a dozen harvests a year. The troupers come once in a lifetime!"

"You're what, nineteen? And they've come twice?"

"You know what I mean. And I know that tomorrow is important, and delaying a harvest is a tough sell, but I think it's worth doing."

"The performance is tonight. They're leaving in the morning."

"Even better!" Linara said, "It's like you're arguing for me."

He grunted. "They're charging an arm and a leg for admission."

"Sell some luma to them. You've seen how much they use on those fancy designs upon the tent flaps—they'll run out before they reach Avorren."

Her father grunted but kept moving. "I won't encroach on another farmer's business. They have a supplier somewhere, a bigger fish than I."

"Oh, come on, do you see a cart big enough to carry all the luma they'd need for a whole tour? The paste is already fading around the edges. They surely rely on the locals."

He paused at that, looking back at the tents with curiosity. "If I know Polt, he already tried. They probably even took the deal."

"Once they see *your* luma, they'll change their minds about any deal they made."

He turned and frowned at her. "Honorable men honor their deals, Linara."

"Since when do you expect anyone else to be honorable men?"

He was silent for a moment before exhaling a long breath into the sky. "I shouldn't have taught you so well."

Linara had to contain her excitement. If there was anything she was good at, it was wearing him down. "So we're going?"

"I haven't decided yet," he said. Then he glanced over and studied her. "Why do you want to go so badly? If you want some excitement in your life, a single performance every decade or so isn't going to be sustainable, you know. You see it once, you've seen them all. You'll see that the buildup is all for show."

"But I haven't seen it once. I have only a few memories, and even then, it's mostly just Mother I remember. And I remember she loved it, and if she were here, she'd want to see it again."

Her father fell silent, staring at his boots while they walked. Linara cursed to herself. It was a mistake bringing her up. It only brought bouts of melancholy.

Then he actually smiled. He shook his head and stared up at the stars. "You're right. She would've."

Linara released her own breath, keeping it as silent as possible. "Then let's go. If not for you, and if not for me, then for her."

He sighed and looked over at her. "Alright, fine. I'll harvest a few bundles today, and we'll head over in the evening."

Linara hung back to silently celebrate. "And if you don't want Skitter in the house, he can come to the show!"

"I've already agreed, don't push your luck."

Frennik Farrow stared out at a darkened field. He had sent Linara ahead to the house, wishing to be alone. How long had he been standing now? What was probably only minutes felt like an hour.

Within the wetlands, most of the ground was too fertile to be devoid of life, but not this particular field. Blighted. Tainted with the touch of feld fungus, and left to rot. It thrived when his wife's brother purchased the deed. It thrived until he died.

That was what . . . ten years ago? Frennik tried not to think of it, but life was dredging up painful memories. Jenora often lingered in his thoughts, but now she hovered like a ghost, haunting his steps. Linara was right, she did always love the troupers. Would she still, if she knew what they did, now that she was dead?

Feld fungus was a wicked thing, but Beorn did not decide to grow it on his own. He was stupid, but not that stupid. Who placed the idea within his head? To taint the field for generations, for a spike of profit? Questions like those kept Frennik up at night.

All he knew was tainted ideas like that seldom came from within. Nelbren was a small village, self-sufficient. That sort of darkness spread from afar, on the backs of wagons and travelers disguised as friends.

CHAPTER TWO

All traveling troupers lived and performed out of their carts. They were entirely wooden, completely enclosed, and were often painted with designs to set them uniquely apart from one another, or so Linara had been told

The troupers in Nelbren, however, followed a theme throughout. Dark greens and blues were the palette of choice, the tops of their carts built with curving additions that made the caravan look like the back of a great serpent. Or, in Linara's mind, a dragon.

Lanterns and banners hung from strands strung above them, illuminating the pathways between the seats. Tents formed a ring around the stage, a flat section of wood made up from the detached walls of a few carts.

Linara and her father arrived early, finding their seats before many of the others. The seats, of course, were nothing more than small crates they used for shipping. Even then, some of the villagers elected to sit on the ground. Linara tried to peek inside, but her father stopped her short. They were probably just full of food supplies anyway, but a few smelled strangely bitter.

Soft music played in the distance, carried over by the wind from behind the stage. Most of the chatter was confined to outside the camp. Nearly the whole village had turned up.

Linara's stomach growled as the smell of cinnamon swirled throughout the camp. Not a few people were walking by with bags of spiced nuts from the vendors. Her father shot down the idea of getting any before they even got to the camp. She knew how much they would upcharge for something so simple, but it didn't matter to her. The luma he harvested paid for tickets, and very little more, so she didn't protest too strongly.

But the smell then reached a little farther, and Skitter scampered out of her sleeve. Linara barely caught him before he could get far, flinging her hand out awkwardly to curl Skitter into her palm. She glanced up at her father, who eyed her suspiciously. She tried to ignore him, running her hand through her hair and letting Skitter bury himself inside.

"Linara?" he said calmly. Her head twitched as Skitter rustled around. The smuggling operation had been going so well, too. "I hope that's not the same mouse scrambling on your scalp that I specifically told you *not* to bring with you."

"What if I told you it's a different umbrin?" Linara asked.

"Do you really think that argument would benefit you more than the alternative?"

Linara grimaced. "It's . . . the same umbrin."

Her father scowled, his mouth opened to respond when a voice called out from ahead of them.

"Ah, Mr. Farrow, you made it after all." Mayor Vahn stood just ahead of them, acknowledging them with voice only. His eyes swept over the banners, the carts, and everything else around them.

The two young men at this side, near Linara's age but not quite, were almost mirror images. Jon and Fenton, all uncalloused fingers and builds that screamed wealth without the efforts of working for it.

"I expected you to ignore such festivities in favor of a quiet evening at home," the mayor said with a bare smile.

Linara heard her father release a long breath, silent enough for only her to hear. Then he plastered on his best smile. "Hello, Vahn," he said, "I trust we have you to thank for this event?"

"I believe the nature of our village and its appeal to travelers has left a fine opportunity for these guests to stay for a length of time beneficial to the both of us," the mayor said.

Which was a fine way of saying, *"I have no idea why they're here, but I will continue to say it was my doing as long as it suits me."* Jon and Fenton smiled at his words, as if they were impressed. They noticed Linara's scowl, and glared at her.

"I hope, then, this new opportunity finds you well," her father said, flatly.

Vahn offered little more than a nod in thanks before ushering his boys toward their seats, right before the stage.

"I don't know how you can act so friendly around them," Linara grumbled. "Their air of superiority. Did you see the way Jon was staring at me?"

"It is easier to force amicability than the alternative. You would be surprised by how much inconvenience they can create for us if we make enemies out of them."

"It's not like we ever start it," Linara said.

"It doesn't matter who starts it. Vahn is the mayor and has the authority. Regardless of how small that may be."

The luma lanterns above them dimmed, dropping the stage to shadow. At least the show was starting before Linara's mood soured too much. A hush fell over the camp, soft whispers still hanging in the air as the rest of the crowd found their seats. Even Skitter poked his head out of her hair, now that he was comfortable.

Then at once, silence fell like a stone as a man stepped out onto the stage. A long cape trailed behind him, hanging from wide shoulders and thick leather armor. His head was bald, skin the color of caramel with a long, pale scar running from eye to chin.

His voice projected clear and strong, carrying the authority and weight of a mountain. "Welcome, yonder folk, to the opportunity to forget your present woes, to be transported to a land that is not your own. A land where light shines brighter than any lantern, higher than any star. A place none often leave, and yet the ones who visit rarely stay."

He, of course, was talking about the Illumination, where the sun shone every hour of the day, and blinded the eyes of any who saw it. At least, according to what most of the villagers said. Most of the peddlers, and the troupers themselves, came from out east, and seemed fine enough.

"Even further, we will visit a land lost to time, a place so deep in history, records do not stretch. A place where only art remains. Where shadows stalked, and the dead walked."

In sequence, patterns of colored light appeared upon the crowd, and on the face of the performer. Everyone around her seemed enamored by the show, but Linara frowned. She could see the short spindly silhouettes clinging to the posts, removing the caps of the lanterns in rhythm.

"Oh yonder do thou shadows grow, onward toward the fleeting dawn. Ever present is thy coldest cut, the greatest of thy blanket embrace. For death cometh to us all, but some sooner than thy neighbors.

"Eidgar the Deceiver laid wicked plans among wicked men, and so carved history in his favor. Until the truth rang among the folds of song and story, unveiling a horror too great, and a power too evil."

Linara yawned and let her head fall into her hand. Everyone had heard the stories of the Seven Odious, but she was never very fond of them.

Most of the other village children requested their stories often from Mr. Trel, but she usually found herself tuning out. There was only so many times she wanted to hear of evil magic killing a great multitude of people.

The man on stage finished his monologue and departed the stage. A flurry of others took his place, and the audience clapped lightly. They each wore costumes of their own. One wore a dress of dull purple, one with a crown, and another in servants' robes.

The Deceiver wasn't a popular story, but Linara still knew it well enough. The performer in the crown was a great king or emperor, something of the like. The servant was an assassin, who infiltrated the palace staff to get close to the emperor.

Once he found his chance, his Odious powers created a dome of darkness so thick no light could penetrate. Within its grasp, he killed the king, and fled into the wilderness. The dome stayed behind, growing until it engulfed the entire city. Once it vanished, everyone within was dead.

A story to scare young children, nothing more. And yet, it still created a strange dread within her. A primal discomfort she didn't often feel, and hardly understood.

The play was longer than it should have been, but ended with great applause. The performers bowed, and a juggler replaced them. Linara glanced up at her father, who looked all too sarcastic with his smile.

The juggler started with a collection of stones, moving to sticks, and then a set of knives. Probably dulled. It was all remarkably average. There was more excitement from the village's year-end festivals than this. And those were free.

Even Skitter was growing impatient. He had started nestling further into her hair, stamping down and readjusting every few minutes. It really made concentrating on an already boring performance that much more difficult.

Then the wind shifted, and Skitter stiffened at the smell of bitterness on the air. Before she could stop him, Skitter leapt from her hair, hitting the moss with a soft thump and scurrying under feet toward the edge of the stage. Only a few people noticed, and made their discomfort clear.

Linara followed, sliding through crates and legs to chase the small umbrin toward the stage. The juggler ignited a set of flaming torches, and Linara saw Skitter scamper under the fabric of a tent near the stage. She followed after, the audience too focused on the show to notice.

Linara froze just inside. The scarred man from earlier stood in the center, still in his thick leather armor, long cape pooling on the moss behind him. Jon and Fenton, the mayor's sons, stood before him, staring with shock and anger.

The tent smelled bitter and acrid, pulling on faint thoughts and memories buried deep within her mind. In Fenton's hands was a leather pouch, partly open, revealing a collection of glass vials. Jon held one now, full of a bright red powder.

Feld powder. Memories of blood red fire, and her uncle's mad, fearless howling flooded her mind. The source of death that killed her mother.

Linara was ripped from her shock, feeling the anger rise like pools of sludge. A heat formed in her shoulder, from the birthmark beneath her shirt. Why was Jon holding such a thing? What had these two fools gotten involved in?

Skitter scampered up beside the scarred man's boots, sniffing at the specks of red powder that stained the leather. The man flinched back when he noticed. Then, with one massive boot, he stomped on Skitter with a sickening crunch.

Linara gasped, and Jon broke out of his own daze. He took a step toward her. "Farrow," he growled, "what are you doing here?"

The scarred man inspected the bottom of his boot, smeared with blood. "Fucking mice . . ." he muttered, scraping the remains on a nearby stone.

Linara couldn't help but watch, unblinking. "I—I was just—"

Jon glanced at the dead umbrin, and at the scarred man. He rolled his eyes and waved his arm. "Just get out of here."

"No," the scarred man said, turning fully toward her. Under his gaze, Linara squirmed. Her anger was doused, and she shrunk back toward the tent flap. She didn't care what was happening here, she just wanted to go back to the show, to watch boring performances and enjoy her father's birthday. "She saw too much."

Jon realized he still held the vial of feld powder, as if on display, and quickly stuffed it within his shirt. "We'll take care of it," he said, his eyes growing to a fury. She'd seen that look before, locked behind the cooling glare from his father, or the protection of a public setting. Here, enclosed by tent cloth, nobody would prevent what was coming.

Linara glanced behind her, but Fenton had blocked her escape. At least he looked a bit hesitant, but it wouldn't matter. He would do whatever Jon told him.

The scarred man glanced at Linara one last time before disappearing out of the tent flap behind Jon, leaving them completely alone. Outside, on the stage, a band had started up, horns and strings sending a melody into the Blackness that already muted most of the sound within the tent.

Linara backed up slowly toward the edge wall as the two boys closed in on her. Her foot knocked against something hard, and she almost lost her balance. A clay bucket full of sand, not unlike a few others holding the corners of the tent down.

Jon kept moving forward, until her back was pressed against the tent wall. Linara felt the fabric, and something stiff beyond it. The walls of a cart, most likely.

"I saw you staring earlier today," Jon said. "You and your pa think you're better than us. Always acting like *we're* the fools."

"I don't know what you're talking about," she said, trying to find another flap leading outside.

"We're not fools," Jon said.

Linara gave up finding an exit. The only way out was through them. "Handling drug deals with shady travelers in the back of a dark tent makes you the stupidest people here. I'm sure your father would be thrilled to learn about this."

"You won't be telling anybody anything."

"And you're going to beat me senseless and blame it on what, exactly?"

Fenton hesitated, and glanced at Jon for an answer. Linara didn't wait for one, darting toward Fenton's flank to slip by him. His size was too much, and his long arms grappled her to the ground before she could make it four steps.

Linara thrashed out of his arms, crawling forward, searching for the bucket, a stool, anything at all she could use to bash his face in. Jon stepped on her hands, and she cried out in pain, though the sound fell mute upon the noise of the band outside.

A warm heat flushed through her left shoulder, but Linara ignored it, as Fenton flipped her over and sat on her chest, holding her shoulders flat into the dirt. He was laughing now. More like his brother than he liked to admit.

Jon pulled at her belt, but it held fast. She struggled, squirmed, trying to loosen Fenton's grip. She yelled into the darkness, but the music was rising now to a fever pitch. Fenton's eyes bore into hers. All bitter anger and justice. This was no justice.

The cold steel of a knife pressed against her skin as Jon cut the belt in two. She thrashed and kicked, but Jon held her legs down now. Only a faint whimper escaped her lips as he tried to pull the waistband down. But then his grip vanished as he yelped in pain, the smell of burning flesh filling the air.

Fenton turned back to her with rage in his eyes. He let go of her shoulder, just to wrap his too-soft hands around her neck. But not for long. The moment his hands touched her skin, she could feel a surge of warmth from her birthmark, and his hands burned like wax. Fenton screamed and toppled over, thrashing and rolling in the dried moss, clutching at his bubbling hands.

Linara felt sick, but she kicked her feet and scrambled away. She couldn't see straight, not with that acrid stench and the haze that filled her mind. By the time she found the exit, Jon was back on his feet. He stared at his singed hands, and then at Fenton, whose screams had died to mere whimpering.

His fury returned in an instant, and he started toward her, death in his eyes. Linara backpedaled, holding up her sliced pants with one hand, until her feet stumbled on the clay bucket once more. No time to think.

Linara heaved the bucket up and around, shattering it upon his head. He crumpled to the floor, his scream dying upon his lips.

Linara stumbled back, watching the blood pool around his head. Was he dead? Did she truly kill him? Fenton was standing now, ignoring the pain in his hands, staring at his fallen brother.

He grabbed an axe leaning in the corner, blood oozing from his fingers. "You roaring witch."

Linara slumped against the floor. No escape. Vengeance had burned hot in her own heart, risen once that knife cut into her belt. But now it was quiet, snuffed out the moment the bucket collided with Jon's head. The music had stopped, a grim silence hanging in the air. And Linara had not the strength to scream.

Fenton hefted his weapon, ready to strike her down, but before he could take a step, a form darted in through the doorway. Her father loomed above, bathed in shadows. He struck Fenton upon the head before the axe came down.

The boy slumped to the ground, the axe tumbling to the dried moss. Her father cursed and rushed to both boys' crumpled forms, checking for a pulse. "Still alive," he breathed, ripping a strip from his own shirt and wrapping it around the wound on Jon's head.

She did that. Elthraal Dragonmother. *She* did that.

Voices called from outside. Footsteps rushed closer. Her father glanced toward the flap, then back at Fenton, inspecting his hands in the dim light. "Do you remember what I told you about this?" her father asked. She didn't answer, and he asked again, more firmly.

"You can't hide from the truth," Linara mumbled, staring at the blood soaking into the moss.

"That's right," he said, taking a step back and kneeling upon the moss, hands clasped in his lap. Waiting. Linara could hear the yells from outside, the searching voices. "I promise, Linara, I will help you," her father said, eyes glancing out the door. "I promise, just stay strong. I will help you."

Then he called for the searching men, and they came at once. All the people she ever knew. Curious eyes, searching eyes, furious eyes. All Linara could remember was the shattered clay and sand-splattered blood, even as they carried her away.

Frennik Farrow rushed through the curtain of their mound, making straight for the corner nook. Hours had passed, a flurry of activity. The troupers quickly left the village, hoping to be as far away from the mess as possible. Nobody blamed them. Then they dragged Linara to the holding cell beneath the hall. The very same Beorn had been sent to . . .

Life was catching up quickly. There was no hiding it now. He should learn to follow his own advice one of these days. Seventeen years they'd hidden her mark. He'd been such a fool. How could it not have caught up to him, eventually?

He flung blankets and clothes behind him until he found the small wooden chest tucked into the mud. A relic of a past life. Inside, he pulled out a long white quill and a bottle of black ink. He flicked the top free and scrawled a long, hasty note on the page. Then a drop of wax, stamped with a long-forgotten seal.

Linara had few options now, but hopefully this letter would be her salvation. If he left now, he could run to Tunhollow and send a griffin to the capital. Maybe then it would arrive in time. He cursed and grabbed his coat from a hook on the door.

Stars above, let it arrive in time.

CHAPTER THREE

Linara awoke, gasping for breath. Her eyes darted around, searching for familiarity, but she was not at home. She was beneath the village hall, trapped in the tiny cell that was hardly ever used. She had passed out after they took her, memories and nightmares clawing at her mind already, but she was unable to tell which was real.

Pale moonlight shone through the tiny slit near the ceiling, illuminating the cobwebs dancing in the corners. Water dripped slowly from outside, a dreadful rhythm that formed puddles upon the floor. Tiredness and hunger crawled at her, but she did not know how long it had been.

She sat up, crawling into the driest corner and huddling in on herself. Sorrow and anger blended here. The last person to touch this ground was her uncle Beorn. Was this how her uncle felt when he awoke this very prison? When the feld fungus left his system? What thoughts ran through his mind as he remembered killing his own sister?

Linara missed her mother.

She grit her teeth and punched the floor. All she could do was think, left alone with her thoughts. She hoped Jon was okay. That simple swing of her bucket cracked his skull. Did he even survive the night? That look in his eyes, though. Stars, he would have done the same to her. But did he deserve to die for it? Linara pulled her knees in tighter. Maybe. Maybe not.

She rubbed the birthmark on her shoulder. Both of their hands burned at the slightest touch of her skin. How did she do that? She'd seen Mr. Pen slip and touch his oven, and that didn't compare to the wounds on their palms. No fire can bubble and blister that quickly.

What *was* she?

Linara looked out the window, barely spotting the stars of Elthraal in the distance. Elthraal, the Dragonmother, celestial sign of justice and fury. Justice was in her blood. She was born into it. But her tongue felt heavy, and her chest hurt at the thought. If he died, she'd never forgive herself.

From the dull light of the window, Linara could see a small bowl of water and a tough loaf of bread, several days old. They must have slid it inside while she slept. Linara ate all of it, the water washing down the ashen taste.

A door ground open from above, and Linara pressed her eyes to the slit in the wall leading to the hallway. A luma lantern led the way down the stairs, bright compared to the near darkness of the cell. Linara's father appeared next, face hung low, sleepless and grim. He stopped at the opening, face unreadable.

"Did you sleep well?" he asked, voice steady.

"No," she whispered.

"You never did in unfamiliar places . . ." he said.

"How long has it been?" she asked.

Linara's father sighed and set the lamp down. "Two days. I'm not sure anybody knows what to make of all of this."

"Do you?"

"What I know is what I saw," he said, as he stared at his boots. "Fenton was able to share what had happened. Stars, I should've killed him and taken the blame."

"Father!" Linara said, eyes darting to the stairs, but knowing nobody was overhearing. "Don't say that."

"Those slimy eels," her father said, slapping his fist against the stone of the wall. "This is such a small town, did they really think they'd get away with it? Practically in the open, too."

"It doesn't matter now," Linara whispered. "What about Jon?"

"He's alive, but . . ." her father trailed off. "He can move, barely, but he can't speak."

"Where are they being held?" Linara asked.

Her father hesitated and looked at his feet. "They're not."

Linara took a step back. "They both walked free?"

"They're seen as the victims here, especially with the state of their hands." He sighed and shook his head.

"What about the troupers?" Linara asked.

"What about them? They left as soon as possible, putting in as much distance as they could. I don't blame them, either."

"I walked in on a deal they were making. It's why they attacked me."

Her father furrowed heavy brows. "Fenton spoke nothing of this."

Linara closed her eyes, trying to focus through the events, wincing at the reality of her memories. "The man in the furs, with a scar across his face. He was giving Jon a pouch of feld fungus."

"You know this?"

"I saw it. A pouch of vials. It smelled like . . . like Uncle Beorn."

Her father was silent for a long moment. "They didn't find anything on them. And of course they didn't. An easy thing to cover up, I'm sure. Just like last time..."

"What do you mean?"

His lips formed a line. He wouldn't budge on subjects like this, especially related to Beorn and her mother. "It's nothing important."

"I'm sure it is," Linara pressed.

He sighed, and glanced back at the stairwell. "I've always suspected Beorn was supplied by the troupers the last time they came."

"The same ones?"

"No, I wouldn't have been so kind if they were." He shook his head. "It doesn't matter. The troupers are long gone, and it's your testimony against Fenton's. I won't be able to prove that, but I'll use it if I have to. There's going to be a trial. Everybody's gathering above."

In that case, there really was no chance. Mayor Vahn had the final say of guilt and punishment, and he was not known for his mercy. Especially if Linara left one son maimed and the other could fabricate any story he wished.

"I took the defense on your behalf," her father said. "I don't think anybody else would've. I don't know what I'll be able to do, but I will fight until my last breath."

Linara swallowed, unwilling to say what came to her mind. She remembered those same words ten years ago, standing beside her father. Her uncle's sunken eyes had stared back from the same tiny slit in the wall. Her father was his only defense then as well, even after everything. But feld fungus made monsters of men. An inexcusable, wicked evil to grow in your farmlands. For Linara, there was no explanation for burned hands, and that might just be the greater sin.

Her father slammed his fist into the wall again. "I couldn't help Beorn, but this is different." He collected his temper. "I won't press you, but I need to know what happened. It started with that damn mouse."

Linara didn't answer. Skitter's death seemed like a lifetime ago, and inconsequential compared to the rest of it. "I hardly remember how it started. I just know I tried to leave, but couldn't. They held me down, and cut my belt. But when—" Linara cut off, words catching in her throat.

"It's okay, you don't have to continue."

"I felt," Linara began, but hesitated. She cleared her throat. "My birthmark was glowing hot, like it does when I touch a steam vent. I ignored it, but when they touched me—" Linara choked on the words. "It was like my skin was fire to them."

Linara's father grew silent, staring at his feet with heavy breaths. He always breathed heavy when he became frustrated.

"Please say something," Linara said, tears forming in her eyes.

"I have truly failed you," he said. "I have tried to protect you, but I have failed you."

"I know I was supposed to keep it hidden. I tried, I did! I didn't know it could—"

"Linara, I failed you because I have tried to ignore that mark on your shoulder, hoping that it would no longer exist if I never acknowledged it to be there."

"What are you saying?"

"You have the mark of the Odious, Linara. I've known it for years but haven't made it clear to you. I didn't want to lose you if the kingdom found out. That is no birthmark, nor is the ability to touch fire without a burn a simple family trait. That is why I told you to never mention it."

"I'm an—" Linara began, stepping back from the cage, hand rising to where her mark lay. One of the Odious. World changers. Destroyers. Of the very same power they portrayed in the show.

Linara burned their hands like wax, without even knowing. What other destruction was she capable of? A power surely too dangerous to be kept alive. "What do you mean 'lose me'?" she asked, scared of the answer. Would she have died by the king's hand instead of Mayor Vahn's?

Her father opened his mouth to speak, but the door slammed open above them. He cursed and turned back. "This is all the time they've given me. I will try to save your life, but do not be afraid. I believe hope will come."

Linara stumbled back until she hit the wall. Her father's words rang hollow. There was no chance of saving her now. Even if she could be cleared of Jon's injury, being Odious was a death sentence. Maybe it would be best if they ended her life before anyone would die by her hands. Every terrible story, earthquake, or disaster always had roots with an Odious, mad with power and hungry for domination. A good reason for the king of Aldebraan to want to end her life as well.

The steps of the Carlo twins—identical only in their massive builds—echoed down the stairs. The clink of heavy chains carried between them. Linara's father stood in their way, a farmer facing off against the mountainous sons of Nelbren's blacksmith.

They answered with cold, impassive stares. Her father sighed, stepping aside as they unlocked the door. Despite their size, the twins hesitated in the doorway, almost testing if she would run. She wouldn't.

The thick chains they wrapped around her chest thrice over. Each touch was brief, scared of the heat that was not there. Did they know she wouldn't fight them?

They led her up the stone steps, her father trailing behind. Through the curtained doorway, the luma chandelier lit the faces of everyone she'd ever known. Those who didn't glare in open hostility just looked terrified. The twins led her to a simple stone stool in the front corner, dark and speckled with moss.

She glanced toward her father, standing resolute behind one of the two tables nearest her. The only man in Nelbren willing to defend her in this trial. He was the only person she would *want* to defend her. He tried to offer a reassuring smile, but it just came off scared and uncertain. Somehow, that was more encouraging.

Mr. Lionas, a thin, hawk-faced man, brooded at the table with the mother of Jon and Fenton Fairgrave. Fenton stood beside him, hands wrapped in thick bandages, like oversize mittens. Mayor Vahn sat just to Linara's left, on a tall podium at the front of the room, glaring daggers into her.

He had always walked with a lighter step than the rest of them, propped up on the arrogance of his position. Now, sitting in his chair of office, he wore it like a cloak.

Mayor Vahn slicked a hand through his oil-soaked hair and cleared his throat. "Well, let's get this over with. If all goes well, this should be a quick trial," he said, unable to keep the thick contempt out of his voice.

"Sir, if you don't mind—" her father said, trying to project his voice loudly, but not quite succeeding.

"Yes, quite," Mr. Lionas said, interrupting cleanly. "Would you like me to bring in the evidence now? Or shall we keep a fraction of formality?"

"Everybody here knows the circumstances, Lucian, but, yes, yes, let's keep it civil," the mayor said with a dismissive wave of his hand. "At least to keep the paperwork clean," he muttered, glancing over at Linara.

Lucian cleared his throat and straightened his shirt at the neck, stepping forward and spinning toward the village crowd. "We all know the Fairgrave boys," he began, voice like jagged stone. "Young. Sweet. With dreams and aspirations larger than this little village could provide. They wanted to create, in whatever way they could, tall buildings, wide farmlands. It didn't matter to them, the world was their playground."

Linara could almost hear the roll of her father's eyes.

"All that was cut short in a flash of anger a few days back. Who knows if they will recover fully. Who knows if they'll hold an axe like they used to. Or a shovel, or a plow. What livelihood they had was laid in the hands of that girl, and she burned it all and tossed it aside. Their innocent lives, their innocent dreams, dashed by a blow to the head, and wicked burns upon their palms."

"Innocent?" Linara's father interrupted. "Those boys have been tormenting my daughter for years, always scheming when I'm not around."

"Please, Frennik, do not slander the morals of these boys in front of them," Lucian said, smoothly. "But even so, did a pair of tormenting children deserve to be clubbed in the head, hands burned to the bone? Certainly not."

"This was no simple torment—" Her father began, but the mayor banged on his podium, dropping the room to silence.

"Mr. Farrow, do not interrupt Lucian again, or I will throw you from this room," the mayor said. "You may continue, Lucian," he said, calmly returning to his seat.

"Thank you, Mayor Vahn," Lucian said with a sweeping bow. "But I think my opportunity for a fair and civil trial has been overruled by the defense. I'd like to end this and be home for supper."

The mayor waved him forward. "Agreed. Do what you must."

With a gentle hand, Lucian led Fenton to the front of the room, toward a simple chair near the mayor's podium. The boy lumbered to the chair as thick-skulled as ever, but now he overplayed a limp and a sad, wincing expression. Linara's father hadn't hit him across the head *that* hard, especially not to nurse an imaginary wound to his legs.

"Mr. Fenton," Lucian began, pacing in front of the room. "Are you well enough to speak in front of the town this morning?"

"Aye, sir," Fenton said.

"Very well. Can you tell me what occurred the night of the troupers' performance?"

"Well, Jon and me were exploring the campsite. It was the first time we've seen the troupers; that is, we were too young to remember the first time. Mr. Thatcher took notice, you see, and wanted to show us the other tents."

Linara squirmed, teeth clenching. Thatcher. That must be the scar-faced man. Somehow, Linara didn't doubt that most of that was true, with just an omission of one detail. Surely he would say nothing of the feld fungus.

"Mr. Thatcher was the leader of these troupers, correct?"

Fenton nodded.

"What happened next?"

"Someone called Mr. Thatcher away, and he left us in one of the stage tents. We were waiting for him when she just burst in. She saw us and..." Fenton shook his head. "She got that look in her eye. That angry look, you know? Like when you done something wrong, but you don't know what? She started attacking me. And Jon. And we tried to defend ourselves. We got her pinned to the ground, trying to talk sense, you know? But then our hands started cooking, like she turned into some kind of fire."

As much untruth lay within his story, he did not lie about their hands. Linara breathed in deep, hand rising to the mark upon her shoulder. Thankfully, she felt no warmth from it now.

Lucian crouched low, meeting Fenton's eyes. "I'm sorry, Fenton, but I need you to continue."

"Our hands were burned," he said, lifting his cloth-covered hands. "And while we laid on the dirt, she clubbed Jon in the head with a bucket. I remember it shattered. And the blood. And now he can't speak, or hardly move." Fenton breathed in deep, trying to find his voice. "I picked up an axe on the ground. A nice axe, I remember cause I could see myself in the metal. I thought she killed my brother, and I . . . I was so mad."

Fenton covered his face in his hands, and Linara stared, the anger bubbling. That part. It wasn't even false. He had picked up that axe with intent to kill.

"Aye, all men succumb to anger every now and again. It *was* good thanks to Mr. Farrow for arriving when he did."

Fenton wiped a fake tear from his eye, glancing at Linara with the same rage she saw in the barn. "Without him, I would've done something I would've regretted for the rest of my life."

"And that is the difference," Lucian said, turning on the rest of the crowd. "Where one acted out of vengeance for a fallen family member, having not fully committing the act of fury in his heart, the other nearly murdered her peer out of pure malice."

Linara sank deeper in her chair, knowing that every eye in that crowd stared upon her with hatred. It would only get worse if they discovered the truth behind her mark.

Lucian bowed to the mayor and returned to his seat.

Linara's father stood and straightened the collar of his shirt. His jaw was set, his broad shoulders lifted and commanding. It was a side of her father Linara had rarely seen. He usually avoided conflict when he was able. A disarming tone and a quick escape. But when he was cornered, he flashed into a different man. One that never used more words than necessary. Frustrated. Precise. Lethal.

With no hesitation, he pulled a length of leather from his bag. Her belt, sliced in two. "What is this, Fenton?"

The boy squirmed in his chair. He looked to Lucian, but the man nodded for him to answer. "A belt."

"Do you know who it belongs to?"

"Dunno."

"It is my daughter's. I found it in the tent, sliced in two. According to Linara, you cut if from her waist as you pinned her to the ground."

Fenton stared back, expressionless. "Perhaps it was cut on a rock."

Her father shrugged. "Perhaps. But it looks like a real fine cut," he said, holding it up to the light. He whistled as he ran his finger along the edge. "I've never *seen* such a fine cut. It would be a hell of a knife that made that. To make stone tools so sharp must be a genuine talent."

Her father turned and showed the belt to the crowd. Keff, the village blacksmith, leaned forward to inspect the cut himself. Keff didn't forge knives, or any cutting edge. Any metal that came through went straight into hoofshoes.

"I can show you if you'd like," Fenton said from behind him, squirming with excitement. He reached into his belt and pulled out a small gleaming knife, struggling to get a good grip with his thick bandages. The hilt was covered in a reddish wood, the metal swirling and shining, even in the pale luma light. "It's real steel. I could never get a stone knife so sharp."

Her father stared in surprise that his scheme worked so well. "Why, that's a beautiful knife. May I see it?" he asked, and Fenton obliged, flipping the knife and handing it over hilt first. Her father held the belt out to the crowd, and with the knife, sliced away sections of the belt with ease.

"Idiot boy," Mayor Vahn muttered.

"Cut on a rock, he says? I think not. Where, I wonder, does cutting my daughter's belt from her waist fit in Fenton's story?" The crowd stared back in silence, and her father wheeled back on the boy. "Would you care to answer, boy? Why did you cut my daughter's belt?"

"I didn't!" he said. "I mean, I wouldn't. It was Jon. He was just borrowing the knife . . ." The more he said, the farther he slunk down in the chair.

"Then you lied? How much else of the story did you lie about, I wonder?" He turned back to the village. "You all know Linara. We've been here all her life. She does not act out of aggression, you all know that! The Fairgrave boys, however, have tormented every child and animal this side of the province. In an act of self-defense, no one deserves the axe, or the stake, or the noose, or whatever you had planned for her."

"Self-defense is never an excuse for attempted murder," Lucian shouted. "Or do I need to remind you of your brother?"

It was a low blow, but Linara's father did not falter. "My brother was family, and I defended him because he was family. Even so, his consequences were set the moment he planted the feld. He deserved the noose. I do not deny that, but my daughter is a *child*, and they almost *raped* her, Lucian."

Lucian sniffed. "That is speculation."

"It isn't if we bother asking the only other person who was there," he yelled, pointing to Linara.

"Enough!" the mayor roared. "I'll have order in this house of law. And Frennik, I must remind you I only accept witnesses that are *not* of the accused party."

"No, I remember," her father said, eyes like cold knives. "But what other reasons do two boys have in cutting the belt from a woman, then to more easily take her, struggling, and defenseless?"

"Defenseless?" Lucian asked. "Skin that burns hands like fire is not defenseless. How would you explain that? I see it as nothing less than black magic, pure and simple."

"Black magic is nothing but myth and legend," her father said. "A sad excuse to put fear in common folk like us to avoid what we do not understand."

"But here we are, staring at a girl who can burn the skin of men with nothing but a touch," Lucian said. "I see no explanation that doesn't lead us to a spike through her heart."

"I was not finished," her father said. "Black magic may be smoke and fiction, but the Odious are very real."

The room fell silent, tension growing like mold. Linara's heart pounded in her chest. He was just going to reveal that openly?

"I'd sooner believe she's the daughter of a dragon," Lucian sneered.

The mayor held up his hand, cutting off Lucian and quieting the soft mumbles spreading through the room.

"Don't invalidate it, Vahn," her father said. "The evidence of the world changers are everywhere, and history does not lie."

"I will not deny that possibility," the mayor said. "But we haven't seen a Mark in two generations. Their like is dead."

"Linara," her father said, gesturing over. "If you would."

Every eye turned to her, and her heart froze. It came to this, after all. Her fingers moved to the laces on the collar of her cotton shirt, but she hesitated. Did she trust her father? What was the alternative?

Linara stood and released the knot, sliding the shirt off her shoulders. She held it firm to her chest, covering her breasts, but still revealing a dark-red splotch upon her shoulder, like a crystal ruby set in her flesh. Tendrils spiraled and webbed across her arm and across her side, thin and wavy. Even now it pulsed with heat, responding to the flush of red in her cheeks and anger burning in her lungs.

The room fell silent. Even Lucian said nothing in response. Linara pulled her shirt up again to hide the unnatural glow.

"That is a mark my daughter gained shortly after her birth. It glows in the firelight and has done nothing but grow every year. Have you seen a birthmark the color of crimson? Have you seen such a web of lines on the flesh of men that pulsates with the energy of the world? The Mark is real. Same as dragons, same as the Kingdom of Aldebraan, same as any of us."

"Even so," the mayor said. But he paused, just long enough for the room to know that he lost that point. "That mark, it's powerful, it's evil, and we cannot stop it if we let her go. At least with her bound here, we can tie her to a stake and stab her through the heart while we still can!"

"Don't be ridiculous!" her father roared. "Get a province arbiter in here at least. This is bigger than any of us."

"There's no time for such ridiculous claims," the mayor roared, rising to his feet. "This will be handled now, right here." He pointed to Linara, hate in his eyes. "Remove her from my sight! Bind her, club her, throw her out by her hair, whatever it takes to see her stoned!"

The crowd swelled, rising to their feet in opposition. Linara stared in shock. The same crowd, glaring death into her soul as she entered, now defended her life. Linara looked to her father, visible relief easing tension across his shoulders.

But the twins were already upon her, lifting her from her seat with no regard to her comfort. The crowd cried out louder, but the mayor did not sway, nor did the twins falter in their steps toward the door.

"See this, Vahn?" her father yelled. "If you follow through with this, the entire village will riot. She does not deserve to die."

"What, then?" Mayor Vahn said. "My son is crippled and their hands are maimed. All for what, so she can walk free?"

"From my perspective, the boys who harmed my daughter are walking free. There are no innocents in these events, Vahn. Listen to reason."

Silence passed through the hall as the twins stopped in their path, looking to the mayor for guidance. Linara clamped her eyes shut, offering a silent prayer to the stars above. Death would have been a peaceful end to her potential to destroy, but the fear of that black void gripped her heart like a vise.

"Fine!" the mayor cried out. "She will not die this day. Tie her up to the post and lash her for all she's worth. Seventeen whips across the back, one for every year my son has lived, thinking he had a future."

The crowd hushed, falling to agreement. Even her father said nothing in response. He saved her life, and that was something they both could be happy about. Linara let their hands carry her along, free from the deathly silence of the crowds and into the open air beyond. Clouds blanketed the sky, filling the air with vague darkness. She didn't even have to feel the moss to know it would rain soon.

The twins threw her to the dirt, pulling the chains away with little grace. They tied her wrists to a single stone post, taken from its place by the inn, and stuck into the earth at the center of the village. Her bonds were loose enough to escape if she truly wished it. She didn't.

Slowly, quietly, the entire village circled around her. Was it courtesy to leave so much space, or was it fear? Fenton and Mayor Vahn stood at the front of the crowd, arms crossed, watching her, almost daring her to resist.

They ripped the shirt from her back, leaving her bare to the damp, to the wind, to the watching eyes. For the briefest of moments, she felt vulnerable. Open. Embarrassed. That didn't last long before the whip came down.

Crack.

She took it without even the slightest grunt of pain. She stared at Fenton, and he stared back. She'd stare into those eyes until the lashes were done, and he'd know that she wouldn't break.

Crack.

Crack.

Crack.

Her breaths rushed out between her teeth. She'd take the punishment without weeping like a child. They wanted that out of her, but she wouldn't give it to them. She'd bend, but she would not break.

Crack.

Crack.

Pain lanced up her back, more than she'd ever known. Her eyes shifted down for the briefest of moments, and the mayor cracked a smile. Fury raged in her chest, and she rose a little higher. She may deserve the whip, but she wouldn't let him win.

Crack.

Crack.

Crack.

Tears welled in the corners of her eyes, but she willed them not to fall. She latched on to the fury and hung tight. This whip deserved to fall on both her and the Fairgrave boys. She just hoped they could feel the same pain. A warmth spread from her chest, and she felt her mark glow with unbridled heat.

Crack.

Crack.

Crack.

Crack.

The smell of burning leather filled the air, but Linara paid it no mind. Each strike stung more than the last, more than it should. The pain spread through her entire body now, and she slumped against the post. Her eyes wavered and fell to the moss below.

Crack.

Crack.

How many more awaited her? How many more until they tossed her aside? Just a few more to bear, and it would be over. A punishment well deserved, but she would've won.

Crack.

Crack.

The last strike fell, and the whip fell limp. A single tear fell to the ground below, sucked clean into the moss. No one made a sound. Their eyes fell on the whip, lying on the moss, lengths of leather charred and singed to ash. They stared at Linara, back broken and bloody. They stared at the mayor, waiting for him to give the order. Any order.

But Linara wouldn't let him have the last word. She stood, naked and broken, and stared at Vahn and his son. The mist began to fall. Her father stepped through the crowd and gathered the tattered remains of her shirt, but she was already walking back to the farm, shoulders raised high, gritting away the pain and letting the tears fall once she was free from the watching eyes.

Orvinth Vinhower III shuddered in the frigid wind, pulling the dark cloak farther around his shoulders. The same air that once would've warmed his bones now chilled him to his core. Such a curious thing, aging could be. He plunged one hand farther in the feathers of his griffin, hoping the warmth in his fingers could spread up his arm. He had hoped to leave ages ago, if not for the tardiness of young knights.

He pulled a worn and faded paper from his coat, studying the hasty script within. A curious thing with curious news. And from that deep in the Blackness? No wonder they never heard of her. Rumors led to disappointment at times, but he knew that with every rumor came a fraction of truth.

Another figure walked through the open doorway onto the platform, two thick bags swung over her shoulder, and a bronze stag helmet pressed firmly around her head. Better late than never . . .

CHAPTER FOUR

A gentle wind blew across the village of Nelbren, rustling Linara's clothing, sending pain stinging across her wounds. Even without the slightest movement, the pain was constant, a reminder of what had happened. She tried not to let it get to her as she walked between the mounds of a place she was once welcomed.

Seventeen lashes across her back. Yet there was no pain greater, no punishment worse, than the watchful, hateful eyes that peered from the dark of Nelbren. Nothing could hide the sound of shutters closing, or the scraping of chairs as people moved back inside.

Nobody wanted her dead, but they certainly didn't want to see her alive. Linara didn't even blame them. She was afraid of herself.

But it had been six days, and she had been cooped up for far too long. Though, if she truly wanted fresh air, she should've just walked into the fields. Or south down the main road until she felt like turning around. But no. She had to see for herself, knowing what to expect but foolishly hoping it to be different.

The wounds were still fresh. For everyone.

Still, Linara kept her head up, shoulders back, teeth gritted tight against the pain as if she wasn't wrapped in three layers of bandages. All things considered, she was recovering better than her father expected. The physician from Tunhollow wouldn't even make the trip to see her. So she powered through the sleepless nights and the restless days.

A rolling cloud passed overhead, darkening the sky. Luma bloomed into light around the path and across the hills. Linara breathed in deep the smell of damp—the earthy taste of the land just before the rain fell. But the rain did not fall. Clouds swirled and swelled, but they never released the mists. Rain would have filled the silence.

Linara stopped at the center green, watching the fungal blooms bob in the soft wind. They weren't quite full yet. It would be another few weeks for that, but it was beautiful enough. As a child, she always wished her father grew them more. She could've sold them to the travelers, to help with the monthly expenses.

But Nelbren never saw many travelers, and outsiders hardly enjoyed the sight and smell of fungal clumps as much as she did. Or Old Jinny Fentil, for that matter. As a child, Linara would cross into the center green to sneak a touch of the flowers, just to be chased away with a wooden spoon by the old woman.

If Linara stepped into the center green and trampled the flowers all to the ground, would Jinny chase her away? Would she even open her window to yell? Her shutters were drawn now, and the curtain to the door shut tight. Linara wanted to push those limits, to see if somebody would notice.

She sighed and stepped away, back down the road toward home. Best not to stir up any more trouble. Father was right, as always. There was nothing to be gained from coming back so soon.

"Ho, Linara," a voice called out from the mist, followed by the slight clapping of forearms, just quiet enough to hear, but not to echo across the village. It was Mr. Trel's soft voice. She paused there, staring out into the darkness, but saw nothing.

Still, if she listened enough, she could hear the soft scraping of a knife upon clay. Linara approached slowly, and found Trel where she always did, perched in his chair outside his door, carving a block of clay with a thin knife. Like Linara, he also did not wear his family sigils upon his sleeve. A lot of sneaking to be done today, even among the elderly.

Tiny shavings of clay littered his lap and the surrounding moss. Three completed pieces sat on the table beside him, carved into bats and likenesses of a few constellations.

He smiled as she approached, the first to meet her eyes in a full week. "How are you, Miss Linara?"

"I've been better."

"I could have guessed that much."

Trel wanted a deeper answer, and Linara considered whether to give one.

"It's strange here," she finally said. "Father hasn't told me much, but I could tell something was off. He doesn't head into the village anymore, and he's not much to let a grudge impede his business."

Trel nodded with a heavy sigh. He was holding something back, but she wouldn't press for it.

"I had to see for myself," Linara said, her words hanging in the air like a great weight. "I'm not welcome here."

"You are to me."

"But not to the rest."

"There are some who've made up their own mind, and some who let Vahn decide for them."

Linara let the silence hang for a few moments, unsure of what to say. "How are the boys?"

"Hands heal as they do," he said with a shrug. "But don't concern yourself with them. Talk will die down, as it does, and normal will return, in time."

Linara shuffled her feet, picking at the bits of clay with her boots. "What do they say?"

"Nothing you need to concern yourself with," he reiterated, waving his hand away. "There are strangers in the village, though, visitors from out east. Arrived a few days ago."

"Troupers?"

"No. Just travelers."

"From the Illumination?"

"They wouldn't say. Their skin is dark enough, though. Quiet folk, they are. Won't say why they're here, or for how long."

"You've talked with them?"

"Oh no, I'm too old for such snooping. Others do it for me. Word passes through."

Linara hesitated. "Are they here because of me?"

"Hah, surely not. Such news spreads within our homes, but never outside them. Nobody wants such commotion here, of all places," Mr. Trel said. "They're probably merchants, or some sort of priest. Nobody's given them much talk to find out."

"I'm sure Ms. Mera's trying to sell half her store, though."

Trel chuckled. "Nothing truer. Even Pen has been making his pitch for a few extra loaves."

Linara stared off toward a large central mound, where the visitors stayed during their travels. Hardly a soul lived within throughout the year, but now the single glass window was lit with luma.

"I wish I could talk with them," Linara said softly. What stories they must have from the Illumination, the land of sun and light.

"Aye, that I know," Trel said. "But even under normal circumstances, your father would not be pleased if I let that happen."

"If they heard the news, they'd only be afraid," Linara said. Just like the rest of the village. "Are *you* afraid of me, Mr Trel?"

"I'm old, Miss Linara," he said, brushing stray clay from his carving. "There's nothing much left to fear."

"That doesn't stop the rest of the village . . ."

"They'll come around. Just wait until another calf runs off or Old Jinny whips another boy to tears again. People will forget. You were too young to remember, but the same happened with your uncle."

"But my uncle is dead. I'm still alive."

"And thank the stars above for that," he said. "Trust me, Miss Linara, it's better to be hated than dead."

Linara rubbed absently at her shoulder. That may apply to anyone else, but with a mark so dangerous, how many others would she hurt before her life was over?

"All stories are rooted in truth," Mr. Trel said. "But the longer one is told, the more it becomes exaggerated. It grows a life of its own, twists free from the facts and becomes a thing of fiction. Don't trust all you are told during stories in the night. Always wonder where the seed of truth lies."

"How do you know this, if the only history we have is what we're told in the stories?"

"I told you, I'm old. The stories I've told my children, they've passed to their children, the smallest detail of untruth growing in size with each telling. That pattern exists among all things." Trel brushed away the clay shavings from his lap. "Do you remember the story of my adventure fighting the leatherboar?"

"Of course."

"What if I told you there was no leatherboar? It was nothing more than a wild hoofbeak. But that's not quite as exciting, is it? And I never even fought the beast. It charged me and I ran. You know why? Because I'm smart enough not to wrestle a wild animal. You tell it once and it's exciting, but by the time your kids want to hear it a fifteenth time, you find yourself bored by your own story. You'll find out when you're my age why we do the things we do."

"You're saying most of the stories of the Odious aren't true?"

Mr. Trel shrugged. "I know enough to suspect they're exaggerated, but I know not by how much. All of us discovered in this last week that the Odious are very real, and it doesn't change who you've been these last years."

"Ignorance can keep a lot of things hidden," Linara said softly.

"Only seven Odious in the history of this world have made such an impact to be remembered. Seven out of hundreds, I'm sure. You might be remembered in this tiny village, but I very much doubt your name will be known throughout the world."

Linara glanced around at the mounds and the fields, and the watchful eyes she could still feel upon her shoulders. Was there much of a difference? This village *was* her world.

"Now go home, Miss Linara," he said, staring out into the village. "Grudges can fade, and some may fester, but nothing is more dangerous than fresh anger."

Linara nodded and started away. "Thank you, Mr. Trel," she said, hearing his knife scrape across clay as she turned the corner. Even if her trip to the village brought less than she expected, it was at least nice to know not *everybody* hated her guts.

She passed by the mounds of old Finber and the Valaen's, their family sigils above the doors long since faded and grown over. Now that she noticed, most of the mounds in the village were fading. It would be time to reapply soon. Father always grumbled about that job.

The sigils on clothing were a small thing, despite needing year-round attention, but the painting of every mound in the village was a large project. So much that a good portion of their fields wouldn't even leave Nelbren this harvest. Assuming her father gave the best price out of the bunch again. And for that, he never made much of a profit.

Nobody in Nelbren focused on luma as much as her father, but Mr. Polt was creeping into his business of late. Maybe he'd swoop in and steal the village painting this year. Her father understood the value of being on good terms with the mayor, but after all that had happened, he might just abandon that contract entirely.

"Psst!" a voice called out nearby. Linara's heart flipped and she glanced around, finding nothing moving in the village behind her. "Over here, Linara," it called again, and Linara focused on the small alley between two mounds. A cloud moved away from the moon and illuminated the shadows, revealing a man pressed against the wall.

"Mr. Pen?" Linara gasped, taking a step back. "What are you doing skulking about?"

"I would ask you the same question," Pen said, waving her forward into the alley. Linara checked her surroundings and stepped into the shadows. Pen shifted awkwardly in the dim light. "Anyway, I thought I heard you in the distance. I have a gift."

Mr. Pen handed her a bundle of cloth, heavier than Linara expected. She unwrapped the edge, revealing a corner of a dark, dense seed loaf. By the weight and size, there must have been at least five wrapped within. She shook her head, trying to give it back, but Mr. Pen pressed it farther into her hands.

"You need it more than most. Those scars won't heal without proper food."

"I don't have any eggs to give you," Linara said softly.

"Don't bother. You've given me enough over the years to last until I die."

"Except eggs spoil," Linara said softly, but Mr. Pen didn't respond. He only turned back around and picked up another bundle, this one rounder and flatter.

"It's a bit old, and stale, but I bet it's still better than those dry loafs." Linara unwrapped her father's cake, now a week old and a little stiff.

"I had forgotten about this," Linara said, feeling a bit of hope enter her chest for the first time since the whipping. "Thank you."

"It's the least I can do."

"It's more than most."

Mr. Pen glanced around at the village. "A shame, I think. Goes to show who really knows you, I suppose."

"You aren't afraid of me?" Linara asked.

"Scared of a little heat?" Pen raised his hands, calloused with thick blisters and scars, splotched with old burns.

"I know, but . . ." Linara choked on the ball in her throat, quickly rising as she stared at the loaves in her hands.

"I know you. I know the Fairgrave boys. I know enough to make my opinion."

That couldn't be said of most of the village, it seemed. At least Pen and Trel risked speaking to her, though. "Do you know about the strangers in the village?" Linara asked.

"Not much. I've seen them a few times. An old fellow, and a woman, as far as I can tell. I've only talked with the man, and he asked me about the local news. I don't spread idle talk. I just offer them bread and I leave, that's all."

"Do you know why they're here?" Linara asked.

"Nobody does. We assumed they were just passing through, but they've been here a few days now." Pen sighed and shook his head. "Your father's always pretty good about rooting out that stuff. Saved us from a few hustlers and the like over the years."

Linara started at that. She couldn't remember him going closer than a hundred yards to any travelers, unless it was to pull her away from one. But she always suspected she knew less about him than she thought. "Speaking of," Pen continued. "I'm surprised he let you out of his sight, let alone to walk to the village."

"He . . . doesn't know I'm here," Linara said.

Mr. Pen sighed and shook his head. "You've always been the restless type. But please head home and rest. I'm sure your back can't be that well so soon."

True enough, the pain was growing unbearable. "I was heading back already."

"Good," Pen said, nodding slowly. "Don't let me keep you."

Linara nodded and backed out into the street. "Thank you again, Mr. Pen."

"I will try to make it out to the farm in a few days with more supplies."

"You don't have to. We can last, I promise."

"If I could, I would've done it sooner," Pen whispered, glancing out into the street before ushering her forward again. "Now go, and be quick about it."

Linara squeezed out of the alley, bundles tucked firmly under her arms. Mr. Pen was always the anxious type, paranoid over the smallest of issues. The arrival of peddlers would have him on edge, so the strangers in the tavern probably had him near bursting.

The path home was lit by moonlight and stars, but Linara still couldn't help but feel not entirely alone. Over her shoulder, she could feel a creeping edge of eyes watching her that never ceased. She stopped, turning her ears to the sounds of the air.

Bats fluttered above, tiny ripples through the sky. The sliding whispers of mosskimmers she heard a few yards beside her. But nothing else. Linara sighed and kept moving, but the feeling never left. Twice more she stopped to listen, twice more she heard nothing, and twice more she kept walking, ignoring the anxiety rising into her chest.

Her eyes drifted to the ashen fields beside her, but she quickly glanced away. She didn't dare cut through her uncle's fields, not even if somebody was truly trailing her. The stars themselves ignored that land now—she'd find no protection there. To the sky she turned her eyes, fixed upon the celestial twins, Irn and Ilnuth, the Watcher and the Warden. With them above, she could walk the long way.

Her mother would have been able to tell her why the twin protectors kept watch. She'd be able to tell Linara a lot of things about the sky. But her mother was beneath the ground, far from the heavens. The stars only accepted the dead as smoke and fire, and nothing much burned in the Blackness.

If only they could've afforded the wood. Instead, her mother was now the life source of her father's fields, blessing the growth while her legacy still breathed.

It was funny, really. Linara had always hoped to live a noble life, deserving of a pyre for herself. Now she wasn't even sure if her body would burn.

Linara took her eyes off the stars only briefly to check the path before her. Once her hands felt the moss of their mound, she let herself relax.

She took one step down into the doorway, turning one last time to the road, watching the shadows of the surrounding hills. Nothing moved, not even a lost umbrin. She shook her head, clearing a mind full of ghosts and shadows, as she stepped down and back up into her home.

The main room was in darkness, the luma lantern by the door taken by her father into the fields. Linara shoved the clutter on the table aside to make room for the bundles of bread, wincing at the pain in her back.

She started pulling her shirt over her shoulders, careful not to pull too hard at the dried blood soaked through the bandages. She reached for a small mirror, only a simple disk of thin polished metal. In the dim light, she could barely see the blood tinging the tips of her hair. Deep lines of red crossed her back, some worse than others. Her bandages would need changed soon.

Linara had just pulled her shirt back on when her father appeared in the doorway, old, dingy axe hung over his shoulder, bound by fresh tanglegum sap. His lantern lit the room with a soft-blue light. His eyes moved from Linara's bloody shirt back to the mirror in her hands, then to the basket on the table. He let the axe fall to his side.

"You went into the village, didn't you?" he asked, voice soft, and flat.

Linara did not answer.

He turned to hang up his lantern and axe. "Do you remember what I told you before I left?"

"Yes."

He turned back, face soft. There was no anger there, just something sadder. Linara was more afraid of that. "This isn't like before. You're not a child any longer. I'm not telling you to stay inside until the mists clear, or until your chores are done. I'm not restricting you because I'm your father, but because you are not safe."

"I didn't believe you," Linara said. "And I still don't know if I do. It's quiet, sure, but I don't think anybody would try anything that stupid."

"No? Do you think Vahn is above taking justice into his own hands outside of the hall? What about Fenton? Do you see how easily his words sway their thoughts?"

Linara shrank back. There was some truth behind those words. She could feel it in the air on her walk home, lingering behind every shadow and hill. But, stars, she just wanted to feel the open air again. Feel the moss on her feet, and hear the night.

"Mr. Pen gave us a few loaves," Linara said, hesitantly pointing at the bundles of cloth.

Her father reached for them, peeling back the corners before swearing under a heavy breath. "The old fool. He surely put himself in danger from the rest of the village."

"Do you really think they'll kill him, too?"

"Nothing so extreme," her father said. "But you were too young to remember the backlash from Beorn. People will forget, eventually, and move on. But not so soon."

"I would know more if you ever talked about it," Linara snapped. She immediately regretted it.

Her father's face grew long, shadows deepening across his jaw. "Those were dark times."

"They're dark times *now*," Linara said. "Are we not going to talk about *this* after it's done?"

"You don't understand. No peddlers came through for months. No news, no trade, no anything. The people always want somebody to blame, and when that person is gone, they turn to the next best thing. It was a miracle we managed to make it free without complete exile."

"So forgive me if I don't *talk* about it. I just—" He stopped himself, clenching his fist and swallowing his anger. "I just don't want to lose you. Not you. I will do whatever it takes to avoid it."

Linara lowered herself into a chair, all her frustration doused before he even responded. All she could feel was the stinging pain and a heavy weight of loss. She wasn't sure which was worse. It didn't feel like it would ever truly be gone.

"There are strangers in the village," Linara said absently. And her father grew still. "You said there weren't any traders back then. At least there are travelers here now."

He was growing pale, his jaw clenched. "What do you know of them?"

"A man and a woman. Nobody knows much, not even Mr. Trel."

"How did they arrive? How long ago? Did you speak with them?" He was speaking quickly, stepping closer with eyes growing wild. Linara shrank back, suddenly afraid.

"No, of course not," Linara said. "Nobody has. Mr. Trel said nobody would, either."

Her father blinked away those wild eyes and started pacing in the center of the room. His fingers fiddled with his old wedding ring, a smudged and stained piece of metal, too tight now to remove. "I cannot think clearly," he muttered, "I must seek guidance."

Linara stared for a moment, but quickly realized he was serious. She moved to clear away the center of the room. Her father pulled closed the curtain on the door before dumping the luma in his lantern in a cloth sack. The room dropped into near darkness. Then, a burst of light, as he pulled the rope upon the wall, lifting the tiny clay cap from the top of their mound. Stars bathed the room, dotting every surface.

Her father stared at the collection of lights—a mirror image of the sky above, cast through the tiny hole at the top of their mound. It took an expert to read the signs, experience Linara did not have, and her father barely touched upon. She could recognize Elthraal from anywhere, and a few others if she looked hard enough, but nothing that gleaned any useful information.

Minutes passed, and Linara watched the stars shimmer upon the floor. They rarely opened the stargate anymore. Her mother was the one who watched the stars, gleaning wisdom from their positions above. What could they possibly find there now?

Her father pointed to a collection of stars, shaped vaguely like a prowling dog. "Fordring, the Wanderer, already making his exit. Lucin, the Imposter, barely visible, riding on the horizon."

Linara rolled her eyes. Of course Fordring was making his exit. Her father was born under that sign, and his birthday was only a few days prior.

"If I'm not mistaken, doom approaches. That should be Caron the Leper, from the west," he said, pointing to a faint edge of stars near the wall. "Our two travelers, perhaps. I do not know."

That could be debated, but Linara said nothing.

Her father stood for only a moment more before pulling on the rope a second time, bathing the room back in darkness.

"It's decided then. In two days' time, we will leave Nelbren behind."

"What?" Linara asked, shooting up to her feet and wincing as pain lanced through her back.

That decision came far more quickly than it should have, even from the stars. How long had he been thinking of this?

"We cannot stay here any longer. It's time to start over," he said, returning the luma to the lantern.

"Just like that? From a collection of stars? Since when did you ever listen to them?"

"Now's not the time to nitpick our beliefs," her father said, grabbing a few empty pots and bags from hidden places and laying them throughout the room. "The stars have clearly spoken, and I must listen."

"But we can't just *leave*. What about your crop?"

He rushed past her, pressing a thick burlap bag in her hand. "It can be replanted. Wherever we go, there's always something to be grown."

"And Mother?" she asked.

Her father gritted his teeth, shoving a drawer of clothes in a bag with increased intensity. "She'd understand."

"Just like that? You'll abandon her now?"

Her father whirled back. "She's dead. There's no changing that. I *wish* we could have sent her to the stars, but we couldn't."

"She's feeding the luma."

"There's nothing left for us here but bad blood and worse memories. Our crop has been good, and I'm thankful, but I won't let us both starve from my own stubborn pride."

Linara rolled her eyes. "Starve? You said it yourself, it'll pass."

Her father wouldn't meet her gaze. "Mayor Vahn is tightening his grip. Nobody will trade with me. I'd have to be the first to greet every caravan that comes within ten miles to get my word in first. Otherwise, none of this luma will be going anywhere. And we certainly can't eat it."

He stopped for a moment to stare out the small window at the rows and rows of healthy luma. He never had a chance to harvest on his birthday, and the tops were growing thick and wide.

"It would take three days for a full harvest, especially if I cut the roots clean." He shook his head and cursed. "There's no time and no room. We'll take what we have, load the wagons full, and head west."

Linara stared at her feet, feeling the weight in her chest compound until she could hardly stand. "I can help."

"No. I'll have to walk the lands for anything I've left behind. Stay and prepare the chickens. If they survive the journey, it'll be a good start. If they don't, they'll be part of our rations."

Linara watched him move around the room, numb to the pain.

He glanced her way and shoved a cloth sack into her hands. "Pack what you can. The morning after next, we're riding off, prepared or not."

Her father stormed out into the darkness, leaving behind half-packed bags and empty jars. He was never this unfocused, never this paranoid. Whoever those strangers were, it scared him beyond anything she'd ever seen.

Orvinth Vinhower III looked out the tiny glass window onto the ground below. It was probably the only window in the entire village. Ordered, shipping, and installed just for the guests accustomed to such amenities. Orvinth, as much as he wished to be comfortable without one, had found he quite enjoyed the simple pleasure of staring into the outside world. He simply could not keep his mind organized without one.

His journey brought him to the depths of the kingdom, chasing a story that an entire village believed to be true. But stories and tales were often layered in falsities, even the ones birthed in current events. The evidence was not apparent, but that did not eliminate the possibilities of truth in the letter, now sitting on the tiny stone table.

If there was an Odious here, then the burned bits of leather scattered in the moss outside spoke of some punishment. The villagers were tight lipped, and Orvinth believed they were bent on fixing the issue themselves. That's what he was afraid of. If pressed against a wall, there would be another event.

If Orvinth moved too recklessly, he would hasten the inevitable, but too slow, and he wouldn't be able to stop it. They would need to find solid evidence of the child's gifts before it was too late.

CHAPTER FIVE

Linara lay uncomfortably upon her bed, staring at a shelf cluttered with rocks and small clay carvings. A collection she started when she was barely old enough to stand. She hadn't added anything to it in years, but of all the things being left behind, this one left a strange, sour taste.

Perhaps it wasn't the rocks she'd miss. Every night when she was young, Linara would add a new rock to the pile, from wherever she had wandered that day. Every night, her mother would ask its importance, and Linara would describe every detail. Every night, her mother would listen. She would smile and kiss her forehead before the buzz of insects carried Linara to sleep.

When she was buried, they made a promise to never leave her. If only they could've built a pyre. If they could've sent her to the stars, they wouldn't have to break that promise. But nobody in Nelbren could afford that honor. Not the mayor. Not even the baker.

Tomorrow, nevertheless, they would leave. All the preparations were finished. Linara never realized how much they owned until they had to choose what to leave behind. Their cart wasn't very large and would barely fit the chickens, which were worth far more than anything else they could've packed. Most of their money was in luma, still buried in the dirt outside.

The furniture they'd leave behind. The beds, cabinets, and casks, all collecting dust before the next inhabitants moved in. *If* anyone ever moved in. They'd probably just board up the mound until the story of the Farrows passed into history. The land was fertile, though, unlike her uncle's.

Linara gingerly lowered herself down the ladder and stood in the center of the dark, empty mound. Father would be back soon enough. They'd have to rise early, to finish the preparations, but it wasn't like she'd sleep. If the burning pain didn't keep her up, the dread and anticipation of a cross-country move certainly would. That probably wouldn't change for a while, probably long after they were finally settled in a new home.

Outside, the moon was hovering just above, barely midday. Would the grim omens in the stars follow her to their next destination? The stars journeyed endlessly across the Blackness. Never ceasing. Eternal.

A thick blanket of clouds crossed in front of the moon and stars, closing them off with some finality. In the silence, she could feel a certain tugging, an ingrained call, from out in the fields. Linara knew where it came from, and followed it slowly, deep into the bright blue of the luma fields.

She let her hands hang by her side, brushing each luma cap as she passed. They flickered and pulsed at her touch. It would've been a great harvest, too. But he was right, it would take a week before they packed them tightly enough to survive a long journey, ready to continue producing light. And the stars had shown that was time they didn't have, apparently.

At least the luma wouldn't go to waste. Once news of their departure spread, one of the other farmers would swoop in to harvest the field for themselves. Probably Mr. Polt. He wouldn't hesitate. He'd probably even adopt the land himself until someone bought it. Heck, maybe *he'd* even buy it.

Linara stepped into the back corner of the field, where the light shone the brightest. The caps near her mother's grave grew almost as far as Linara could stretch her arms, leaving almost no room to walk between them. Once cut, they would last for months before dimming. They sent them off to the bigger cities, like Tunhollow, or Elaan. Unlike the smaller clumps near the outskirts of the farm, which never left Nelbren.

The grave was overgrown now, covered by moss and luma spores. It was a minor miracle Linara could even find it still, but there were certain markers that guided the way. Rocks, tipped at odd angles, familiar divots in the dirt.

Linara knelt and pressed her palm upon the moss and breathed in deep. Father was right. She would understand. In death, she sustained their crop, and it was what had kept them alive some seasons. Now, what would keep them alive would be to leave.

The stars spoke, and they listened. Her mother would respect that most of all. She would even be content with supplying some prosperity to the next family to move in. Even if it *was* Mr. Polt.

Stretching her legs, Linara looked out across the hills, at the land spreading far around her home. There was nothing spectacular about those particular hills, really. Just a lot of moss, and light, lit with stray spores from their field. But they were unspectacular hills of moss and light she'd never see again.

It deserved something more than just a last look. There were still a few long hours to kill before she had to be back. Perhaps one last walk to one of the tanglegum groves. Who knew if there would even be any tanglegum where they were headed? Well . . . there was tanglegum *everywhere . . .*

They could use some branches, though. If she learned anything from the travelers that passed through, you could never have enough rope on the road. It was why Mr. Trel always kept a steady supply.

Yes. More rope. It was decided then. A walk through the hills, all for the sake of being prepared. Linara had already started walking before she could convince herself otherwise. It would be a mostly blind walk, outside the reaches of a normal path, into the mossy hills behind her father's field.

She passed by Nela, long trunk pressed to the moss, searching for bugs and other crawlers. Linara stopped long enough to run her hand along their heffen's smooth, leathery hide. Did Nela know what was coming tomorrow? She never wandered the hills for this long, and never ate quite so well, but she'd need her strength to pull the wagon tomorrow. As if in response, Nela's trunk moved over to suck up Linara's pant leg before she moved along.

The air smelled damp. It usually did this time of year, when the misty rain fell more than it did not. A few hunting owls fluttered overhead, searching for signs of life across the hills. The downhill slopes aggravated the wounds upon her back, but it felt good to move around again.

Linara's foot brushed past a clump of orange fungus, and it bloomed open, spewing spores across her boots and pant legs. It was close to the time of year where a good wind would pick up the spores from all around, carrying them like snow throughout the countryside. It wasn't at all dangerous to those who lived here, but travelers tended to stay inside, or risk getting sick.

Linara crested the final hill, long gangly limbs of the tanglegum trees waving to her in the soft breeze. The sweet, sticky smell greeted her like an old friend, but it brought forth a distant sorrow. It was strange how much she missed Skitter. Missed the days before all of this.

Her foot knocked against something hard in the moss, and she knelt, finding a small glass bottle, slightly clouded and covered in dirt. It held nothing inside except a few drops of muddy water.

Linara let it be and moved on deeper into the grove. Most of the trees had grown long, nearly touching the ground. She didn't often go this far out of her way to harvest, but thankfully the branches still weren't clogging most of the paths deeper inside.

Linara stepped into the center ring of trees that circled each other like a set of graceful dancers. No tanglegum grove was ever planted by human hands, and yet, every single one followed the same strange pattern, like a twisting pinwheel.

There was something relaxing about the groves. Peaceful. No wind made it through the trees, and no hunting animals dared come close. A quiet that nothing often broke.

Linara froze as she saw a figure slouched on the ground across the ring, not a dozen paces away. They made no sound, probably asleep. Or worse. She inched closer, peering into the darkness. It wasn't often someone got lost in the hills and ended up dead, but surely she would've heard of someone missing.

It was a man, shirtless and disheveled, stinking of bitter decay. The fierce stench of feld fungus. That smell lingered in her memory like a sharp thorn. The surrounding moss, torn up from a night of mad ramblings, was soaked in his own filth and sick. The clouds moved away above, revealing Mayor Vahn's sleeping face.

She suppressed a gasp, everything in her body telling her to flee. But in that lingering moment, her own boiling anger rooted her to the vomit-soaked moss. The same man who condemned her uncle for growing it, now lay in the same stupor. A stupor that would one day lead to utter madness.

Vahn was playing with fire. Was that why he came all the way to this grove? So he wouldn't harm anyone near him? No distance would bring safety if that same feld stupor caused him to kill.

Then the answers crashed down like a wave. He surely wouldn't be stupid enough to be growing it himself. It must have come from somewhere, and the thought sickened her.

Jon and Fenton weren't buying from Thatcher for themselves, in some strange sort of childish rebellion. They were loyal to the end, always at the beck and call. If their father wanted feld, of course he wouldn't dare be seen getting it himself. He would send his sons.

A heat flared in her chest. She'd seen the corruption before. It struck at the heart of even the righteous. What more could it do to a monster? Under Vahn's own rules of justice, she should kill him now, before he brought danger upon another. It was what he wanted to do with *her*, right?

Linara had no weapons, no knife or axe or tool to end him. Except one thing. It would be so easy. To let go, and be the reaper. Everything called her closer, to take control for once in her life. If he died, they wouldn't have to leave.

She stepped closer, her heart beating wildly. Knees upon the moss, ignoring the bitter stench of feld clogging every breath. Her hands shaking, she brought them around his neck. His breath felt ragged. His heartbeat dull upon her fingertips. Weak.

If he had his way, her whole family would be buried beneath the earth. A village was left hating her just at his word, but now his own folly left him vulnerable. Open to the justice that Linara could bring. From his ashes, she could be reborn. A hero, burying a menace beneath his memory.

A deep heat rose from her chest, throbbing at just the thought. He would die just as he feared, and he would deserve it.

Vahn winced and groaned beneath her grasp, feeling the heat even before she released the fire. The smell of burning flesh replaced the acrid stench of feld.

Linara gasped and snapped her hands back, coming quickly to her senses. Faint wisps of smoke curled from pink welts along his neck, the hairs singed away just at her touch.

What was she doing? If she killed him, she would be no different than him. She'd be worse. She'd be exactly what they thought of her. Now he'd wake with burn marks upon his neck, evidence that she threatened his life.

She had to run. Flee the village before he woke. If they were far enough gone, he wouldn't pursue. Linara stood and carefully backed away, careful not to make even the slightest of sounds.

Vahn's eyes flickered open, and Linara froze. His hands clutched at his neck, and he mumbled meaningless words. His eyes, tinged bloodred, bobbed around the grove, but saw nothing. He was still deep in a stupor, despite the pain.

Linara's feet shuffled faster, disregarding any semblance of caution. If he was sober, she could reason with him. But he wasn't yet. Nothing would stop him.

Vahn wavered and stood, head hung low to his chest as he steadied himself against the tree beside him. He studied the sap stuck to his hands for a moment before wiping it upon his pant leg. Linara held her breath. A few dozen paces away now, almost past the first tree. After that, she could run, and he wouldn't be able to catch up. Probably.

She took one last step back, and a sharp crunch shattered the silence as she stepped on the long glass bottle.

Vahn's head snapped up, red eyes focusing on her in a flash of rage. He fingered the burn upon his neck wordlessly as he stumbled forward, ignoring his barefooted steps through vomit-soaked moss. He had a singular focus now, and Linara wouldn't escape from it.

"Witch bitch," he mumbled, words catching on his thick tongue as he spoke.

"You're not yourself, Mayor Vahn," she said steadily, still backing away.

"I'm more myself than ever."

Linara ran. Her feet scrambled against the darkened moss, blindly rushing into the wilderness. Clouds hung high in the heavens. No stars, no moon to guide her now. Her back burned and stung as if the whips were falling fresh, but she kept on. Shadows crept through the edges of her vision, but she dared not turn, dared not take her eyes off what ground she could find. Footsteps followed close behind her.

She knew what feld fungus could do. Vahn wouldn't slow, wouldn't tire, wouldn't stop until he finished his goal. Right now, Linara was certain that meant until she was dead. Linara could only hope that he would pass out along the way. The way it was looking, she'd collapse from pain before that would ever happen.

Linara crested hills and darted through the valleys between, eyes searching for a way out. A light of blue crested on the horizon, and Linara made for it, disregarding all else. Was it her father's field? Which way had she been running? There were a few natural luma groves around Nelbren. It could be any of them.

After running in such darkness, the bright light might disorient Vahn enough for her to escape, but after that, then what? Where else would she go? Would their farm be safe for her? Would the village? Could they hold Vahn back in his current state?

Her feet pounded on moss and mud, burning from effort and weight. Tears flowed from the pain in her back, but she was almost there. She nearly made it to the first stalk of Luma when a hand tightened on her shoulder. Linara yelped and spun around, finding Vahn, wide eyed and mouth open, staring into her very soul. He said nothing as he flung her to the side. She landed at the base of a luma stalk, bending it beneath her weight, and nearly snapping it off. That strength was truly unnatural.

He was upon her in a moment, hands like iron, pressing her shoulders into the ground. Her wounds ground into the dirt, and Linara yelled out in pain. She could feel the heat rise from her shoulder, just like in the tent, and the smell of burning flesh filled the air.

Vahn's very hands were burning, but he made no sign that he noticed. His eyes were fixed on hers, death at their center.

She wouldn't roll over and accept it, not from this man. Jon and Fenton may not have deserved to die, but Vahn certainly did now. Linara opened herself up to the heat, to the hate and the vengeance. Liquid fire filled her bones. He would feel it now, feel what his power had done to her and her father. They'd finally be free from his petty anger.

A voice called out from the darkness, a familiar voice, a calming voice. Not her father, but . . . Mr. Trel? To the side, she saw Trel and Pen both push their way through the luma stalks. Linara had led Vahn straight to them.

No. She led them straight to *her*.

Linara gasped, scrambling to pull back on the fire within her, to gather what she'd already started to release. It was like grasping at a rush of water; the flames slipping through her fingers.

She clamped her eyes shut as she screamed, blinded by the flash of light that filled her vision, and deafened by the roar of flames. If there were cries of pain, Linara did not hear them.

She could smell the ash and the fire. She could smell the burnt moss and luma, and beneath it all, the burning flesh. All at once she threw up everything she'd eaten onto the smoldering dirt. Then she dared to open her eyes.

The world around her was far too wet to burn. The fire scorched through everything it touched, but did not spread. Three bodies lay before her, in a ring of ash within dim luma. One, on his back just before her, was Vahn, hateful eyes upon her no more. Two others were blasted against the trunks of dark and ruined luma. Trel and Pen.

A single basket survived the flash of fire, wrapped in cloth, slightly burnt around the edges, covered by Pen's withered form. He had said he'd bring more bread for them. Even Mr. Trel came. Kind, gentle Mr. Trel, bringing nothing but his company, knowing nothing about their leaving.

What had she done? They'd come to show her kindness, and she killed them. Burnt them to ash and cinders. Would they still find their way to the stars like this? Did she ruin that for them?

She looked back to Vahn. Part of her wanted to blame him, to pour all her anger out onto his broken body, but she could not. It would have been better just to die. Why couldn't she have just laid still and died?

Another voice cut through the chaos, calling her name. Her father. How could he see her like this? Half her clothes were burned away to nothing. She covered herself with her dirt-smeared arms, leaving the bright ruby mark pulsing in the gentle darkness. They'd find her naked and guilty before the stars themselves. Justice would have to come, and they'd kill her this time.

A day too late. Tears fell as darkness overtook her.

Orvinth Vinhower III sighed, sliding the few books he brought back into his pack. Time had proven that they were too late and too early indeed. Their journey was at an end, with a whole cart full of rumors to show for it. They'd have to speak to every suspect directly. They'd call for the carriage, talk to the girl, and they'd be off, with or without her. It was done, but he truly hoped he was not impatient. The Stag Knight tapped her spear against the mud impatiently, but the more she tapped, the slower Orvinth moved.

A flash of light lit the sky through the window, almost blinding compared to the pitch darkness around them. The young knight was already out the door before Orvinth could catch his bearings. Heart thudding, he reached for his cane, hobbling out the door as quickly as his old legs could take him.

Old fool, he was. So scared of being wrong, he ended up being late twice. And who would pay for his caution this time? Whatever happened in that flash of light would rest on his conscience until he died.

CHAPTER SIX

Linara awoke in a cell of stone, far too small. A taste of ash layered her mouth, and her back ached. Her mind caught up in an instant, racing with thoughts of fire and smoke, of the dreams so vivid and real.

But they were not dreams. Vahn, Trel, and Pen were all truly dead, and the memory of blackened corpses hung like a thick miasma. If there had been anything left in her stomach, she would've thrown it up. This time, there wasn't even a plate of food for her.

The air smelled just as damp as before, but a cold layer of smoke hung in the air. It wasn't her clothes—those had been changed—but it clung to her skin. A layer of death that no water could scrub clean.

Linara sat up, wincing as the scabs cracked and shifted beneath her shirt. Thick chains clamped her arms to her side. She tried to catch a glimpse through the window but saw no moon. Was it the middle of the night? Surely it couldn't have been too long. There'd be nothing to prepare this time. There wouldn't even be a trial. Who would be there to judge?

The scrape of boots echoed softly from the stairwell, and Linara's heart shrank. Her judgement came. She forced herself to her feet, resolved to die with *some* dignity left.

But it was not judgement that came to greet her. It was her father, face clouded and dark. He hadn't slept. They both stood in the opening, saying no words between them.

"You were right," Linara finally said, choking out the first words with a slight laugh. "Vahn would take things into his own hands."

Her father shook his head. "It doesn't matter now. You did as I asked and stayed clear of the village."

"He didn't come looking for me, you know," Linara said, and her father looked up in surprise. "I found him drugged up on feld fungus. I barely even had a chance to run."

"If that's true, without your mark you'd already be dead," her father said. "Surely all evidence was burned up with him . . ."

"But Trel and Pen," Linara muttered, shivering at the thoughts that she shoved quickly back down.

"Yes, the fools," her father said. "Such simple kindness only got them killed in the end."

"No, *I* got them killed in the end," Linara said. "And they won't have mercy on me for that."

Her father nodded in agreement, though for which part, Linara wasn't sure. There was a part of her that hoped he would disagree.

"I'm surprised they let you visit," she said.

"They didn't. They only posted one guard through the night."

Linara paled. "You didn't."

"We had plans to leave the village, and I intend to keep them."

"Father . . ." Linara took a careful step back, away from the door. "What if I don't want to run?"

"They're going to kill you, Linara."

She was silent for a moment, considering the words for longer than either would have liked. "Maybe it's what I deserve," she muttered.

Her father locked eyes with her, all his fatigue and sadness evaporating in an instant. She stood up a little straighter at that look. She had no choice. "Linara Farrow, you're my daughter, blood of my blood. You are no killer. You are no monster. You are no faceless story told to children in the night. If you die here in this cell, your story will be finished, but if you come with me, you'll have a chance to redeem yourself."

Tears welled in her eyes, voices in her head trying desperately to oppose the words he spoke. "I don't know how I can."

Her father was silent, but he glanced aside just briefly, enough for his face to grow softer, eyes welling before he even spoke. "I don't, either, but there are those who do. Those strangers that came to the village, they're from the capital."

Linara took another step back. From the capital? What purpose would the king have for her? Surely they would want her dead, such danger stricken from his land. But why would her father seek them out if that were true? "What are you saying?"

"I know this because I was the one who sent for them," he said, face twisting in all sorts of sorrow. "I was terrified of your fate before the trial. I didn't think they would spare you, so I sent for the only ones who could help. But they arrived too late. After that, I thought we could start over. I thought we no longer needed their help, and I wished to flee. Now I know I was far too rash, and I've paid the price."

Her father stepped to the side, and an old man appeared in his place. His skin was dark and wrinkled, like old bark. His robes, dark as mud itself, hid stains of dirt and dust. His smile was warm and comforting, not entirely unlike Mr. Trel. But Trel was dead.

"Good morning, Miss Farrow," the man said. "I'm sorry to be meeting you this way, but despite what it may seem, I am a friend."

Linara didn't believe him. How could anyone be on her side? A sharp crack split the silence, and the bark-skinned man slowly pushed open the door with one hand, the other leaning on the gnarled cane propped against the cobbled stone.

He knelt before her, taking her hands and inspecting them in the dim light. "Such softness for a girl of the farm," he said. "I am sorry for what you've been through."

Then he grabbed the thick padlock, clasping her chains together. After a moment, the metal cracked and fell to the floor, a thick branch breaking through the lock. The man smiled and winked, unraveling the last of the chains and dropping them to the ground. He worked with a strange gentleness. Perhaps they would not kill her after all.

The bark-skinned man grunted and creaked as he rose, cane unsteady on the smooth stone. "I'm sure you have more questions than I have answers," he said, with panting breath. "I will do my best to hear them all in due time. For now, know that my name is Orvinth, and I have come to take you to my home."

Linara shrank back. "To *Avorren*?"

Orvinth looked at her, sadness in his eyes. "I wish to show you that you're more than what has happened here. For that, we'll have to leave this place behind."

He reached out his hand for hers, and she stared at it for a long moment. Everything within her groaned that it would be impossible. And yet despite it all, Orvinth felt gentle and kind. No deception, no lies. If her father trusted him, Linara could too.

She breathed in deep and took his hand as a dull thrum of noise grew in the distance, outside the window. She tried to catch a glimpse as Orvinth led her out, but saw nothing but stars, no clouds or storms in sight.

Her father stood against the far wall, face unreadable. A woman stood at the stairs, wearing a bronze helmet shaped like a horned stag. Linara's breath caught, staring at the wide metal shield and the set of spears slung across her back. A Knight of Alde, in the flesh. She'd heard the stories, but barely considered them to be real. Was Linara truly such a threat that they sent one all the way here?

The Stag Knight nodded in greeting before turning up the stairs. Orvinth placed a gentle hand on her shoulder and led Linara up. They emerged in the empty town hall, chandelier cold and dark. She'd never seen the meeting hall without light, and she'd never thought it could be any more unsettling.

In the corner was the silhouette of a man, slumped in a pew. Her father's axe, the one Trel had made just a week prior, lay by him, the handle cracked in two.

A touch of moonlight glimmered through the crack in the doors. The crescent moon had just breached the horizon. Barely morning, then. The same morning she and her father were supposed to have left. Well, in a way, they still were.

A twin line of luma lit the ground outside, placed intentionally through the center of the mounds. Was that the strangers' doing, or her father's? The Stag Knight waved them out the door and around the mound to the edge of the village.

The deep thrumming noise was louder out here, unimpeded by dirt and stone. It grew like the wind, blowing in a strange rhythm. She could feel no breeze on her skin, but with each passing moment, it grew closer. The stars flickered and darkened above her, a long line of shadows breaking the light.

Her father shrank back against the wall of the mound. The bark-skinned man and the knight, however, did not flinch as the noise grew closer. The shadows formed into the shapes of wings, griffins pulling a great mass behind it. A carriage? Surely not; that would be impossible.

A rush of wind nearly bowled Linara over as the griffins landed all around them. Soldiers rode atop some, carrying long pointed lances. At the central patch, where the spiral maze of perennial flower-fungus grew, now floated a wheelless wooden carriage, held off the ground by a great cloth sack. A twin line of griffins stamped and pecked at the flowers impatiently.

A few feathers blew all around her in the calming wind, sticking to the moss and her hair. Brown, white, and black, of all shades and patterns. Other than the chickens, she'd hardly seen an animal that wasn't just a muddy gray.

"Have you ever seen a griffin before, Miss Farrow?" Orvinth asked.

"Only as a shadow over the moon," Linara said absently. "They're eating Jinny's flowers."

"Oh," Orvinth said, surprised. "I'm sorry, we didn't realize. There wasn't much space for a clean landing."

"No, it's fine," Linara breathed. "I don't actually care about them."

Orvinth chuckled curiously and continued leading the way forward. Linara didn't quite know how to explain. Just a week ago, Old Jinny was chasing a few kids into the hills for just touching those flowers. Now a herd of griffins were eating them like second breakfast, without a care in the world. Griffins. In Nelbren.

In the distance, the driver of the carriage hopped off onto the moss and glanced around, locking his eyes on Orvinth and frantically waving him over. Orvinth sighed and stepped after him, offering his apologies and leaving her behind before she could catch up.

That left Linara alone. Even her father was nowhere to be found. Soldiers scrambled all around her, offering only brief glances in her direction.

A griffin walked slowly by, sharp beak sweeping the moss for bugs to devour. A leather bridle was wrapped around the base of its beak, stretching back to a simple saddle set between two powerful wings. Dew glistened upon white feathers, pressed down from the top of its head all the way to leathery birdlike feet.

They were beautiful, up close. Linara inched forward, a strange curiosity driving her. The griffin froze when she noticed her approach, watching cautiously as droplets of dew dripped from its feathers. A long feathery tail flicked anxiously. The griffin clicked its beak together a few times in anticipation before letting out a sharp cry and backing up a step. Linara leapt back in surprise.

"Sorry, Aria's a bit skittish," the Stag Knight said, coming up behind her. The knight removed her helmet, revealing her long, sweat dampened hair, bronze as the armor she wore. She couldn't have been more than a few years older than Linara herself. "Especially in unfamiliar places. Come, she'll let you touch her if I'm here."

The knight walked briskly to Aria's side and slid her hand through the feathers in her neck, the griffin's back arching in enjoyment. "Come closer. I promise, she's no different than a horse."

A horse. Another thing the knight didn't realize never came much into the Blackness. The griffin, now held by her owner, still watched Linara curiously, but she stepped closer. The feathers were gritty and thick at the top layer, but the undercoat was soft like cotton. Weather proofed and insulated against the cold, just like father used to say. Aria nuzzled her shoulder and stared with great blue-marble eyes, studying her intently. Linara could see a lot of wisdom in her gaze, a steady caution.

"I'm Lorin, by the way," the knight said, thrusting out an open hand.

Linara stared at it for an uncomfortable amount of time, trying to remember how to return the gesture. She settled for grabbing the hand in both of hers. "Linara."

Lorin chuckled as she pulled her hand away. Linara stared at Lorin, at the griffins all around. At the carriage, and Orvinth, and the village being torn apart. Nothing was making sense. "Why did you come?" Linara asked. "For me?"

Lorin's brows knit together. "To bring you with us. Didn't Orv tell you? He's your teacher now."

"My teacher? Is he . . . an Odious?"

"Only living one in Aldebraan. Well, second living now."

Linara stared at the ground. Was that what those branches were in her cell? Could an Odious be so kind and gentle?

For nineteen years, Linara and her family pretended the burning mark above her heart never existed. They never talked about it, except to tell her not to talk about it. It went from a curiosity to a monstrous danger, and now what? She would be taught how to use it? She wasn't really sure she wanted to.

One of the guards, a tall, dark-skinned man with a thick iron helmet, appeared next to Lorin, whispering in her ear. "The village awakes," he said, still loud enough for Linara to hear. In the faint light of the moon, she could see a crowd gathering over by the mayor's mound.

"Then we're leaving now," Lorin said quietly, before pulling Linara away toward the carriage. Griffins and guards started moving back toward the carriage, forming a perimeter around them. Orvinth quickly joined them, hobbling on his cane as fast as it would take him.

Just as quick as it formed, the village crowd surged against the line of guards, voices raised. Those that weren't rubbing the sleep from their eyes held axes and hayforks with intent to kill. None of them knew if they should be attacking the soldiers or Linara, now huddled behind Orvinth and the Stag Knight.

Questions rang out from all sides, mingling together in the morning air like mud in the rain. Linara tried to tear her eyes away, but she could not. Within those angry, rage-filled faces, she saw friends and neighbors. Now fully turned against her.

"Where are you taking her?" A voice called out louder than the rest, and the crowd yelled in agreement, finally finding some unified voice. The crowd slowly parted, allowing Fenton Fairgrave to press forward, followed closely by Lucian Liones, the hawk-nosed farmer turned prosecutor.

"We demand answers," Fenton said, over the noise of the crowd, "What about my father!"

"And old man Trel!" another voice called.

"And the baker!"

Lucian held up a hand to silence the village. "We deserve a trial. This village has lost loved ones to this witch."

Orvinth sighed and turned to face the crowd. "We are saddened by the death of your mayor," he said, projecting his voice as far as he was able. "As well as the potter and baker both. We are regretful we were not aware of the circumstances earlier, but we have come prepared to pardon this girl of all involvement."

A roar of outrage rose. "Under whose authority? Who are you?" Fenton demanded, and the rest of the crowd echoed in anger. Orvinth reached into his sleeve and pulled out a small scroll, tightly wound and stamped with red wax. He held it out to Fenton, but Lucian grabbed it first. They both read the missive under the light of a nearby lantern.

"We have a king?" Fenton mumbled just under his breath, turning to Lucian. The hawk-nosed man snapped at him quietly, and Fenton turned back, adopting his anger once again. "What about my father! And my brother!"

"We hope that the compensation we've prepared can begin the bridge to forgiveness." Orvinth untied a pouch from her belt and tossed it to Fenton, who barely caught the pouch with his bandaged hands.

He managed to untie the pouch and glimpse inside before quickly snapping it closed. He seemed satisfied until Lucian jabbed him in the side. "A pardon can cover her crimes, but it cannot save her from who she is. You cannot keep us from executing a known user of black magic."

It hadn't been even a day, and he already sounded like his father. Or maybe he and Lucian practiced in the mirror. Orvinth sighed and pulled out another thick scroll from within his sleeve. He unraveled it and scanned the contents.

The Stag Knight rapped her spear against the carriage until the crowd fell to silence. Orvinth read aloud, "Under decree number seventy-nine, paragraph one, made by King Tivangian the Third in year 104 NK, all children born under the mark of Eion, or 'Odious', are henceforth conscripted by the king, for the king's service, with compensation of fifty gold tiles per child, no exceptions for birth, titles, or previous service."

Orvinth returned the scroll to his sleeve and pulled out a thin pouch of tiles. "Which reminds me"—he scanned the crowd—"where's Frennik Farrow?"

A voice called out from the edge of the crowd, standing alone by the edge of the village. Her father pushed his way through the crowd.

Orvinth tossed him the pouch, and he caught it just to toss it straight back. "I won't take your money."

The Stag Knight reached for the pouch from Orvinth and pressed it firmly into her father's hand. "It must go to somebody," she said, glancing at Fenton, still counting the coins in the pouch given to him. Her father sighed and slid the tiles into his coat pocket.

Lorin glanced at the crowd and leaned in close to Linara. "I suggest taking the moment for goodbyes. We don't have much time left here."

And then Lorin and Orvinth moved off, leaving Linara and her father alone in the center of a ring of guards. The villagers still mumbled amongst themselves, uncertain if their anger had been settled.

She and her father both looked at each other, not knowing what to say, or what to do. How had it come to this?

"I'm sorry, Linara," her father said, at last. "I've tried to hold on to what I could not. My stubbornness in trying to preserve your old life only caused more harm."

Linara nodded, voice catching in her throat. "I'm sorry too." She wasn't sure if she agreed with him. There was nobody to blame but herself. "Will you be okay here?"

Her father shrugged and looked around at the boiling crowd, still watching them a few dozen paces away. "I can take care of myself. Who knows, maybe I'll even stay."

Linara glanced back at the Stag Knight, helping the guards hold their line around the carriage. And then to Orvinth, already making her way back over, a comforting smile never having left his face.

"Will you come with me?" Linara asked, turning back to her father. It would be a transition for both of them, but they'd get through it together.

"I'm afraid that would not be wise," Orvinth interrupted, with a soft hand upon her shoulder.

Her father nodded sorrowfully. "Even if I could, my place is here."

"So is mine," Linara said softly.

Her father laughed at that. "No, I don't think that's true. You'll find that out, eventually. You're more of me than your mother at your age. I was your age when I left home, and it took a dozen years until I settled down again. Maybe a year, maybe ten, but you would've left on your own. I'm sorry it had to be this way, instead."

Orvinth tapped gently on her shoulder and gestured toward the cart. "We must be leaving."

Linara nodded, feeling the tears well up within her eyes. She rushed forward one last time, holding her father in her arms. They both breathed deep and held tight.

"I'll come home soon," she said, pulling away.

Her father took a step back and shook his head. "Don't do it just for my sake. Come only when you truly wish to, when you realize you're not meant for such a small life."

Was farming luma too small a life to live? What if that was what she wanted? But he slipped back into the crowd, swallowed by the pressing shapes. She took a step after him, but Orvinth was already pulling her away.

"I wish I could ride with you in the carriage back to Avorren," Orvinth said to her. "But I'm afraid I have other business deeper in the Blackness. I must speak to the herald of Elaan before the day is out."

Linara, again, said nothing. There was too much happening to make sense of it all, and she didn't care enough to understand. To her, the herald of Elaan had always been their king. Their land tax went straight to her. All news and laws of the land came from her.

"Be careful, Orv. You won't have my men to catch you if you fall," Lorin said.

"I'm resilient, Master Lorintus, and I still have some strength left in these old bones," he said, mounting a deep-brown griffin. "Linara, I will see you at the Golden City, and there I hope to answer your questions. For now, safe travels, and I pray you may have a chance yet to rest."

He kicked his griffin forward, and the beast leapt into the air, catching the wind and shooting off far into the sky. Lorin watched briefly, unimpressed, but Linara couldn't tear her eyes away. The shape dropped to shadows on the horizon until the darkness swallowed him and he was gone.

Lorin had her stag helmet back upon her head, shortspear held firmly in her grip. "We must be going as well," she said, voice ringing behind her helmet.

She rapped her spear three times on the doorframe of the carriage, the sound echoing out over the shouts of the crowd. At once, the soldiers who weren't keeping the crowd at bay mounted their griffins.

The Stag Knight quickly ushered Linara into the open carriage door, trying to steady the wobbling structure as Linara collapsed hard on the bench inside. She latched the door behind her, taking the seat opposite Linara. The coach lurched forward and threw Linara against the wall.

They gained speed, the mounds of the village rushing by in a blur. They passed the last boundary of the village, and then the fence line for Fairgrave farm. Linara was pressed down against her seat as the carriage rose into the air.

Linara leaned her head out the window, watching her home fall farther and farther away with each passing second. And then the village was gone, replaced with the rolling mossy hills of the Nelbren countryside. Off, gone and away, flying farther into the sky and away from her home. Forever.

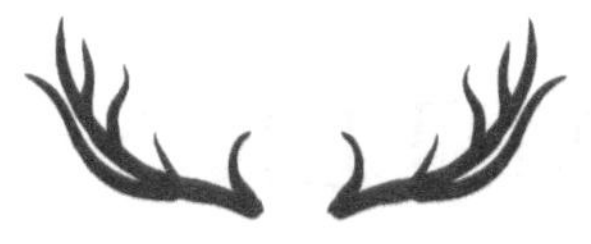

Frennik Farrow barely stayed to watch the carriage lift off into the sky. His heart ached, but survival hung on tighter. He slipped through the shoulders of old friends, fiddling with the pouch of tiles. Blood money for all it was worth. But it was more money than he ever made farming. It would certainly keep him alive. After that? He hadn't the slightest idea.

He had to leave the village. The thought of staying was fleeting, a lie told to comfort his daughter. As soon as they realized Linara was truly out of their reach, their anger would turn to another source.

Already, shouts began to rise from behind him. Shouts for his blood. Frennik turned his walk into a run. Out into the hills, away from his farm and away from Nelbren. A week's stay in Tunhollow will do everyone some good. At least until the anger died down.

The Farrows, fleeing home.

Chapter Seven

The flying carriage shuddered and creaked, Linara's grip tight upon the bench. Houses and distant villages drifted by like tiny insects, seas of luma fields like cracks of lightning. Her entire world was just one of those fields only a day ago.

They'd been flying for ages, the moon now on its descent somewhere on the other side of the carriage. They stopped to rest once so far, to sleep and to give the griffins a rest. Lorin snored the whole night, and Linara's eyes never closed. In an unfamiliar carriage, in an unfamiliar land, with unfamiliar people, she wasn't too surprised by it.

"If you lean out any farther, you'll be one hard lurch from falling out the window," Lorin said, lounging in the corner of the opposite bench. Her helmet was off, resting beneath the bench with the rest of her spears, hair billowing in the wind from the open window.

Linara forced the window closed and forced herself away from the edge of the carriage. She was certain they wouldn't let her hit the ground, even if she tried.

They were alone in the carriage, enclosed by smooth wood on all sides. The wood of the door rattled in the blustering wind, held in place by a few strips of leather. So much wood. A deep auburn brown, smoother than stone.

The door to the meeting hall had always been a point of pride for the village. A slab of wood, bigger than a heffen and twice as heavy. Linara remembered when it arrived. Trel, Pen, and the other men stood and watched that door for hours, all beaming smiles. Now, Linara knew that the door was nothing more than scrap. Rough, warped, and rotted.

"Do you know anything about Avorren?" Lorin asked. She had taken a thin-bladed knife from her belt and was picking the dirt from her nails, despite the bumps of the carriage.

Linara had heard plenty of stories. Of the sun, and everything beneath it. Grass, fruit, trees the size of buildings. Even dragons, horses, and griffins. But stories could not prepare her for everything. There was plenty that never made its way to Nelbren. "I know a little. But nothing about flying carriages."

"Neither did I until a few days ago," Lorin said.

Linara stared at the knight. "This is . . . new?"

"It's never flown before yesterday."

Linara clutched the seat tighter, her fingers turning white.

Lorin glanced over. "I wouldn't worry; it made it to your village alright."

She glanced outside at the griffins flying in formation all around them. Soldiers watched the carriage and the sky ahead of them. She counted at least a dozen. "Why take it at all?" Linara asked.

"We weren't sure if you were in condition to ride," Lorin said. "And two days in the saddle is not something many people can handle."

"I think I've ridden worse," Linara said, thinking of the boars that roamed the Blackness. It was only once, over ten years ago, but she rode it longer than the other boys.

"I thought the same thing. My first time, I passed out six hours in and woke up with a nasty bruise on my back, sprawled across the back of a different griffin."

"You fell off?"

Lorin nodded grimly. "They had someone beneath me in case I fell."

Was that why they brought so many soldiers? To ensure the carriage didn't plummet from the sky?

"Then I'm sure this wasn't the best experience for you," Linara said absently.

"Oh no, this was great," Lorin said, brightening slightly. "I can fly to Mahnbusa and back, no problem now. Any trip outside the city is a good day in my book."

"Is Avorren that bad?"

Lorin shrugged. "For you? I doubt it."

Linara sighed and brought her knees close to her chest, hugging them close. Except, wasn't this what she had wanted for so long? She used to sneak away to pester every traveler for stories of Avorren. To hear of the roads of liquid silver, of the towers and walls paved with bricks of gold. She could finally see Avorren for herself, and yet the nerves within her were still bound tight.

Hours passed, and questions swirled endlessly within Linara. Of Avorren, of their purpose for her there. She didn't dare ask any of them. Lorin hadn't moved, chin in her hand, staring out the window at the landscape below. That same view was the only distraction for Linara, as the signs of a looming sun showed on the horizon.

She'd seen a map of Aldebraan once before. Avorren lay just into the Scarlet Band, the area where the sun just kissed the horizon. She'd heard it painted the sky like fire. Now, she wasn't sure she liked that imagery.

Her legs itched to feel solid ground again, but her heart shivered at the thought. The sky was brightening by the minute, and the stars were fading away. They would not be there to watch over her now.

An orange glow settled upon the sky, and Linara shifted to the edge of the carriage again, risking another glimpse outside. The sky was darker than before, layered in thick clouds, but there was a deep light glowing upon the ground.

Was *that* the sun? It certainly wasn't as bright as she expected. She breathed in the passing wind, catching dry Blackness air. So far from home, yet it still held that familiar earthy taste. A lot less damp, though. And was that smoke she smelled? Did the sun really burn the very air?

Before Linara could ask, the carriage rattled and shuddered, throwing Linara against the opposite wall. She heard the faint cry of the griffins in the wind as a wall of smoke blew through the open windows, a hail of tiny knives erupting through Linara's eyes and through her chest as she hacked and coughed.

Lorin was over her in a flash, slamming the windows closed and pushing Linara to the floor, where the smoke was thinner. Linara's head swam, and she struggled to find a clean breath, looking around for any air untainted by the thick smoke.

The air smelled familiar, an acrid stench of burnt grain. Maybe not the sun. Just a fire, then.

"Can't you take this smoke away with that mark of yours?" Lorin asked between hacking coughs.

Linara's hand instinctively fell to her shoulder. Could it do that? She wouldn't even know where to start. What if the carriage caught fire? Nobody could catch them then.

The smoke was too thick to think. It choked out every breath she tried to take. Her vision grew fuzzy, the darkness creeping from the corners of her eyes. She fell to the carriage floor, eyes drifting closed.

Visions swirled before her. Of small translucent beings hopping across the smoke before her. Their feet were like pins, sending ripples through the smoke with each step, like waves across a pond. Little faceless men, the color of rust and blood.

One turned to face her, halting in the air above her chest. The air seemed to clear around where it stood, and Linara's breathing came easier. Her eyes screamed for her to blink, but she didn't dare take her eyes away. Slowly, carefully, it reached out its hand, passing through her shirt until it touched the mark beneath.

A rush of heat erupted through her, and all the air gasped out of her body. Power filled the space it left, and it was like she was torn apart at the seams. The smoke and embers ignited in a single flash of light.

A fine powder settled upon the bench and floor, coating them in a thin layer of white ash. Linara breathed in deep, nothing catching now in her throat. Even Lorin glanced around wearily, taking what breaths she could.

They both collapsed on the bench.

"I didn't really know it could do that," Lorin said, rubbing her fingers across the boards. "What did you do, burn the ash into smaller ash?"

Linara really wasn't sure *what* had happened, only that it certainly wasn't *her*. She searched the cabin for . . . whatever it was that touched her mark.

"I don't know. I didn't really—I thought I saw . . ." Linara said, but trailed off. Whatever she saw, it was gone now, and she wasn't sure she wanted to know any more than that.

The coach lurched down, and Linara's heart slammed into her throat. Her head hit the side of the cabin, then the edge of the closed window before she slammed into the floor. Lorin's stag helmet cracked against the bench above her, nearly crushing her leg.

The carriage leveled out, and Lorin was on her feet. She slammed open the tiny hatch to the driver and shouted out into the harsh wind.

An ash-covered head peeked in a moment later, thick goggles covering much of his face. "Sorry, ma'am. By the time we saw the smoke, it was too late." His voice was scratched and mumbled, as if he'd been shouting the entire trip. "The hot air above the fire played havoc on the balloon. Very fascinating, if you ask me. I've already made a note to discuss with—"

"Yes, very interesting," Lorin said flatly. "Could you warn us next time we're about to crash into the ground?"

The man scratched his chin in thought for a long while. "If it's unplanned, how am I to warn you?"

"Right. Thank you."

The driver tried to respond, but Lorin slammed the hatch closed before he uttered a word.

"I suppose that's my fault having a Magister drive an oversized experiment across the kingdom," Lorin huffed, gathering her spears, now strewn across the floor. "They can build a flying carriage, but they're terrible pilots. Can't see smoke in a Blackness sky? Please."

"A field fire?" Linara asked. There weren't often fires in the Blackness. Not with the mist rolling in nearly every day.

Lorin stuck her head out the window for a moment and grimaced. "Dragon fire, if I had to guess. Nothing like the stories, either. It's basically a thick liquid, and too hot to put out easily."

"A fire's a fire, right? How hot can it be?"

Lorin frowned. "I heard a story once of a man who put a piece of dragon hide in his forge for a week. It came out cold. But if you touched that same hide to its own fire, it'll melt like wax."

"That seems . . . counterproductive. For the dragons, at least."

Lorin shrugged. "I don't ask questions about things I don't understand."

"How far will the fire spread?" Linara asked.

"Not as far as Nelbren, if that's what you mean."

Linara sat back. That was all she cared about.

"Your village sure chose land far out of the way of everything," Lorin said. "You probably don't see many travelers, I would imagine."

"I was told everyone stayed because they liked the quiet, and those that don't end up leaving." Linara paused and stared at her boots. "I could never decide what I liked."

"Avorren is loud and hardly stops moving, but it has its own charm."

"I've heard stories, but I don't know how many are true," Linara said.

"Depends on which ones you've heard."

Linara fidgeted, questions swirling so deeply, she couldn't pick out just one. "How big is it?"

Lorin thought for a moment. "Your village would fit comfortably in the entry hall of the Spire."

Linara fell silent. One of the few things she knew about Avorren was the giant tower in the center of the city. A glorified palace, built to touch the clouds. She wasn't sure if that meant it truly was that large, or her village was just really small.

"It's not all bad, though," Lorin said. "They don't call it the City of Artisans for nothing."

That was something Linara *could* understand. Peddlers came through occasionally with artisan work. All of it beautiful, and far more expensive than any of the villagers could ever afford. But would the homes of such artists be carved of solid wood? The streets inlaid with crystal and gold?

Her mother once had a blue-crystal vase. It was a common item for sale among the peddlers, but she had never used it once for fear of shattering it. Even after she died, it barely left the tallest shelf of their mound. Neither she nor her father dared to go near, not even to dust.

Linara sighed and rubbed at her head. Between the smoke and all the rattling, a pain was forming between her eyes. She just wished to stop and rest.

But they never did. The coach kept flying, and Linara kept thinking of home, her new future, and of Avorren, creeping closer with every passing moment. Towns formed in the distance, each growing larger than the last. Her heart turned at each one, thinking they'd finally arrived, but the carriage never slowed, always keeping on toward the brightening sky.

And despite it all, the pain, the guilt, the aches, and the dread fell away when she laid her eyes upon the sun.

The blue and silver glow of luma and moonlight turned to a touch of faint yellow, then to a brilliant burn of red and orange as the clouds burst apart with light. Linara leaned out the open window, caring little about the dizzying drop, just to watch the sky shift and brighten. A collection of colors, of art so grand. How could she fear something so beautiful?

It did not take long for the light to become blinding. She had to cover her eyes; the light burned beneath. But she couldn't tear them away. How had nobody carried stories of the light to Nelbren? No words could explain such a thing, but why had nobody tried?

Of *course* Avorren was meaningless to someone like Lorin, who was raised beneath the sun. But to Linara, the moon was the brightest thing in their sky, and it didn't even compare.

Linara felt Lorin's grip gently guide her back into the carriage, and Linara was suddenly aware of the headache now pounding beneath her eyes.

Lorin smiled to herself as she closed the window. "Thankfully, we're not going much farther into the Illumination."

"Farther?" Linara asked, rubbing the sides of her head. "It gets *brighter*?"

Lorin laughed. "Reginaan and Mahnbusa are worse."

Stars, it was so bright already. So bright, and so . . . warm? Was this what *warmth* felt like? The *sun* could do *this*? How could such a thing exist? And still, it did not stop. It was like the carriage was on fire, with no destruction, no pain. A thousand bundles of luma couldn't light a room like this.

Lorin peeked her head out the window. "We're almost to the city. Do you want to see it yourself?"

Linara considered for a long moment, staring out at the sliver of sky she *could* see through the open window. Her head was already pounding. How much worse could it get?

Pain be damned. She would put the stories to rest and see the city for herself. Slowly, she inched herself closer to the window as Lorin slid out of the way.

Her eyes focused first on the ground, flat plains of gold that stretched infinitely into the distance. Caverns and holes pocked the surface, as if giant fingers had once pushed into the earth. It all seemed to stretch forever, all the way to the sun and back.

A great shadow fell upon the carriage, and Linara turned to the source, gasping in a long breath as she finally saw the Golden City. Compared to her village, every town was a metropolis, every city its own kingdom. Avorren was a new world entirely.

On a field of gold, a single mountain rose to touch the sky, obscuring the sun behind rock and building alike. Everything she imagined the city to be was false, and yet it was more than she could wrap her mind around. Even stuck behind the mountain, the light of the sun cast a hundred shades of orange and yellow across the smooth stone of every tower and rooftop. No, a city not made of gold, but pearl-white brick that simply caught the light. City of Artisans indeed, it could be created by no one else.

They flew over wide ponds and lakes, vines and plants bobbing all across the surface, covering most of the view of shimmering water below. Houses and paths were carved into the fields, few and far between, even from so high. Windmills, sheep, and horses dotted the grassy fields between each one, recognized from the picture books.

Linara wanted to look away. It was nearly too much, but every new fantastic view kept her held firm. The shadow of their carriage flew over the city wall, bobbing over the snow-white stone of each building they passed. People cluttered the street, dressed in all sorts of colors.

Linara leaned out farther. Up toward the mountain peak, where a large stone spire rose into the sky, Linara could see faint splotches of patrolling guards upon the towers. Dozens of griffins flew through the sky, most with riders, but some with none at all.

"One thing they learned in Nelbren," Lorin said, grabbing Linara's arm and pulling her down to the bench. "Is that the landings in this thing can be a little rough."

Linara braced herself against the wood, thankful for a brief reprieve. As amazing as it was, she was overwhelmed, and the pounding in her heart returned with fervor. She was moments away from arriving at her new home, to a new life. That thought made the headache worse, and she wanted to throw up.

Hooves touched stone, and they were both nearly thrown from their seats. The carriage came to a sudden stop, but Linara held fast to the bench. All fell still, and Lorin stood and donned her stag helmet, one hand pressed to the door. She looked at Linara for a brief moment before shoving it open. No more rest. No more waiting.

It took a moment for Linara's eyes to adjust as she stepped out of the carriage. Light pooled across every surface, blinding her from every stone and white polished rock. All she could tell was that they stood upon a long flat platform, high above the city. The stone was gray and dimpled from years of use.

Ahead of them stood two men, Knights of Alde like Lorin, but much taller and thicker of arm and chest. One wore a helmet of a silver lion, the other of a gold bear.

Lorin saluted, and the two men saluted back. They barely looked Linara's direction, which was all fine, considering Linara could barely keep her eyes open to say hello. They turned and marched toward the massive set of doors against the wall, just as the other guards landed on griffins around them.

Linara wasn't sure if she should follow, but Lorin's gentle hand guided her forward. But that was where all comfort ended. As Linara fell in line behind her escorts, Lorin fell back to walk behind her. Were they flanking her so she wouldn't run? Where would she even run to?

They passed beneath the set of stone doors, twice her height and nearly as wide, and the world fell back into sweet, comfortable shadows. In contrast to the stark white of the stone outside, the walls of the spire were instead a muddy gray. The floors, of the same color brick, sloped like a huge spiral in both directions.

Linara expected the two guards to lead them down—how much higher could they possibly go?—but they turned their boots upward and continued on. Past the first turn, Linara noticed the strange panels on the wall, glowing with a strange white light. Certainly not luma.

They stopped before a set of doors so grand, Linara nearly froze. A griffin, lion, bear, and badger were carved in the four corners, in such detail Linara couldn't comprehend. How much could such a door cost? A century of harvests? Two? It must've taken years just to carve it.

The two guards knocked gently upon the wood before opening the doors. Inside, Linara's steps *did* falter. The room was impossibly large, but Linara had come to expect that. What surprised her was how *full* it seemed. Pillars bridged between floor and ceiling. Great, colorful tapestries hung from the walls, with symbols and pictures she sort of recognized. One was the flag of Elaan, she knew, but the others were a mystery.

A girl glanced up from the couch against the wall, curious eyes watching Linara from above the pages of her book. Her skin was tanned and smooth, framed by shining black hair tied back with a long ribbon. The dress she wore, of the purest whites, pooled upon the carpet at her feet.

The girl turned and whispered to the sleeping man lounging beside her. He lifted his head, square-jawed and commanding, to look at Linara before dozing off again. He shifted a sword of faded blue across his lap.

The two guards ahead of her stopped suddenly and spun, facing back at the front of the room. They stood stoic and firm, hands resting comfortably on the weapons on their belts. Linara's eyes fell upon the wooden desk between them, occupying most of the back wall.

A man sat behind it, scribbling upon a page with quill and ink. His hair was just as black as the girl upon the couch. Wrinkles of stress and age were stretched across his face, but somehow they suited him. His shirt was a deep blue, like the brightest core of luma, but without the same luminescence. A simple crown of silver sat on the desk beside his paper, and Linara's heart skipped a beat. The king.

Moments passed in silence, and Linara shifted uncomfortably where she stood. She dared to glance at the two guards who led her in, but their helmets hid everything beneath. Even Lorin stood just over her shoulder, stoic as ever. She had dropped all familiarity as soon as they arrived in the city.

Linara was alone once again.

Slowly, her eyes wandered, to the tapestries on the wall, then back to the king. The carpets, to the shelves, filled with books of various sizes and colors, neatly arranged as if nobody had ever even read them. Back to the king. Still, he scribbled away, showing no sign that he knew of her presence. Should she say something? Surely not.

Linara noticed for the first time the fire burning gently in the hearth against the wall. A real fire. She stared into it, watching the flames flickering across the logs in an endless rhythm. The logs cracked and popped, shifting as they turned slowly to ash. Real logs, burning for no other reason than warmth and comfort. It seemed alive. The colors shifted as they moved, chasing something, dancing endlessly, endlessly.

Linara was suddenly aware of her heart thudding in her chest, and the entire room staring at her. She took a panicked step back, face growing hot, as her eyes darted to the floor. No, not just her face, she could feel the heat spreading from her chest. She quickly stuffed it down, feeling it return to normal. She glanced up at the king, now studying her curiously, and she stared even harder at her boots.

"Curious," he said, pulling on a cloak that hung upon his chair. "Forgive me, I've been preoccupied, but welcome to Avorren . . . Linara, was it?"

Linara hesitated, then slowly nodded her head.

"You've taken longer to arrive than I expected," he said, dipping his quill back into the inkpot before folding the paper in front of him. "I hope your trip was not too strenuous."

"We encountered a field fire, sir," Lorin said, voice ringing in her helmet.

The king glared up at her, mouth tightening in a line. That look was not directed toward Linara, yet she still felt equally cold. "I will ask for your report when I need it, Stag Knight."

The silence that followed felt palpable. The king held a thin stick of red wax into the candle flame upon his desk before letting it drip upon his page.

"Do you know why we brought you here?" he asked, stamping a small metal seal into the wax.

Linara cleared her throat, not daring to even glance back at Lorin for any sort of support. "Here with you, or here in Avorren?"

The King smiled, the same sort of warm smile that Orvinth had given her back in the village. Linara's shoulders loosened ever so slightly.

"You're here with me because I wanted to meet you. It's the least I can do after moving you halfway across the kingdom." He looked at her, expecting her to say something in return, but Linara had nothing to say. "No, I wish to know why you believe you are here in the city. I am unsure of what Orv could tell you."

"He just mentioned that I'm to be trained."

The king pondered her words. "Perhaps that can be said. You see, your kind can be dangerous if left unattended, but valuable if guided in the right way."

Was that how she saw her? Maybe it was her fatigue, or the headache, or the countless other things swirling through her mind, but her emotion got the better of her, and the words flowed, unfiltered. "Something to be used or tossed aside, depending on how I turn out?"

The king leveled that same glare that shook her to her core, and she shrank back. Her mouth cracked open, but no words came out. The events of the last few days welled up. The strangeness of the city, the bright sun, the new people, the sudden aloneness. Linara felt herself wither down deep.

But then a knock rapped upon the door, and the hinges slowly cracked open, revealing a familiar bark-skinned man. Orvinth, robe dark and disheveled from travel, hobbled in, his cane moving swiftly across the carpeted floor.

Despite it all, Linara's heart suddenly lightened, thankful for some familiar face, especially as his eyes locked upon hers, a deep smile pressing into her. He turned and bowed quickly to the girl upon the couch before stopping just beside Linara, wrinkled hand falling gently upon her shoulder.

"I apologize for my tardiness. I was held up in the skies above Northrow. Horrendous field fire, I'm afraid. How was your journey? Not too bumpy, I hope," He said, and Linara took a long moment to realize he was talking to her.

"Long," she choked out, consciously aware of the king just a dozen steps ahead of her, watching her with stone eyes. "And smoky."

"Thankfully, that'll be the last cross-country adventure you'll be on for a while. I hope." He finally turned to the king. "Did I miss anything, old friend?"

The king folded his hands under his nose and shook his head. "They had only just arrived before you had."

"Excellent timing then," Orv said, clapping his hands. "May we retire, then?"

"I have many questions," The king said. "And she has much to know."

"Yes, as we all do," Orv said simply. "But she just flew across half the kingdom, which, until yesterday morning, was twelve times farther than she's ever traveled before. Her head's probably pounding, she's probably a bit blind, and it's more than likely she hasn't had a proper sleep in a day and a half." Orv leaned back slightly to glimpse her back. "And it appears she needs some medicinal attention from prior wounds."

Linara suddenly remembered the pain throughout her body. Her back *did* sting, and she could feel her shirt stuck to dried blood even now. Her headache had faded to a dull throb, thankfully. She even suppressed a yawn.

The king studied her, face loosening slightly. He sighed and rubbed at his brow, nodding slowly. "Yes, you're right, my friend. Further introductions can wait. It was a pleasure to meet you, Linara Farrow. We'll talk further at a later date." He waved his hand dismissively and reached for his quill, scratching upon another sheet of paper. "Please stay, Stag Knight. I will hear your report now."

Orv led her by the shoulder away from the king and his desk. Past Lorin in her stag helmet, and the girl and her knight, into the hallway where no other eyes were upon her. Once the doors closed shut behind them, Orv sighed and relaxed his posture, rolling his shoulders with audible pops.

"So much riding really does a number on these old bones," he said with a dusty laugh. "I'm not quite as young as you anymore, but I'm sure you're not faring much better, eh?"

"No," Linara said. "The journey was fine, it's just . . ."

"Everything else?" Orv guessed, and Linara nodded. He smiled somberly and led her down the slope of the spire. The click of his cane echoed across the stone, following their voices down the endless, round hallway. A few guards and other people passed them, none paying them any mind.

"Your room and mine are not far from each other," Orv said. "I would give you a tour of the Spire, but as you've been rushed around without a chance to catch your breath all day, I think some true rest would do us both well."

Linara stifled a yawn in reply, and Orv laughed. "Excellent! We'll get you to your rooms, I'll send for a physician to tend to your wounds, and then I will bid you farewell for the evening. I will return in the morning, of course, and we can begin a proper tour then."

That did sound nice. Within the confines of stone, the Spire itself felt far less overwhelming than the rest of the city. Despite their new plan, Orv didn't hesitate to explain the entire layout of the palace as they walked.

It all fell on deaf ears. There was far too much floating around in her head for anything more to fit. All Linara truly wondered about, as they passed windows glimpsing the fiery sky outside, was if she would ever see the stars again.

The door of Linara's room closed behind Orvinth, followed by a swift rush of cold air. He allowed himself to shiver as he rubbed his cold arms back to warmth. A fascinating child, he thought as he began the walk back to his office.

He'd never taught a student so old. He'd never taught a student at all. Just a few dozen steps before his goose pimples settled back, and he relaxed, letting his old bones settle with the usual warmth of the Spire.

Brought into a strange land, with a strange sun, in a strange place, with a strange man, and already she was pulling the heat within herself. Was she aware she did such a thing at all? Had nobody told her that the air around her was considerably colder when she was stressed or afraid?

Orvinth fiddled with the small pile of seeds in his pocket. Such a different thing, fire could be. Already he felt lost for the first time in a very long time. He redoubled his pace. His library was extensive and held many answers. It was time to delve deep once more, even if it meant a sleepless night.

CHAPTER EIGHT

Linara stared out the wall-length window in her room, unsettled by how far she could see. From so high, most of the city was visible. Slate-blue rooftops, running all the way down to the city wall—a thin strip of white far below. Even a distant range of mountains hung upon the horizon far to the north.

The sun wasn't nearly as painful to look at as the day before, but it wasn't pleasant. Still, she couldn't keep herself from watching a new world wake for the morning. A woman hung her laundry on a line strung out her window. A man rolled a cart of produce through the city streets. Two broad-shouldered men climbed across the rooftops replacing sections of tile.

Perhaps, in some ways, Avorren wasn't too different from Nelbren. The same jobs always needed done, no matter how big the city, or how they lived with their light.

But there was no central green. No flowers. No Mr. Pen to bake pies and give away bread. Here though, it seemed everybody did only one thing, and nobody did everything. Not to mention, everyone was so *dark*. Skin so tan and leathery, every shade of brown she could imagine. Linara studied her arms, a bleached white in the sunlight. Some peddlers had dark skin, but she never expected *everyone* in the Illumination to be so similar.

But despite all of it, Linara felt hopeful. If she could find some familiarity under the bright gaze of a new world, maybe she could make it work.

Linara stifled a yawn and rolled her shoulders. She barely slept. The bed was too big, and too soft. The curtains let in too much light, and when Linara did find some rest, it was after she moved to the hard stone of the floor. Then the deep echo of a ringing bell had woken her, a final reminder she was no longer home.

A platter of food had been waiting for her in the sitting room, piled high with more fruits and bread than her family could afford in a week. As well as her handmaid, Meyla. Orv had mentioned her the night before, but the thought still made Linara uncomfortable.

The only servants she was familiar with belonged to kings and tyrants in storybooks. Linara was little more than a farm girl, and she definitely didn't deserve to be waited on. Orv had said she would be there for any questions or needs, and would be as invisible as Linara wished. The Spire could be a confusing place, he had said, and Meyla would ensure she would never have to wander.

Shortly after waking, Meyla had led her to the bath, a hidden chamber in her room larger than most mounds back in Nelbren. Linara couldn't remember the last time she had bathed, and it took an hour to feel like the ash was truly scrubbed from her skin.

Now she wore clothes far softer than she deserved. Meyla had set out a few options, including a long flowing dress of blue silk. It reminded Linara of a dress her mother had sewn for her when she was a child. She had outgrown it quickly, and they never sewed another. Nobody wore dresses in Nelbren. They were impractical, and cloth was expensive.

Linara had almost put it on. Instead, she left it draped over the couch, embracing familiarity in a plain shirt and trousers. Except even they were too soft. Everything was too soft, or too bright, or too nice.

A knock at the door broke Linara from her contemplations. Orv waited for her on the other side, warm smile seeming to have never left his face. "Good morning, young one. Did you sleep as poorly as I suspect you did?"

Linara stepped out into the hallway, pulling the door closed behind her. "Worse, probably."

"It's been seventy years since I stood where you are, and it took nearly three weeks to not have to sleep on the floor. Or without a pillow over my eyes."

"You came from the Blackness?"

"A town in Feorn, a few times larger than your village. I was a third your age, probably, when they took me here. Twice as scared, too. This city was so bright, I thought it unnatural."

"Do they have rooms with less sun?" Linara asked.

Orv considered. "Sure, but your chambers were my suggestion. It'll help, I promise. The sun is no terrifying thing; it's just different. You should see men from Reginaan study luma, or even a heffen. It really rots their carrots!"

"I suppose they're scary if you don't know they only eat moss," she said. Nela did like to eat her pant legs, though. "Do they have harder mattresses at least?"

"I never thought to ask," Orv said, scratching his chin. "Though I suggest getting used to it as well. These beds are wonderful after a day of sore travel. The larger adjustment, however, is life spent in an unfamiliar city. The more you discover and explore, the more it'll become natural."

"Except when my bedroom is the size of my old home."

"Quite so," Orv said with a faint smile. "It is why I intend to simply embark on a tour of the city this morning. I once explored every street, alley, and building until I could map the city with my eyes closed. That would be a difficult task today, however; the city has expanded quite ambitiously."

Orv led her down the spiral slope of the hallway, allowing her to silently take in the Spire as they descended farther than she'd gone the night before. He told her where each hallway led, and the purpose of each room they passed, but Linara knew she would remember almost nothing. Some parts were simple, though. The higher you climbed, the more important the rooms.

The king's chambers and his office were at the top. The kitchens were near the griffin platform, but that she remembered smelling the night before. At the bottom lived the guards, then the cooks and servants and their families.

The final stretch of hallway opened up suddenly to a chamber larger than Linara had ever seen. The inner wall fell away, replaced by a simple stone railing and a long drop a hundred strides or more. Below, carpeted in lavish red and lit by a huge metal chandelier, was the Spire entry hall.

Tapestries hung from the walls, with embroidered shapes of all types of animals. The only one Linara recognized was a brown stag, with Lorin's name stitched beneath it. A hundred people walked below, the conversations blending and echoing across the wood and stone. Lorin was right. Nelbren *could* easily fit inside the entry hall.

Linara's steps were faltering, trying to take it all in, but Orv had a hand upon her back gently guiding her along, talking at length about the Spire libraries.

Great statues of soldiers greeted them at the bottom, thrice as large as any living man. Some wore helmets of strange animals, others with crowns. Weapons of all sorts—swords, spears, axes—were pressed firmly into the ground at their feet. They stood stoic and watchful, lining both walls, stretching back to a set of closed double doors at the end of the entry hall.

"The throne room," Orv said, following Linara's gaze.

Then he turned and strode out through a black-iron gate. Despite the overwhelming amount of stone in the city, a small field of grass spread from the base of the Spire to a tall white wall a hundred paces on every side. Birds flew between the bushes, growing in scattered places, chirping wildly into the air. Trees, the types that only her father's stories had taught her about, waved with the steady breeze across the mountainside.

Linara rubbed her fingers through the blades of grass. A thousand tickling plants, growing like moss. She plucked a blade and popped it in her mouth, mulling over the taste. Horses ate this stuff? At least moss was *edible* when it dried. Maybe it needed to be cooked?

Orv studied her just as she studied the garden. She wished to stay there forever, but knew there was much more to see. Orv led her out through the next gate, and into the true city of Avorren.

The sun flashed gold across the white bricks, changing with each step, the windows shining like mirrors. Even the bricks of the path seemed scrubbed clean of dirt. It was almost blinding.

Orv moved quickly, through, paying no mind to their surroundings. It was the wealthy district of the city, the Cloud Peaks, he called it. Linara gawked at the size of the manors within. Did the rooftops and buildings she saw from her window all belong to this area? And were the woman washing clothes and the man pulling his cart just servants, like Meyla?

Linara didn't have a chance to ask. A wide path, with metal railings pounded into the rock guided their way down the side of the mountain. The smell of rich oil and leather greeted them when the road leveled off again, the sharp ring of hammers cutting through the dense chatter of the crowd. The Artisan's Pass, as Orv explained.

Here the city felt natural. Used. Worn. Lived in. The buildings were tightly packed, and the roofs a bit lopsided, but Linara could tell the people here preferred it that way.

Linara always imagined the artisans of Avorren to be snobby jewelers and lonesome painters. Instead, it was blacksmiths and sculptors, noses to their work as the crowd walked by. Any apprehension from walking in the upper parts of the city began to fade.

"Most people live above their shops here, hardly ever leaving the district for anything at all," Orv explained, stepping around a pair of shoppers. "A carpenter may need leather for her work, and she buys it from a tanner down the road, who buys his hide from another man a few blocks away, who supplies the whole city."

"It's like its own huge village inside a city." Linara could've spent an entire month in the Pass and still not see everything.

A voice began to rise above the drone of the crowd around them. Linara tried to crane her head to see the source, but found nothing. It grew louder, and louder, until they came across a man standing upon a crate on a street corner. His hair was thick and matted. His robe, patchwork and covered in mud, pooled at his feet..

"Woe to the people who follow these destroyers," the man shouted above the crowd. "You, who rely on their power for safety and comfort! Woe to those who live in ignorance, under the thumb of oppression! Listen to the winds, as they blow! Listen to the earth as it shakes! They destroy kingdoms and level cities, and yet you live with them in your very midst!"

The crowd hardly paid him any mind, but Linara was transfixed. She knew what he spoke of before he even mentioned them by name. She knew he was speaking of her.

Then the man's wild eyes fell upon her. Her heart began to race. He knew. He must, why else would he be staring so deeply into her very soul? He could see the blood on her hands, and the guilt in her eyes.

Then his gaze moved on. "The Odious *scourge*, pressed upon us like a hanging weight, a sword ever to our throats! Is it peace, to be held at sword point? Is it peace to be the one with the bigger monster? I say nay, you people! We must be brought out from under their grip, into true freedom, away from their black magic and terror!"

Orv placed a hand upon her back and guided them farther down the street. "Do not listen to him," he said, not even offering a glance back at the man. "He preaches of ignorance, but I would not put much weight behind a man who does not recognize the very person he speaks against when he stands within his midst."

Her chest felt heavy, and the feeling of eyes upon the back of her neck wouldn't fade. "He wouldn't be speaking so passionately if it wasn't true," she mumbled.

"People stand upon untruths every day. It is not the words he speaks, but how much people listen, which isn't often a good metric, either. If you noticed, nobody was paying him any mind, because they know he speaks nonsense."

Linara tried to glance back, but he was lost to the crowd now, voice muffled in the wind. "Do you think he knows I'm here in the city? That the news already spread out of Nelbren?" Linara asked. Mr. Trel had said that nobody would spread village business, but now she wasn't so sure.

"I very much doubt anybody in this city knows who you are," Orv said. "I doubt many people know who *I* am."

"Good morning, Master Orvinth!" a man shouted for him from a stall across the street, and Orv smiled and waved a hello.

Orv passed a quick glance at Linara and sighed. "Perhaps I am often more humble than I realize."

His words meant little to her. All it showed her was that the Odious weren't just fairy-tale stories to the people in the real world. They were distant threats to places like Nelbren, but now that she was in Avorren and the threat she posed was very much real.

They continued through the city, Orv speaking more about the various districts and shops, but Linara had stopped listening. The thought grew like mold upon her chest that Avorren would never feel like Nelbren. Despite how similar they may be times, her old life would be incompatible. There would never be a return to normal. Orv told her she'd grow comfortable once she knew the city. But there was nothing for her down here. At least in her chambers it was quiet, and she could pretend to be back home.

The buildings grew stranger the farther they walked, away from the usual style everywhere else in the city. Murals and splotches of color broke up the usual snow-white brick.

They stopped in the center of a small courtyard. The bricks were worn and cracked, and the few people who walked through stepped with purpose. Water poured from the mouth of a stone griffin in the center, pooling in a wide fountain.

Orv mentioned something of a surprise and an errand to run, and asked her to stay put. Linara agreed, knowing she had nowhere to wander off to. She knew the dangers of getting lost in unfamiliar places.

She thought she'd be thankful for the rest. The calmness of the morning air here, and the relative quiet was peaceful. But the faint sound of hammering, still echoing across the city, just reminded Linara of the beating of her own heart. It was a warning call, that at any moment the few people walking through the square would know who she was, and turn on her, like they did back in Nelbren.

A man walked through, balancing a bundle of scrolls under his arm. He smiled and tipped his cap at her, and Linara forced a smile back. She didn't wish to be in the open any longer. Under the light of the sun, there were no shadows to hide in.

Linara glanced around. The buildings around were squat and quaint. They were all colored a mismatched batch of hues—purple and green or unpainted brick. Linara saw a saddlemaker on the corner, hanging leather on a line outside his shop. And a gem cutter beside it, whatever that was.

The last building, however, caught her eye. The red brick looked similar to the rest, but the doorway was dark, and unlit by candles or luma. A large wooden sign hung above the door, a faint-green painting of a green wolf and a red bird outlined in elaborate script. *The Last Free Menagerie.*

Linara glanced back at where Orv walked off, but did not see him. The shop was still in the courtyard, and she needed someplace to hide away, if only for a moment. It wasn't even a good option, but it was what she had. Linara went inside.

Candles and lanterns hung from the rafters within, only a few lit to cast the room in a dim, fiery glow. A white-haired wolf slept right by the door, fur constantly shifting from wispy hair to thick green vines. Perhaps it was just a trick of the light. Linara shook her head and walked on.

Each step brought an unfamiliar smell of earth, manure, and flowers. Plants hung in bundles from the rafters, and the tables and shelves were full of jugs and pots of various herbs.

An orange-and-black cat watched her from the top of the shelf. Two massive birds, chromatic like the surface of oil, squawked loudly from the corner. A lizard darted between her feet, but she was mostly used to things like that.

At the counter, a woman stood hunched over a large oblong rock. Thick, curly hair framed a pair of eyeglasses, which balanced precariously upon her nose. Linara breathed in a cloud of dust and sneezed.

"Hello again, dear," the woman said, barely glancing up at her. "Could you hand me that malwollop, please?"

Linara started, then looked around. No one else was in the room. "Do I know you?"

The woman narrowed her eyes. "Do I? Are you not Deni?"

"No. I'm Linara."

"Ahh, I see!" the woman said, nodding firmly to herself. "Pleasure to meet you. I'm Nerissa. Could you hand me that malwollop?"

Linara stared at the table Nerissa gestured to, filled with vials, plants, and jars of colored sand.

"What's a malwollop?" Linara asked.

Nerissa stared up again. "It's the slimy green one that smells like foot fungus."

Linara opened her mouth to ask again, but thought against it. She reached for a thick leafy stem and carefully sniffed at it. It certainly smelled like feet. To be sure, she checked another, and then another. They all smelled of feet.

"It looks like a fuzzy-haired man with his legs twisted together," Nerissa said.

Linara saw a leafy bulb with a wide tangle of branches at its base. She found if she stared long enough, it looked like a person. "This one?"

"Aha, yes! Bring it here."

Linara weaved through the shop and handed it over. Nerissa inspected the bulb carefully, flicking off a few specks of dirt as she found them. Then she whacked it hard against the countertop.

The root exploded, showering orange pulp across the counter and Linara's clothing. The woman reached a finger inside the burst root and slathered the orange paste upon the strange rock in front of her.

"Thank you for your help!" Nerissa said, wiping her hands clean and beaming up at her. "Oh, did I get you with the root? Don't worry, it washes out with cold water. And it might leave minor tingling sensation." Nerissa grabbed a handful of the paste and rubbed in on her arms. "I rather like it myself."

Just then, the pulp began soaking through Linara's clothes, and tiny pins began dancing across her skin. She tried to ignore it. "What are you doing to that rock?"

"It does look like a rock," Nerissa said, holding it up to the light. "I'm ninety-five percent sure it's a dragon egg."

"There's a five percent chance it's still a rock?"

"That percentage *has* been getting smaller. So I'm either slathering it in malwollop root to better insulate and simulate a mother dragon, or I'm making a rock all numb and tingly. I'm mostly just hoping anything works at this point."

Linara glanced around the shop again. A bottle hung from a rope in the corner, dripping water into a large basin surrounded by many small furry creatures. "You don't know how to hatch a dragon egg?"

"Of course not," Nerissa scoffed. "Nobody knows anything about them! Only that their leather is highly sought after. They don't let us get close, you see, not enough to study them. They've decided humans are lesser beings and don't deserve their time. Not anything like my relationship with the pygmy bladehoppers," she said, gesturing toward the basin. "They get quite needy."

Linara laughed. "You make it sound like the dragons decided this formally."

"Don't let *them* hear you say that. Dragons are smart, maybe even smarter than us. Wiser, definitely, but that happens with age. They have a council, a seat of four from each of the corners of this continent, and you better know nothing happens without their approval."

"Like kings?"

"No. Well, maybe. Who knows? North, south, east, and west, they are the dragon seat! But it's a title really, the dominant in each region. Some reign for centuries, some for months, depending on if they can live long enough to defend their seat from others with ambition."

"You seem to know more than you let on."

"You don't need to befriend a dragon to know how their hierarchy works. We can watch those disputes from the ground as they tear up the sky. Quite frightening, I hear."

Linara leaned in close to inspect the egg. "Has anybody tried to ride one?"

"If you did, you'd be on a very exclusive list as the only living rider on Irea. And then you would join the rather extensive list of dead ones."

"Oh. I think after seeing so much already, I figured somebody learned how to tame them."

"I'd settle for just touching one, even," Nerissa said, staring longingly at the egg dripping orange paste onto the countertop.

"Then where'd you get a dragon egg?"

"One of my merchant contacts found it near the silent coast. He brought it back here hoping it wasn't a perfectly oblong rock." Nerissa paused and studied her for a long while. "You're not from around here, are you? Wait, let me guess . . . Mahnbusa?"

Linara glanced at her arms. She'd met a Mahnbusan once. He had dark skin and thick, curly hair all over his arms and legs. To protect from the sand, apparently. "No; Nelbren. It's in the Blackness."

"Fascinating," Nerissa said, eyes brightening. "Have you ever seen a fungalow before?"

Nerissa took her arm and led her to a small shelf behind her counter, where a red, five-legged creature bent itself completely backward as it plucked at its fur with a long thin tongue. Linara had helped birth Nela, and a dozen cats, but this was far stranger. How did it even reproduce? "Does it create milk?" she asked.

Nerissa studied her with wide eyes. "You're the first person to ask me that! It has nipples underneath its armpits so its young can hang on to each leg and never have to move."

"That's so cool," she said. That would explain why she set up her shop in the Artisan's Pass; these creatures were truly works of art, and Nerissa treated them as such.

"Have you met Ferin?" Nerissa said, gesturing toward the sleeping wolf creature Linara saw on the way in. "He's a vinewolf, native to most deep forests and jungles, protectors of all things nature and balance. He likes my shop."

Before Linara had a chance to catch up, she was already across the store again. "And you *must* meet Hector, our resident Fire Phoenix," she said, pulling her to the center of the shop, where a huge flaming bird sat perched on a wide wooden rod suspended from the ceiling. "He's not really on fire; his feathers glow and slowly pulse through various colors, imitating flames. They do radiate some heat, though. I've tried to release him on multiple occasions, but he always comes back within the hour with a roasted rat on the counter, as a gift."

Linara cocked her head and stared. "Like a cat."

"Like a pseudo-flaming, feathered cat," Nerissa agreed.

The bell rang at the front of the shop, and Orv strode in, bowing in respect toward Ferin in the corner as he stirred from his slumber.

"Master Orvinth!" Nerissa said, leaping up.

"Good Morning, Nerissa," Orv said with a wide smile. "I see my young apprentice has made her introduction here. I'm not too surprised."

"Apprentice?" Nerissa asked, staring curiously at Linara before gasping loudly. "You have a mark."

Linara shrank back and nodded slowly. Nerissa scrambled over, wide eyed, and started prodding at her skin. "Fascinating! What color? Source of power? How big? Where is it? Nothing too . . . inconvenient, I hope."

"Uh . . . it's on my shoulder," Linara said.

"Can I see it?"

Linara hesitated, pressing her hand to her shoulder. She glanced at Orv, who had already turned around, inspecting Hector on his perch. There was something strangely comforting about Nerissa, though. Linara unlaced the collar of her shirt and slipped her arm free, revealing her ruby mark pulsing across her shoulder. Nerissa's eyes widened as she moved closer.

"Ahh, *nearly* in an inconvenient place, yeah?" she said, poking at her breast. Linara blushed and held her shirt tighter.

"Very red, very fire, hmm, yes. Full structure, long webs, interesting . . . Have you made anything explode yet?" she asked, wide eyed.

Linara's blood went cold. Before she thought about it, she answered. "Yes," she muttered, eyes glancing at the floor.

But Nerissa didn't shy away. Her eyes softened and she held tighter on to Linara's hands. "I'm sorry to hear that," she said. "You must forgive my excitement, Eions fascinate me as much as most creatures."

"What's an Eion?" Linara said, quickly tying her shirt back into place.

"In due time, Miss Farrow, in due time," Orv said, beckoning her forward. "Thank you, Nerissa, for your hospitality, and thank you, Ferin, for your protection, as always." He said, bowing to the wolf, now fully awake and watching them. Linara whispered a gasp as the wolf bowed back to him, the vines upon his back rippling in a steady pattern.

Once they were outside, Orv smiled at her confusion. "Ferin is more intelligent than he lets on."

"He's not a normal wolf, is he?"

"Vinewolfs are often guardians of world powers. Or in some cases, assistants to the guardians. Ferin lost his many years ago, but has since struck up a relationship with Nerissa I don't fully understand. Perhaps she doesn't, either."

Orv glanced back at Linara and frowned. "I apologize that my task took longer than expected. She didn't make you uncomfortable, did she?"

"Not at all," Linara said. It was the opposite, really. Meeting two sides of the same spectrum so close together was jarring. One, afraid of her, the other merely curious.

That was the difference between Nelbren and Avorren, really. The same people, with varied opinions. Only here, with so much light, she could just see more of it and from farther off.

Linara wasn't sure which was more comforting, to live in ignorance, or to live in the light. The more she could see, the muddier it seemed to get.

Nerissa watched the girl disappear into the crowds outside her shop. Not a very large crowd, but a crowd nonetheless. A crowd that may, one day, lock eyes with the sign above her shop, and be so captivated, so motivated, so entranced by the very idea, that they finally make their way inside.

Today was not that day, however. Nor was it the time to fantasize about such pleasantries. It was a new day, full of a new person! Glancing at Ferin, Nerissa noticed his vines pulsing and moving in a peculiar rhythm across his back. They rarely danced like that these days. Ever since those tiny adolescent drollops started bullying him. Poor thing, no self-confidence, none whatsoever.

"Why Ferin, you're smitten!" Nerissa said, folding the window shades over and blocking out more light. Ferin's vines stopped suddenly and returned to their usual melancholy stir. What a drama queen. "Well, I like her," she said, folding her arms. He opened one eyelid and gazed up at her momentarily before shutting it again. "Yes, I agree. We should stick to that one like vines on fur." She paused as his vines twisted and flickered in irritation. "You're right; poor analogy. I apologize."

CHAPTER NINE

Orv led Linara further down the main thoroughfare to the final stretch of road that led to the base of the mountain. They didn't step through the gate, lest they be swept up in the traffic and end up at the bottom.

The Labor Valley made up the rest of the city, expanding around the entire base of the mountain. Full of warehouses, taverns and other various shops, it was easily the largest section. A fine place to explore, if one had the time, but dangerous if someone didn't know which areas to avoid. For now, Orv left the tour there, and they continued back up toward the Spire.

By the time they made it back to the heart of the Artisan's Pass, the street preacher was gone. His box remained, shoved back against the wall where it probably belonged. Still, his words echoed through Linara's mind, of swords and terrors in the night. It probably wouldn't soon leave, despite Orv and Nerissa's comforting words.

A cart lumbered just ahead of them, pulled by a single ox, assuming Linara remembered the name of the animal correctly. It reminded her much of Nela. Most of the other travelers moved on around it, but Orv seemed content in a slow pace back up the mountain. Linara was thankful for it. Her calves burned something fierce, but she was finding her back hardly ached. The physician's care the prior night did wonders.

Linara wondered if Orv even noticed the cart at all. He'd been rambling about the history of the city, among other various topics of study, since leaving Nerissa's shop. It was growing a bit overwhelming, and she was no closer to understanding why she was truly brought to Avorren at all. She knew it wasn't just to be educated. But she wouldn't ask, more afraid of the answer than the uncertainty.

"We'll start right into the basics. Geography and important histories, I think. Albeit, my list will be far shorter than others would agree upon. Perhaps a few other miscellaneous topics could be useful. Stately etiquette, points of travel and trade, griffin riding, etcetera, etcetera. Let's skip all that for now, though."

Linara perked up. "Griffin riding?" One thing she was discovering was how much she truly missed the feeling of flight from the day before. Not to mention, the way Lorin had described it, she was sure griffinback would be even better.

"Yes, of course, I'll make that a point to the stable master then. It can be relaxing to some, and a chore to others, but I'm thinking it will be one of your lighter lessons."

Still, all this talk of books and learning and she had not the slightest idea of why. Was she plucked from Nelbren just to read about history?

Orv seemed to notice her fall behind, and he glanced back, worried. "Is this all too overwhelming? Shall we continue this tomorrow? Or do you perhaps already know of all of this? Hmm . . . Surely not, Nelbren is pretty isolated . . ." Then he slapped his forehead. "Oh, sun above, I forgot to even ask! Do you know how to read?"

Linara scrambled, trying to interrupt. "No—I mean yes. I mean, no, that isn't it. It's just—" she paused. "Are books and history like that really the best place to start?"

"Well . . ." Orv grimaced. "I don't really know. It's where *I* wish I had started. It's important to know the failings of our predecessors to build a foundation of success."

"I think I already know firsthand about the mistakes involved," Linara muttered.

"True . . .true . . ." Orv said, considering. "I don't have much experience in teaching. As much of a great man my mentor was, he was not very great at having pupils. He was a man who could learn by watching, and assumed everyone else was the same way."

The cart ahead of them hit a bump in the road and lurched awkwardly along the path. Orv didn't seem to notice, but Linara felt a weight in her chest, a strange terror of a sound that echoed faintly off the walls around them. Maybe it was the snap of leather, or the crack of wood. It could have been the cry of the ox pulling the cart.

But the cart started moving back down the road, gaining speed as it tumbled down the mountainside.

A yell rang out from ahead of them, a desperate cry from a desperate driver as he dove from the cart's front bench. The few men and women ahead of them quickly leapt out of the path of the cart as it careened down the slope, jostling and twisting out of control.

Linara grabbed a fistful of Orv's robe and tried to pull him away, but he stood fast to the pavement. Eyes fixated, he stared at the cart with only a hint of a smile. Was he mad? A cart moving that fast would crush him without even slowing. Linara never stopped tugging, however, unwilling to leave him behind.

Orv thrust out his cane, and vines sprouted from the tip in a flash. Roots, thick as barrels, met the cart like a great sinuous hand. Linara clamped her eyes shut, feeling the impact thump through the bricks and into her chest. She dared a look, vision obscured by a cloud of dust pluming out from the cart, now stopped in the net of roots.

The cloud settled, and Linara could feel the silent crowd staring at them both. Mouths agape, they watched the vines and cart, uncertain if they should be afraid or amazed. Or a little of both.

Orv stepped forward and pinched the end of his cane, breaking off the growth of roots. He dusted off the end and tapped it against the stone a few times, satisfied. The driver, a short man with a drooping mustache, rushed forward with tears in his eyes. He threw himself at Orv in a tight embrace, sobbing his thanks into his robes.

The crowd loosened at that, deciding at once that Orv had, in fact, done well. Two sweat-glistened men from the smithy beside them returned with the ox, frayed leather lead and broken yoke trailing on the stones behind. A few others were already pulling the cart free from the roots, dragging it back uphill and into an alley, where it wouldn't roll away so easily.

All very village-like. When something needed done, count on everyone to get involved. When the cart was finally free, the crowd dispersed, reminding Linara that they were still in Avorren, after all.

Orv spent some time comforting the driver before urging him to tend to his ox and cart, now left alone in the alley beside them. Then Orv took a moment to inspect his new creation. He walked around the furl of roots, frowning at a few curves and dents in the new wood. Then he placed a hand upon its surface, and within moments, the healthy roots shriveled and turned to dust.

He turned and winked at Linara before waving her to follow. She skirted around the pile of dust settling upon the bricks, staring wide eyed at Orv as they climbed back to the Spire, as if nothing had happened at all.

"What was that?" she asked.

"That, young Linara, was what being Marked truly means."

"Odious, you mean."

Orv grunted. "I've always hated that word. Odious. It means we are something to be feared. In reality, we are a gift. We are imparted with power to change the world. Often it is used for great evil, but not always. We *are* imparted. It is a shame that term will never stick. At least not in my lifetime."

Linara grunted. "You make this power sound like a good thing."

"Did I not prove that it is?"

"I would find it difficult to stop a runaway cart with fire."

"Yes, I would probably agree. But there are many problems you might solve that I could not."

"Like what? Will I stand in a room to keep the king warm? Will I light up the shadows of the Spire until I wither and die?"

"Ahh, life would be too easy if I knew, wouldn't it? That is part of our journey, to discover the depths where we are needed, and to fill them as we see fit."

"I can think of only a few good uses for a flame, and none of them I wish to think of for long."

"Fire is used to temper steel," Orv said after a bit of thought. "To heat metal to forge and refine. It's used as an avenue of artisans, a medium for art upon wood and stone. It's a light, a flicker of life, the heart of heat and comfort. Even the burning power of fire in a forest can be the catalyst for new growth. There are new and creative ways to apply all sources of power, and it took many years to find mine."

"Nobody seems to remember the good deeds," Linara said.

"Aye. There are plenty of tavern ballads and folktales of the world-changing Odious, like Talar the Splintered, who shattered the

Deydalus coastline to create the island nation of Arkya. In the center of every exaggeration is the truth, despite how ancient its origins. There are some who irresponsibly shattered nations and kingdoms with their power, and those are the stories that everyone remembers. In reality, there are many more who have done nothing with their gifts, and some that have made history in better ways. They carve cities, protect forests and other primal sources of power. For every nightmarish Odious, there are twenty who fade from history unnoticed. Like all authority and power, it needs to be treated with wisdom."

Orv gestured to the mountain they walked upon. "Like Avorren, for example. This was no natural creation. A mountain sprung out of the plains where none other exist? An oddity that smells like Odious influence. But my predecessors, including Master Korion, came to this mountain with their gifts and carved the stone like clay."

"They had the power over earth?"

"Not exactly. We will explore that aspect later, but know for now that they could send great spikes of force into the ground and crack the stone with precision. It took many years and had some interesting consequences for the landscape around here. I'm sure you noticed the pits and ravines as you flew in? All the rumbling from this mountain collapsed not a few underground caverns."

Linara nodded and stared out over the city and the burning sunset beyond. She heard stories of the sun being a great bonfire thrown into the upper reaches of the heavens by an ancient Odious, a constant light and source of heat, flickering red hot across the clouds in the Scarlet Band. Perhaps she could do that.

"I will leave you with one last thing for the day," Orv said as they crested the final hill, entering back into the Spire gardens.

He stepped off the path and into the grass, combing the ground with his foot. Then he lowered himself to one knee, carving out a small hole in the dirt. He worked meticulously, nudging aside small rocks and apologizing to the bugs and a thin earth worm as he displaced them.

Satisfied, Orv reached into his satchel pocket and pulled out a thin leather sack. He smiled and gingerly reached in, pulling out a tiny, familiar seed.

Is that—?

Orv passed her a glance and a knowing smile before pressing the seed to his lips and then placing it in the hole as carefully as he had dug it. Before Linara could speak, Orv inhaled deeply and placed his palm over the seed. Linara could *feel* something from him. Almost like a soft breeze, gentle against the skin, blowing toward Orv and into the ground.

A few seconds passed, and then the dirt shifted and moved. A thin black stem emerged from the ground between his fingers, rising steadily higher into the air until it burst open to form a web of thin branches. Taller it grew still, until the branches burst apart, and the stem formed a rubbery bark. Orv shifted his hand upon the tree's trunk as it grew too big to fit between his fingers, still doing . . . whatever it was he was doing.

Finally Orv took his hand away and gasped, his breathing returning to a normal pace.

"A tanglegum tree," Linara said, inhaling the thick, sweet smell of the branches. It was almost impossible to plant them with human hands. They only grew naturally, spread by some strange twist of fate to nearby hilltops.

Orv stared at the thin syrup coating his fingers. "I wanted Avorren to have a bit of your home in it. It's something I wish was done for me," he said, cleaning his hand with a thin rag he pulled from his pocket.

"They take decades to grow to season." Before that, the branches weren't strong enough, or flexible enough for proper cordage.

"Twenty-five and a half years, technically."

"How does your mark do any of this?"

Orv placed a hand across her shoulder. "After many years, I wonder the same. I accept what it can do and do with it what I think will help the most." He stepped back and pulled up his shirt, revealing a small part of a deep-green mark across his left side. It webbed out across his body like Linara's but looked over ten times the size. "I will show you how to do as I did, though with fire instead of trees and nature."

Linara searched Orv for any deception. He truly believed being Odious was a gift, and that Linara truly had something to offer the world besides death and destruction. Perhaps it was the sweetness of the sap, or the comfort of the hanging shadows of a tanglegum tree, but Linara suddenly began to believe him.

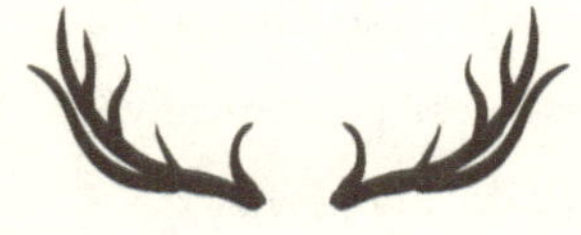

Orvinth Vinhower III, now alone in his office, rubbed at the sticky sap on his hand, careful not to touch the bare skin of his good hand. He was already in a rut as it was. His hand, now balled into a fist, was stuck tight from the tanglegum sap. Even the rag he used was now permanently adhered to his robe pocket. He tried to play it off at the time, to seem competent for his new apprentice, but soon he'd have to crawl back to her room and ask how to unclench his fist.

He sure deserved it, after showing off like that. Orvinth sighed and dunked his hand back into the basin of water. Water, oil, soap, nothing worked, even in the slightest. He cursed under his breath as he worked his stuck fist under the water. He still had a few things left to try before that walk of great shame down to young Linara's room. Always a few things more.

CHAPTER TEN

Linara woke in the morning like any other since arriving in Avorren—uncomfortable and restless. Names and histories swam in her head like buzzing insects; pictures of maps imprinted on her eyelids. The only comfort she had found was with her morning meals and a bath before her lessons.

Three weeks had passed as quickly as they usually did, much to Linara's surprise. She had no chores to do, no work to keep her on her feet, but her studies with Orv filled more time than anything back home.

After returning from their tour, he'd scoured his library for books on histories and sums, making up for a lost education growing up in the middle of nowhere. Her mother had taught her some things before she died, but everything she needed to know she learned on the job, doing the chores her father needed done.

This type of work was far less appealing. At least at home she knew why the jobs needed done. Nela always needed milked, and it was good to keep the chickens clean and healthy. But why a knowledge of Mahnbusan economics was important was beyond her.

Trapped inside most of the day, she could not even see the faint moon enough to gauge the passing of the day. A set of bells rang out through the city at key points, but Linara still wasn't able to remember the different tones.

Orv hardly followed a daily schedule, and his pace was relentless. Linara was certain they would take more breaks if she asked, but she wasn't sure what she would do with them. She spent most of her free time beneath the tanglegum tree, but that often got boring rather quickly, and she only had enough courage to venture out to Nerissa's shop a handful of times.

Today, though, was different. Before she even stepped out of her room, she found a note upon the table in Orv's own script. He was caught up in a sudden morning meeting, it said, and to return to his office after her midday meal. With scant idea of how to pass the time.

As much as she wished to sleep away the day, she knew it would do little good. Tiredness seemed to cling like a stubborn rain, but she still couldn't accustom herself to such brightness yet. It grew easier by the day, but even the nightmares shook her awake most nights.

She didn't even have Meyla to talk to. The woman barely made herself known, besides the platter of food and a fresh set of clothing she left every morning. The few times Linara *had* bumped into her were very short and as awkward as expected.

Meyla was easily thirty years older, but when had Linara ever gotten along with anyone her age? If Linara was going to have somebody waiting on her like Meyla was, she at least wanted to know more about her. Meyla, evidently, thought differently.

It was times like this, alone with her own thoughts, Linara missed the stars the most. She longed for the guidance, for the comfort. She never realized how much she relied upon them, now that they were gone. Well, they were never truly *gone.* They were still somewhere above the bright and blinding sky. But if the sun blocked her sight of them, did it block their sight of *her* as well?

Maybe even Trel and Pen were up there. Maybe they could forgive her one day. It was a small comfort, imagining her actions sent them to the heavens. She hoped they were deserving enough. Their bodies weren't even fully burned, but maybe it still worked.

Linara shook the thought away. It was never good to dwell on such things, especially when she had nothing to distract herself with. Whatever she did, she'd find no good staying locked up in her chambers.

Linara pushed open her door and stepped into the hallway, resigning herself to heading into the city after all, hoping this time not to get lost on the way to Nerissa's shop.

Out on important dragon business
No loitering or snooping, stealing or conniving
Ferin will know of it!
Be back soon. ish.
Nerissa

Linara sighed, her breath fogging in the morning air. It was just like Nerissa to up and leave with hardly a warning. She had been talking about taking a trip with the dragon egg, but it never sounded like she was entirely sure where she'd even be going.

Nothing to be done about it now. Linara turned back to the square, watching the griffin statue in the center pour out water into the pool. Koin, the balding saddlemaker, waved to her. He slid a long metal blade along a stretch of leather, pooling hair and fat at his feet.

Out of the corner of her eye, Linara spotted Ferin the vinewolf trotting out from beside the building. She frowned at him. He'd never left his perch by the door, let alone walked all the way outside. He left behind patches of mossy ground where he stepped that quickly withered and faded back to stone. No one else in the square seemed to even acknowledge him.

He paused by the fountain, glancing back at her. He studied her for a moment, like he was waiting for her to follow. Maybe this was the guidance she sought, after all. Not the stars, but something just as ancient.

Ferin led the way through the square, trotting up against the wall and down a minor road. Buildings and cliffsides rose, casting deep shadows on the streets below. Ferin turned sharply, leapt up a small set of stairs, and disappeared through an open doorway.

Linara paused and looked up at the filthy, crumbling walls. She glanced around, noticing no other living souls in the surrounding street, suddenly feeling quite alone.

Well, Ferin seemed to think the shop was safe enough. She glanced at the sign nailed above the door, script long faded. *Past and Ancient History*. Could a store sell history? Linara stepped through the door and found the answer.

The air smelled old and musty, like a long-abandoned mound, finally reopened for cleaning. Very little light filtered through the door and windows. A small luma lantern hung from the highest peak of the ceiling, casting a faint, blue light. Crates and barrels were scattered around the floor, topped with cracked vases and old plates. Linara shuddered at the wall of raggedy books, reminded of her studies she'd been trying to escape.

Dust scattered at her movement through the doorway. Ferin was nowhere in sight, but a man stood against the wall, eyes unfocused, staring at a large slab of stone propped on a small table. The strange symbols on the surface of the stone were nothing she recognized.

The man turned to face her, entirely unsurprised by her presence. "Welcome," he said, pushing his eyeglasses farther up his hawk-like nose. He brushed a stray hair away from his face, one of the few hairs left upon his head. "You are not from here."

If that was a question, Linara didn't know how to answer. But the man was already moving, studying her features in the light of the lantern above.

"You are pale," he said. "Black hair, thin build." He furrowed his eyes and lifted her arm to stare into her armpit. "Little hair growth." Linara clamped her arms down at her side. "Not tall, but not squat, either." He sniffed the air deeply, smacking his tongue upon the roof of his mouth. "Hmm. Quite . . . mossy. Damp, as well." He stared at her, eyes growing unfocused again. "The southern hills of Elaan?"

Linara took a step back. Could he figure all that out just by what she looked like? And what she . . . smelled like? "Nelbren."

The man brightened. "Never heard of it!" He slapped his palms across his forearms. "I am Artoris. It is a pleasure to finally meet you, Linara Farrow of Nelbren."

Linara smiled and slapped her palms across her arms as well, a welcome familiarity since arriving in Avorren. "Do I know you?"

"You've met my wife. Now please, I must see your mark!"

Linara flushed, stepping back and glancing toward the door. The windows were filthy, covered in grime and dust that obscured all view, but anybody could walk in at any moment. "Your wife? I haven't met many people . . ."

"Nerissa," he said, waving the statement off. "She left this morning on a long journey. I suspect that's why you're here. And worry not about privacy. Nobody visits my shop this time of day. Or any time of day."

Nerissa was married? She never made any mention of it. Linara reached to her collar, but hesitated. Artoris didn't seem at all dangerous. Only just as curious as Nerissa was the day they met. She sighed and began untying the neck of her shirt, pulling it down just enough to reveal the swirling ruby of her mark, softly glowing in the faint darkness.

Artoris furrowed his brow and pushed his eyeglasses down his nose as he examined her skin. "Very red, yes, very fire indeed. Have you made anything explode yet?"

"Why is that the first thing people ask me?"

"It is within my realm of study, of course!"

"You study explosions?"

"Ahh, close." He scampered off, waving her forward as he squeezed between a pair of broken statues and cobwebs. Artoris stopped at a large painting against the wall, faded with time and dust, half obscured by boxes and piles of books. The object of the painting was still clearly visible, a smoking crater formed in the center of a ruined city. Buildings smoldered in such detail, flames still burning the painted countryside. A true ruined landscape captured on canvas.

Linara felt sick, even without knowing the history behind it.

"This is the city of Yarldin, lost now to time and destruction," Artoris said.

"What happened to it?" Linara breathed

"Fen of the Hidden Flame."

He was one of the Seven Odious, but one whose story Linara hadn't heard told often.

"To answer your prior question, I study history. And none have left more of an impact than the Seven Odious," Artoris explained, "The *true* world changers. Eidgar the Deceiver. Thien Earthshaker. Rradgar the Lifestealer. Fen of the Hidden Flame. Talar the Splintered. Storm Maker Pol Drun. And Liza Burnfeather."

"Orv has been looking for a book from Liza," Linara said absently. She wasn't entirely thrilled to read it, but he had overturned every bookshelf in his office to no avail.

"Ahh, a lost tome," Artoris said. "It does not happen often for him. Perhaps one I'd be able to find in my shop."

"I assumed his library had everything."

"Nearly everything. Orvinth has tried to gather the materials of history, just as I have, but the difference is I am actually able to leave the city to find them."

"He came to my home to find me," Linara said with a shrug.

"And you must have been quite the find for that rarity to occur."

"I don't think he knew much about me before I came."

Artoris snorted. "If it is not obvious by now, Orv is not a man to gamble. He must have known what he'd find before he left."

Her father did write him a letter, but she'd probably never find out what exactly was written.

"You know, I was but a young boy when I met Orvinth Vinhower," Artoris said. "He was at the peak of his life then, and now I am an old man myself. I devoted my life to setting history straight, just as he had. It was when his body started to degrade that he realized he hadn't even attempted to protect the most important history of all. His own. At a certain point, he realized expecting to find a pupil would be foolish, so he started writing everything down."

"That's why he has so many journals," Linara said.

Artoris bobbed his head in half agreement. "Well, that's also just who he is. I, of course, knew from the start that if he were to truly finish, he would've had to start a decade earlier. Now I suppose it doesn't matter, for you've arrived just in time."

Linara listened in silence, following his gaze back to the painting, his eyes still studying every detail. If his idea was to make her feel better about being here, it wasn't working. "Why do you tell me this?"

He turned to her then, studying her face. "What do you fear, Linara Farrow?"

Linara's eyes glanced toward the picture before she could think. She feared being like Fen, immortalized in history, accidental or not.

"Ahh, you fear your purpose, then?" Artoris said.

Her eyes snapped back to his, studying his face. That was certainly not how she would have phrased it. "What do you mean?"

"For what other reason would you have been brought here than to be a warning to others? The *Razing of Yarldin* always hangs in the back of every king's mind. Imagine the sort of danger an Odious of that power can be to your own people. But when they're loyal to you? A powerful force to have at your disposal. Kingdoms these days are forever locked in a stalemate of power, at the whim of who has the strongest Odious."

Linara's eyes widened. Of course that was the case. She was foolish to think they sent a knight to kill her back in Nelbren. Why destroy something dangerous when you could use it to your advantage?

The walls began twisting upon themselves as she glanced back at the painting. She steadied herself against the counter.

"I would not fear, however," he continued, "No one dares use these weapons at their disposal, otherwise a mutual destruction is assured. Just being alive and present is all the purpose that needs to be served. Orv is old, and everyone knows it. Reginaan, to our north, has grown bold because of this. A war has been approaching, but now, perhaps not. Now that you're here, such a weakness has been patched, so to speak."

The ravings of that mad street preacher came back to memory. He spoke of swords and forced peace. She'd slowly forgotten his words, but what if he was more accurate than even Orv let on?

"Is that why I've been brought here?" she breathed.

"King Cindivaar is a wise and strong man, but often one dimensional," Artoris said. "But who am I to say?"

"Orv made it sound different."

"Orv often disagrees with the king."

Ferin pushed his way through the aisle then, stopping at Artoris's side and staring up at Linara. Artoris scratched above Ferin's ear, whose vines endlessly twisted and curled in on themselves. They both stared at her, and the tightness in Linara's chest grew by the second. She wanted to leave now, run out the door and out of the city, never to return.

"Why have you come here, Linara Farrow?" Artoris finally asked.

"I was following him," Linara said, nodding at Ferin. The vines suddenly shifted and curled in a different set of patterns, and Artoris frowned down at the wolf.

"An interesting choice." Artoris hummed curiously to himself and turned his attention back to the painting. "Purpose is a fickle thing, you know. Heavy as a dragon, but harder to catch than a mouse."

"That dragon has been thrust upon me, I think," Linara said.

"Some truly are locked in those situations, and they have not the power to change it. Do not fall for the fallacy that you are in the same position."

"I'm . . . not sure what you mean."

Artoris pointed at the painting, but his eyes looked straight into hers. "Power brings choice, and choice is power. With that mark of yours, you have all the power in the world."

Linara entered the Spire with her shoulders slumped. It was a long, lonely walk back up the mountain. The midday bell had rung out over the city a long while back, and her stomach growled.

Orv would be searching for her, but that was hardly important now. She didn't want to go to her lesson, that much was certain. At least finding a meal was convenient enough of an excuse.

Letting her stomach guide her, Linara hiked up the Spire slope, sniffing out the kitchens like a hunting cat. She ventured for the first time into the branching hallways, following useless signs and the light from the strange glass panels.

Orv had said that somewhere in the endless hallways of the lower levels lay the kitchens. But finding it amongst the larders, the library, the servant quarters and the sitting rooms was like finding a silver tile in a pile of luma.

How confusing did a palace need to be? Anger simmered below the surface. Toward the city, her mark, and the endless, confusing hallways. At least if she were home, she'd be able to find her way in the dark. But there, she'd be searching for cold mushrooms and stale bread, where in Avorren she'd be getting some warm food.

Linara turned the corner into an enormous room, lit by a half dozen blazing hearths against the walls, and a line of simple chandeliers, burning candles. This was surely the guards' meal hall, but at the moment, most tables were empty.

Against one wall, a cauldron was set above the flames, a young cook slowly stirring with a long wooden stick. Food was food, no matter who it was meant for.

The cook turned toward her as she approached, face expressionless. His skin was blue as luma, even in the firelight. A Luman-Viri? She'd heard of them before. A race from Arkya, apparently ageless. Though, he looked youthful, no older than she was. And besides the blue tone, nothing else about him seemed all that different.

"We do not receive many guests after the bell," the Luman-Viri said. His words were slow and deliberate, monotone, yet almost melodic. "At least those who are not from the watch. Most send for their servants, but it is always nice to find a new face in the kitchens."

"I usually eat in my room," Linara said hesitantly. "But I've been out."

"You've come for my stew this day?" he said, Linara almost missing that it was a question. She nodded, and he turned, finding a bowl and filling it slowly with his ladle. "I've heard your name uttered throughout the Spire. Are you Linara Farrow from Nelbren?"

Linara furrowed her brow and stepped back. How did everyone know so much about her? How much else did they know? "I am," Linara said hesitantly, stretching out her hand like everyone else seemed to.

The man cocked his head, staring at her outstretched hand for a few brief moments before forcing the bowl into it and bowing low. "My name is Raastivarlin. Every person around here calls me Raast. It is easier to say, I believe, and every person likes to be in a hurry."

"I've noticed that too," Linara said.

"As much as I love this land, I miss the slowness of my home island," Raast said, musingly.

"Is your home in the Blackness?" she asked, taking a seat at a nearby bench.

"We do not call it such, but yet, we live in a place where the moon lives," Raast said, standing curiously close to her. "That is the only place a child of the moon *must* live."

"Then why are you in Avorren?" Linara decided he wouldn't be going away anytime soon, and started eating anyway.

"I've come to prepare food," Raast said with a solid nod. "Be wary, the stew is still quite hot."

But Linara ignored him, shoving spoonful after spoonful into her mouth. "If you've made this, you've done pretty well," she said between mouthfuls. She had to force herself to keep her pace slow, avoiding tipping the entire bowl and drinking it. It was the best meal she'd had since she'd arrived. It was the best meal she'd had in years.

"I thank you for your compliments, but I must be the best. No, wrong word," Raast said, pondering. "I would *like* to be the best."

"There are better cooks than you?" Linara asked, scraping the bottom of the bowl clean.

"There is always room to be better," Raast said, staring off as if he were recalling a memory. "I do not think the guards are knowing that I prepare the meals for them while my master focuses on the high section of the Spire. The more I cook, the better I will be. That is what every person is saying."

"Have I been eating your master's food since I've arrived?" It would explain why this stew tasted so much better than her last meals.

"I am to believe that you stay near Master Orvinth? So yes, Master Dent prepares your meals."

"I think I'll come down here every morning instead," Linara said with a laugh.

Raast considered the statement for a short while. "The men grow rowdy in the morning, especially when visually appealing women are involved."

Linara blushed and spluttered over her next words until she realized he wasn't flirting with her. He spoke with slowness and age, but also with a strange naivety. "Would Meyla fetch my meals from you if I asked her?"

"I am to believe that all maidservants will do most anything you ask of them."

Linara paused. "Surely there's a reason they use the other kitchen. I don't like the idea of giving orders unnecessarily . . ."

"They are not slaves, Linara Farrow. The king pays them for their service, just as he does for my stew."

Linara said nothing, unsure of how to phrase how she disagreed. Did she disagree at all?

"I can leave whenever I wish to," Raast continued. "But I have come for a reason, and I stay for the same reason."

"To become a great cook?" Linara asked.

"I believe so. I remember little of how I came to be here, except I longed to cook for kings," Raast said, pointing his ladle to the ceiling. Then he turned back to stir the cauldron. "Why have *you* come, Linara Farrow?"

"I'm not sure I had a choice," Linara said, grimacing.

"Do you wish to leave?"

Linara hesitated. She wasn't even sure of that. If her true purpose in being trained was to be a sword, she certainly didn't. But Orv thought otherwise. "I don't know. Maybe."

"What is keeping you from doing so?"

"Where would I go? How would I get there?"

"I do not know, I am only a cook," he said, rapping the side of the cauldron with his ladle.

"They would come after me. I'm too useful to let roam."

"If you believe so."

"And . . . even if I left, I'm sure I would just repeat what had already happened. I'm too much of a danger to have a simple life."

"If you are not too much danger for the king of this land, then you are not too much danger for any person else," Raast said.

She supposed he was right. Linara now lived in a section of the palace filled with the more important people in the kingdom. Orv placed her there because he believed in her ability to control her mark.

Linara stared at her hands. "I just miss home."

"No place feels like Arkya to me," Raast said with a sad smile. "Not even in the other places where the moon truly lives. Places try very hard to feel comfortable, but I always long for Arkya. But there is no king on Arkya, so my dream does not work there."

"There are some places that seem familiar enough," Linara said, "Orv even added to his garden outside for me. It was the nicest thing anyone's done for me."

Raast turned to look at her, curiosity filling his eyes. "Then perhaps there are places like Arkya in the city too? I haven't been outside the Spire in a long while. I have no memories of it."

Linara gawked. "You haven't had a day off?"

Raast shrugged. "My days off I spend cooking."

"You haven't at least wanted to *see* outside?"

"The city is quite large, and I don't know where I'd go, I think. But Avorren is not the reason I came here. I came to cook for kings." He paused again, to consider. "Perhaps, Linara Farrow, if familiarity is not helping, you might instead find your own reason you should stay?"

Linara pulled her knees close to her chest. "I just don't want to hurt anybody."

"A good goal to have. How will you know when you achieve it?"

"When I die and nobody else has been harmed by my hands."

"You would have to never leave your room, Linara Farrow, to never hurt somebody," Raast said with a laugh.

"That'll be made a lot more difficult when I'm sent to wage war."

"Are we at war?" Raast asked.

"Not that I know of. At least not yet."

"Then what is there to worry about?"

Linara opened her mouth to object, but closed it. He was right, in a way. She had time. Time to plan. Time to figure out the details. And more importantly, time to learn. Maybe that was what Artoris meant, and what Orv intended.

Power brought choice.

"I suppose you're right," Linara said softly.

"About what?" Raast said. He had gone back to stirring the deep pot.

"Your advice," she said, frowning at him.

The Luman-Viri stared at her for a few moments. "If it was helpful, I believe it was unintentional. I just wanted to feed you."

They both turned as a group of guards sauntered through the archway behind her, voices slurred and loud. Voices called for Raast to prepare bowls. So far, they seemed to ignore her, but Linara still felt unnerved by the smell of ale already drifting on the air.

"Ahh, the end of one shifting of the watch," Raast said, staring after them. "I will have to leave you and serve them."

Linara breathed in deep and stood up to leave. "It's fine, I should head back."

"Good afternoon, Linara Farrow," Raast said with a low bow.

Linara made her way back to the central ramp. What a strange fellow. He seemed so old, and wise, and yet so strangely young.

Still, his words seemed to find purchase. She did have time, and if doom and destruction waited for her at the end of this long path, she could at least walk it until she had the strength to leave it.

If Orv disagreed with the king's own purpose for her life, then he'd be an ally. He knew that fire could be more than destruction, something of life, something of creation, but they were things Linara knew nothing about. Orv had mastery, to tame the wild nature that could destroy stone and crack foundations. He found control, and he did nothing but create. Linara desired that control.

She wouldn't be helpless, and she wouldn't be used. She would learn to tame the heat and the wildfire, so when the day came that she'd be forced to use it, she'd be gone.

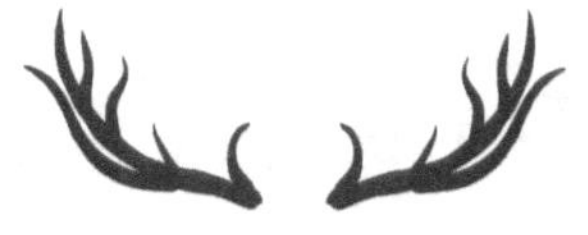

Artoris stood at the Razing of Yarldin, *the colors melding as one into his mind. An event lost to time, but not to history. So long ago, but so fresh. He sniffed and looked around, remembering the girl. How long had it been? An hour? Twelve? A strange girl. She smelled of change. What kind of world would Linara Farrow create? He studied the painting. The blackened sky, the crimson strokes.*

Hopefully not that one.

He spun and stalked between his aisles to a nook in the corner covered in rags and tapestries from a bygone era. Beneath the materials lay a chest, rotted and broken. Inside was a book, edges charred and cover faded. A biography of Liza Burnfeather. Could this help? Could a mouse stop a rolling boulder? Perhaps at the top of the hill. Catalysts and reactions.

It was a book Orvinth did not possess, at least not after Artoris had taken it from him. That was a dark time, full of grudges and mistakes. Perhaps it was time to let it lie and be useful for once. Artoris set his jaw and plucked the book from its hiding place and made off out the door toward the Spire. Back to its rightful home. But whether that was with Orv or with young Linara, Artoris did not know.

CHAPTER ELEVEN

The horizon outside the city burned a deep orange, clouds bursting aflame by the distant sun. Linara had been in Avorren for nearly a month now, and only recently had the sun not given her a headache. It really was amazing, and she understood why no peddler or traveler could quite describe it.

Lorin stood beside her, bronze stag helmet held awkwardly under one arm. The other was plunged into the feathers of her griffin, Aria, who was quietly grazing on the long golden grass. She wasn't paying much attention to the colored sky. Nobody was. It was a strange reminder that Linara didn't quite belong.

The stronger reminder, of course, was that she wasn't allowed to train with the guard recruits. Two dozen men and women, ranging from grizzled laborers to simple children, stood a hundred yards beside, all in the basic yellow vests of the Avorren guard—minus the coats that would prove their status as full soldiers, of course. Even a more spindly group of folks stood off to the side. Future city messengers and field scouts, mostly.

A week ago, Orv had written to the commander of the griffin watch, petitioning for a seat in the upcoming batch of training, but it was swiftly declined. It was never explained why, but Linara suspected that she was too dangerous to be kept close to the other recruits. But before Orv could petition an appeal, Lorin stepped up to train her personally.

Their journey together in the carriage from Nelbren was what inspired Linara to want to take up the saddle, so it was strangely fitting. Every day since, she'd met with Lorin outside the city gates to learn the basics of flight. It was a slow process, leading up to a few days before where she rode a *horse*. They were just hoofbeaks with teeth. She knew enough about them to know that they could not fly, and that was all Linara really *needed* to know.

Apparently, falling from a griffin in flight hurts more than falling from a horse, but what better way to learn than with the risk of plummeting a thousand feet? That, of course, was why Linara would never be allowed to teach a class.

At least now they were finally moving on from horses. That was more than could be said of her training with Orv. Despite a renewed motivation to learn, they still hadn't left the grueling history of the geographical changes of kingdom borders. She shuddered even at the thought, and turned her attention to the field ahead.

Three dozen griffins grazed a quarter mile off—off-duty messenger birds and retired guard mounts, chewing on moss and grass between their claws or staring curiously their way.

Linara and the rest of the group would pick their mount for the day soon. Linara already had one mount in mind. A graying bird separate from the others, walking slowly and methodically as he stared longingly into the sky. They were all saddled, and knew what awaited them, but some looked all too indifferent about it, enjoying retirement more than they should. Linara's bird, though, wanted to fly forever, she could tell.

One of the trainers, standing a full foot taller than the rest, not even counting the golden griffin helmet upon her head, paced in front of the recruits. Commander Nilya, the woman who rejected Linara's training, and Lorin's commanding officer.

Her voice carried effortlessly across the field, but being so far, Linara couldn't understand a word. Lorin translated, though, having been through enough courses to know it by memory.

"She's giving them a rundown again on the difference in vertical motion," Lorin explained, digging her boots into the dirt. "You, of course, picked up on that almost instantly, but the recruits are full of rocks and need reminded a few dozen times."

One thing about being personally trained was that Lorin's own advice was a step away from the basics and further into trade secrets. Wind-whips left the skin cracked and dry, but keeping the body and low and arms covered almost negated that entirely. She showed where to put her hands if she lost balance, and how to quickly gain the trust of a wild griffin before trying to ride it. Griffins were prideful beasts, same as any other animal in Linara's mind. If *she* could fly, she wouldn't want to carry just anybody.

Would that old gray bird allow her to fly with him? He seemed stubborn, like a cat who never quite enjoyed doing as he was told. She could see it in his eyes, though: he would do anything to fly again with a rider on his back.

Nilya stepped aside and motioned behind her. The line of guard recruits broke into a run toward the group of bunched griffins. Linara started, distracted and unaware of the release. She glanced back, and Lorin nodded in approval. Nobody moved toward her old bird, though, and Linara walked with ease, knowing well she had no need to hurry.

The griffin noticed her approach, wizened eyes studying her every move. He was far older than she expected, feathers rough and graying even at the top of his head. She stepped forward, resting a hand on his neck, sliding a few fingers beneath the first layer of feathers.

A glimmer passed through his eyes as he stared at the sky, Linara following his gaze to a guard patrol far above, returning to the Spire. He longed for it again, she could feel it in every feather. Her own flash of excitement must have set him at ease, for he bowed his head low and sidled up beside her, a permission to ride along on a launch to the sky.

She climbed up the straps against his front leg and lifted her way onto his back. Griffin saddles felt strange compared to a horse's, or even a hoofbeak's. Her legs tucked in slightly farther back on themselves, compensating for the massive pair of wings still folded against its body.

She grabbed the short reins and guided the old bird back. Some of the other eager recruits stood mounted in a line. Only the timid ones still stood awkwardly near grazing griffins, instructors prodding them forward with words or with backs of spears.

"Dresborn, aye?" Lorin said, hopping up on Aria. "He doesn't choose just anybody."

"Dresborn?" Linara said, stifling a laugh. Weird name for an animal.

"He's old, and ornery, but energetic. He was my pick for my first time. We'll see if he's a good fit for you, as well." She smiled and put on her helmet. "Might kill your eagerness for flight. Might not. Guess we'll find out."

Was that a challenge? Linara could feel Dresborn constantly shifting his weight and scratching at the ground. Anxious to be on with it, then? She rubbed her hand down his neck.

A long moment passed, longer than it needed to be, but Lorin wanted to wait until the recruits were in the air before they went off. The timid ones took the longest to even saddle up. Those had more than a few experienced riders with them, ready to coach — and to catch—any falling recruits.

Then one by one, the griffins went off. Years of built instinct drove each griffin forward, all but ignoring the rookie riders on their backs. Their leaping strides were long and fast, enough to build up speed quickly so their final leap could take them into the sky with a few flaps of their wings.

Linara watched with envy, bouncing slightly in her saddle, heart already beating quickly. The last of the recruits took off, and Lorin gave the all clear. Linara barely urged Dresborn on before he gave a loud cry and bolted forward.

In the long line of recruits racing beside her, she outpaced them all, a small spark still left in Dresborn's old bones.

They built speed until his gallop was full. Linara flicked the reins and felt her gut lurch as he leapt off the ground and unfurled his wings. One flap, two, and they were above the city wall, Dresborn already curving off toward the city, knowing the route before Linara could guide him.

Dresborn rose higher and higher without instruction, an old, proud bird showing off. Linara's heart thudded wildly, but she could hardly feel it now. The city zipped by at dizzying speeds, but he continued to build momentum. Old bird? Sure, but he certainly had fire in his veins.

Linara didn't try to stop him, and he kept rising higher and flying quicker. He opened his beak and threw out a joyful call. Dresborn was no grump. He was a fire-spark ready to be lit, but hadn't had the rider to free him. Not for a long while. All Linara had to do was suppress that primal fear and hold on, letting Dresborn live in freedom as he wished, and fulfill her dream with hardly any effort.

The wind blew harsh and fast, whipping her hair and tugging at her shirt. She could feel an energy there she couldn't explain; like awakening from the rare night of complete rest.

She grew numb to the pain and the wind, feeling only that elation. Not even in the Blackness did she feel so blissfully alone. No one to injure, to burn, to worry about or to think of. She was alone with her thoughts for the first time since she'd gotten to the city, and that itself was like lifting the weight of the world from her mind.

Confident Dresborn could guide himself in their lap around the Spire, Linara closed her eyes and let go of the reins, feeling the wind tug at her palms. It tried to throw her away from its domain, but she held fast with her legs. Lorin thought this would quell her eagerness? This only fueled it further.

But she could only stay there for so long. Even with the love of open air, the depth of the unknown, of seeing nothing of where they flew, caught up to her.

She snapped open her eyes to scan the ground and the surrounding sky, before fully relaxing again. It didn't look like anyone else was even *near* comfortable enough to fly above the peak of the mountain, but the higher Linara flew, the safer she felt. They were nearing the Spire itself now, and Linara scanned the windows in search of Orv's office. She wondered if he'd be able to spot her. Though, he usually had his nose too far in dusty tomes to ever glance out the windows.

Lorin, bronze helmet catching the light with a blinding intensity, flew up fast from behind. She laughed into the wind, giving a firm nod to Linara.

"You proved me wrong," she said, voice barely audible. "You're a natural."

"Really? It doesn't seem that hard," Linara said, readjusting her footing in the saddle. So far, the most difficult part was finding the limited comfortable positions. It wasn't quite like fitting on a horse, with the wild movements of wings getting in the way. "Dresborn's doing all the hard work."

"That's what I thought, too," Lorin said, "I didn't realize that until recently."

"Well, you've been flying for a lot longer than I have."

Lorin shook her head. "Only a year or so."

Linara opened her mouth, but closed it again. Only a year? She had learned more about the Knights of Alde since she arrived, enough to know that each had their own roles within the system. The Stag Knight was always a griffin rider, leader of the Ebon Wings, a small but elite fighting force that traveled all over Aldebraan. Including to Nelbren.

And Lorin had been flying for only a *year*? She always knew Lorin was young to be promoted so far, but that truly didn't add up.

"I served on the ground for most of my career," Lorin explained, laughing at her confusion. "I took flight lessons, just like everyone else here, and they offered me a spot on the messenger team, almost immediately. That's the usual path to a patrolman, but I declined. I wanted to serve on the streets, where it felt like it mattered."

"How'd you end up back in the sky then?" Linara asked.

"The old Stag Knight retired last year. It's a pretty big deal when a knight grows old enough to have to. Usually they promote the standout member of the team, but this time there was none. So they held a tournament—aerial jousting, sparring, that sort of thing. It was supposed to be just for the Ebon Wings, but nobody ever specified. So when I showed up, they couldn't turn me away. Maybe they thought I'd get thrown from the saddle on the first tilt."

Linara faced forward, mimicking the motion of a lance in one hand, and the reins in the other. She'd seen those long spikes of metal and could only imagine how heavy they were. And not to mention having to maneuver enough to spear a different rider, traveling just as fast? It must take years of experience to even fly straight enough.

"You won, didn't you?" Linara asked.

Lorin's head dipped a bit, and she paused. "The whole thing. Every joust. Every ground fight."

"That's amazing!" Linara said, "I'm sure they regretted allowing it. I'm surprised they didn't try and change their mind."

"I was the fan favorite. A wild card. Youngest soldier to ever ascend. It would have been difficult to deny that." Somehow she sounded almost sad about that. Regretful? Linara didn't have a chance to ask. "Let's head down farther, back toward the rest of the group."

Then she was gone, banking down with Aria to join the recruits. Linara joined, thankful to Dresborn that he listened to her promptings. They were gathering near the Labor Valley now, gradually climbing higher, but still hovering near the base of the mountain.

Back near the group, she could feel Dresborn fall into a rhythm. To him, this was just another routine patrol flight, but they both could still feel the pleasure of the air. Most of the others, she noticed, felt it, too, their smiles wide, straight backed to feel the wind fully. Some, though, heads bowed and faces pale, wished nothing more than to feel the ground again.

Linara allowed her thoughts to drift away in the wind, tuning out the barking orders from the instructors to the men drifting away, or fumbling in their saddles. She belonged here. Why was she born without wings?

This could be a life to enjoy. Free from danger, from the pressure brought by her mark. Just her and a griffin, living in the sky. It could never be, however. Even a griffin had to return to the ground, eventually.

A piercing cry cut through the wind. Her eyes shot to the sound, toward a riderless griffin and the shape of a man hurling toward the ground. She acted in the hair of a second, pressing her body forward, angling her griffin toward the ground. Dresborn reacted faster than she did, folding in his wings and diving after the fallen trainee.

Together, they cut through the air. They were gaining fast, but the ground approached far faster. From a quick glance, Linara could see several Ebon Wing soldiers diving around them, but Linara was closest.

The blue of the rooftops grew, taking up her complete vision. Linara squeezed her legs tight, trusting Dresborn as he slid seamlessly below the falling guard. His body landed with a muffled thump behind her, his screams now silent and his body limp, having blacked out long ago.

Dresborn unfurled his wings to catch the air, but Linara could tell it wouldn't be enough. She closed her eyes and tensed for an impact, yelling wordlessly into the wind. She felt the heat grow in her chest, and they lurched upward, Dresborn catching a final bit of wind to glide just above the rooftops. Linara cracked open her eyes to find them still alive, gliding smoothly to the top of the city wall, one hand on the reins, the other supporting the guard recruit behind her.

Her heart thudded strongly as she searched the ground below. She felt the fire and the heat leave her body, but nothing was scorched or burning. Where did it go? Somehow, did it save them?

Linara barely felt them land upon one of the city walls, and barely heard the thunder of hooves on the surrounding stone. Members of the Ebon Wings scrambled around her, lowering the recruit to the ground to check for injury.

They came for her next, helping her out of the saddle. Someone asked for her name and what company she belonged in, but she wasn't sure how to answer any of them. They said she was falling too fast to not have crashed, but Linara felt fine.

Mostly. The ground felt wobbly, and she was suddenly exhausted, but that was a familiar feeling. The same feeling after the encounter with that strange thing in the flying carriage, and even back in Nelbren.

She had used her power somehow, tapped into her mark. There was no fire, nor smoke, but she felt drained. Dresborn even seemed okay, and very pleased with himself now that he was the center of everyone's attention.

Lorin landed nearby where Linara leaned against the wall, and checked her and Dresborn quickly for injuries. Linara's heart raced in her chest still, feeling the eyes upon her, watching her, waiting for her. The small-village part of her, the Blackness part, just wanted to be away from all the attention.

Commander Nilya landed a moment later, golden griffin helmet shining in the sunlight. Her eyes gazed over the scene for a moment before turning fully toward Linara. She stiffened as the commander removed her helmet, revealing a pair of holes where her nose should've been. Nilya ran a hand through her short, sweat-matted hair as she studied Linara. "Well done, Farrow."

"Thank you, uhh . . . ma'am. But, I think it wasn't me," she said, looking at her nose again and snapping back up to her eyes. "Thank Dresborn. Uhh—he kind of . . . came alive."

"Griffins are habitual animals," Commander Nilya said, nodding. "But it doesn't take just anyone to prod an old beast to flight like that. Or to convince him you'll pull that trick of yours at the end there."

"Trick?" Linara asked without thinking.

The commander was silent for a moment, her lips pursed. "I will choose to believe that it was intentional. That flash of light that pushed you above the rooftops did not seem like a mere accident."

"Oh, that," Linara said, suddenly both panicked and relieved that it *was* real and nobody was hurt. "I just don't think all of it was me."

"Certainly not. I don't think any other bird could've pulled it off, but there's not a rider within this sorry batch of recruits that could've done it, either," she said, glancing back at the soldier who fell, now leaning up against the wall, eyes wide in shock. "None of my Ebon Wings were close enough to catch him, a mistake that, thanks to you, somebody's only getting a long stint of latrine duty for. You saved a life, and a guard from facing the whip."

Then she slid her helmet back into place, wheeling around with fresh orders on her lips. Linara released a breath she hardly realized she held. Lorin was right, the commander *was* terrifying, but for hardly the reason she expected.

Another man approached just behind the commander, a timid recruit with a leather cap wrung between his hands. He was a few years older than Linara, his cheeks plump. His eyes deflected off hers, and he cleared his throat before speaking, his voice thick and accented. "Thank you for saving Elbert," he said, and paused. "I've heard stories of you Odious, but I saw what you did up there. It was amazing. You're one of the good ones."

He bowed his head in quick thanks before jogging off toward the fallen recruit. Linara stood against the wall, the compliment leaving a sour taste. It was the same churning in her gut that came from every stare since she arrived in the city, the manifestation of the same fear of herself. Even on the wall, she couldn't help now but notice that he, like everyone else who looked at her, assumed she was a monster before they even met her.

Lorin Kartridge, Stag Knight of Avorren, future commander of the Ebon Wings, and youngest Knight of Alde to serve beneath the crown of Aldebraan, stood upon the wall and watched Linara try to catch her breath. She had been confident in the air, free from the chains upon the earth. Now, though, she was a mouse. Lonely and afraid.

Lorin tried to stay close, giving her space, but blocking the view of the others, as well as the guard being carried away. Some of his ribs would surely be broken. Maybe even his back. Linara didn't need to know that. She was still in shock, her mind not quite catching up to the events.

Soldiers were still landing around them, trying to help, or whispering shadowy things under their breaths. Her soldiers, she had to remind herself. But they hardly listened to her. She may have sent each one of them to the dirt to prove herself, but it was difficult to lead after that fact. Especially when she herself couldn't save the recruit in time.

It ended up being Linara. A recruit herself. A damn good flyer by any standard, but still a recruit. The commander's look still hung in the back of her head. It wasn't respect, and yet it wasn't condemnation. She wasn't sure what it was, and that was the most terrifying.

Lorin did take some comfort in knowing she was right, however. Training Linara one on one was the right call. It took a good deal of convincing to make it happen. Nilya almost sent Linara into the ranks with the others, but she would've just been bogged down. A spark like hers needed to be coaxed and tended.

It paid off, in the end. The boy was safe, and alive. But the alternative still felt so close, balancing on the breadth of a hair. Lorin shuddered. It was best not to dwell on the alternative. The boy was alive, no matter how close he was to being otherwise.

CHAPTER TWELVE

Linara stared at the page in front of her, vision blurry and unfocused, unsure what she had just written upon it. Orv paced endlessly in front of her, book in hand. Whatever words he spoke fell on deaf ears, and her eyes hung heavy.

She had poured every ounce of energy into learning the past few days, but determination and riding breaks couldn't help the topics of discussion. Orv taught his own lesson plans. This morning he started on the economy and founding of Aldebraan, and after a dozen or so tangents, came to a full stop on the nature of the local fauna on Arkya.

Linara had tried to interrupt, attempting to rein the conversation back into *something* relevant, but Orv knew his share about almost everything, and it only led to more rabbit trails.

What she did want to know, Orv had given her books upon. Her father had taught her letters long ago, but these tomes were far beyond her comprehension. It took hours to get through even a page at times, and most were far more unhelpful then they let on.

By far the most interesting, however, was the biography on Liza Burnfeather. Orv did end up finding it after all, and despite Linara's reservations, it contained a lot of insight into her story.

A few hundred years back, Liza walked through a port city in Mahnbusa, and burned the entire place down in three days. She would toss burning goose feathers into the wind, and chase down the embers where they went out.

It was sickening, to say the least, but Liza left a comprehensive amount of notes about her life leading up to it. Translating them from her language into theirs brought its own challenges, apparently, and the gaps in understanding left Linara with a mind full of images she didn't wish to face. At the center was that damned painting, and all the possibilities she could think of where she'd create the same scene somewhere on a battlefield, or worse.

Linara sighed and blew a strand of hair away from her eyes. A guard patrol rode by on their griffins outside the window, and she watched them with envy. She had thought riding lessons with Lorin would help her productivity, but it seemed to only make it worse. Every minute she sat in the Spire she spent watching messengers fly by.

In a breath, the griffins passed, leaving her alone with Orv and a clustered office. The entire wall was made of glass, but every inch was covered in bookshelves, except for a tiny sliver just beside Linara's desk in the center of the room. She could tell it took a fair bit of energy for Orv to make space for even that. The floor was layered in dusty ledgers and loose papers scattered everywhere, leaving only a small square where she could see the rug—just under the chair she sat in.

It didn't smell nearly as musty as Linara would have expected. She had Orv's collection of plants to thank for that, neatly trimmed in their clay pots scattered all around his study, even the tangle of vines crossing the shelves, the walls, and the ceiling. Somewhere around the walls was a door leading to his bedchambers, and probably a hidden room for his bath, like Linara's.

"Are you paying attention, young one?" Orv asked.

Linara flushed and turned back. "You were explaining the importance of borders in trade agreements?"

"That was a half hour ago."

"Oh. Then I wasn't listening."

"Ahh," Orv said with a heavy sigh. "Is the unique dye production of the Collis Province not as interesting as I think?"

"Is it to anyone?" she asked.

"Of course!" Orv said. "I figured you'd want to hear of the tense political situation in a more relatable subject field."

Linara shrugged. "My father grew and sold all our crops. Not much controversy over luma, at least not something to hold a grudge over."

"Ahh, so you were paying attention," Orv said. "But with luma, you sold it to your own province, or at least to others living in the Blackness. Now imagine growing it year-round, and not being able to keep any of it for yourselves because you need to trade it for food."

"Sure, but that's with dye. Having fancy clothes is different than being able to see in dark places."

"But that's why it's more complicated than that. From the gaudy clothes for the nobles to the guard uniforms, a lot of the materials come from the Collis province. There's a new demand for the huge feathers from the Cliff Peckers, and dye makers are paying less and less for the berries."

"So people are starving?"

"Not quite, but it won't be long until they are. That's why they are unhappy. The minor tension in the provinces is important for you to know." He sighed and placed the book back upon his desk. "Not to mention the conflicts growing on the border. Reginaan is growing rather bold."

Linara tensed. It was the first he'd mentioned anything related to the conflict Artoris spoke about. "I've heard there's trouble on the roads," she said cautiously.

Orv nodded solemnly. "Caravans are being attacked. Groups of soldiers are sneaking through the border, attacking merchants. It's not the first time this has happened over the decades. Things will pass, as they always do."

Artoris made it sound like it would come quickly to violence, especially as Orv grew older. It would be on Linara to quell the tide, once they made her name and face public news. Then she'd be expected to do her duty, prepared to burn whatever the king saw fit.

"Is something the matter?" Orv asked, bringing her out of her thoughts.

"No," Linara said quickly, and grimaced. She had always been a terrible liar. "Yes. But it's nothing." She grimaced again, hoping Orv didn't see through her lies.

Judging by the look he was giving her, he could see through like glass.

"I went into the city the other week," Linara began, trying to avoid the topic entirely. "I met a man. Artoris. He said he knew you."

Orv's face brightened. "Did you? He's the one that found that biography for me." Then he stared out the window, his face darkening. "Did he . . . unsettle you in any way?"

Linara wanted to say no, that it wasn't *Artoris* that caused such discomfort. "I don't know," Linara said. In reality, her time with Artoris still sat on the fence-line between helpful and scary. "He told me a bit about the Seven. There was a painting as well."

"The *Razing of Yarldin*," Orv said, nodding grimly. "A truly wonderful find. A terrible piece of history, albeit necessary to know."

"Is it a true story?" Linara asked.

"A valid question," Orv said, pondering. "Probably. From what we could discover, Yarldin was very much a real civilization, and now it is not. It can be deduced that there was an event that triggered its downfall, but the severity and motivation are likely lost to time."

"Motivation? What other reason could you have for blowing up a city?"

"What reason do people have for anything they do? People kill to protect their homes, their families, and their beliefs. Some invade distant lands for honor, some for resources to feed their people. I'm finding that very few people start wars for malicious intent. The very same, I think, can be said of the Seven. Did Fen destroy Yarldin because he wanted to, or was there some other reason? Something more personal than that? That is what I want to know, and that is what we may never find out."

"It's funny, you and Artoris sound very similar."

"We're cut from the same cloth, both of us searching for the truth of things amidst the ruins of lies and exaggeration. In our younger years, we used to explore the deepest recesses of Irea. Delving deep into old castles, cities, and caves, searching for history. We found much, of course, some more helpful than others."

Orv opened a drawer at the bottom of his desk, stuck firm from age. He pulled out a dusty tome, larger than any book Linara had ever seen, probably older than Orv himself.

"Artoris is a storyteller at heart, and I cannot blame him for that. His motivations behind history are his own, even if our goals are the same. The stories of the Seven Odious of Irea have been told through generations, very little changing about their tales within the last hundred years."

Orv flipped a few pages. "But history has seemingly forgotten the thousands of others. Odious whose deeds have gone unnoticed, whether that be of good nature or bad, or simply by lack of witnesses. There is Killin the Cracked, who created great fissures around a village to protect from a wildfire. Or Terron the Brave who faced a horde of marauders single handedly to protect his farmstead. Noble, powerful stories, but not quite grand enough to last the flow of time. Fear, terror, and anger are powerful motivators. Enough to have their stories survive generations."

"If no one else remembers, how did you find these things?" Linara asked.

"Long ago, Artoris and I followed a hunch to the Cliffs of Remembrance in a distant corner of Deydalus. We were lucky enough to find the ruins of a tower there. We still do not know what it once was, or who lived there. It must have been home to great scholars and scribes throughout its life, for we found many tomes of written events throughout the world. Wars, battles, random events of varying importance. The library in that tower laid the foundation of our work."

"If the stories aren't fully true, how do you know those books were?" she asked.

Orv flipped the tome closed and shrugged. "Ahh, well, we don't. Some items match different accounts from all over Irea, but for most, a small assumption must be made. I choose to believe that the men and women of that tower went to great lengths to only record the truth."

Orv slid the heavy tome back into the drawer and shoved it closed with a rattle. He waved his arm dismissively and lowered himself in his chair with a heavy sigh. "All of this to say, sometimes you can't believe everything you hear, despite even having seen it in a painting.

"But if you require more substantial evidence of my point, I have something a bit more recent. My master, Korion of the Stone, they called him, made a sizable living of carving stone with his Mark. He built his house in the Artisan's Pass, far before it was called such a thing. Most say it was because of him the name stuck, that after generations of artists flocking to his home, they settled and began work of their own."

"What do the others say?"

"Some know the truth, that his house was actually closer to the Cloud Peaks, and his work was inspired by the artists arriving in the city, not the other way around. Even the stories that have a more favorable ending are often not entirely accurate."

Linara threw up her hands. "So the only thing that's true is what's written down, and even that might be false. And, on top of *that*, people will just tell whatever stories they want to hear, or what sounds more interesting?"

Orv laughed a bit grimly at that. "It does sometimes keep me up late at night, wondering what people will say of me when I am gone from this world. I can leave written accounts, but very few might read it. Eventually I conclude that no matter how much I try, stories shift like the winds, and that is life."

Linara sat back and sighed. No matter the outcome of her life, she would vastly prefer to be left to the unknowns of history than remembered as a scourge on Irea. "When I first arrived you promised you'd show me how to control all of this. How long before we start? If I can't control what the people say, I'd at least like to control what I *can*. Other than this book, I'm no closer than when I started, and ignorance had been a better tool than not, up until a month ago."

Orv fell silent, eyes drifting down to the wood of his desk, and the open pages of his journal, spread out before him. "Perhaps you are right. Ignorance *can* be a tool, but you are not ignorant any longer, are you?" He sighed and rubbed at his fingers. "I heard about your flight experience the other day."

Linara looked up sharply. "You did?"

"I think the entire city has. The stories are growing a bit of proportion, but that's how it goes, I'm afraid. I doubt you conjured a storm cloud to catch the falling man, and I also do not think you sprouted wings."

Linara paled. "Is that what they're saying?"

"More or less, depending on who you talk to. A common theme is that you looked angelic, like the wind was your servant."

"All I remember is we were falling too fast, I thought we would hit the rooftops for sure. Then there was a gust of wind, and we were fine." Linara breathed in deep, past the anxiousness growing in her chest, "But the point is, I don't know how I did it. I just as easily could have done the opposite."

Orv sat back in his chair and let his fingers brush along the leaves growing upon his desk. "This is true," he said after a long moment, "and I believe you are right."

A soft knock came from behind her, and the door opened.

"Ahh, our young Stag Knight," Orv said, forcing a smile as Lorin stepped in. "This is good timing. I'm thinking a break will be good for us both."

"I'm sorry to interrupt," Lorin said, peeking her head in the door, frowning apologetically. "I've just come to let Linara know I'm canceling our lesson for the day. Aria's saddle blew a strap and is out for repairs."

"That is most unfortunate," Orv said, letting the cover of his journal fall closed. "I was planning on canceling the rest of your lessons for the day, but if there is no reason to break for the afternoon, we might as well cont—"

"But I'm sure Lorin meant that with the lesson canceled, she'll be showing me other important things, right?" Linara said, scrambling to find words, and Lorin frowned at her. "You know . . . like how to . . . brush a griffin when their saddle is . . . broken?"

"Yes, of course," Lorin said, taking the lead. "How could I forget, you don't know that yet. Never a dull moment, and all that." She grimaced and shrugged at Linara.

But Orv already had his journal open, and he was scribbling furiously within. "Fine, fine," Orv said, waving a dismissive hand. "I must have time to ponder on what you've said. Find me in the garden tomorrow morning, young Linara."

Linara scrambled from her chair and closed the door behind her before he could change his mind.

"It's going that bad, huh?" Lorin said, once they were out in the hallway. Linara mumbled some half response, unsure of how to answer, before Lorin laughed and interrupted. "Oh, don't worry, I understand. I took a few months of tutoring from him when I took the stag. It was agony, really."

"It's not *all* bad. Some of it is useful," Linara said, but trailed off. "So a strap really broke, huh?"

"Thankfully not mid-flight, but I caught it during inspection this morning. Probably from the scare with the recruit. We banked hard, and that probably started the tear. It's nothing to worry about. It'll be a day or two before Aria's airborne again, though." She paused, her jaw tightening. "It's funny, in the end. If that strap broke fully, it would've been me needing saving . . ."

There was a certain sorrow behind her words, an anxiety that it seemed that everyone felt that day.

"I hope the commander wasn't too harsh on everyone," Linara said. Despite her words of praise, it still felt like a strange form of rebuke. She didn't want to know what true punishment looked like. "It's hard enough to look her in the eyes as it is . . ."

"With the nose thing? Yeah, it's pretty gross," Lorin said.

"How did it happen?" Linara asked.

"She doesn't say. Or at least, the story changes every time she tells somebody. But you should see when she gets *really* angry—the hole wriggles, and it's really hard not to look."

Linara tried and failed to keep that visual out of her memory.

"Did you actually want to learn how to brush down a griffin when a saddle's broken, or whatever nonsense you said back there?" Lorin asked. "It's the same as any other time, I promise."

"No, no, I was just looking forward to a break all day, no matter what it looks like."

"I have no other plans, truly," Lorin said. "Has Orv given you a tour yet?"

"Not entirely."

"I'm sure he stopped at the Pass. The road down the rest of the mountain is probably a bit much for him at his age," Lorin said. "In that case, let me show you my old stomping grounds. It'll be good to stretch my legs, and any excuse not to catch up on paperwork is good enough for me."

Some fresh air always sounded nice. Lorin led the way down the Spire, talking at length about her time growing up at the base of the mountain. They passed the mouth of the kitchen hallway, when the pale blue of a Luman-Viri caught her eye.

Linara hadn't seen Raast since that day in the kitchens, but his words had never left her thoughts. Both of his advice, and of his admission that he had never left the Spire. She needed to pay him back.

"Raast!" Linara called out, running to catch up. The cook turned and smiled at her approach, bowing in greeting. "You said you wanted to see the city, right? We're going down, come with us."

Raast looked to her, then to Lorin, catching up from behind. He brightened, then frowned, a confusing blend shifting by the moment. "I . . . well . . . who will tend the stew?"

"There are other cooks in the Spire, aren't there?" Linara asked.

"Well, yes, but none who know just how to stir . . ."

"I'm sure it'll be fine," Linara said. "You haven't yet taken a day off. I'm sure nobody will mind, you're long overdue."

"But Master Dent will need to approve, of course. This is not precedented for me to leave so suddenly," Raast said.

"Will he even notice? I've never seen him in the lower kitchens even once," Lorin said, "The stew will be here when you get back."

"But the midwatch meal will go on without me," Raast protested.

"As the only officer who still has their meal down here, I can attest that they will be fine." Lorin paused for a moment as Raast considered more. "I doubt I have any authority over the cooks here, but if I gave you an order to come with us, would that make you feel better?"

Raast nodded firmly. "I will return my apron. Give me one moment." Then he turned and rushed down the hallway, back to the kitchen.

"You know Raast, too?" Linara asked as he turned the corner, out of sight.

"Everyone does, he's the best cook in the Spire."

"That's what I said. He doesn't seem to think so."

Lorin shrugged. "He's a Luman-Viri."

Raast returned a moment later, still in uniform, without the apron, just as he said. Linara expected him to change, but if he never really left the spire, he probably didn't own much else. At the very least, his apprehension before had been replaced with giddy excitement, even before they got to the entry hall.

Lorin took them straight through the city, and into the Labor Valley, the bottom area of the city Linara hadn't yet visited. She suspected why the moment they crossed the threshold. It was a strange place, full of strange people and dark shadows.

The busy thoroughfare was clogged with travelers, the cries of food vendors and peddlers rising high above the din of the crowd. Bolts of cloth and jewelry were shoved into their lines of sight if they ventured too close. With how tightly the road was packed, it wasn't too difficult to fall into their traps.

The Artisan's Pass seemed familiar to her, a slice of Nelbren in the capital city. Here, though, nobody smiled as they passed. There was no connection, no familiarity. This was the city Linara had always expected.

Raast, though, was thrilled with every second he spent outside. He saw everything with a childlike wonder. A set of eyes seeing things for the very first time. Linara saw herself in his expressions, like when she had seen the sun for the first time.

"Do you truly not remember anything from when you came to the city?" Linara asked as they weaved through a parked cart in the middle of the road. They had to drag Raast away from the horses harnessed to the front. "Not even from looking out the windows?"

"I catch glimpses through doorways, and through paintings in the hallways," Raast said, staring at a pair of women showing far too much cleavage, "But I am Luman-Viri. I remember much of what I am doing, and where I am walking, but none of what and where I do not."

"I—" Linara said, furrowing her brow, "don't quite follow."

"You spent your early days a Blackness farmer," He said, sniffing the air as they passed by a pair of food-cart vendors. "You are human, and you will not forget what your home looks like, or what you have learned there. I have cooked for so long, but if I decide to become a painter, I will lose all semblance of culinary taste. Perhaps not the foundations, just as I have not forgotten the way to my home island, or forgotten our native tongue. Some things stay, some things become us."

"You forget everything you've ever done? That sounds terrible," Linara said.

"The people we meet, the places we go, all are nothing but faint impressions after some time," Raast said, a smile still on his face. "But we remember very much of what we experience recently."

"You don't even remember your family?" She asked.

"I could see some benefit to that," Lorin mumbled.

Raast stared up into the sky a curiously long time. "I do not think I ever had a family."

Linara didn't know what to say to that. Stuck in a world, remembering nothing about your own family, or any of the friends you met or the places you went. Linara often wished to forget what brought her to Avorren, but it was good to remember those things, as a cautionary tale.

There was peace in ignorance, it seemed, however. Raast walked with a certain serenity, taking in every sight and sound. Everything was just as fascinating as the first time he saw it. Every walk new, every place fresh.

"I am smelling such a blend of food and spices," Raast said. "We must stop at all of them."

"These vendors will get you a fast ticket to food poisoning," Lorin said with a scowl, "I'll take you deeper. Trust me."

Raast was clearly skeptical, but followed her anyway. Linara, though, made eye contact with a man across the way. He beckoned her closer, smiling, inviting. Stacks of flatbreads steamed from a tray strapped across his shoulders. Linara's mouth watered as she drifted toward him, but Lorin tugged her away and down another street.

She'd better be right about this.

Lorin led them through the winding paths, down small roads and alleys deeper into the city. Linara's impression of the Labor Valley seemed to shift with every turn they made. She had thought it was where the tougher citizens of the city worked the warehouses and storage depots, but in reality, it seemed to be where everything else in the city was dumped. Butchers, busy taverns, and even entire alleys were stacked high with trash.

Lorin's journey finally led them to a stop in a courtyard paved with broken bricks. A dry fountain stood at the center, caked with dirt and grime. A man with skin as dark as the Blackness sky sat on the ledge, stoking a small campfire. Even sitting, he was a full head taller than the both of them. He silently watched the scarce crowd pass, tending to a row of meat skewers grilling atop the fire.

The man brightened as Lorin approached, extending his arms with a deep, wordless cry.

"It's good to see you, Durlo," Lorin said, clasping his arm at the elbow. Durlo cried out again, gesturing with his arms in a way Lorin apparently understood. "Yes, I know, it's been too long. I'm here now, though, aren't I?" She stepped aside and gestured to Linara and Raast. "I've come to show my new friends what foods Maasin Luut has to offer."

Durlo smiled wide, plucking two sticks off the grill and handing them over. Linara stuffed the first bite into her mouth, hunger getting the best of her. The meat was tough to chew, but the spices were rich and filled with flavor.

"It's delicious," she mumbled through another bite, looking up at the large man, his smile deepening even further.

"This is not beef," Raast said, mulling over the taste. "Nor is it pork. It is too tough for poultry, and yet I have not tasted anything like it."

Durlo shrugged for a moment before motioning with his hands at Lorin.

"He says it's camel," she said.

"What's a camel?" they both asked.

Durlo gestured again, but Lorin shrugged. "An animal? He says it wanders the sands of Mahnbusa."

"Camel is delicious," Raast mumbled, his mouth full.

"Do you believe me now?" Lorin asked.

Raast locked eyes with her. "I would trust you with my life."

"Well, I'm flattered," Lorin said. "I suppose I'll have to prove it again in a month, though."

Raast was no longer listening, his eyes closed in deep concentration as he chewed. Linara reached into her pockets and slid a pair of copper tiles to Durlo for another pair of skewers of her own.

Lorin thanked Durlo and led them back through the winding streets. Raast continued on about other exotic foods he struggled to remember—memories of the rare times the Spire ordered anything new into the kitchens.

Linara was right to trust Lorin, though. She knew the city better than anyone she'd met so far. Better than Orv. Years patrolling the streets would do that. Lorin even shared a few secrets to finding the quality vendors. She always watched for the silent ones, the ones who looked like they cared about their trade. The desperate ones always had something to hide. Linara knew that applied to everything, even luma.

They passed a street bathed in long shadows. The sound of music and cheering drifted through the air. The road curved into an open expanse, where a multitude of stages were lit with both oil lanterns and luma. Wooden platforms were constructed in open plazas, filled with performers dressed in armor and costumes of all sorts.

There were several sets, all dispersed among the various stages, but Linara's tongue was still soured at the memory of the troupers in Nelbren. They weren't the same, they couldn't be; she was halfway around the kingdom now. But the smell of spiced nuts poked at the memory of burning flesh as Jon's and Fenton's hands melted backstage.

Linara looked to Lorin, hoping to catch her arm and turn them back toward any other area of the city, but she had already darted out of reach. She was headed straight toward a nearby performance, and a low section of wall separating the road from the audience.

A girl knelt in the alcove, peeking her head just above the wall to watch the stage. She wore a simple shirt and trousers, not unlike Linara's, and her jet-black hair was tied in a tight bun. A soldier knelt just beside her in a thick gambeson. He watched the crowd with an attentive eye, his hand never leaving the pale-blue sword at his hip.

They looked strangely familiar, but Linara couldn't quite place them. She had met a great deal of people since arriving, and remembered very little of them, after all.

"Princess?" Lorin whispered sharply, "what are you doing out here?"

The soldier elbowed the girl as Lorin approached. "Oh, hello, Lorin!" the girl said, before turning fully to Linara and Raast. "Who are your friends? Hi, I'm Cirena." She smiled wide, reaching out a hand to the both of them. Raast took it first.

"I am Raastivarlin, I am a cook!"

"You work in the lower kitchens. I've heard great things about you," Cirena said, and Raast brightened.

"You know me?"

"You're the only Luman-Viri in the city; it would be hard not to."

"Have we met before?" Linara asked, studying her face.

"Rhoam and I were in my father's study the day you arrived," she said. That was right. She wore a long white dress then, adorned with jewelry, like a painting. The knight beside her, Rhoam, looked exactly the same. "You made the room uncomfortably warm for a moment. It was quite fascinating."

Linara flushed. Had she really?

"You still didn't answer my question," Lorin asked. "You don't often leave the Spire. Especially unattended."

"I'm not unattended; Rhoam is with me," she said, before glaring at them each in turn. "And by the way, I was never here, do you understand?"

"Your suspicious nature is not helping," Lorin said.

"It's not like you'll turn me in," Cirena said. "Because I suppose you're not doing anything you're not supposed to right now?"

"Hey, don't turn this around on *me*," Lorin said. "Just because I tend to procrastinate doesn't mean I am right now."

"She's been teaching me how to fly," Linara clarified.

Cirena stared at the both of them, then at the sky, and then at Lorin again.

"Aria's. Saddle. Broke."

"I didn't say anything!" Cirena said, feigning ignorance.

"We have good reason to suspect the troupers behind us have been smuggling a large amount of feld fungus into the city," Rhoam interjected.

Cirena rolled her eyes. "Always the secret keeper, Rhoam."

"Okay, and?" Lorin said, and then frowned. "Don't tell me you're planning on doing something about it? Sneaking backstage and arresting them yourselves?" Cirena and Rhoam both looked at her as if she wasn't joking. "You can't be serious. And you're okay with this, Rhoam?"

"I've found it's best to just agree early. It gives me the most amount of time to prepare for what she's just going to do anyway."

"And it's not like this is the first time," Cirena said, rolling her eyes.

"I think we're up to . . . six busts in the last few months?" Rhoam said.

"Seven if you count those twins," Cirena said.

"Good point," Rhoam said.

"You've been parading around the city as . . ." Lorin stammered, waving her arms in wild motions. "Vigilantes? And I'm just *now* finding out?"

"You told us yourself the city watch has grown lax in this part of the city," Cirena said. "You said you wish my father would do something about it."

"And you're saying he approved of this?"

Cirena laughed. "Oh, sun above, no. I'm tired of my father's passivity lately, so we're doing it ourselves."

"How did you find out about the smuggling to begin with?"

"I told you we were in the study the day you arrived," Cirena said. "We heard Lorin's report, and figured they'd be coming here soon enough."

"So you thought you'd try and find them?" Lorin said. "There's probably a hundred trouper caravans in Aldebraan alone. What makes you think you can find that one?"

"Well, if this isn't the same one, we found *another* one," Cirena said.

The crowd hushed from over the wall, but no one else seemed to notice. Lorin and Cirena continued in their argument while Linara crept toward the stone wall. She peeked over the side, just as a man in a fur cape took the stage. Linara jaw clenched, an angry hiss escaping her lips.

Cirena was right to suspect them after all. His skin was the color of caramel, a pale scar running from eye to chin, visible from even so far. She'd recognize him anywhere.

Thatcher.

My dearest Linara,

I hope you're finding Avorren more pleasing than I did. I am a cynic at heart, and that city was the first I visited away from home. You, though, always were apt for new adventures. I trust you'll find this to be just another one of those in the end.

With the money given, I finally bought the proper arrangements from the peddlers. I sent your mother to the stars above, just as she would have wanted. She always looked to the signs for guidance, and now I will always be looking to her. I wish you could have been there.

Nelbren is a home for me no longer. Tomorrow I will leave it behind for good. Perhaps we were both wrong. Neither of our places were truly here. Perhaps they never were. In my youth, I traveled the corners of this kingdom and beyond. I may just venture out again. The kingdom was generous to me, and I will not waste away my years.

I will continue to write to you, and hope that these letters reach you. If nothing more than a hope for this tired old soul that perhaps someone is still listening to my rambling words.

Peace below the stars,

Frennik Farrow

Chapter Thirteen

I t was a strange feeling, seeing him again. She didn't think she ever would, and had been perfectly fine with that. After all, he was not the object of her ire, at least on the surface. But the longer she watched him, the more the anger bubbled.

When she traced everything back, it all started with him. With four simple words, he let the Fairgrave boys end her peaceful life. If he'd never come, if he'd bypassed their tiny village and continued on to Avorren as planned, she'd be back at home, helping her father with another harvest.

"You recognize him," Lorin said from behind her. A hand fell on her shoulder, gently guiding her away from the wall. Linara's grip stuck to the bricks for a moment before she let it go. Thatcher's voice still carried over the crowd, deep and commanding.

Rhoam and the Princess were looking at her now, and Linara was suddenly aware of the waves of heat rising from her mark. She quickly stomped it down, and nodded confirmation to Lorin's question.

"I *told* you," Cirena said. "We've done our research."

"Yes, yes, you were right," Lorin said with a dismissive hand.

"That man, Thatcher, is the ringleader here," Cirena said. "He starts every show with a monologue. One of his men is waiting just off curtain with a report. They'll talk for a minute or two, and no longer, before he retreats straight back into his cart. He doesn't even take off the costume."

"He's in there for a few hours at a time, sometimes more," Rhoam chimed in. "I haven't seen him exit before the show ends."

Lorin rolled her eyes. "And you've been watching him this whole time?"

Cirena pointed to a window across the street, a building looming above them a few stories up. "We've been renting the top room for a week or so. It gives us a nice view into the courtyard behind the stage."

"Okay, so you'll, oh, I don't know, break down his door, tie him up, and throw him on the guardhouse steps, with a few vials of feld fungus for good measure?" Lorin asked.

Cirena looked at Rhoam and shrugged. "Yeah, exactly."

"What about the scores of audience members, and the whole troupe standing in your way?" Lorin asked.

Rhoam reached down and lifted the edges of a brick in the road. Linara stumbled back, as her feet rose with it, an entire section lifting on a hinge. They all peered down the trapdoor, leading into darkness.

"This leads backstage," he said. "It's mostly used for magician acts, and some specialty performances."

"Halfway through the show, they perform the 'Ballad of Garadhur,'" Cirena said. "It's all hands on deck, and everyone in the troupe is onstage. We'll head under, and once the ballad begins, we'll pop out backstage and make it to the courtyard before anyone's the wiser."

Lorin frowned and rubbed at her chin. "I'll admit, you've thought this through."

Rhoam shrugged. "I told you, it gives me more time to prepare."

"I want in," Linara said without thinking. Cirena looked thrilled, but Lorin already was full of concern.

"This isn't a good idea," she said. "They can get into whatever situation they want to, but—"

"I have the biggest reason here to want to see him arrested. The city watch isn't going to do it, and you're not going to stop them," Linara said. "So I can either sit here and watch, or I can be there firsthand."

"Thatcher is a big guy," Cirena said, with a shrug. "An Odious on our side will be helpful somehow, I'm sure."

"If even just intimidation," Rhoam said.

Lorin blew out a long breath. "And the Stag Knight."

Cirena brightened. "You're coming, too?"

"If I can't stop you, I'll have to come along. I promised Orv to keep her safe."

"That's strangely heartwarming," Linara said.

"I just mean if this goes south and we end up arrested, Orv better find me in the cell with you."

"And I will come, too!" Raast said.

"Five people in this tiny tunnel?" Lorin said, glancing down into the dark.

"It really couldn't hurt," Rhoam said. "The more people we have, the better chance he won't fight back."

"I really doubt he'll go quietly either way," Lorin said.

"Then I suppose Raast being there or not doesn't really change anything, does it?" Cirena said.

A blast of music rang out from beyond the wall, and they all craned their necks. Thatcher was gone, replaced by a group of troupers in various costumes. They were acting out a different story than in Nelbren, one Linara didn't recognize.

"No time to argue now," Rhoam said, gesturing into the hole. "We better get into position while we still can." Then he was gone, leaping feet first into the darkness, with Cirena following closely behind.

"After you," Lorin said, gesturing down. Linara hesitated. There was no going back now.

The drop was farther than she expected, the ground sending a sharp shock through her legs on the impact. The floor was compacted dirt; the walls were old, crumbling brick. Raast landed just behind her, followed by Lorin, who closed the door above, dropping the tunnel into shadow.

Linara could see well enough. The faint blur of slithering shadows as the others fumbled in the darkness. The scrape of their hands echoed strangely in the darkness, broken by soft cries as they stepped on one another's toes. There was a faint trickle of light on either side of the tunnel, where the trapdoors didn't quite sit correctly. Could the others truly not see enough from it?

They came to a stop at the end of the tunnel, just below the other trapdoor. An orange-ish light filtered through, blocked occasionally by the moving figures above. Footsteps resounded all around them, at least a dozen pairs rushing and blending together in the dark. Nobody dared to speak.

Then a great blast of a horn signified the start of the ballad. Footsteps stomped, a flurry of sounds that shook the door. A few moments passed, and silence returned once more. Cirena reached up, but Rhoam stopped her. Another set of footsteps ran above, and then the music shifted.

Then Rhoam slowly pushed open the door until he could peek through the crack. Then he shoved it open the rest of the way, leaping through the opening and helping the others up, one by one.

Linara came up last, into a long room lit by shadowed daylight from the open doorway, and a lantern burning in the corner. Long racks of clothing filled up every inch of the wall.

Through a thin curtain, Linara could see the stage. Cirena was right, there were probably three dozen people moving around within, the music swelling from somewhere beyond. The sound was familiar, and Linara recognized it from back home. The backdrop to the Fairgrave boys cornering her in the tent.

"The traveling troupers enjoy their games of pretend," Raast said, holding a thin blue dress to himself, a wide smile across his face. It matched his skin color quite well.

"Guard uniforms from Reginaan," Lorin said, pulling a sleeve from out of the rack. It was a long, billowy piece of cloth, layered with bits of metal, likes scales. The fabric looked scratchy and rough, a light brown that seemed to blend in with the wood behind it.

"Probably for a different show," Cirena said. "There's all sorts of costumes I don't recognize from their other performances."

"Stay focused," Rhoam said, creeping through to the other doorway, leading outside. "We have one goal here."

They followed him out into the courtyard behind the stage, a relatively quiet patch of land set between a pair of rising buildings. Stumps and crates surrounded a small fire in the center, which was burning low. Raast stared into the cook pot simmering in the coals. "A good stew needs constant tending. What a shame."

The familiar blue and green trouper carts Linara remembered from Nelbren filled the back side. Now, in the light of the sun, Linara could see the bright, vibrant colors for what they truly were. It was beautiful, in a way, even as worn and faded from travel as they were. Did this group start out as performers, Linara wandered, or did they simply learn the trade to hide their smuggling?

Packed so tightly, they truly looked like a long coiling serpent. A barrier to the rest of the city. They were all almost identical, with limited variation in paint and style. A luma lantern glowed through the cracks in the curtains of most, and no other movement showed from within.

Rhoam and Cirena evidently knew which one was Thatcher's, as Rhoam stepped up to the cart in the center and rammed his sword into the gap of the door with no hesitation. Linara and Raast barely had time to catch up before he cracked the doorframe and slammed it open. Lorin rushed in, knife raised.

A moment passed, and she appeared again. "He's not here."

"What do you mean, *he's not there*?" Cirena said, throwing her hands up. "The cart is tiny."

Lorin slammed her knife back into her belt and waved them inside.

Cirena was right, there wasn't much room to move inside the cart. A dim luma lantern hung from a shelf on the corner, but the rest of the space was piled high with crates. There was barely enough room for all of them to stand, and the proximity had Linara feeling tense.

"Your intel was wrong, Princess," Lorin said. "He never entered here."

Rhoam shook his head. "He entered this cart every time. No variation. Ever."

Linara's eyes began to water, and she tried to blink away the pain. The air smelled off. An acrid smell so strong, it burned. She could recognize the stench of feld fungus anywhere, but she'd never smelled it so potent before.

Lorin cracked open a crate with the flat of her knife, and pulled out a small clear vial, topped with a bright-red powder.

Linara's breathing grew fast, and ragged. The air felt clogged, the room too small. Could the others not feel it?

"This isn't Thatcher's cabin; it's their storage cache," Lorin said, tossing the vial back and closing the lid.

"Well, it still doesn't change what we've seen," Cirena said. "Our intel wasn't wrong."

"No, not wrong. Just incomplete," Rhoam said, staring at the wall covered in fabric and pictures. "Maps of Aldebraan. And Avorren."

Lorin stepped up, jaw tense. "Those are air-patrol routes. Nobody should have these, save for a few of the guard officers."

"This looks like an old list of drop-off points or caches," Rhoam said, passing over a small weathered page, frayed and brown with age.

"These aren't some second-rate smugglers," Cirena said, picking up a stack of notes. Linara leaned over, trying to read them, but the letters were in some sort of code.

A crack of sunlight appeared as Raast opened a hatch hidden in the floor. Lorin knelt down, poking her head into the opening. "Maybe he did come through here. It leads underneath the cart, and into the alley behind us."

"Truly gone, then," Cirena said, kicking one of the crates. "He retreats to his cabin at the end of the show, then parades off into the city. We can't wait for him; the show will be over soon."

Linara swayed and she caught herself on the edge of the crate. She tried to breathe, but choked on the terrible air. It was in the cart. Within the city. Within the stench upon Vahn's breath.

Thatcher was going to get away. Again. Somebody needed to answer. She just wanted justice. Vahn already got what was his, but the corruption ran deep, stretching all the way to Avorren now.

Images of fire and ash, charred and broken corpses filled her vision. Of Thatcher and the Fairgrave boys in that tent. Of her uncle and mother, both dead at the end of that path, taken so long ago.

It was evil. All of it. Feld fungus caked the boots that killed Skitter. It was the order that caused the boys to attack, and Linara to burn their hands. Without it, Vahn wouldn't have chased her so far, wouldn't have threatened her life. Without it, Linara would be back at home, harvesting branches and wishing for a better life.

Trel and Pen would still be alive.

A heat rose from her chest, filling her fingers. It burned. But it felt so . . . sensible. A justice so hot she could taste it. What good could a fire bring? How about a cleansing? Burn away the impurities of this world, leaving behind clean ash.

So let it burn. Let it all crumble to dust before her. Rising on the smoke she would find her justice, written in the flames as their carts burned. Thanks to them, she wouldn't fade easily from history. Now she would really give them something to talk about. Let future smugglers speak of Linara, burner of feld and vanquisher of evil. What good was power if she didn't use it?

Something struck Linara across the shoulder, and she lurched from her rage. Wood smoke curled from the crate she clutched, and Rhoam waved a fire out from a plank of wood he held in his hands.

The others crouched against the far wall, shielding their faces. From her.

"Oh, stars above," Linara gasped.

"I thought we lost you there," Rhoam said, forcing a smile.

"I'm sorry," Linara breathed, backing away. "I'm so sorry."

"It's time for us to go," Lorin said, reaching a tentative hand out. She gestured to the trapdoor, to fresh air and freedom. Linara hesitated, but forced whatever heat still lingered away and grabbed her hand.

They pulled her from the carriage and out into the alley. And all Linara could remember was a blur of streets and shouts, her feet moving with no instruction.

She almost killed everyone. Again. She almost lost control and burned them all to cinders.

That was a reminder she wouldn't forget. Thatcher didn't kill a single soul. Feld fungus caused nothing. *She* burned their hands. *She* killed Vahn. And Trel. And Pen. Their deaths were because of her, and her alone.

And all that talk of righteous justice . . .

What did she expect to do? Burn their carts, and their feld? And then what? Even *if* the others made it out alive, what was she to do? Expect them to turn and bow to her? Renounce their ways and serve at the whims of some maniacal, burning monster?

They would've turned on her. The troupers, the audience, the whole damn city. They'd see a wicked girl rise from the fire she started, and stone her in the streets.

But that wasn't the worst of it. If she had continued, the others *wouldn't* have made it out alive. She'd be standing on their graves, and the king would've killed her himself.

Lorin's grip relaxed, and Linara looked up to find them all back in the Spire. Sweat pooled on their brows, but Linara didn't even feel warm. Another reminder that she was an aberration. They laughed, and panted for breath, leaning on each other on the plush red carpets of the entry hall.

Great statues loomed above them, a line of old soldiers and heroes immortalized in stone for honor and glory. They looked upon everyone who entered, a silent protection against any ill intent that might walk those steps. They were just statues. Linara had passed their dead gazes a dozen times.

But now she felt their eyes upon her. Watching her. Condemning her.

She couldn't stay under their watchful eyes. The others laughed, full of joy, but none of them looked her way. Linara couldn't tell which felt worse. A dread filled her chest, she couldn't think any more. Back to her chambers, where she could be alone. Truly alone. And safe.

Lorin turned toward her, arm outstretched.

Linara ran.

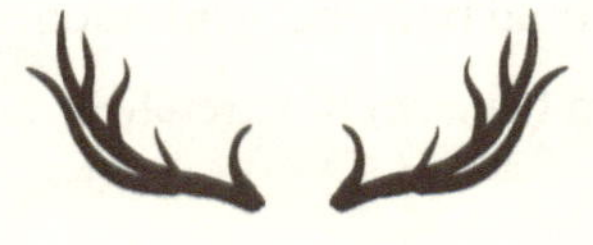

Raastivarlin sat deep within his memory, reminiscing about a wonderful day. New sights and sounds. To see a horse up close! And all the people! The sound of chaos, a cacophony of noises with no pattern. What a paradox! He loved the walk more than he ever expected. More than . . . cooking? Moon and stars above, surely not! Would such a walk eliminate his other memories? His dreams?

Perhaps he should not walk any longer.

But the camel! The delicious camel! A glorious combination of spices. Cinnamon! What a strange choice. A beautiful choice! He mulled over the taste once more, melting into the memory like wax. It would be good then. A new addition he must add to his book. But where to find camel?

Raastivarlin opened his eyes, back in the Spire entry hall, watching his new friends catch their breath. He didn't feel winded in the slightest. Where had Linara Farrow gone? He was very thankful for her on this day. She remembered how he wanted to see the city, to find something familiar. He could not remember Arkya, not enough to know if he had succeeded. But what he found was friends, and those he surely must have had back home.

She had grown quite warm. Smoking like a well-cooked roast. Very interesting indeed. Perhaps that was what she was speaking of that day? Very curious. The others weren't concerned, so it must have been nothing.

Laughter and joyous voices sang out among the hall. Raastivarlin stood with his new friends, wishing to never forget the memory of this day.

CHAPTER FOURTEEN

Linara did not sleep. The night passed slowly, full of ruminations and terror, until the morning bell marked the beginning of a new day. Meyla came with her morning meal, as usual, and Linara dragged herself through a bath before her lessons.

A weight hung over her, a deep realization that she could never truly deviate from her schedule. Raast had said that to never hurt anyone, she would have to never leave her rooms. He was right. She could never trust herself to leave her routine. Maybe not even to fly.

There was a strange comfort in that now. Her time with Orv was isolated and safe, despite how much she usually dreaded it. At least with him there was no risk of doing anything stupid.

Once she opened her door, however, all the blood fled from her face. The princess, Cirena, stood in the hallway just beyond. It didn't look like she had been waiting for her, but she had stopped all the same. Her shirt and trousers had been swapped back to a flowing blue dress, her hair tied back with braided silver.

Linara took a half step back into her room, wanting to get out of their way so they could pass. But Cirena just smiled at her, stopping in the hallway. Even Rhoam didn't move between them, or shove her back. He just stood a step behind the princess, a long maroon coat draped over his arms.

"Good morning," Cirena said, glancing awkwardly between Linara and the doorframe around her. "Are you headed up to Orv's office, then?"

"I . . . uhh—yes," Linara said quickly, then shook her head, "I mean no. I'm headed to the garden . . . ma'am." She winced.

Cirena rolled her eyes and sighed. "Please don't start, now that we're back in the Spire. Rhoam and I are headed to the library, and the garden isn't too much farther. Shall we walk together?"

Linara nodded and fell in pace beside the princess, fully conscious of every breath and beat of her heart. Her mark did not thrum with power, but she was certain if this became a regular occurrence, the stress alone would cause her to combust.

"Are you feeling better?" Cirena asked.

Linara glanced up at the princess. "I'm . . . not sure what you mean," Linara said softly.

"Well, after you ran straight to your room, we assumed you were under the weather. I'm sure those experiences of yours can be quite taxing," Cirena said. "And I especially understand now that you're being forced to take flight lessons."

"I don't know about *forced*," Linara said. "I volunteered, after experiencing it on the way here."

Cirena shook her head. "Another one fallen to the dark side, Rhoam."

"I prefer flying, actually," Rhoam said.

"That's not true, and you know it," Cirena said.

"I prefer horseback with *you*," he clarified. "A griffin is preferable when you're absent. They get skittish around you. I think you pull their feathers too hard."

Cirena sniffed. "In other news, Lorin followed up with some of that evidence we grabbed in the trouper camp. She took a whole squad down to bust them just a few hours later. But they were gone already."

Linara couldn't hide the scowl that crossed her face. "No thanks to me."

Cirena laughed. "Maybe we should've let you burn it down, in hindsight." Linara looked on with horror, even as Cirena glanced back. "What?"

"I almost *killed* you," Linara said.

They both studied her for a moment, as if they didn't realize it before.

"I almost burned down the whole caravan." Linara said.

Then Rhoam grunted and returned to watching the others in the hallway. "You don't strike me as the type."

"It doesn't matter, I almost lost control."

"But you didn't," he said.

"If you didn't strike me with that beam, I probably would've."

"Oh, that's good to know," Rhoam said. "I didn't strike you so you wouldn't kill us. If I was that concerned, we wouldn't have stuck around. I struck you so you wouldn't do anything reckless."

Cirena clarified. "Despite their crimes, burning down their caravan would've landed you in more trouble than them. Arson is still a crime, no matter who committed it."

"Well," Rhoam said, "trespassing was already a crime at that point."

"Not one easily proven, Rhoam," Cirena huffed. "What I mean is combusting a whole cart full of feld fungus would've left you in a terrible situation with my father, and we can't very well be friends while you're in prison."

Linara only noticed she stopped walking once the princess turned around and looked at her. "Friends," Linara said softly. "With me?"

Cirena's cheeks flushed. "Well, that is . . . we had a good time, and I was only hoping, that . . . you know."

"No, no, it's not that, I just thought . . ."

"Oh, and I almost forgot." Cirena gestured behind, and Rhoam handed over the long maroon coat. "I snatched this from the caravan before we left. I thought it would make for a fine consolation prize, since we didn't grab Thatcher in the end, but you ran off before I could give it to you."

Linara stared at it for a moment, surprised, before slipping her arms through it. It went down to her knees, and had sleeves too long for field work. Even the buttons were a bit ornamental for her taste, and had far, far more pockets than she could find use for. But it was strangely comfortable. And the thought itself warmed her heart.

"I—" she said, but words began to fail. "Thank you."

"It fits you well," Rhoam said.

"Oh, and just as well, there's still unfinished work to do!" Cirena said, gesturing behind her again. Rhoam handed over a stack of papers. They were the same she was looking at in the cart yesterday. The encoded messages and strange drawings. "Rhoam and I are spending our morning reading up on them."

"Troupers?"

"Code breaking," she said. "And if you tell me that it's not a very princess-y topic, you won't be the last," Cirena huffed. "We'll have to sneak past the librarian."

"Again," Rhoam added.

"Again," Cirena agreed. "In any case, Linara, when you're done with your studies, you should join us."

"In the library?" Linara asked.

"We'll be there awhile, I'm sure," Cirena said, "but I know how long Orv can go on if you let him. Just come and find us; the Spire is a small place."

Cirena waved and walked off down a large, wide opening in the hallway, toward the central library.

She thought the Spire was *small*? Linara shook her head, realizing she was standing in the middle of the hallway as servants and guards moved around her like fish in a stream. And she truly wasn't afraid? What was wrong with them?

There wasn't much time to even think upon it. The bell rang above, marking her tardiness. She rushed the rest of the way down the slope and out the front gate, finding Orv leaning on his gnarled cane in the middle of the garden path.

He held a book under his arm, a copy of a similar tome she found on the table that very morning. She could barely understand the title. *The Subcutaneous Attribution of Eionic Impression: An Account of Findings and Observations of Orvinth Vinhower III*. The first page wasn't much different.

"You're late," Orv said, smiling at her.

"I know, I'm sorry."

"It's of no consequence," Orv said. "Did you get my book?"

"I left it behind. I could barely read the title."

Orv laughed and nodded in understanding. "I sent a copy to Cindavar years ago and *he* couldn't even read it. I apologize, I had spent the last several years of my life prepared to pass on my knowledge in only my writing. I wanted to make *some* use out of it."

"I'm sure it'll be useful eventually," Linara said with a smile. That book was probably the culmination of all his notes, which will make more sense as time goes on.

"That is kind," Orv said, moving off into the garden. "I thought a new topic of teaching deserved a change of scenery. Here begins the meat of your lessons, and the reason you've come to Avorren."

Linara's heart skipped a beat. She had almost forgotten, overshadowed by the rest of the prior day. A primal fear began to rise, but she knew the importance of facing it. Especially if Cirena wasn't going to leave her be, she could at least do her part in making sure it never happened again.

"Then what are the tools for?" Linara asked, pointing to a small pile of gardening equipment beside him.

"I thought it might make a nice instructional parallel," Orv said, stooping over for two pairs of metal shears, and handing one to Linara. She had used her father's pair only a handful of times, but his were rusted and notched, barely worth using.

"It is also the season to trim back the ferns." Orv glided over to a bush growing just off the path, and with careful motions, cut away stray lengths of twigs and leaves. "It is good for a plant to be pruned away, allowing the bush to flourish in the shape I have for it." He paused and glanced her way. "But I'm sure you know this already."

Linara nodded and moved to the bush beside him. She had helped her father trim back the luma before. Fungus was different than these strange bushes, but she was sure the process was the same. Linara snipped off a huge section, surprised by how easily the shears cut through the plant.

"Even the harvest is healthy for luma," Linara said, moving on to another section before Orv could spot her mistake. "Skipping a harvest lowers the collection for several months."

"While we're not growing any fruit, the process remains the same," Orv said, taking a step back and inspecting the bush with a firm nod. "I've heard the guard you saved is recovering nicely."

"Was he injured?" Linara asked. It was the first she'd heard of it. She never thought to ask about him, too concerned with wanting to remain free from the spotlight of the whole situation.

"He had a few broken ribs, but nothing serious. He'll be sticking to the ground from now on, though. Griffin flight isn't for everyone. I'm sure you've noticed."

Linara sighed and rolled her eyes. "I could've picked the timid ones out on the first day. They were scared to touch a feather. Have you ever seen a longstrider? Try climbing its legs just to get your grain shipments from the peddlers. They're two stories tall!"

Orv chuckled and lifted his hand to a low-hanging branch. "All men fear something. Some are afraid of heights, some are afraid of insects." A small green caterpillar scuttled onto his finger, and he let it crawl across his hand. "But all guards must train in the saddle."

Linara almost wished she feared flying. Then, at least, she could just avoid it. Fearing the outcome of her life was not something she could flee so easily, it seemed. She almost became the *Razing of Yarldin* without even realizing it. It ended up being far simpler than she ever imagined, falling into that trap.

Linara took a step back and examined the bush. It didn't look nearly as good as Orv's, but it wasn't terrible either. "What are you afraid of, Orv?"

Orv inhaled deeply and allowed the bug to scurry back beneath the grass. "Death."

Linara said nothing, allowing the rustle of branches and the leaves in the wind to occupy the void. She looked to him, and he stared long at the bug, still squirming through the grass.

Then he inhaled deeply and smiled, looking back at her. "Worry not about me."

"Is it death itself you fear?" Linara asked. "Or the fear of what you've left behind?"

Orv exhaled a long breath. "Do you know of the lilies that grow in the ponds outside the city walls? They purify our water; It's what makes this mountain a viable city center. Without my direct touch, the lilies would die, and the city would quickly run out of fresh water.

"But there are now plans in place to address this when I am gone. I also did not wish to leave this life without passing on my knowledge. To die having never met my successor." He smiled at her then, and Linara wanted to shrink away. "Now you've come along, and my legacy will no longer fade."

A silence spread between them, birds singing overhead. Then Orv inhaled sharply and moved on, clipping away at the branches as if nothing had happened. "What are you afraid of, young one?" Orv asked.

Linara looked at her hands. His honesty set a precedent, and she wasn't sure she'd be capable of lying about it. "Becoming the eighth Odious."

He nodded grimly and turned back to the tree. "I do not believe that will be your future, if it is not what you wish. Once you understand how you create fire at your fingertips, I believe it will become less frightening.

"You see, all of Irea is composed of energy in some form or another. Some are free as the breeze, others constant as the sun or mischievous as fire. Where these places of energy are concentrated most, you will find tiny beings called Eions. They gather like night bugs to luma. They feed on it, taking the excess as it pours into the world."

Linara watched him work, his concentration unwavering as his hands moved deftly across the branches. How could he pay attention to both at once? Linara was already struggling to keep up.

"They don't need it to survive, but they cannot resist it, especially in such large quantities of it. It's why you won't find them floating around your hearth or in a small garden like this. It's not enough for them. They need something to match their appetite. Head to the surface of an active volcano and you'll see them by the dozens or the hundreds."

Linara thought back to the carriage ride to Avorren, to the flood of smoke and the fires below. Something familiar struck out in the memory. "What about dragon fire?" she asked.

Orv scratched his chin and thought. "Perhaps. But dragon fire is no consistent source. You probably have not seen one. Even with the steam vents near your home being a sizable source, it is still far underground."

"But I think I did. On the ride here, some small creature touched my mark, and a heat blew out from my chest and cleared smoke from the carriage."

Orv's eyes widened. "Why didn't you speak of this before?"

"I hardly remembered," she said. "And honestly, I thought I imagined it."

"Fascinating," Orv said, face brightening in excitement. "I've never heard of an Eion interacting with an individual's Eionic Impression after the bond has formed!"

Orv was speaking too quickly now for Linara to follow, his words almost blending together. "You see, Eions are what give us our power. They fuse to us, so to speak, creating a mark on the skin. Why or how, we don't quite understand, but when an Eion is full of energy from a source, it tends to leave, searching for another meal or something that interests it. Perhaps that is the reason itself: fusing with a human is, at its source, sating its curiosity for the unknown.

"But the bond creates a curious interaction, something beneficial to both of us. Eions lose energy constantly, like a hole in a bucket. The human body plugs that hole. It does nothing but grow, gathering the small amounts of innate energy all around us, though, quite slowly."

Linara lifted the edge of her collar and peered down at the glowing mark upon her shoulder. If she looked closely, she thought she could see it pulse in a strange sort of rhythm. Was it truly alive? A being bound so deeply to her? Such a small thing, the source of all her trouble.

"Now, wherever an Eion was before it bonded with a person determines what power they can manipulate, and therefore, its color. I, for example, lived very near the Valley of Blue Sun, and naturally have a very green mark and an affinity toward nature-based energy."

"My mark is a deep red," Linara said. "So . . ."

"I suspect the steam vents are a source of great thermal energy. But keep in mind not all of this is exact. We all have some measure of power over all the known energy sources, even if it means I can only make a flame flicker out every couple of years. If an Eion is filled half with the power of heat, and half with the power of the sun, then the man it bonds with can manipulate light and heat equally well, but not as strongly as if he had just one."

"How many types of energy are there?" Linara asked.

"As far as we know, four. Thermal, the manipulation of heat, often in the form of fire. Kinetic, the energy of moving objects, from a thrown ball, to the power of the ground grinding against each other. Natural, using the energy given off by all life, mostly in plants. And illumination, the light given from the sun and other sources."

"What about darkness?"

"Aha, good question! Darkness has no energy because darkness is just the absence of light. The same with hot and cold. The only difference between the Blackness and the Illumination is that the sun is in one and not the other."

There were nights in the Blackness so dark that it clung to you like a thick blanket. Light certainly cut through it like a knife, but was that not a battle of two forces? Linara shrugged it away. Who was she to know?

"I thought you said that a group of Odious made this mountain?" Linara asked.

"There is a misconception that there exists a power over the earth itself. It is kinetic energy that allows people to toss rocks like rubber balls," Orv explained. "The Island of Arkya, for example. Hit anything with enough force and even the ground itself will crack and break. It is how this mountain was carved. Like a chisel taken to a slab of granite, they split the rock with kinetic force."

Linara stared at the ground beneath her feet. "I'm surprised it turned out so well."

Orv chuckled. "The founders spent half a lifetime on research and experiments, and a full lifetime gathering the necessary energy to complete it."

"It took that long?" She asked.

"You are lucky. Fire expends a significant amount of power. Stick your hand in a flame for an hour and you could keep a room warm for an afternoon. Someone with a kinetic aligned mark can catch a thrown plate and send it back with nearly the same force. Trying to store up a great deal of power takes a great deal of intentionality that way."

"And yours?" Linara asked.

"Nature is very efficient with its energy, keeping much of it for itself. But—" Orv reached up for a long branch hanging above his head. Within moments, the wood shriveled to dust, the leaves falling gently to the grass. Then he pressed his hand to the ground and grew the patch of grass up to his ankle. "It's all a system of give and take. I sometimes walk through one of our greenhouses and take some from the thriving and give to those that are not."

Orv looked around at the vines growing along the bricks of the Spire, and the grass growing thickly beneath their feet. "If you haven't noticed already, nothing grows entirely well in this part of the world. There's not enough sunlight for most of the Illumination foliage to flourish, and too much for the Blackness to spread its reach. Moss, though, grows especially well between both worlds, and I use that to my advantage. Everything in this garden will die without me, and I kill acres of moss a year to keep it alive."

Linara let the shears dangle by her side as she considered all of it. Nothing quite lined up with stories she was told. The Odious were spoken of as creatures that could snap an earthquake into existence. With a wave of a hand, a storm would come, and at a word the sun would die.

"So we're not all powerful?" Linara asked.

"Given enough time, we can, in fact, change the shape of the world as everyone fears. But that would require a lifetime gathering the necessary energy. This city was a lifelong project for many Odious, and the product was made in a matter of weeks."

"That doesn't seem to be common knowledge," Linara said.

"It's difficult to explain the truth about something people deeply fear. They long for something, or somebody, to blame. Some Odious use their power irresponsibly—destroy a village, kill some cattle—but the majority don't do much at all."

That would be her plan. To fade into the background and die without touching her mark again.

Orv smiled and gestured to the shears hanging limp in her hand. "This was a bit of a test, I must admit, to your ability to multitask. Most people struggle to listen and work accurately, but as an Odious, you must learn to focus on two things at once."

Linara grimaced and turned back to her bush. She really hadn't trimmed anything yet, she realized.

"You will learn with time," Orv said. "To always have one eye to the world around you, and the other looking inward, always paying attention to the flows of power around you. Being conscious of your emotions, or even when you could absorb excess heat, will only increase your control.

"Though I suspect you've done this already. Have you noticed that fire doesn't seem to be that warm around you?" Orv asked. "Perhaps you touched a flame when your mother told you not to, but it didn't quite hurt?"

"I sat on a steam vent when I began to walk. My clothes singed off, but I was perfectly fine. My parents told nobody."

"How much of the heat do you feel? From a fire, or from that steam vent?"

"It doesn't burn me, but a flame feels barely warm when I touch it," she said.

"It seems like you've been instinctively absorbing this energy since you were born."

"How much do I have?"

Orv shrugged. "Not even I could tell you that. It's hard to say if you'll ever find out, unless you use it all."

"Yours seems to cover your entire body."

"Most of my torso, half of my left leg, and a bit of my neck. I don't know how much I could do with it, but I suspect I could probably grow a sizable forest if I wished. In the same way a wandering Eion will be drawn to places of power, so will we. Build a house on the lip of a volcano, and

I'm sure you'll find your mark growing to my size in a decade. I spent a great deal of my middle years at the World Tree, and I haven't even come close to tapping into what I gained there."

Linara stepped away from the bush, realizing she cut away far more than she meant to. She'd gotten lost in the work. Now it was lopsided and hideous. She grimaced and glanced toward Orv, who had already finished another smaller tree.

He peeked around to her side and smiled. "This will be a healthy bush in a few months."

"Could you grow it out now?" she asked, glancing around at the path and the guards walking into the Spire, embarrassed.

Orv considered, checking different angles of the bush. "No, I don't think I will. Trimming a hedge is an exercise in control and patience. It will be a stepping stone to taming wild naturally occurring energy."

"But fire is different than plants," Linara said.

"That may be," Orv said, considering. "But this is where I started. Perhaps the lesson will be the same."

He walked over to a particularly tall tree, growing nearly to one of the taller Spire windows. One hand he placed upon the trunk, and at once, a dozen limbs fell from the canopy, trimmed in an instant. He turned and winked.

She threw her hands up. "If you can just trim these plants in a second, why are we doing this?"

"There are a few simple pleasures in this world I have not abandoned," Orv said. "This is one of them."

Linara rolled her eyes. "You have boring hobbies."

"True," Orv said, eyes glistening with laughter. "I used to explore the hollow caverns around the city in my youth. They spread for miles underground; they were quite the adventures. I'm a bit too old for that now, so I don't have much of a choice, do I?"

He waved her over to a long hedge, leaves small and needlelike. "This will be easier to focus on. Trim back the lighter color of needles, and keep it nice and square."

He left her there in total trust, moving on to his own project. She got to work in the same way as before, with only a slight understanding and a complete lack of confidence.

Still, such mindless labor allowed her to process through her conflicting thoughts. She'd always heard of the Odious as a great terror on the world, but that didn't seem to be the case. She could still burn, harm, and kill anyone close to her, though. Minor victories in understanding, she supposed.

"Did they ever explain how that flying carriage works?" Orv asked.

"Something about a fire in the balloon?"

"Smoke drifts into the sky because it rides the hot air above a flame. Fill a balloon with the same hot air, and it will drift off the ground. I believe you may have done something very similar to your griffin's wings the other day."

"By heating the air beneath his wings?"

"A flash of light, I hear, could accompany such a spontaneous and sudden expenditure of energy," Orv said, smiling. "Perhaps there is some natural talent within you, after all."

"But I had no idea that would happen," Linara objected.

"Humans have a natural talent for survival, pulling on skills our conscious minds could not pull off. You proved that back in Nelbren, no matter how unfortunate the circumstances."

"I've been trying not to think about how close I came to burning a building down and lighting Dresborn's feathers on fire. It's at least good to know I probably don't have the stores of power to burn the whole city down, even on accident."

"Correct. Maybe when you're my age, and by then it would only happen if you wanted to do it on purpose."

She used to think she would never find herself in that place, but now she wasn't certain. It would be so easy to fall into that fallacy, to think herself morally upright. It already happened less than a day prior.

But it was time to move on. It was a mistake that, thankfully, didn't have lasting consequences. Linara breathed in deep, feeling a bit of the fear subside, ever so slightly. "How do we start?"

"That's something I've been eager to find out," Orv said excitedly. "No matter how many texts and ancient journals there are, the first intentional manifestation occurs differently for everyone. It's like finding a new muscle. Once flexed, it falls into place, but how will you unlock it? One hand plunged into a flame for weeks on end? It would certainly terrify the servants."

"I'm pretty sure they're all afraid of me, anyway."

"Perhaps so, but I doubt it. I've been growing strange and unusual plants on every level of the Spire since I arrived."

Orv clipped the last branch and tossed his shears to the side with a satisfied smile. "That, however, is a problem for tomorrow. I'm sure your mind is too full to coax any power from you today."

Linara sighed and clipped the last section of pine branches. This bush looked a *little* better than the others, but she had much to learn. Well, that was assuming she would want to trim more hedges in her lifetime.

"I have an extensive list of ideas to start. We'll dip our feet into a lot of ponds to see what sticks."

That seemed manageable. It terrified her, of course, to face her mark head on, but Orv's attitude toward it comforted her. If he wasn't afraid of her, why should she be afraid of herself? Memories of just a day before still lingered, but at least he was confident that she could control it one day. She would use that thought as fuel, a motivation to work hard.

She didn't trust herself, but she trusted Orv, and that would be enough.

Orvinth Vinhower III slumped in his chair with a heavy sigh. The mountain was crossed; the lecture was over. He shuddered at the memory of his own mentor teaching him of the mark. They knew far less about it back then. Orvinth had to delve into the darkest corners of Irea to find proper information. Once, he thought it wasted time, but now he had a pupil, and he was thankful for it.

The differences between them couldn't be more great, however. Nature was rigid and defined. Fire, all chaos and passion. Not to mention Linara did not learn with books. Orvinth knew that. Maybe some of his words stuck, maybe not, but once she had her fist in a flame, things would click home.

At least, he hoped. There weren't many writings on that topic. The thermal marked of Irea were far more vilified, that was true. Any accounts on their behalf were barely accurate, hardly educational, and often destroyed.

But that didn't mean it wasn't worth trying. Orvinth cracked open a book on his desk, brittle and dusty. There was some truth behind fiction. He just had to find it. It might take months, maybe years, but he would see Linara through her training before the end. He would not die, not yet. That was his promise.

CHAPTER FIFTEEN

"I apologize for my absence," Orv said, pushing open the door and hobbling through. "I did not mean to leave you by your lonesome for so long. We're apparently expecting dignitaries tonight."

"It's not like this is strenuous," Linara mumbled, allowing her finger to fall slowly deeper into the flame until it snuffed out the wick. "It's not really anything at all . . ."

A month had passed since Orv started Linara's true training. Weeks spent plunging hands into all sorts of flames, and other sources of heat, to no success. Candles, lanterns, hearths. They were all the same. Different fuels, different feelings of warmth, but all required a touch that Linara couldn't give. At least not on purpose, and nobody was about to put her in enough danger for her to do it accidentally.

Initially, they never left his office, but it had only taken a week to change their scenery. Orv had hoped to strike new inspiration, a sense of purpose and being. All it did was bring further embarrassment. Linara remembered the look of every face that had passed by the dining room as she stood on a bed of coals spread out on the stone. They even had taken a trip into the city to watch a blacksmith heat a chunk of iron so hot it burned like the sun. Orv had her pick it up. Whatever he thought would happen didn't, and the blacksmith had been sufficiently freaked out.

She had spent one early morning in the kitchen with Raast, trying to light his cook fires. Orv had figured it would be a more comfortable environment. His stew had a very rigid schedule, apparently, and Raast's impatience had been the closest thing she'd seen to murder since leaving Nelbren.

Hanging from her feet, submerged in water, balancing on one leg, all of them ridiculous and equally ineffective. At one point, Orv had her read the entirety of a book on star signs, one hand grasping the blackened end of a torch. Linara was left with nothing but strained eyes and a fist full of tar.

For every box of candles left unlit and cold, there were three more Orv had her watch burn for "inspiration." He claimed the process was almost a subconscious effort, a hidden muscle never touched before. Once flexed, she'd be able to do it again with ease. Until then, she was left staring into nothingness, one finger plunged in a candle flame, the other pinching an empty wick, hoping her mark just knew what to do.

It didn't.

Orv swept the candles from her desk, and into a nearby drawer. "I had an idea on the way back," he said, crossing over the hearth. "And by *idea*, it's more probable that I mean a *craving*."

He poured half a pitcher of water in his small copper kettle, followed by a few clumps of leaves into the teapot beside it. "Maybe if we aim smaller. Instead of igniting an open flame, let us see if you can heat the water for our tea."

"With my hands?" Linara asked.

"Well, I don't suggest blowing warm breaths against the metal," Orv said. "Though I suppose that *could* work, but I believe that would be far more difficult than simply using your fingertips."

Linara slid her hands around the smooth metal and focused her mind on heating the liquid within, whatever that was supposed to look like.

"I'll continue searching for journals and histories concerning other thermal marked," Orv mumbled, walking back to his desk.

"How many are there, anyway? Odious, I mean."

"Currently?" Orv said, scratching at his chin. "Deydalus has two, Reginaan just one. I believe Mahnbusa is down to one as well. It's been a strange phenomenon; there used to be many more. Seven in Aldebraan alone, when Avorren was founded."

"What changed?"

"Who knows? It could just be the way of things. There could also be many more in hiding nowadays. I'd imagine there's probably a dozen or more like you, hidden out in the remote places of the world. Oblivious, or otherwise."

"I'm surprised there's no great manhunt for these missing Odious."

"How would you go about doing it? Rounding up every civilian in the nation? We keep eyes on population centers close to places of power, but it gets difficult. People slip through the cracks. Maybe other nations have figured out better ways, but we'll never know. Nobody even liked to catalog their knowledge from ages past, let alone what other kingdoms are doing *today*. Anything that can be used for advantages are deemed 'kingdom secrets' and are kept locked tight. Makes teaching new generations rather difficult."

Even the passages Orv had written about with his own journey were entirely useless. He was no abstract thinker, and tapping into a store of energy was pretty abstract to describe.

"If everyone is different in how they manifest, why would other biographies even be helpful?" Linara mumbled.

"The first step is always the hardest, to find your footing in the darkness," Orv said absently, returning to his notes.

It was a phrase he'd said more times than Linara could count. She wasn't even sure what it meant anymore, other than knowing that there was nothing more Orv could explain that he hadn't already.

Tapping into ones mark was like explaining color to a blind man, or the sun to a Blackness dweller. The only thing that would make sense would be for them to just see it.

She sighed. Why couldn't her mark be kinetic? Throwing a rock across the room at barely a touch seemed easy enough. That could be destructive, but nothing like a fire. And nobody was afraid of plants, or light. Linara hated the sun at first, sure, but *everybody* hated fire once it burned something they loved.

Linara shook her head, stamping out the tendrils of thoughts that would creep in her way. She tried to remember Orv's lessons, the blending of mantras creating a strange vertigo. The well of energy was a mountain to push through, a barrier to cross. She had to focus her mind like a knife, pressing through the wall to release the pressure.

The pot in her hands felt warm. Just a trickle, a faint impression. It felt like her imagination. The more she focused on it, the colder it got. Linara released a breath and steeled her focus. She fought to keep it, wrestling with the warmth. But the more she tried to grasp it, the further it fell. She pushed harder, reached deeper.

Then it was gone.

Linara collapsed back into her chair. She'd been at it all day, and her mind was mush. She needed a break, a breath of fresh air. A walk around the Spire, a flight through the city. Anything at all.

It had been a few days since she'd seen Lorin or Cirena. They were probably still in the library. Three weeks had passed since they tried to take on Thatcher's troupe. The princess's requests for Linara to join them in deciphering the coded messages had been constant until she had finally given in. It was becoming clear she truly didn't care about Linara's shortcomings, after all.

Having friends to pass the time with was a great improvement on Linara's day to day, but the work involved with their own research was probably more than anything Orv could concoct. And yet, Linara suddenly felt a strange desire to dig through strange maps and letters. A desire far stronger than one to remain clutching a cold teapot.

Linara glanced up at Orv. He was still pouring over notes piled high upon his desk. He was in one of those intense moments of focus, where he hardly paid any mind to the world around him. Sometimes it went for hours, Orv skipping entire meals as he went on a wild chase through tomes on his shelf in pursuit of a question.

He didn't notice when she stood. He was very particular about how long his tea steeped, but she knew it didn't matter. She poured out a cold cup and handed it over. He took it without complaint, not even looking up from his book. Then she hung the kettle above the smoldering hearth, so he would have a proper cup when he realized his was no good.

Then she crept out of the room with steps as quiet as an umbrin.

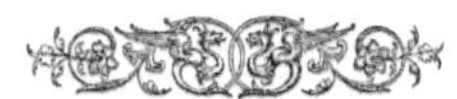

Linara groaned and thumped her head upon the table. Upon the back of her eyelids, swimming in that intimate darkness, was a sea of nonsense letters. How could she think this would be a better alternative? At least with trying to light a fire, she could see straight after she was done.

From the far wall, Lorin tossed a rubber ball, thumping it against the door to the tiny library nook. "I agree with her, you guys should have given this up ages ago."

Cirena scowled at her, but Lorin hardly noticed. She caught the ball, and threw it again, the rhythmic thumping more than a minor annoyance.

They all were piled in a small private study in the main library. Lorin had given up helping pretty quickly, but still joined them most days. Linara didn't really blame her. Still, the space was probably meant for only one or two at a time, and every inch of the table, and some of the floor, was piled high with books and blank sheets of paper.

"They're not so stupid as to use a cipher so easily broken," Lorin said, "There's a reason we have entire teams devoted to it, and they're unsuccessful most of the time."

"We're too far to give up now," Cirena said, furiously scribbling on the remnant of white space in the corners of her sheet.

"She may be right, Princess," Rhoam said, tracing the trim work on the cover of a thick book with his finger. "Perhaps we should move on."

Cirena scratched a harsh line on the page and glared up at him, a fierceness in her eyes that Linara had rarely seen. "They bested us, Rhoam. I won't stand for that."

Lorin rolled her eyes. "And I know Linara has some grudges to see to completion, but this is a bit extreme."

"It's more complicated than that," Linara grumbled, rubbing at her eyelids. "It's more than just Thatcher." She opened her eyes, finding them all looking at her, as if she had more to say. She didn't, but they weren't going to leave her be.

"It started way before him." They continued to stare, and Linara sighed. "My uncle was caught growing it a while back. Filled his whole field with feld, really. Supplied half of Elaan, they used to say." Linara sat back, too deep in the memory to leave it now. "Though, I know now that isn't true . . . The people of Nelbren have a tendency to exaggerate."

"I'm surprised," Cirena said, "It seems hard to hide."

"With enough luma scattered within, it just looks like any other field," Linara said. "Though, my father would make fun of how poor a farmer he was, because his land was always so dim. Uncle Beorn would laugh and blame it on a poor work ethic."

Linara's smile fell. "He would've gotten away with it, too, if he hadn't started taking his own crop for himself. He stumbled into the village one night in a stupor. Nobody could stop him. My mother came. Tried to calm him down. He killed her right there, in the middle of the village square."

She looked up, and they were all staring at their laps. What did they expect, pressing for the details? Linara sighed and crumpled up the sheet of paper in front of her before reaching for another. "So yeah, I want to see Thatcher behind bars. Or at the very least, his supply stores destroyed. Or his contacts arrested. Or all three. Is that so much to ask?"

Lorin shrugged and threw the ball again. The thump as it hit the wall broke everyone else from their dazes, and Cirena and Rhoam quickly went back to their own work.

No one had a chance to get far. The door to the study creaked open, as a messenger peaked his head in. Lorin's ball sailed through on her next throw, disappearing down the hallway beyond. Lorin scowled after it, but the messenger was too busy staring at the letters in his hands. He glanced up first at Cirena, and went deathly pale.

"My apologies, your highness," he said bowing so low Linara thought he might tip over. He quickly stumbled over and handed a small, worn envelope to Linara, and the other to Lorin before retreating out the door.

Linara didn't have to open it to know it was from her father. The corners were smudged and worn, not unlike the type of paper that found its way that deep into the Blackness. Except the page didn't smell like the usual mossy dampness, instead like . . .

Linara crinkled her nose, not wanting to speculate. She flipped the page over. It was addressed to Lorin.

"Here," Linara said, tossing it over. "I think you have mine." Lorin reached into her vest pocket and swapped them out, stuffing hers back inside without a second glance.

"You're not even going to see who it's from?" Linara asked.

"It's from my parents," she said, staring at the door. "Do you think he's coming back with my ball?"

"You don't seem thrilled about it," Linara laughed. "The letter I mean."

Lorin rolled her eyes. "It'll say the same thing it did four times before. They wish I were home, because they have a big order and they need help to finish it before the deadline."

"Oh," Linara said. "What do they do?"

"They make belts," Cirena said, when it was clear Lorin wasn't going to answer.

"Like . . . leather belts?" Linara asked.

"To hold up pants, and to fasten armor, yes, those belts," Lorin said with a scowl.

"And I'm assuming you're too busy here to give them a hand?" Linara asked, sarcastically.

Lorin sighed. "I didn't expect you to understand. There's always an order, and there's always a deadline."

But Linara *did* understand. The harvest never truly stopped, and missing a single month meant the next two would diminish. There was always the expectation for Linara to be there, regardless of whether Linara realized she would ever have a choice in the matter.

"The problem is not that they *need* help, or they can't *find* help; it's that they can't accept that I don't *want* to help. We're a large family, a lot of cousins and siblings, and nobody strays very far. It makes for a lot of mouths to feed, scraping by as belt makers. Every. Single. Family member. So when I left to join the city watch, they weren't thrilled."

"Even after so long?" Linara asked. "Youngest Knight of Alde, and all that? It has to count for something, right?"

Lorin grunted. "To the average citizen, it's an enormous feat. To my team, it's a liability. To my family, it's just another checkbox in the list of transgressions."

"Do you regret becoming the Stag Knight?" Linara asked.

Lorin scoffed. "Certainly not. Do you know that all Knights of Alde receive land when their charge is finished? My family were on the brink of poverty, and now they're in a farmstead outside the walls. But the one thing about being the youngest Knight is you quickly find you've peaked pretty early on."

"Surely there's more to it than *that*," Linara said.

Lorin sighed and fingered the letter in her pocket. "Eventually, Nilya will hand over command of the Ebon Wings in full, but before that? I have a silver helmet waiting for me someday. Maybe even gold."

"You could always sacrifice your life in such a way you'll be immortalized in the Hall of Heroics," Rhoam offered. Were those the big statues in the entry hall? Linara had read the plaques only a few times, but did remember a lot of them were old Knights.

Lorin laughed and rolled her eyes.

"What's wrong with that?" Cirena asked.

"The only people who'll get to see it will stand beneath it and wish I was a belt maker." Lorin finally pulled the letter back out of her pocket and looked at it briefly before putting it back again, thumping the back of her head against the wall. "I'm sorry, I'm in a bit of a mood today."

Cirena cleared her throat, trying to change the subject. "Well, anyway. I wish *I* got mail."

"You do get mail," Rhoam said absently, reading a book at the end of the table. He looked up a moment later, at Cirena staring wide eyed. "What? I know with absolute certainty you wouldn't want to read them."

Cirena sniffed. "And how would you know what I would or would not like to read?"

Rhoam shut his book and folded his hands over his lap. "Princess, in all the years I've known you, you've consumed every page of fiction in this entire library. From top to bottom, poring over the shelves. You've crossed through fairy tales and adventures as you've aged, all the way through the entire shelf of romantic interest. It still has not prepared you for the sheer volume of love letters you've received in recent years. Even before you were of proper age where it wasn't considered completely disturbing."

"Love letters?" Linara asked. "I always figured you two were . . . well . . ."

Cirena's face paled. "Oh, sun above, no."

Rhoam reopened his book, scanning the page to find where he left off. "I've been at the princess's side since her birth. We're practically siblings."

Linara frowned, studying Rhoam's face. He couldn't have been much older than them. Maybe mid-twenties, at the very most. Then she laughed. "You had to have been . . . five?"

"Four and a half," Rhoam said. "I could barely lift a sword."

"What did they expect out of a child?" Linara asked.

"Well, I wasn't her only guard back then. My job was just to grow up with her, learn to never leave her side. I had to prove myself before they handed that duty fully over."

"But what if you weren't good enough?" Linara asked. "Would they have just found another?"

Rhoam shrugged. "But I was."

"His family has guarded the royal line for centuries," Cirena said. "It would've been a real tragedy if he was the first to fail."

So he was born into it. A purpose so grand, thrust upon him. In a way, his story seemed similar to hers, just far less . . . dangerous. "So you had no choice, either," Linara muttered to herself.

Rhoam chuckled. "It's not like I would choose anything different. I'd be a soldier either way."

Linara reached for the pile of books in the center, searching for something new. Most were code-breaker guides or some story on espionage. She flipped open the cover, revealing page upon page of maps, ranging from Aldebraan all the way to Deydalus.

"Why did you grab an atlas?"

Cirena shuffled through the notes on the table and handed a few over. They weren't messages, but drawings. One was of a galloping horse, the other of a griffin. It was a peculiar sketch, made with no color, but just a single line stretched and curved into their respective shapes.

"I read about a man once who hid maps in sketches like this," she said. "Guard paths as the pattern on butterfly wings, or locations of encampments as the veins of leaves. Things like that."

"Why would they bother to hide guard patrols if they had simpler maps hung on the wall right next to them?" Linara asked.

Cirena huffed and turned the page. "I don't ask questions of hardened criminals."

Lorin grabbed the paper and turned it around to look at every angle. "I think it's just a picture of a horse."

"Maybe they just want us wasting our time," Rhoam shrugged. "Spend all our effort examining meaningless art. Or decoding orders on which play they're going to rehearse next. Or which costume needs sewed. Just in case they got stolen."

"Rhoam, these are drug-smuggling troupers, not Reginaan spies," Cirena said. "I really don't think they planned on having *anything* stolen."

Linara let the pictures fall to the tabletop, and reached for a poster, colored corner peeking out beneath all the clutter. It was an old advertisement for the troupers' show, once plastered on every tavern and street corner a mile in each direction from their stage. A painting of a king wrapped in bear fur faced a giant, with huge script lettering arcing above it. Marlin Manlin's Marvelous Masters, a three-month Blackness tour. Below it was a list of cities, starting with Avorren, ending all the way down at Ohtaka.

Linara frowned at the list, and at the one that came next. "It says they're performing in Blackrest until the end of the week," Linara said absently.

"Well, assuming they kept to their schedule," Cirena said.

She'd seen Blackrest on the maps. It was probably only a few hours ride by griffin. For a whole caravan, maybe a day or more. They would've left the city three weeks ago, and if they used that time to regroup and lie low, they could easily reappear in their next stop like nothing ever happened.

"I mean . . . why wouldn't they?" Linara asked. "I doubt they have any reason *not* to continue."

Cirena opened her mouth to object, but then frowned. "If they left because they knew *somebody* broke into their caravan, they'd prepare for the worst and assume that the city watch would be over to shut the whole thing down."

"Which we were," Lorin added.

"But they would also know that they would stop there. If the Avorren watch cared as much as the troupers *think* they do, would they send a warning to the Blackrest city watch in advance?"

Lorin frowned. "Probably not. They would've closed it when they left the city walls."

"Not to mention, it must cost more than they're willing to part with to cancel their tour just as it starts." Cirena leaned back with a heavy sigh. "And to think we've spent so much time here, and it was sitting right in front of us the whole time!"

"Don't tell me you want to fly to Blackrest," Lorin said. "There's still a lot of assumptions behind this theory of yours."

"But they could be there right now, continuing in their machinations, uninhibited," Cirena offered.

"And what if they *are* there?" Lorin asked.

"Then we finish what we started," Cirena said, slamming a fist on the table.

Rhoam leaned forward and placed a gentle hand on her own. "Princess, I'm all for closure, but we should definitely think more upon this, especially with how poorly that worked for us the last time."

"Last time was a fluke," Cirena said. "That plan was flawless."

"Hence the floor hatch, standard in every trouper's cart built within the last fifty years," Rhoam said.

"Just because you found that out *after the fact* doesn't mean you anticipated it," Cirena said, standing. "It's time to put your money where your mouth is. If you doubt they'll be there, then let's go and find out. Worst case scenario, it'll be a great trip, and I'll drop this hunt forever.

Best case, they *are* there, and we'll do something truly good for once, something the city watch couldn't."

Cirena slapped her hand to the center of the table, staring at them each in turn. "Do we have a deal?"

There was a fire in her eyes, a fierceness that Lorin was quickly rising to meet. "Fine," she growled, setting her hand on top. "I'll take that bet."

Linara reached her own hand out, but hesitated at the last moment. She almost lost control in pursuit of this goal; was she really that willing to step into that possibility again? It was easy, looking back, to slip into that mistake. Just one trail of thoughts of righteous fury, and she'd be gone.

But something had to be done. If it wasn't them, then who? Thatcher and his men would parade around the entire Blackness, spreading their influence to anyone within reach. They'd harvest from the farms that grew it, and convince people like her uncle to follow suit. Families would be destroyed because of their inaction. Would that be on her hands?

Except Lorin and Cirena would go, with or without her.

Linara wanted to see it for herself, but she hardly had anything to offer. Except the one thing Artoris believed she had. Intimidation personified. As long as she breathed, no dared move against them, right? She could provide that. Even if it was a bluff.

But would knowledge of her own pitfalls be enough to avoid them? If she grew too confident, that would be when things failed. As long as Linara didn't lose focus, keeping to their mission, there wouldn't be anything to worry about.

Linara placed her hand on the stack, and Cirena smiled wide. They all turned to Rhoam, who sat back in deep contemplation.

He looked around at each of them and blew out a long breath. "Fine. We'll leave in two days. If they've kept to their schedule, we'll make sure it doesn't continue past Blackrest. But listen to me. We won't have the protection of the city on our side this time. We'll be out of our own territory, and into theirs. As soon as something goes awry, we're gone, no questions asked. Got it?"

"Deal."

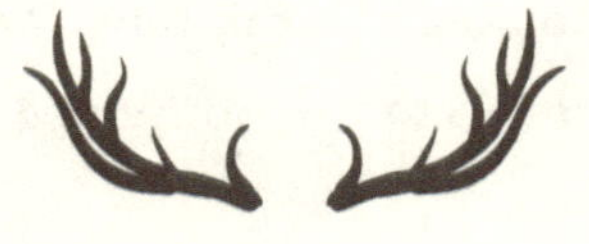

Orvinth sipped from the cup of lukewarm tea contemplatively. It had been his third cup, and he still couldn't decide if he preferred it cold after all. He at first stomached it, not fully realizing its temperature until Linara had long left the room, but now it was growing on him. Perhaps he was not clear in his intention. Was this the way they drank tea in the Blackness? To not waste a source of heat, they took to drinking it cold? Surely not.

Though, she had mentioned in the past her inability to feel heat at all. Perhaps she just truly could not tell whether or not the pot was warm enough yet.

Orvinth frowned at the pot. Perhaps, more likely, she just had not figured out how to heat the pot yet in the first place? She seemed so confident in placing the cup in his hand that he hadn't even questioned it. So confident that she left without a second thought, as if she accomplished her goal, after all.

It really was no matter. He did not expect her to make any sort of progress in even a month. He took another sip of the cold tea and grimaced. No. Cold tea was not very preferable at all.

CHAPTER SIXTEEN

Linara knew the moment she arrived in Avorren that an entire lifetime spent living within the Avorren Spire wouldn't be enough to understand its inner workings. The upper section, filled with offices and living quarters for the nobles, was simple. But the farther down one walked, the chances of becoming hopelessly lost increased dramatically. Even if she did ever figure it out, there were guards posted at the lower levels, blocking doorways that Linara knew led even farther into the mountain.

That being said, the more time Linara spent with the princess, the more she learned to understand its layout. The Spire had its own patterns and systems, if someone paid enough attention. Though, it certainly didn't help that every few decades, a new Master of the Halls rearranged things to his liking. Things like the library and kitchens were never touched during these times, but everything else was apparently fair game to be moved halfway around the Spire just for the sake of efficiency.

According to Cirena, the last change in management was just five years prior, and the dust was only now beginning to settle. With such a large tower, there were often rooms left abandoned, or unaccounted for, which some groups snatched away without a second thought. Including the city watch.

They had their own buildings all over the city, barracks, and training grounds for the thousand or so men stationed throughout the city. And yet they still looked for whatever space they could find within the deepest recesses of the Spire.

The day after their commitment in the library, Linara found her friends in such a room. A hall, really, emptied out and filled with racks of wooden blades and other weapons. Straw dummies were propped against the wall, wrapped in leather jerkins or bits of broken metal armor. A few round targets were painted red, with broken arrow shafts sticking out like pins.

Rhoam and Lorin circled each other in the center, slicked with sweat and weapons bared. They dared not tear their eyes away from each other, even as Linara entered. Cirena lounged on a bale of hay against the wall, a map pulled open on the surface.

"Good, you're here," she said, trying to trace a finger from one point to another before scowling and giving up. "Maps of the Blackness are confusing."

"And you think I'll be able to help with that?" Linara asked.

"Well, you lived there."

"Certainly not in Blackrest," Linara said, peering over at it. It looked like an old sketch of the town, city walls surrounding a block of buildings, much larger than Nelbren. "And not in any place that required a map to get around."

"Your village isn't even *on* half the maps I've seen," Cirena said. "I've checked."

"So why do you think I'll be able to help *now*?" Linara asked.

"I don't know, I just figured it would be universal knowledge." Cirena leaned in closer to the map. "I can't find their theater plots anywhere."

Linara hopped up on the bale, watching Rhoam attack, his arm a blur. He hardly seemed to be putting in any effort, but Lorin was out of breath. "Have you considered the possibility that there aren't any?" she asked.

Cirena frowned up at her. "What did they use in Nelbren?"

"Barrels."

"Surely not."

"Not on any map, remember?"

Cirena scowled and folded the map. "Then I guess you'll just have to be our tour guide. Never having been or not, it'll at least be like visiting home, yeah?"

Linara grimaced. "I still haven't figured out how to leave my lessons for a few days. It's already hard enough to take an hour off."

"I can just draft up a royal decree," Cirena suggested. "That is within the bounds of my small semblance of power."

Despite the lack of progress in her training, she felt obligated to show up and try. Especially after blowing off half her lesson yesterday. Still, this was important, and she wouldn't miss it. "No, I'll just ask," Linara said. "It's possible he'll allow it, I just never bothered to find out. Or I could fake being sick or something."

Cirena grimaced. "I tried that once to get out of etiquette tutoring. Orv brewed up the vilest of potions to help. I think those *actually* made me sick."

Linara thought back to the thick green liquid Orv would drink before breakfast every morning and shuddered. "Good to know."

Raast shuffled in through the open door then, all childlike wonder as he watched the duel between Rhoam and Lorin unfold. He sat on the bale beside Linara, barely acknowledging them as Lorin stepped forward in a brief attack.

"I heard you are leaving tomorrow," Raast said absently.

"Are you not coming with us?" Linara asked.

He turned and studied her curiously. "Am I invited?"

"Of course you are," Cirena said. "That's why I sent the messenger to begin with. You were with us in the beginning."

"I am honored that you would include me," he said, eyes wide in surprise. He stared out before him, as if searching the wells of his mind. "Though, it is only blurred memory that you speak of. I remember a play. A dark tunnel, and lots of sneaking. I remember a smell like burnt meat."

It had been over a month since that little excursion. Had he nearly forgotten already? "That sounds about right," Linara said.

"Excellent! What time shall I be ready?" Raast asked.

Linara turned to Cirena for an answer, who called out to Rhoam, still focused on Lorin and their duel. "Uhh . . . maybe after the midmorning bell?" he said, pedaling back to parry a pair of blows.

"I will need more time to prepare the supper stews," Raast said. "If I leave a big enough pot, I will not be missed."

"Supper?" Linara asked. "That's barely past breakfast."

"A fine stew requires much of a day to simmer," Raast said excitedly.

"Fine, later then," Cirena said. "Rhoam, will you finish up so we can plan this?"

Rhoam nodded silently and launched forward. Lorin scrambled back, deflecting his two blows and stabbing out with her spear. Rhoam easily spun away to land a glancing blow across her side. Lorin cursed and fell to the stones. She threw her spear down at her side, wiping sweat away in defeat.

"If you'd practice like you used to, you'd still be able to beat me," he said, offering a hand up. She slapped it away, heaving herself up and pushing away. "What happened to you, Stag Knight?" he asked after her. "You used to be so spry, so *dangerous*."

Lorin scowled and stalked over to grab her spear, waving him off.

But Rhoam did not let up. "You used to be a terror. Your spear was legendary, now it's just another chunk of wood."

"I still am a terror," she muttered, gasping for breaths. "When I want to be."

Rhoam shook his head and dabbed a few beads of sweat away. After such a one sided display, it was clear he barely put in the same effort. He was just toying with her, all the way until the end. Had they ever been evenly matched?

"Raast, when will you be ready?" Rhoam asked.

"After the lunch bell," he said with a firm nod.

"Then we leave after that. It'll give us time to get settled and find any evening performances. Any objections? Wonderful."

Lorin returned, still grumbling, with an armful of practice swords from the barrels in the corner.

"On another note, I'm only agreeing to his excursion on one condition," Rhoam said. "This is a step up from breaking into a stage play. You two must know how to defend yourselves."

"More training?" Linara groaned.

"Just having a sword on you will make anyone hesitate to attack," Rhoam said. "And knowing how to hold it will probably work a little better. Hopefully."

Lorin tossed a wooden sword her way, and Linara barely caught it. "Alright, up you go, let's see what you got."

"What? Now?" she asked.

"Yeah! It builds character! You, too, Raast," she said, tossing him a sword as well. "Hefting pots builds character, I know, but this is different."

"I am a cook, not a fighter," Raast said, laying his sword against the hay bale.

Lorin rolled her eyes, grabbing it back and pressing it more firmly into his arms. "We won't go long enough for you to forget how to cook."

"That is not what I am worried about. I let the servants kill our chickens. Blood does not do me well."

"They're wooden, Raast; they wouldn't cut a spider."

"But they would crush a spider."

"But we're not spiders."

Raast considered for a moment, and then grabbed the wooden sword, finding the statement to be agreeable.

Lorin turned to Linara. "Have you ever held a weapon?"

"Do pitchforks count? I've stabbed moss before."

Lorin motioned for her to toss back the blade, replacing it with her wooden spear. "Moss doesn't fight back, but it's a start."

"I want to join!" Cirena said, slamming her book closed and running over.

"I've already tried to teach you," Rhoam said. "You're exempt."

"And I'm terrible, I know," Cirena said, quickly grabbing a sword and joining the line. "But I can't miss out!"

Lorin paced along their line, face hardening to stone in an instant. "Alright, you lily-livered assholes," she shouted. "*You* came here to train. *I* came here to beat the soft out of your ass."

Rhoam shot her a glance. "This isn't the academy."

"What's the problem?" Lorin said, spinning back toward him. "Cirena's used to it. Linara was in flight training with Commander Nilya, and Raast...well..."

"You sound very much like master Dent," he said.

"See? It's not the same without the speech."

Rhoam rolled his eyes and waved her forward, playing the part and falling into his best hulking no-nonsense titan look.

"You brought skill and habits that you *think* are going to help you here," Lorin continued, Rhoam behind her, mouthing along to the speech. "You *think* you're special for having a deadbeat father who knew how to whip you with a fire poker. I'm going to beat that out of you and train you *my* way. *My* way is the *only* way. Got it?"

"Yes, sir!" Cirena yelled, Linara and Raast following suit behind.

"Now you sorry lot look like you need to learn how to stand," Lorin said, taking a massive step forward and falling into her usual sword stance. "This is how men stand. Men stand strong. Little boys stand weak. Now stand, gentlemen! And ladies."

Cirena stepped forward with resolve, her posture straight and practiced. Linara tried to match it, but Rhoam had to prod her to straighten in far too many ways to count. Raast somehow did better, but Linara had no time to study his stance before Lorin barked more orders.

"We do not have the luxury of teaching you sorry excuse for snail dung how to walk and talk before you learn the blade, so I hope you have the decency of acting like adults before I treat you as such." Lorin pointed to her sword like it was a foreign object to everyone in the room. "This is the blade of a sword, and if it weren't made of wood, you probably would've hacked off your arms by now. It is used for killing and, if you have no shield, preventing yourself from being killed.

"Now look at me with at least one of your virgin-watching eyes for long enough to grasp these simple concepts," Lorin said, holding her blade above her head, parallel to the ground. "If a sword is coming toward you from above and your infant brains lose all sense of combat focus, just remember to hold your blade like so."

Linara fell into stance as she demonstrated, and Lorin stepped up to her, eyes glaring at every point of her posture. Even though she knew it was an act, Linara could still feel the sweat form on her brow at the iron stare. With a swift movement, Lorin whacked down with her own sword. Linara's spear caught the blow, but the force sent it cracking hard against her forehead.

"Oh, blazes," Lorin yelped, her persona dissolving instantly as she rushed over. "You're supposed to hold it tighter!"

"I think you're supposed to hit lighter," Rhoam said.

"I did!" Lorin said. "I think?"

Linara rubbed her head. "Hard to tell."

Rhoam took Linara's spear and replaced it with his blade. He closed her grip tight and shook it firm. "Now hold it tight. Think of it like an extra length of your arm."

Linara looked at the sword, then at her arm, and back again. "But it isn't."

"I know its not, but think of it that way."

"You sound like Orv, telling me to think like fire," she said.

"Then you should try to think like fire," Lorin said. "While you're at it, think like a sword, too."

"Just hold it tight," Rhoam said. He took a step back and raised his sword high, bringing it down slowly until it barely made contact with her own. A light touch, and nothing more. Then he held it, pushing harder and harder until her arm began to give.

"Good. Now take that same grip and push back when it hits this time."

He swung again, same speed, same power, and when the blades touched, Linara pushed, shoving the blades away and losing her footing as she stumbled forward. Cirena stifled a laugh.

"Good start, but less oomph," Rhoam said, returning to his position and raising his sword again. "I'm going to swing for real this time. Now block it!"

Rhoam swung down. The blade hit Linara's quicker than she expected, and the wooden sword cracked against her forehead. Linara hit the floor, stars swimming in her vision. Rhoam stood over her, eyes wide with shock, apologizing profusely as he helped her up.

Lorin and Cirena were both doubled over in laughter. Even Raast seemed amused in his own strange way. Despite the throbbing in her skull, Linara couldn't help but laugh with them.

"After all that, I swing just as hard as Lorin," Rhoam said, slapping his forehead.

"No, no, I think I'm just bad at this," Linara said, prodding at the welt beginning to form. "It probably wouldn't be so bad if it didn't hit the same place twice."

"Would you like to join my guild?" Cirena asked. "I've founded it for people who cannot hold swords properly. We read books and make fun of the strong burly soldiers."

"Does it have a name?" Linara asked.

"It hasn't needed one until now."

"Don't force a name on my account," Linara said, reaching out her hand. "But I accept."

Cirena shook it firmly. "Three more members, and I'll have to make a formal plea for authentication with the guild board."

"It's a shame you don't have more friends," Lorin said.

"Am I a member if I'm obligated to be at every meeting?" Rhoam asked.

"No, you can't make fun of yourself," Cirena said.

Lorin twirled her sword and squared up to Raast. "Alright, Sir Raastivarlin, you're the last one standing. Will you be joining their wimpy guild, or our regular training sessions?"

"I would like to join their guild," Raast said flatly.

"You have to submit your application," Cirena said, gesturing to Rhoam and Lorin.

"Fine, I will try this sword combat."

He stepped up into position, a perfect mirror of Lorin's demonstration. She went through the basics again, as if he didn't hear it before. Then she stepped back to swing, this time light and smooth. He blocked it easily. Step by step, swing by swing, she increased in power, and it became clear Raast had much more talent for the sword than either Linara or Cirena combined. Perhaps it was just quick learning.

Lorin circled him, sending blows from all different directions and angles, testing him further and further. His moves were fluent, small yet powerful, barely moving his arm at all. Lorin stepped quicker. Harder. Swiping down with greater power than before, but still Raast blocked every blow.

Soon they were far past simple training. He was using motions never taught. Rhoam cocked his head, pacing around them, watching with a strange curiosity. Then he leapt in, striking with his own blade, a flurry between them both. And Raast took every blow in stride. He was a whirlwind, eyes darting between them, unflinching.

Then Lorin and Rhoam both struck out at once. Raast spun, deflecting one blow and twisting his blade to disarm the other. The wooden sword spun off and struck against the wall, and the room fell into dense silence. Lorin stood panting beside Rhoam, stunned at Rhoam's empty hands.

Raast dropped his sword and staggered back. "I—I do not wish to continue."

"That was incredible," Lorin said, still unmoving.

"Fine work for a beginner, even for a Viri," Rhoam said, flexing his wrist where Raast disarmed him. "Are you sure you haven't been hiding this skill from us?"

"No. No." Raast said, staring at his hands, now shaking visibly. "I have not."

"Hah, well, the Luman-Viri's famous quick learning is quite apparent."

"This was something different," Raast said. "Like remembering a dream from my birth moment."

"I thought you forget everything you do not keep up on?" Linara asked.

"I am a cook," Raast snapped. "A cook, nothing more!"

"Right," Cirena said, holding out a calming hand, "that's fine. We won't have you fight anymore."

"Looks like if we run into trouble, it'll just be the two of us after all," Lorin said, slapping Rhoam on the shoulder.

He grunted and folded his arms together. "I'm not so sure. It makes me nervous."

"We've already come this far. We can't just abandon it," Linara objected.

"She's right," Cirena said. "We're not all defenseless. Linara can conjure fire from her fingertips, and Raast, whether he likes it or not, can probably club a few guys with pans before they kill him."

Raast seemed uncomfortable with that. Linara found herself in a similar mood. Conjure fire from her fingertips? She wasn't sure she could toast a slice of bread.

"My duty has proven easier when I am your friend more than just your guard, but there will come a time I must prioritize your safety over my friendship with you, Princess." Rhoam stared firmly into her eyes, then released another long, heavy sigh. "But I do not think today is that day. I must also protect the kingdom, and this feld fungus threat might be a real danger.

"And before you all celebrate," he continued, "let me remind you I have an oath that overrides anything else. If the choice needs to be made of who I must protect, I will prioritize the Princess, every time."

"Relax, we're just scoping out a caravan full of a fungus that potentially creates super soldiers," Lorin said. "It's not like we're breaking into a Mahnbusan oil vault."

"Everyone's still getting a knife," he grumbled.

"Deal," Linara and Cirena said simultaneously. It certainly was better than nothing, especially if they assumed she could burn the place down in a pinch. She just hoped it never got to that point; she'd hate to disappoint them.

Just then, a flurry of footsteps echoed from the doorway as a small crowd of people rushed by. Whispers and shouts mixed together from outside as Linara glanced at Cirena and Lorin. Neither of them seemed to know anything, either. They all dropped their swords and raced out the door.

A crowd led them down the spiraling ramp toward the gates. Servants, guards, and nobles gathered at the railing, peering down to the entry hall below. They all made room for Cirena and Rhoam.

Through the double doors of the Spire walked a huddled mass of people, broken and ashen from travel. Their clothes were tattered, each face a mess of grief and pain. Blood splattered upon even the children as they huddled through the gates. They looked like they'd walked a great distance, but had no relief upon arriving.

A gap formed around them from the passing crowd below, an unspoken understanding to leave the newcomers be. Whether out of pity or disgust, Linara could not tell.

"What happened to them?" she asked, watching a boy stumble on the paved stones and barely keep his footing.

"Refugees, I think," Cirena said softly. "From Bordin. There has been talk about their village. Pillaged and burned a couple of weeks ago."

Linara gasped, and a child looked up at her from below, face smeared with tears and dirt. "Who would do such a thing?"

"According to the reports, a militia group from Reginaan," Cirena said.

Reginaan. If this was the truth behind the conflict the king was so paranoid about, Linara now understood. Everyone talked about the tension at the northern border, something Linara tried to ignore. It reminded her only of her purpose here, to one day be the weapon to end that conflict.

Now she stared at the alternative. Innocent people, caught in the middle of growing war.

"I've been to the border," Lorin said, staring out. "It's never been a quiet post, but it's never been this bad."

Even Raast stared out in silence, taking in every face in the crowd.

"What changed?" Linara asked.

"We don't know," Lorin said.

"Nobody asked?"

"It's not that simple," Lorin said. "Usually they burn one of our caravans, so we burn one of theirs, you know? Small skirmishes to hold off a bigger conflict. This feels different."

"Neither of our kingdoms want war," Cirena said. "Or so we thought. If my father asked for these refugees to come into the Spire, it means he's taking it seriously."

Linara nodded grimly, swallowing the pit forming in her throat. She scanned every face in the entry hall, remembering every feature, stain, and wound. This was the true cost of war. Villages of collateral damage all under the name of justice.

But would Linara truly step aside if she had the power to put an end to it? What she had to remember, was there existed a future where ashen faces like those were caused by her own hand. Simple retaliation could send her into Reginaan to send a similar message, and that thought terrified her.

If that was what it meant to serve Aldebraan, she wanted no part.

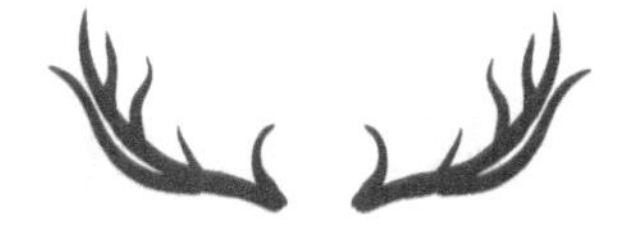

Father,

I'm glad to hear your business is going well. Perhaps it is not so surprising, since you were the best farmer in Nelbren. If you were right that I was not meant for a small village like Nelbren, it's a trait I inherited from you. I can finally read a full letter without Orv's help, so you need no longer worry about any prying eyes.

Those panels you mentioned are made of quartz built to absorb light, usually from the sun. They found recently that firelight and Luma both work, apparently, but not nearly as well. They're all over the city here, but it is surprising to know that they are sprouting up across the Blackness. Perhaps it is good you left your farm.

I did not get a chance to tell Raast about your recipe. He has surely already forgotten about your offer, but he'll be just as excited again when I remind him. Cirena and Lorin both said you're welcome and asked why you seem to be so vague and mysterious. I told them it was because you were kicked too many times by Nela, but you probably have your own explanation.

I hope Ohtaka is as beautiful as the books describe. I hope to visit one day. Good luck on your dealings there, but I know you hardly need it. Oh, and let me know where you are headed next so I can direct any letters there.

Peace below the stars,

Linara

CHAPTER SEVENTEEN

In the end, it didn't take much for Orv to release her early. After mulling over an excuse for half of the morning, Linara opted for the direct approach. It helped that it was a particularly nice day, and Orv himself was feeling particularly antsy for a walk.

An hour later, after only a minor delay, they were all flying toward Blackrest. It was a strange experience, leaving Avorren. It wasn't too long ago she'd arrived, trading the dark comfort of the Blackness skies for the brightness of the sun. Now that she was heading back, she couldn't shake the feeling of unease. After only a few months, was Avorren the familiar place being left behind?

Lorin led their procession through the skies, her griffin, Aria, a stark white beacon upon the landscape ahead of them. They would follow the major air routes to the town, but none of the others knew the way, and once the sun passed beneath the horizon, it would be difficult to follow.

Thankfully, Linara managed to get Dresborn for the flight, and she appreciated the familiarity on such a long ride. He had deep experience in both the patrol routes above the mountain, as well as the longer journeys to places like Elaan and Blackrest.

He was a good choice for first timers, and Raast's elation during the flight matched her own. So much so, she had to constantly remind him not to lean too far out of the saddle as he stared at the passing landscape.

Cirena, a stark contrast, had her eyes clamped shut, pressing her body tightly to her griffin's neck. She was always vocal about her dislike of flying, but Linara always assumed she was exaggerating. After seeing her and Rhoam's griffin, Linara didn't even blame her. Corinth was a snooty bird, having eyed them all with contempt before they took off.

Thankfully, the journey took a few hours and was entirely uneventful. By the time the town came into view, the sun had long passed below the horizon, dropping the sky just barely to black.

Blackrest was built into the darkness like fungus on a dirt road. It was still larger than many of the towns and villages they passed on the way from Nelbren, even large enough to warrant a low stone wall around most of the perimeter. A dark river ran along the edge, like a winding branch of tanglegum on a stretch of moss.

They landed their griffins just outside the town's meager wall, stamping through the moss down to the road. No one paid them any mind, even as they trotted through the gate. No guard stood watch. Hardly any travelers hogged the path.

A man swept dirt from the stoop of a storefront just inside. He waved as they passed. Cirena waved back, but Linara narrowed her eyes in suspicion. Who waved in the Blackness? It was a useless endeavor, usually. No one could see you until you were right in front of them. It was why they clapped their forearms. Sneaking up on someone often communicated the wrong ideas, and sound carried warning farther.

But this town had lanterns hanging from doorways, and from poles in the intersections of every street. Linara could see every surface under the pale-blue light, shadows only a light addition to the moss growing along the road. Even the houses, only *modeled* after the style of village mounds, were unnatural, built of stone and wood. These people lived almost fully in the Blackness, but pretended like they were not.

Was *this* where her father's crop went? Wasted on towns and villages that would rather be a few miles north? All this luma wouldn't even last a full harvest. They'd have to be getting double shipments from several large farms just to sustain their light. And what about when the mist rolled in? Or a new moon? Would they put out *more* lanterns?

Linara glanced down at the road, and the moss crunching beneath her feet. It was bone dry, and she'd have to dig down deep to find any life. Maybe the mists didn't fall here often.

Cirena had thought the town would bring a sense of security to her, a feeling of home, but it only did the opposite. The sky, just a tad too bright. The crowds, just a tad too large. Through the gaps in the clouds, she could see the faint glimmer of the stars peeking through, but that wasn't enough. How far would she have to fly to see them fully? An hour? Half a day? Would it be worth it?

"It's so dark," Cirena said, and Linara almost laughed. "Is this what your home was like?"

"Not at all," Linara said, "It's more confusing than Avorren, here. The moon is near full, and yet they walk under the light of lanterns like they can't see. If it bothers them so much, why live under the moon at all?"

"I don't think you realize how far from civilization your little village was," Lorin said. "I've been all around Aldebraan. Trust me when I say that most major cities light their streets even brighter than this."

Linara scoffed. "There's no farm big enough to produce that much Luma. Every street corner, building and cellar? You'd need a hundred acres just to light it for a week."

"You really haven't left your village much, have you?" Lorin said. "If we flew any closer to Elaan, you would've seen the fields."

"If that were true, wouldn't I know about it? Our family barely had the time to manage two acres on our own. Fields that large would probably be under constant rotating harvest. And even *then* they would shine just as bright as the sun."

"Yeah, that's exactly how I'd describe it," Lorin said.

"Did you think the Blackness ran off just small village farms?" Cirena asked.

Linara's mouth worked wordlessly. "I . . . suppose not," she mumbled. "I guess I just figured we were helping more than we were."

Lorin shrugged. "You probably were, just not for the province capitals."

They continued on, and each building they passed filled Linara with increasing sorrow. All those years of growing luma, she really thought they were doing something important, something meaningful. Lighting a world bathed in darkness. That was their purpose.

At least that was what her father always said. But *he* was the one who traveled in his youth, who saw a lot of the kingdom before settling in Nelbren. He would've known how little impact they truly had, and yet his determination never failed. Maybe it was only because he didn't *want* to be impactful. If he did, he wouldn't have gone back to Nelbren.

And for that, Linara both resented and respected the people she passed. She understood now what it meant to live in Nelbren. Everyone lived there with intention. Those who didn't like it, or wanted more light, simply left. Now Linara wasn't sure *what* she preferred. If these people couldn't decide which part of life to live, they were given an opportunity for both. From that point of view, Linara could understand that.

This place was foreign, yes, but Linara knew the fault did not lie with the town itself. Every place would be foreign to her. Even Nelbren, now. She should be thankful to spend even a day in this place. Away from the noise of Avorren and the light of the sun. The friendly wave of the shopkeeper at the wall was no insult, but a reminder of what life used to be like. Neighbors who knew each other. Bakers and butchers who remembered your name. Her friends were right. This place *could* be a bit of a comfort to her, if she looked at it the right way.

They stopped at a wide building on the main road. A sign hanging limp above the door, script written in luma paste. *The Scared Skipper.* Their little inn in Nelbren never needed a name, but this one was quite a bit larger, and was surely not the only one in Blackrest.

Rhoam helped Cirena down from the saddle and disappeared through the door, while the rest of them stretched their legs. A few other griffins stood in the wooden stables at the back of the building, busily pecking away at clumps of moss and hay. A young stable boy eyed them from the alley as he brushed out the inside of a barrel. Linara didn't envy him, but still missed such simple barn work.

A few moments passed before Rhoam returned. He flicked the stable boy a bronze tile before handing over the reins to the griffins. "We're booked here for the night," he said. "There are posters for the troupers hung inside, but I couldn't find out from the owner how accurate they still are. The best option we have is to scope out the market square."

Linara could barely see the moon through the heavy clouds, but there was still a faint glow just above the horizon. "It's closer to evening than anything else, but it's still early yet."

"Probably better to be early," Lorin said. "Which way to the market?"

Raast closed his eyes and rose on the balls of his feet. He breathed in deep, tasting the very air while everyone watched, waiting for his revelation. "I think it's that way," he said, pointing off down one road.

"Is that a Luman-Viri thing?" Cirena whispered.

"No. Everybody seems to be walking this direction," Raast answered. "And I smell the food."

"Are you sure it's not just tavern slop?" Lorin asked.

"It is different," Raast said, starting off down the path. "More distinct. More unique. More appetizing."

Linara could smell it, but only slightly. The entire town smelled far sweeter than Avorren. It was too overpowering in the capital, but here it had a strange depth to it. That familiar damp, earthy smell was there, hidden just beneath woodsmoke and bread ovens. Just above that was something more profound. It was a delightful addition, really, but it reminded Linara of her hunger even more.

She still had the flatbreads in her coat pockets, but proper food was far more appealing. Both Raast and Linara led the way through the crowd, sliding between peddlers and merchants, following their noses to the center of town.

One food cart in particular, Linara honed in on. It smelled of mushrooms in the best of ways. Her stomach rumbled with every raving imagination. Cirena called out for them to slow down, but once her stomach found its course, it could not be swayed.

The road opened up to a market. Stalls and shops were scattered amid the dirt path, banners and flags hanging on lines set between them. Voices yelled, peddled, and laughed around them, a flurry of sounds that would've overwhelmed Linara a few months ago. Now, she just wondered why it was so small.

She passed two stalls selling various foods. Sugared pastries and whole vegetables would never do. Not when such a delectable smell still filled her nose. Raast found it first, pointing through the shifting crowd to a simple wooden stand against the far wall.

Smoke curled up between the rooftops from a small fire dug into the dirt. A man leaned against the corner, soft white hair running down to his shoulders. His skin, at the strange in-between of light and dark, contrasted with the paleness of the surrounding crowd.

Raast closed the distance before Linara. "What is it you are selling, fellow cook?" he said, trying to lean over and glimpse the long dumpling-looking things sizzling on the grill top above the fire.

"Two, please," Linara said, slapping a handful of copper tiles on the tabletop.

The man paused, looking between both of them, trying to decide who to answer first. Ultimately, money won, and he speared two with a pair of wooden skewers and handed them to Linara. She stuck one firmly in her mouth, and he grimaced, waiting for the burn that would never come.

"It smells of mushrooms and . . . pastries?" Raast said, absently. "What is in them?"

"You cook, Viri?" the man said, glancing toward Raast.

"I cook," Raast said with a firm nod.

The man glanced from side to side, looking for prying ears, then leaned in close. "It's a secret."

"Oh!" Raast said, nodding in agreement. "It is famous, then?"

"Oh yes. Very famous. Closely guarded, and all that."

Linara shrugged. "Tastes like mushrooms," she said between mouthfuls.

The man rolled his eyes. "It *is* mushrooms. The secret is everything else."

"Worry not, master chef," Raast said. "Your secret is safe, as I will forget it eventually, after all."

The man frowned at Linara, then back at Raast. "Yeah, but *she* won't."

"Don't mind me," Linara said, licking the first skewer clean. "I just like to eat." And it *was* delicious at that. She hoped Raast could learn the recipe. Good thing she bought two.

The man grunted. "Fine. But buy one first."

Raast straightened. "I like to know what I am eating before I eat it."

"And you'll buy one after?"

"I can guarantee nothing," Raast said, but then stared at Linara's now empty skewers. "But probably."

The man narrowed his eyes, locked with Raast in a fierce duel. Except from what Linara remembered from a book she had read just that morning, Luman-Viri didn't feel the need to blink quite as often. Eyes watering, the cart owner broke his gaze away, cursing under his breath.

"It is a mushroom puree, spiced generously and mixed with a few choice vegetables," he said, grumbling all the way. "The pastry is my own inclusion, thin enough to bake on the grill. It gives it, if you will, the needed crunch."

Raast's eyes lit up, and he moved even closer, staring with a new light at the other little roll, still grilling upon the fire. "Fascinating! You discovered this yourself?"

The man shrugged. "Inspiration comes from many places, Viri. From my homeland comes the wrap, from Elaan comes the mushrooms."

"What mushrooms? I must know. And the spices! What spices?"

"*That* is as far as I go, Viri. My competition would run me out of this town otherwise."

Linara glanced around the market square, full of shops and vendors, sure, but hardly any who offered cooked food. "What competition?"

"They'll come. I must move first to attract the early customers before other vendors arrive, you see?"

So far, no others had even glanced their way, all but ignoring the poor man and his stall. "Does that work well for you?"

The man grunted and swept the tiles off the counter into a pouch at his waist. "It's been a slow day, alright? Now, Viri, may I interest you in one at last?"

Raast considered for a moment, far longer than Linara did when they arrived. "Yes, you may," he said, sliding a few tiles across the tabletop.

A tug on Linara's sleeve pulled her away. Lorin was behind her, pointing down a length of road. "I tried yelling after you. You both were walking too fast," she said, rolling her eyes. "We found the troupers. Cirena and Rhoam are back keeping an eye on them."

Linara thanked the cook and scampered off to follow Lorin, tugging Raast along as he studied the mushroom roll. They crossed the rest of the market and went down a small road, stopping at the mouth of an alley. Cirena and Rhoam watched from the corner, peeking out across a wide road at a performance set up between the buildings.

Curtains draped from clotheslines, and a long wooden platform marked the stage. A few performers lingered on the stage, and the bench seats were beginning to fill. The show hadn't started, but it wouldn't be long.

There was no sign of their carts, but there didn't seem to be any space within the town to accommodate them.

"We asked around while you were gone," Cirena said. "They're camped outside the walls."

"That's an interesting development," Lorin said.

"It could be," Rhoam said. "It's possible they're being cautious of trespassers, or there truly wasn't any room."

"If that's the case, we won't be finding anything valuable here," Lorin said. "It might even work to our advantage."

Rhoam grunted. "Assuming that they posted no guards."

Raast looked up from his food to notice the play for the first time. "I seem to recognize that one." He said, pointing to a bearded woman in the corner of the stage. "She sparks a memory quite vivid."

A horn note blasted from behind the stage, and a few others joined in, half-heartedly. It was the opening to the Ballad of Garadhur, the band practicing before the true performance.

"They'd be foolish not to keep the camp guarded," Cirena said, "but if they're still doing the Ballad, they can't afford to leave *too* many behind."

Rhoam looked to Lorin, a silent conversation passing between them. Lorin nodded over her shoulder, where her short spear was strapped to her back. After watching them spar back at the Spire, Linara was certain they could handle a few posted guards, no matter their background.

"It's unlikely we'll find Thatcher there," Rhoam said with a heavy sigh. "He'll be with the other performers."

"That's fine," Cirena said. "We'll leave the heavy lifting to the Blackrest watch. We can sabotage their carts so they won't escape, and gather enough evidence for the guards to investigate themselves. We won't have to do anything strenuous."

Rhoam glanced over at the stage, then back at Cirena. "Fine. We'll scope it out. That's all I can promise."

Cirena smiled and nodded in agreement, motioning for Rhoam to lead the way down to the edge of town. Linara followed, guiding Raast in front. He seemed interested in little else outside his mushroom roll. He had taken only one bite so far, spending the rest of his time in intense study, scribbling vigorously in the small journal he pulled from his pocket. Even as they walked.

Compared to Avorren, Blackrest was tiny. The market wasn't far from the edge of town, only a half mile or more. The wall loomed, and the crowd thinned. Very few buildings occupied this side of town. A few houses, and little else. No one stirred within, and even the guards paid them no mind as they left the boundaries of the town, into the wilderness beyond.

Even from so far, Linara could see the light of a campfire burning in the distance, blocked only by a few lingering shadows of motionless carts. The ground was flat between, maybe a half mile or more, but the day was cloudy, and they had the advantage of darkness.

Rhoam led off the road to the flat of the wall, crouching against the stone as if they were simple, tired travelers. Lorin volunteered first to scout ahead. She stayed low, keeping to the dark patches of moss. To her credit, she did remarkably well in keeping herself hidden. Linara could spot her the whole way forward, but if she didn't know what to watch for, she probably wouldn't have noticed. Not to mention, whatever troupers they had keeping watch probably weren't too accustomed to seeing in such darkness, especially if they were reliant on that bonfire of theirs.

Lorin returned a few moments later, reporting a mostly empty camp. A pair of troupers were stationed in the center by the fire, too occupied by their game of cards to truly notice anyone enter.

Rhoam agreed to continue, and they all crept forward. Raast, they kept by the wall, still too engrossed in his food to notice them moving off. He was oblivious to the world, stuck in the experience as firmly as mud.

The first thing Linara noticed as they closed in on the camp was that there seemed to be more carts than she remembered. But maybe she hadn't truly been paying attention. They weren't in the courtyard for long, back in Avorren, and they were packed pretty close together.

Still, Linara counted at least two dozen carts, laid out in two concentric rings. A single bonfire was the camp's only source of light. It illuminated only the inner ring, long shadows cast upon the rest of them.

The night was quiet. Bats fluttered through the air, and their footsteps crumpled dried moss. The sound of the town was mostly blocked out by the wall, and the only real conversation heard was the sound of bickering from the camp, growing louder as they drew closer.

Somewhere on the far side of the camp, Linara could hear the faint stamping and sniffing of a herd of heffen. Probably their draft animals of choice.

They closed in on the first ring of carts, crouching low to the walls. Lorin knelt beside one of the massive wheels, running her hands along the wood beneath, while Rhoam moved off toward the front.

"There's nothing to sever that I could see," Rhoam whispered after a moment.

Lorin frowned as well, wiping her hand upon the back of her pants. "I could break an axle, but it'll make some noise."

They were *already* making too much noise. Linara knew they were trying, but their whispers were hardly quiet.

"We could just subdue the guards in the center," Cirena suggested. "It doesn't sound like they're even keeping watch."

"Assuming there aren't any other stragglers we missed coming in," Rhoam said. "We should be quick about whatever we come up with."

Linara's heart began to quicken, unnerved by the stillness around them. She glanced around, cursing herself for trusting her vision too much after only a few months in Avorren. A glint of light caught her eye from underneath a nearby cart. Linara tried to focus upon it, but the more she narrowed her eyes, the less she could see. She shook her head and turned back to the others.

"We prioritize the important ones, then," Lorin said. "The storage caches, food stores. Anything of value they won't want to leave behind."

"There's two dozen carts here, at least," Cirena said.

Linara glanced around, and saw the glint once more. She frowned into the shadows, before looking toward the others, still huddled against the side of the cart. Then at the dark wilderness around them. Nothing stirred.

Teeth clenched, Linara crept away with all the softness of falling mist, moving toward the back of the cart beside them. She searched the moss but found nothing of note in the dimness of the cloudy sky. Linara scowled. She was getting too used to the sun.

"I'm sure we'll be able to smell it," Rhoam said.

"If only we didn't leave Raast at the wall," Cirena muttered.

"What about Linara?"

There was a pause, and Linara grimaced. They really were too loud.

"Where'd she go?"

Just before she rose, her hand fell upon the source of light. It was a chunk of metal, smushed into the moss, probably from the wheel of the cart running it over. The bonfire light must've been reflecting off at just the right angle. Linara dug it out and brushed off the mud and bits of moss. It was some kind of pin, carved with a symbol Linara didn't recognize. It probably just caught the light from the fire. It looked important, though, or at least valuable enough not to leave behind. She slid it into one of her many pockets.

Just before she crawled out from underneath the cart, a flurry of shadows moved in the space ahead of her. She froze, pressing herself flat against the ground. They passed her position, moving like stalking cats. There was no sound, besides her friends' whispering. Not even the sound of bickering from the center.

At once, the shadows darted forward, converging on the others. Rhoam and Lorin both cried out in surprise. The scrape of steel and the clash of metal followed.

Linara scurried further underneath the cart, trying to stay hidden and catch a glimpse of the action. Lorin, Cirena, and Rhoam were surrounded by a half dozen men wielding spears and worn swords. Every now and then, one would step forward, and Lorin or Rhoam would lash out themselves, deflecting whatever blow came their way.

Cirena looked panicked, trying to search for an escape, a long knife shaking in her grip. Rhoam kept one hand firmly on her shoulder, the other holding his sword with perfect calmness. No blow touched him, but neither did he have the opportunity to counterattack.

Lorin said there were only two men at the fire. Where had these men come from? Was the show over? They didn't look like the normal troupers. They weren't in costume and seemed far more hardened.

Linara squirmed underneath the cart. What could she do? Step out, yell for their attention? And then what? She couldn't—and wouldn't—use her mark in any way useful to them. She couldn't be an intimidation factor, either. In the dark, they wouldn't know who she was, even if they did recognize her face. They'd just rush in and take her too.

But whatever opportunity was there left quickly. The troupers worked in tandem, pressing the group toward the center of camp. Every now and then, there would be an exchange of blows, but Lorin and Rhoam kept a tight boundary, and were led unwillingly.

Linara cursed and punched the ground. She felt so useless. As soon as they were out of sight, she scurried from underneath the cart and slid down under the next one, in the inner ring.

The dried moss pricked her hands with every move. It was a tight fit, but she doubted any other guards would suspect anyone was hiding underneath it. If she was lucky, they wouldn't even know there were others in the camp. Hopefully Raast hadn't heard the fighting, and stayed by the wall.

The bonfire in the center burned low, and the two bickering guards were gone, their game unfinished upon a crate. A low mound of moss and dirt obstructed much of Linara's view, but she could see enough of the fighting from her vantage.

The troupers kept them surrounded in the center, shouting for them to drop their weapons. Cirena yelled out obscenities in response, but Rhoam and Lorin kept silent and focused.

Would these men be ruthless enough to kill them? If they smuggled such qualities of fungus, surely they weren't strangers to thieves. She'd heard stories of severed hands and broken legs in the past. At the very least, whatever would happen to them at the end of this wouldn't be good.

Linara had to help somehow, if even just a distraction. She pressed her head to the moss, trying to focus on her mark, and the mountain to overcome. The sound of fighting was ripping her from her thoughts. Her heart pounded deep, an anxiety building fast. She couldn't focus, not even enough to breathe deep.

There was no righteous anger to fall back on here. Just fear. Despite it all, she didn't want to hurt anyone, including the soldiers. If she let go of all reservations, even her friends would get caught in the fire.

"Lorin, Princess. Prepare yourselves to run."

Linara glanced up as Rhoam straightened his stance. He released his grip on Cirena, facing fully toward their adversaries. The men gathered around him took half steps back, unsure of what to expect.

"That'll be enough!" a voice boomed from beyond the center yard. Rhoam ignored it, but the other men faltered, retreating back farther, their weapons drooping just slightly.

Rhoam launched forward with a burst of speed. The first man fell before he could raise his sword, but the others closed in quick, fighting him back. Lorin took the opportunity to go on the offensive as well, Cirena unsure of who to follow.

Thatcher stormed through the gap in the carts. His thick fur cloak and horned helmet cast wicked shadows on the carts behind him. He walked with the weight of a mountain, and Linara's chest tightened.

"Faaxriin!" he called out, and whistled through his teeth. The troupers immediately darted away as the hill in the center unfolded like a serpent.

Linara suppressed every scream and primal sound that echoed throughout her body. Not a hill, and not quite a serpent, but a dragon, scales the color of moss. Spines across its back unfurled and snapped back. It supported itself on bony wings, stretching back on two thick legs. Talons gouged into the ground like swords, and it lowered its head to stare at the fighting with an impatient eye.

Cirena yelped, and Lorin cowered back. Rhoam was the only one to stand his ground, sword held up at the dragon's snout like a toothpick against a mountain. Behind Thatcher, a pair of guards pushed Raast into the circle. He seemed unconcerned, and unfrightened, even by the dragon before him. So they had found him, after all.

Linara clenched her teeth and pushed herself lower into the moss. Any opportunity for her to help had now passed.

Raastivarlin stared up at the great, magnificent creature, in awe that such a thing could truly exist. The deep shades of green, the heat of its breath. He stared into its amber gold eye, lost in its age and wisdom. He wondered what memories it had. Where it had been and what it thought of them.

Most of all, Raast wondered what it would taste like. Such a thing seemed too horrifying to ever find out, for to kill such a creature just to eat it would be a true atrocity. But to find a creature already dead? Unlikely, but possible. The creature was lean, a physique of strength and honor. No fat to flavor, all muscle. The meat would be tough, and chewy. But slow roasted, or in a stew . . .

Raastivarlin blinked away his thoughts and looked around. A clearing lit by fire, faces bathed in shadows. A polarity of opposites, so delectable. He hardly remembered being led to this place. He was once in the market, tasting such an encapsulating experience, and then he was here. Raast returned to his deep memory, returning to that place. Upon his tongue, flavors like the golden sun of Avorren. Being led by his friends to the edge of town. Then he was alone, with his notebook. A pair of men came. He remembered them from Avorren. They were jugglers.

They seemed now to be in great danger, but Raast hardly felt it. And Linara Farrow seemed to be missing from their company. Where had she gone? What a phantom she could be. They promised him an exciting adventure, so how could he be surprised? To be kidnapped and rescued by Linara Farrow? A true delight!

Raastivarlin watched the dragon, and the guards, listening to every whispered word of his friends beside him, wishing to never forget such an exciting adventure.

CHAPTER EIGHTEEN

"Let's put down our weapons, shall we? Faaxriin can get skittish around sharp objects."

Thatcher's voice echoed around the silent camp. Rhoam didn't listen at first, staring straight into the dragon's eye. But slowly his sword point dipped, until it fell into the moss at his feet.

Immediately the nearest soldier grabbed the pale-blue blade and retreated as others came to tie their hands.

Thatcher rolled the cloak from his shoulders and handed the helmet to a man beside him, his gaze focused on the prisoners around the fire. He spoke no words, but his eyes said everything. Irritated, yet . . . amused.

He reached into his vest and pulled out a small leather pouch. Slowly, methodically, he began unwrapping the leather cords. The dragon broke its gaze from Rhoam and watched Thatcher now with hungry eyes. "Did you know dragons like feld fungus just as much as humans do? It doesn't have the same effects, of course, not nearly so . . . volatile."

He dumped the contents of the pouch into his palm. Raw feld fungus, shriveled and dried, but otherwise unprocessed. Thatcher tossed the whole handful into the air. The dragon lashed out with its long neck, swallowing it whole with a loud clamp of its jaws.

A long, forked tongue flicked across the scales around its jaw, smoke curling from between jagged teeth. Then a shudder passed through its body, and it curled back upon itself. A moment later, and it looked just like a mound of dirt and moss, just as before.

"It relaxes them, you see, and they can't get enough," Thatcher said. "A strange twist of fate, really."

Cirena cleared her throat, stepping forward. Her head she kept high, despite her hands tied tight behind her. "We would like for you to release us," she said, voice wavering. "This is clearly a large misunderstanding—"

"Be silent, girl," Thatcher snapped. A young boy ran forward and handed him a wooden goblet before hurrying away. Thatcher swirled the liquid in the cup for a moment. "Do not think I do not know who you are. Your descriptions were clear in Avorren, but I truly did not think you'd be so stupid as to come back."

"You know us?" Lorin asked.

"The Stag Knight, the Princess of Aldebraan, and her knight protectorate. There's been talk in the capital of a black-haired maiden and her brute of a body guard nabbing smugglers in dark alleyways. A bit overexaggerated, I think, to describe a silly girl who just wishes to be what she is not. Him, though," he said, gesturing toward Raast, "I do not know him."

"I am a cook!" Raast said helpfully.

"Sure. Did you think we wouldn't recognize a Luman-Viri? Did you think we wouldn't tighten security? It's a natural response to a break-in. And you still waltzed up to our little camp like you were simple mice slipping underneath a net."

"That didn't stop us in Avorren," Lorin said.

"That hidden entrance was little more than an oversight that you aren't nearly as clever as you think you are for finding."

"We still chased you out of your selling grounds," Cirena said, and Thatcher laughed.

"You know very little of what goes on here."

"And what would that be?" she asked.

"Do not think I will answer your questions so easily. All you need know is that you've only . . . accelerated what was once lost. I must thank you for that. Enjoy your night, little mice. I'll have plans for you soon enough."

Thatcher motioned for his men. A moment later, her friends were dragged from the fire. Cirena and Lorin struggled, but Rhoam let himself be led away. Even Raast went willingly, but he seemed far less concerned than the others. They disappeared behind a cart, Cirena's muffled yells echoing through the camp for a few lengthy moments.

Thatcher stared into his cup for a long moment before tossing the drink into the fire with a huge burst of flame. He rubbed at his temples, pushing the cup into the nearest man's chest. "Once already, we've delayed our plans because of them. Do not allow it to happen a second time."

He walked out of view, leaving the clearing in a tense silence. The popping of the fire was barely loud enough to drown out the low breaths of the slumbering dragon. It was a sound Linara couldn't remove from her mind, now that she knew it was there.

She didn't dare move from her place under the cart, even after the soldiers thinned. Time passed, and the other performers returned, trickling in as the performance in town came to a close. Logs were added to the bonfire, and the drinking truly began. How they could celebrate so close to the sleeping dragon evaded all sense of reason.

Pressed into the moss underneath the cart, Linara overheard many conversations, whispered and shouted alike. Most talked of their performance, or their dealings in the town. Simple things. Of Cirena and the others, it seemed no one knew anything at all. Thatcher kept his plans close, perhaps because he knew the kind of men he employed. The kind whose voices carried far in the wilderness with drink in their hands.

Her stomach called for food, and she fished out the bread and meat she'd smuggled into her pockets. It was hardly a distraction. Linara worried for her friends. Something was stirring in the camp, and everyone knew it. Plans were shifting, their goals were changing, but no one knew how. Maybe not even Thatcher.

Mostly, Linara worried for Raast. They were foolish to bring him along. His age probably numbered in the hundreds, and they endangered his life. And for what? This whole endeavor was foolish.

Linara released a long breath. There was no point in steeping on that now. She was still free, and whether she could tap into her mark or not, she could still do *something*.

Whoever those new soldiers were, troupers or not, they were well trained, their movements quiet. If Linara had paid more attention, she could've warned her friends before they'd leapt upon them. They were more accustomed to the dark than Linara had expected, but Linara still had that advantage upon them.

She was born in it. The shadows belonged to her. And now they were after her friends. With the dragon only a lingering problem, she found a slim chance once more. Linara would wait, and she would save them tonight, before their plans were fully decided.

Sharper voices sounded from behind her, and Linara managed to twist her body to face out toward the edge of the camp. A pair of men stood underneath a luma lantern, hung above the stairs to a cart just behind her.

One was a soldier, arms outstretched beside him while an older man, stooped over with a significant hunch, hobbled around with a chunk of chalk. A tailor perhaps. The soldier wore a uniform, tightly fitted and slightly muddied. None of the soldiers fighting Rhoam and Lorin wore the same thing.

The tailor inspected every facet and groove of the fabric, tugging at the edges until everything was squared away. Upon the sleeve, Linara recognized a familiar shape of medal. She dug in her pocket and pulled out the dirty medallion from earlier. A perfect match.

"Humph," the tailor grunted, yanking one last time at the front of the man's jacket, nearly pulling him off balance. "It is fixed."

The soldier relaxed and sighed audibly, flinging out the soreness from his arms. "Thank you, Baba."

The tailor grunted and waved his arm off. "It is nothing. Now don't rip it again. And stop getting so much blood on it. And take it off, for light's sake, before somebody sees you."

"We're in the middle of nowhere, Baba," the man said with a laugh. "Who will see me? The bats?"

The tailor spun and slapped the man across the shoulders with his chunk of chalk, spraying white dust into the air and leaving splotches across his uniform. "Tell that to Thatcher, eh? He's not so blind as a bat, eh? You're lucky he paid you no mind! He'll crush you like a slug! Now go wash that off."

The man turned and sauntered off, flinging back a hand sign Linara didn't recognize when the tailor had his back turned. The tailor grunted and picked up a sword from beside the stairs, the sheath a light, faded blue. Rhoam's sword. No mistake, she'd seen none other like it.

The tailor plucked a key from behind the unlit lamp beside the door and unlocked the cart before tossing the sword inside with a dull clatter. Linara made note, hoping that whatever plan presented itself, she'd be able to find it again.

Hours passed, and the sounds of the camp grew quieter . Loud cheers and yells from drinking and games fell still, as one by one, the troupers retired to sleep. The noise that remained was densest near the fire, which helped Linara stay awake and vigilant. She even recognized the tailor, Baba, dancing and spinning around the fire, more lively than the men half his age.

Clouds obscured all sense of comfort for her. Linara knew the stars were closer than ever, just hidden behind a thin veil. What sign would even be above them now? How long had she been in Avorren? Had Ordgar the Smith risen completely yet? Or was it Endval? She couldn't even remember their callings, or their purpose. She only wished to see them.

The door opened in the cart above her, and Linara's heart thudded in her chest. The wood creaked and groaned as footsteps crossed the cart, and she prayed they wouldn't, for whatever reason, open the hatch in the cart's bottom. Then the thump of discarded boots hit the floor, and the movement fell still. Linara breathed out long and slow, counting the seconds as the occupant within fell asleep with the rest of the camp.

It was then she moved, crawling slowly from under the cart back into open air. A few stragglers still drifted around the fire, and she was sure there were guards around the edge of the camp, but she wouldn't get a better opportunity. Linara craned her ears out to the darkness, no longer trusting her eyes, even in the faint light of the lanterns around the camp. There was no true silence, not in a camp like this, but it was still quieter than even an hour before.

One step at a time, Linara moved forward, only knowing which direction her friends were taken, but unsure of how to find them. Would she risk looking through every window to find their sleeping forms?

Knowing them, they wouldn't be resting at a time like this, but how would she know where to look without giving herself away?

Linara peeked around the corner of the next cart, and thanked the stars above for her luck. Two guards sat outside a cart, upon a pair of overturned crates, bickering over a game of cards. Piles of garbage and furniture were strewn around them, as if the contents of the cart were thrown into the darkness from the doorway. To hastily make room for some prisoners, perhaps?

Creeping around and rolling underneath the cart, Linara nearly yelped in pain as her hand came down on a bent nail poking out of the moss. She bit the inside of her cheek and brushed it aside, alongside a few broken bits of wood. She pressed her ear against the seam of the hatch underneath, hearing hushed whispers inside. The words were muffled, but she'd recognize Cirena and Lorin's voices anywhere. They'd clearly calmed since their time by the fire, but their conflict still went on strong.

The hatch was secured with a simple plank, a crude solution for a lock from the outside. They did only have a few hours to secure a batch of trespassers, and Linara didn't doubt the security would be far tighter in the coming days. Just further proof that they didn't have much time.

She grabbed the edges and tried to pry it loose, but it didn't budge. Linara sighed and fell back, feeling the point of the knife on her hip dig into her ribs. Thankfully Rhoam kept to his word, and gave them each a long knife before they left. It didn't help Cirena, but now it would do its job now.

Linara maneuvered around to reach down at her hip, pulling the knife free. It was a simple thing, barely longer than her hand, but sharper than any dinner knife she'd used. She slid the blade gently into the gap between the plank, rocking it back and forth as the nails squeezed slowly out of their homes. It took longer than Linara would have hoped, but moving any faster caused the wood to squeal and groan.

Eventually, the plank gave way with a soft pop, landing upon her chest. Linara sighed deeply in relief, sliding the knife back into her belt. Then Linara pushed up against the door, feeling a slight resistance above, followed by a faint yelp of surprise. Then the weight shifted, and the door flew open above her. Rhoam, Lorin, Cirena, and Raast all stood around the door, ready for a fight. At once, their faces brightened.

"About time you showed up," Rhoam said, hoisting her up.

"Forgive me, they seem to party late around here."

"It doesn't matter, you're here now," Cirena said, almost bursting with excitement. "They have a dragon, Linara! A real *dragon*!"

Linara brushed the dirt from her coat. "I know. I was under a cart the whole time."

"Oh," Cirena said. "How'd you get so sneaky?"

"One moment you were behind us, and the next we were being wrangled by a bunch of ghosts in the night," Lorin said. "They had to have known we were coming."

"I got distracted," Linara said, "And I think that much is obvious. All of you were way too loud to begin with."

"I am a cook, not a thief," Raast said, flatly.

"*None* of us are thieves," Linara said.

Rhoam grunted. "That's obvious enough."

"He's just mad we got caught," Cirena said.

"I still don't think you understand the severity of our situation, Princess," he said, spitting out his last words. "This little ploy we wandered into is much deeper than we anticipated. I don't know how I could have been so stupid, allowing this idiotic game to go so far."

"That reminds me," Linara said, digging in her pocket for the pin she found in the mud. "I found this in the moss outside the camp."

"That's a military pin," Lorin said, stepping closer. "From Reginaan."

"They were tailoring a uniform after they captured you. They had the same pins."

"What did the uniforms look like?" Lorin asked.

"Light brown in the center, straight but a bit billowy, like robes, I suppose. There were patches of metal maybe, kind of like scales."

"An older style," Lorin said. "But that checks out."

"What if they're preparing for their next play?" Cirena asked.

"With uniforms caked in blood?" Linara asked. "Does that really seem to be the case?"

"Curious," Rhoam mumbled. "Whatever the reason, this is clearly more dangerous than we expected."

"You don't think they're involved with the raids along the border?" Cirena asked.

"Like the one that destroyed that village of refugees?" Linara asked.

"These troupers are not from Reginaan," Rhoam said. "If they *are* involved, it could change things."

"It might explain why there's more carts here than in the capital," Lorin said, "They could've easily split up, to return here afterward."

"If we get evidence, we might stop a war," Cirena said.

"With all due respect, Princess," Rhoam said, spinning back on her. "Our priority should be your safety. The extent of their involvement is still unknown to us, so even if we escape with this pin, or even a uniform, that alone will prove nothing."

"Thousands of people have suffered from what these people have done," Linara said.

"And thousands more if we do nothing, I understand, but think of the cost if Cirena dies here tonight," Rhoam said.

"I agree with Rhoam," Lorin said. "Let's get out of here first, and we can think about our next steps after that."

"That works for me," Linara said, lifting the floor hatch. "Let's go."

"It's not that simple," Rhoam said, grabbing her arm before she leapt down. "Despite everything within me telling me it's impossible, they have dragons on their side."

While terrifying, she hardly questioned it. Her expectations were rocked ever since leaving Nelbren. "I didn't realize it was that unusual," Linara said.

"What they don't eat, they leave alone, unless it's a threat to them," Lorin said. "Humans have always been little more than a pest. Every griffin knight in Avorren is trained to fight them, but those battles never end well. They've never attacked the capital directly, thankfully, and only a few scouts have ever gotten ambushed. But very few ever survive."

"The Collis province is a testament they can be beaten, but only if you're prepared," Rhoam said. "They built their capital city in the center of the Dragoncrest mountains, and have fended off dragon attacks for at least a hundred years."

"They're pretty awesome," Lorin admitted.

"Who knows how many dragons they have here," Rhoam said. "I can't imagine it would be more than one, but at this point, I don't know what to believe. Not to mention how many men are truly here."

"There are twelve more than usual, if that's what you mean," Raast said. "They arrived in Blackrest two weeks ago, until the rest of them met up. They'd been up north, but according to the men guarding our door, nobody knows why." Everyone looked at him, and he took a step back. "Was that not helpful?"

"How do you know this?" Rhoam asked.

"The men outside are very talkative."

"You can hear them?"

"Oh, yes. They've been arguing for hours. I can start from the beginning if necessary."

"No, no, that's alright," Rhoam said.

"If there are more dragons, they'd spot us in the dark a mile away," Lorin said. "We wouldn't make it back to the town."

"And if we did, we'd be helpless on griffinback," Cirena said.

"If only I had my lance . . ." Lorin mused.

Cirena scoffed. "Please, you couldn't take out a single one."

"I'd probably die, but I'd *definitely* take out one," Lorin said.

"Focus, you two," Rhoam said. "Brute force obviously isn't an option, but we're in a bind if we don't know what we're dealing with."

"Perhaps we can create such a noise in the wrong direction that we may escape in the right one?" Raast suggested.

Rhoam and Lorin both opened their mouths to object, but paused to consider. It was straightforward enough.

"Yeah, that might work," Rhoam said.

"What kind of noise?" Cirena asked.

"Oh, I do not know. I merely had the idea," Raast said.

"It needs to be something more complex, more chaotic," Lorin said. "Something to wake the town, perhaps."

"A crowd to slip into. Good idea," Rhoam said. "Maybe a fire? It would gain a lot of attention. People would watch and flock to help. Linara, can you light a fire big enough in the camp to wake the town?"

Linara slumped against the wall. The one thing she could contribute, and the one thing she knew she wasn't able to do. But were there any other options? She very nearly did so before, back in Avorren. But that was an accident. Could she do it again on purpose?

She thought back to that moment, standing in the cart, so helpless. The ashes rising, and the fire spreading. Burning what laid within. Even now she could feel her mark stirring, warming her from the inside. Back in the Spire, she couldn't even heat a pot of tea. Perhaps tonight, though, it would be different.

"Once we're out into the town, they wouldn't dare pursue us," Rhoam said. "Worse they can do is pin the fire on us, but we'll still end up in the city's custody, and then back to Avorren in the end."

"It's simple enough," Lorin said. "Are you up to it, Linara?"

She nodded, despite the well of doubt in her gut.

"Great!" Cirena said, "Let's get on with it." She moved off toward the trapdoor, but Linara stopped her.

"You all are too loud," She said, "You'll wake the whole place before I even light it. I'll have to go alone."

Lorin reached out a hand. "Let me at least come with you. I can move quietly if I try, and I'll buy you time if we're caught. I'm sure Raast's memory of this place can help lead Rhoam and Cirena out."

Linara took a deep breath and nodded. She took each of their arms in turn, clasping tight in farewell before Rhoam opened the hatch and Lorin slipped out. He helped Linara down, but just before he let the door close, he leaned in close, hesitant.

His arm held lightly onto hers, and he glanced back at Cirena and Raast, conversing softly in the corner. "They have my sword. I told myself I will accept the consequence of losing it if I must, but . . . it is important to me."

Linara nodded. "I know where they put it. I'll see what I can do."

"The Princess is more important," Rhoam reassured. "Only if it is not out of your way."

"I'll make it part of the plan."

"Thank you," he whispered, and the door closed.

Lorin let Linara take the lead. It didn't take long to retrace her steps back to the tailor's cart, and Lorin was proving herself to be as quiet as she claimed.

Whatever time of night it was, there was some stirring among the guards posted along the fringes of the camp. Perhaps a changing of the watch. Or just the time of night when the restless sleepers stirred. Either way, Linara didn't want to spend any more time in the camp than they needed to.

The only thing she could think to burn that would cause enough commotion was one of their carts. On an ideal day, she'd burn their feld supply, like she wanted to in Avorren. But they didn't have the luxury of searching it out. That left a problem, since she also wouldn't dare burn a cart with anyone inside. Nobody deserved to die for their crimes here. At the least, Linara wouldn't be their judge.

They approached the tailor's cart, the luma lantern at the door still pouring a soft light into the shadows. Linara left Lorin behind, crouched in the nook of the back wheel.

When she'd left her perch by the campfire, Baba, the old tailor, was curled up beside the logs. She doubted very much he had woken since she left, with how much she saw him drink. Even so, her fingers shook as she sidled up the steps of the tailor's cart, reaching behind the lamp beside the front door. She felt the brush of sharp metal, and plucked the key free, sliding it into the lock with a soft click. She disappeared within before anyone could turn the corner.

The cart was lit only by the faint crack of firelight through the gap in the window curtains. Racks hung along one wall, full of the brown uniforms of the Reginaan guard. Most were in pieces, or incomplete. Tattered remains of broken sleeves or bloodied shirts were scattered upon the crates and counters. Against the back wall was a pile of clubs and other weapons. On top was Rhoam's blue sword, discarded like it was nothing more than a souvenir. She grabbed it, the steel heavier than she would've expected.

Voices sounded from outside, and Linara dropped to a crouch. She waited for them to pass, but they only grew louder, until she heard footsteps on the stairs outside. Her heart quickened, and she ran her hands along the floorboards, searching for the latch that would lead underneath the cart.

"Where's that key?" one voice asked.

"Do you have the right lantern?"

Linara's hand caught the edge of the wood, and she traced the seams to find the handle.

"It's always the left one," the other grunted.

"Well, hurry up, it's cold."

The latch stuck out from under a barrel, and Linara carefully slid it aside.

"Tell that to Baba. He probably kept it, that senile bastard."

"Maybe he's inside?"

Her heart raced as she lifted the hatch as quickly as she dared, praying to the stars above that it wouldn't creak.

"He's passed out by the fire."

"What if it's unlocked already?"

In one smooth motion, she tossed the sword to the moss and swung herself underneath the cart.

"Try it, then, if you're so sun-damned impatient."

She reached up and pulled the door closed just as she heard the click of the door outside.

"Why didn't you try it in the first place, clod brain?"

"Do *you* remember when Korin left this cart unlocked? Missing damn near both his ears now."

"Just grab that sword, and let's be gone before Baba thinks we're the ones who lost the key."

"Where is it?"

"Do I look like I know?"

"Well, I don't see no blue sword."

"It's got to be here somewhere."

"It ain't, so who's telling Thatcher?"

There was a clatter of swords, followed by a long silence. "I'd rather wake Baba first."

Footsteps retreated from the cart, and the door closed behind them, leaving Linara alone in the moss. It would've been helpful to take some of the uniforms, if even just scraps, but she didn't dare take the time to delve back up. It wouldn't take long before they came back, and there needed to be a fire lit by then.

Linara took a deep breath to ease the tension in her chest. No time to think about it. She grabbed at the moss, rolling a small patch into a tight ball, compressing it down.

Back home, her father would ignite a ball of moss if they needed light for a few short moments. It wasn't often, only after particularly poor harvests, where there was no luma to spare. The moss would burn quickly, but not so quick he wouldn't be able to get his task done. It wouldn't usually work with fresh moss, but Nelbren was always wet, and they'd hang it in sheets for months even to be decently edible.

The mists didn't come to this part of the Blackness, though. The moss was dry, and scratchy. Almost devoid of life.

Linara took a deep breath and wiggled her finger into the center of the dense ball. She *was* capable. She'd done this before. To a cart just like the one above. She let her mind drift from the present, trying to remember that moment of lost control. The rage she felt in Nelbren, the desperation in the sky on Dresborn. Those moments of violent focus.

She thought of her friends, and the dragon curled up just a hundred strides away. Thatcher and his face of calm malice twisted at her chest, yet her mark only flickered now. She pushed, trying to clench every muscle in her body in the hopes of accidentally pulling the right one.

Nothing.

Linara released her breath and pressed her head against the ground. Orv's lessons were swimming in her mind. All his guiding words. He described a mountain that needed pushed through, but the more she pushed, the quicker it left her grasp.

But she couldn't fail now. The night was full of terror, and she had the key to their escape in her fingers. Fire would be light in their darkness, it would be warmth. It would burn and destroy, but it would consume all that was wrong in this world. Dangerous men with dangerous goals stood before her friends and freedom. This fire would be their escape, and she *would* create it.

Eyes closed to the moss, to the camp around her, and to the shadows, a certain calmness took over. An inevitability. An emptiness she couldn't quite describe. Then, with a strength she could not yet grasp, Linara breathed out, and the moss flicked over.

She could feel it burst aflame like the flare of the sun. A glimmer of heat rose around her, but not from within. She could feel it from above, and around, like a blanket. Linara snapped open her eyes, seeing the entire bottom of the cart engulfed in flames. The moss was shriveled and smoking in a circle around, spreading as the flames consumed the wood above her.

Linara's heart beat wildly, a weight falling upon her chest. She just wanted a small fire. A small flicker to ignite slowly. But it was like asking for a drop of water from a dam.

She crawled out from beneath the cart, stamping a bit of lingering flames at the edges of her shirt. Thankfully Lorin had backed away long before. She stared wide eyed at the cart fully engulfed now. Eyes full of horror.

Linara ran past her, Rhoam's sword clutched close to her chest. She heard Lorin's steps alongside her, but she dared not meet her eyes. Just the sound of their feet pounding against the dirt, the wind rushing through her hair. Yells rang out from the camp behind her. She turned, if only to ensure they weren't yelling after them, but her steps faltered, and she froze.

The fire of the cart roared, a great beast of light that split the darkness like its own little sun. It grew past just the one cart, now engulfing two around it. Troupers poured from the carts, fleeing into the night.

Uncontrollable, destructive, a blast of heat that would tear through all wood and moss until the night consumed it once more. It was Linara's doing. From her hands came the flame that grew to such ruin. She couldn't be trusted for such a small task. It couldn't be done. Who was she kidding? Fire couldn't save, it could only bring irreparable destruction.

Whatever life was lost this night was on her hands. Again.

Lorin tugged at her shoulder. They had to keep moving. Already the town stirred. The quiet folk, awake at the dim hours of the night, poured out past the wall. The night watch stood by, some more eager to help than others.

Nobody paid them any mind as they disappeared within the crowd. The light of the fire enrapturing all stares. Linara searched those faces for her friends, but found no trace of Cirena, or even Raast.

There was a certain comfort to reaching the edge of the town, behind the safety of the wall. The crowd was growing thicker now, as the houses woke with the commotion. Bucket crews ran out, water sloshing to the dirt path in their panic.

Linara was jostled at every turn. She and Lorin were the only ones running in the wrong direction. Each step brought her forward, but she had no idea where she was going. Avorren was confusing at the best of times, and Blackrest was no different. Lorin snaked through the streets with ease, and she followed blindly along.

Were Cirena and the others even free from the camp already? Were they able to escape? They knew the plan, but at the back of her mind, all Linara could do was worry.

They turned the final corner, into the intersection of roads that held the tavern. Before they even reached the doors, a flurry of feathers erupted out, Rhoam and Cirena wasting no time in taking to the air on Corinth.

Dresborn and Aria weren't too far behind, saddled and anxious to follow. Linara tossed the sword up to Raast, already seated upon Dresborn, and grabbed his reins before he darted off down the road.

Lorin was already in the air by the time Linara heaved herself into the saddle, but the old bird needed no prompting to follow close after.

Any other griffin might have hesitated, or been wary of the distant flames, but Dresborn knew better. He could sense the danger and the panic. His feet were gliding just above the buildings before Linara made herself comfortable.

Linara chanced a look back at the burning camp. From the blinding light of the flames, a single shadow rose from the center, a hulking mass of scales and wings unsinged by the flames roaring around it. Screams rose with it as the town fled in fear. It opened its jaws and split the sky with a roar. A bone-chilling, ear-thudding sound that almost jolted the griffins into the dirt.

They kept control, however, and kept low to the ground, past the town and into the bare land between danger and home. Linara kept her focus forward, the flames behind her casting red light upon the sky. A fire she left behind, but a fire that saved their lives. A fire she created. On purpose.

That thought was a twisting sensation. The *Razing of Yarldin* flashed through her mind, and she tore her eyes away.

She fingered the medal in her pocket, thinking back on the refugees in the tower. A trouper caravan or an enemy village, it didn't matter. All that was clear was she doubted her ability to trust herself any longer. Hopefully the medal would be enough to stop a war, because if it came to that, she wouldn't have the strength.

Linara tried to rest, pressed forward against Dresborn's neck as the rhythm of his flight prompted her to sleep. But the roar of the dragon wouldn't leave her mind, and she couldn't stop the anxious glances, expecting to see the shadow of dragons pursuing them into the night.

All she could see was the darkness. Linara had lived her whole life in the dark. It was once a comfort, to know she could remain hidden. Only now, she knew what else laid just out of sight. Thieves, soldiers, and dragons, skulking in the silent places.

Thatcher stood in a field of ruin, rubbing the edges of a single copper tile between his fingers. What an annoying stench feld made when it burned. Harsh and bitter. Nothing like when it was ingested. Or so he'd heard. He'd never partaken.

None died in the fire. It burned fast, but his men were used to waking quickly. Faaxriin's rampage, though. Three dead and too many wounded. Even the heffen scattered into the wilderness. Damn dragons. Half a pound of feld wasted just to calm it.

"Two crates of product left," Kurtrus said beside him. A good smuggler. A better performer. "The rest went to the flame."

"What of the wardrobe cart?" Thatcher asked.

"Gone."

"And the uniforms?"

"Those, too."

Thatcher grunted. Every performance must come to an end. Some more abruptly than others. Without the uniforms, they could not continue. He let out a long breath, slipping the tile into his breast pocket.

"What now?" Kurtrus asked.

After the end, where left to go but to the beginning? Their work wasn't finished, but perhaps they'd done enough already for the boulder to move without them. There was only one way to tell.

"Back to the mountains."

CHAPTER NINETEEN

No one fully relaxed until their feet touched the safety of city stone. Dresborn collapsed upon the landing platform the moment Linara was out of the saddle. Corinth sauntered away to find a quiet place to sleep. Aria stood alert, but her wings hung low, each step slow and labored.

Linara rested her head against Dresborn's rising chest, whispering quiet praises as he rested. His age was showing now, but he was braver than most. Surely not many griffins could claim to fly to Blackrest and back in a single day, with the threat of dragons on their backs.

Even now, despite the safety and comfort of the light, and of home, Linara's eyes still found the horizon, searching for the silhouettes of dragons. Instead there were only the sparce shapes of griffins, on late-night messenger runs.

At least, Linara assumed it was still the middle of the night. She had no idea how much time had passed. The city was quieter than usual. It never truly slept, but it wasn't quite awake, either.

Lorin stepped over, helping her to her feet. Her eyes couldn't hide a tiredness they all felt, but she still walked with a strange confidence. A soldier just escaping a battlefield. While Linara had spent the whole flight afraid, Lorin was surely prepared to turn around and fight, without the slightest hesitation.

"Is everyone alright?" Lorin asked the others. Rhoam slammed a pair of saddlebags beside her, and glanced up at her, jaw set tight. "Raast?" she asked, and the Luman-Viri just smiled back, happy to be alive.

"I'm excellent," Cirena said, far too awake for her own good. She finished stretching her legs in the center of the platform, and practically skipped over to Linara. "Nicely done, by the way; that fire was incredible."

A sour taste filled Linara's tongue. That was not how she would've described it. Not how she remembered it. The flight back was long, and left plenty of time to ruminate on how many men she injured or killed.

"You did well," Rhoam admitted, looking up from the bags. "Better than I expected."

Linara forced a smile and nodded.

"But I hope we all agree that we'll be forgetting this ever happened," Lorin said. "We tried our best, got too reckless, and delved into things we didn't understand. Petty revenge ended a long time ago. It's time to let it lie."

Linara nodded at this, relieved to hear someone else say it.

Cirena's smile faded. "No way. There's something huge going on here, and we're only scraping the surface. They have a *dragon* on their side. That fire wouldn't have even scratched its scales. We have to go back and find out what's really going on."

Linara grimaced at the memory. That blackened shape rising above the inferno. The roar of anger it sent into the sky. Linara knew she only sent it into a frenzy. If the fire didn't kill the troupers, surely the dragon did.

She clamped her eyes shut, trying to calm her breathing. The fire was meant to be slow. A distraction, nothing more.

"We don't," Rhoam snapped. "We have the medal, and five testimonies of their business. Let your father handle the rest."

"He won't do anything," Cirena said. "I know him too well."

"We burned down their caravan, Cirena," Lorin said.

"*Linara* burned it down," she said.

"Which is exactly why we can't go back!" Linara yelled, louder than she would've liked. That had been building for hours, and now that it was out, there was no reining it back in. "At least not with me. Everything I've done, regardless of how it ended, had been an *accident*. All of you have to leave me be, get as far away as you can, before I hurt you too."

"What do you mean? You lit the cart fast enough," Lorin said. "Before anyone returned."

"I didn't mean to! I wanted to just create a spark, you know? Instead it just . . . exploded."

"And what, you think it's only a matter of time before you blow us up?" Cirena asked, and Linara stared at her, dumbfounded. Of course that was what she thought. How could it not be an inevitability?

"You saved us today," Cirena said. "Without you, we'd still be in that cart, and without the fire, we surely would've been pursued."

Linara stared at her feet. "It happened to be the most convenient, sure, but you would've figured something out without me. I don't think you realize that if Lorin had been any closer, she would've been caught in it too."

Lorin looked at her boots. She would've had to have been thinking the same thing. Linara saw it in her eyes, just before they fled the camp.

"Even so, at your side is probably the safest place in the entire kingdom," Rhoam said. "I mean, maybe not now, but eventually—"

Cirena's elbow caught him under the ribs, and he gasped out the last word.

"But right *now*, it doesn't matter, does it?" Linara said, her temper flaring. "It just takes one mistake. I don't want parents whispering my name to their kids in the dark. I know that many of the stories that survive are from the type of people who wouldn't mind being talked about for eternity, but how many are because of accidents?"

They were all looking at her now, knowing not what to say. They just held the same type of look they always had. A blend of sorrow, and pity.

"And yeah, even if I did manage to help us escape — or however you want to look at it — there's still a pissed-off dragon we left behind, and a whole troupe who have nothing left to live for than to vilify me, probably." Linara clutched at her head. She was so tired, and her thoughts weren't making sense.

"Every time I try to do anything for myself, I end up on a knife's edge, one small step from a tragedy. Raast was right when he told me I'd have to never leave my room. So if you're not going to do me the decency of never seeing me again, I guess I'll have to."

Linara tried to move off, but Cirena stood in her path, fists clenching. "Do you think it's easy, finding friends? Like I can just replace you whenever I wish? With just a wave of my hand? Is it so hard to believe that we actually *like* you?"

Linara stared at her. "Yes?"

Cirena scoffed and stalked off. Lorin actually laughed.

Before the princess made it to the end of the platform, the doors to the Spire creaked open, and two men stomped through. Their shoulders were broad, thick metal armor covering much of their body. One hand rested upon their blades upon their waists. Linara recognized them from the day she arrived in the city, one wearing the helmet of a silver lion, the other a gold bear.

They blocked Cirena's path, and she sighed impatiently. "Let me through, Boltan. I'm not in any mood."

"My apologies, Princess," the bear knight said, dipping his head ever so slightly, "but your father summons you to his study."

"Oh, he *summons* me, does he—"

The bear knight stamped his boot upon the ground, silencing her next words. She took a step back, startled. Rhoam walked up and placed a hand upon her shoulder, guiding them both forward with a stoic sort of dread.

"Oh. *That* kind of summons," Cirena muttered.

Then the bear knight turned his gaze upon Linara, Lorin, and Raast in turn. "You three, as well."

"I cannot even begin to understand why that idea passed through your mind in the first place," the king said, his anger palpable, like a thick fog, inescapable. "To bring my daughter out of the city in a time of impending war? To have an idea, so idiotic, and then to *go through with it*?"

Linara dared not look anywhere but his calm, burning eyes. It was the same stare that flickered in his gaze when she first arrived in Avorren, an anger with such authority that struck her down to the last bone.

And she wasn't even the focus of his anger. Rhoam, straight-backed and stoic, took every word like the soldier he was. Linara was used to punishment. She had scars on her back to prove it. Cirena, though, hadn't looked up from her boots from the minute they stepped in. Tears already glistened on the carpet at her feet, but Linara risked only the briefest of glances to spot that much.

Whatever determination the princess had on the platform was now gone, quenched by her father's ire. Though, to her credit, she was right about the medal. He dismissed it out of hand, claiming it nothing more than rumors and riffraff, the mumblings of addled children who took it upon themselves to throw themselves into disastrous harm for nothing more than whimsical fancy. Or something along those lines.

He barely believed them about the dragon, if not for the troubling rumors already spreading around the countryside. As well as Raast's detailed testimony. It was hard to dispute a Luman-Viri's memory, after all. For it, Raast evaded all punishment, deemed to be an innocent party, not fully aware of the actions at large.

Still, the news that they brought did not lessen the brunt of rage. Even Lorin was facing her own trial across the hall with Commander Nilya, a fate that no one here envied.

Rhoam cleared his throat. "I take full respons—"

"I was not finished," the king bellowed, slamming his palms upon the table. Whatever shred of calmness he'd had vanished. The first morning bell struck just above him, and he paused, jaw clenching, as he waited for the echoing throngs to die down. "I should have you thrown in the lowest depths of our prison, or reassigned to the Diamond Tower. There is no punishment fitting to what you've done to my daughter."

"Father, no," Cirena said between sniffles. "It was my idea."

His eyes shot over like lightning, and he growled a fierce roar that sent Cirena staring straight back at the carpet. Even Linara flinched, but her eyes flickered only a moment, finding the king's eyes once more. He glanced her way, and her heart dropped.

"Not only that, but to bring Linara, our *untrained* Odious, with you? Do you understand the ramifications of your actions? Answer me, boy!"

"I know now, sir."

"I hope you do." The king lowered himself, his breathing loud in the silence. "The list of punishments before me is endless. I trust you understand that," the king said, resting his forehead upon his knuckles. "You've served my family for nearly two decades without issue or complaint, which is why I will not exile you to the farthest outpost on our borders."

Linara could see Cirena and Rhoam both breathe out in relief.

"But that does not mean you've escaped this unscathed. I will need time to think on this. I am not such a foolish man to believe I am of right mind to enact a decision. Unless you have any advice, Orvinth."

At his mention, Linara glanced to the side, at Orv standing beside the table, arms folded across his back, trying his best to seem disappointed. When telling her story of their escape, he seemed to brighten when she told how she lit the fire, the opposite reaction she expected. Not even the king made any mention of the cataclysm Linara wrought.

"I know what will be done with my young apprentice," Orv said. "But as for the others, I will leave that to you."

The king grunted, fiddling with the medal upon the table. "Then you two may leave."

Orv gave a slight bow and glided out from around the table. He motioned for Linara to follow, which she did with haste. She wouldn't waste a second on leaving. They squeezed through the crack Orv managed to open, and Linara shoved it closed.

Orv continued down the hall without her, expecting her to keep up. The Spire seemed to groan with the wrath of the king. The hallways felt empty. Servants scurried about quickly, stopping for nothing. Even the few guards and soldiers said no words to each other. It would be a solemn day, it seemed, for everyone under the watching eyes of the Spire.

"Are you upset?" Linara asked, after a moment.

Orv sighed a long, drawn out breath. "I am immeasurably disappointed, in a way. That you felt the need to hide your plans from me. I had hoped I had provided enough reason for you to trust me. I could've helped you."

Linara swallowed the ball in her throat. Somehow, that hit deeper. "We figured it would be easier to do it ourselves. Cirena believed her father to be too passive."

"Her father is the ruler of an entire nation. *I* don't have that same hindrance. I may be old, but I have resources available to me. I would not have let something that still bothers you that deeply to simply run rampant within our borders."

He sighed and shook his head. "Don't misunderstand me. What you four did was reckless and foolish. I do not think it needs to be said, and I truly wish it didn't have to be, but you shall no longer leave the city limits without my knowledge."

Linara nodded at that. It was a fair punishment.

"I am thankful, though, that you do not remind me much of myself. I got into more trouble at half your age than you probably ever will."

Linara stared at her feet, an anxiousness within her still unsettled. "And what about that other way? With the fire?"

"I'm proud that you did what you needed to do. You accessed your mark with intent, and safely."

"Safely? I almost killed Lorin, not to mention how many of the troupers I burned alive."

Orv was silent for a moment, chewing on his words as his cane clicked across the stone. "We do what is necessary to protect those closest to us," he said cautiously. "It also highlights the complexity of true control. It's more than learning how to access that well of power, but also how to navigate the great surges of emotion that can often hinder our ability to grasp it."

"But I wasn't under any great surge of emotion," Linara said, "Not like with Dresborn, or in Nelbren, or even in that cart the first time. Trust me, at first I wished I was, but there was hardly any anger to fuel it back there. I just did what you told me to. Pushed through a mountain, and what I got was an explosion."

Orv frowned as he pushed open his door, his next words upon his lips, but froze at the threshold. A thin man stood within, focused upon the books upon Orv's shelves. His hair was slicked back, barely touching the collar of his deep-green robe, which was draped down to hang just above the clutter of the floor. He turned slowly as Orv entered, a wide set of eyeglasses pressed low on a sharp nose.

"Ahh, Nymin," Orv said, moving inside. "I forgot about our meeting, my apologies."

"Do not fret, Master Orvinth," Nymin said, closing the book in his hand and sliding it back upon the shelf. His words were slow, deliberate, and nasally. "I often underestimate the extensive nature of your library. I forgot about the time entirely."

Linara hesitated in the door, but Nymin's eyes fell upon her, and he smiled widely. "You," he said, moving closer, "you are Linara Farrow."

"I am," Linara said, stepping back slightly. "Do I know you?"

"No, but I know you," he said, flourishing into a low bow. "I think everyone in this city knows *you*."

"That's encouraging," she mumbled.

"Linara, this is Nymin, one of our magisters," Orv said.

"A carver," Nymin said, bowing and extending his hand.

Linara took it. "A carver of what?"

"Of quartz, of course."

Orv frowned and rubbed at his chin. "I have had the intention of taking you to their lab, but it always managed to slip through the cracks. You see, the magisters work with a type of quartz that can emulate our marks."

"A demonstration, perhaps?" Nymin said, reaching into the pocket of his robe and pulling out two perfectly round chunks of crystal, the size of small plums. He twirled them in one hand, like a performer, showing off the contrast of the two colors. One glowed a deep, shifting red, the other perfectly clear.

He grabbed a candle from Linara's desk and handed it to her. Then, with one swift motion, he tapped the edge of the glowing quartz with a stone ring on his finger. A flash of light burst from the crystal, like a hundred sparks compressed into a pinhead. The wick ignited, burning steady and slow. Then, with another flourish, he took the clear sphere of quartz and touched it to the flame, pulling the fire into the gem.

"Amazing," Linara breathed, staring at the small ribbon of crimson flowing through the new gemstone, like a fish through a pond.

The magister handed her the clear gem and stepped back. "Now try to fill it."

Linara opened her mouth to object, but hesitated. After Blackrest, who knew what could happen. But the quartz had absorbed the candle flame like a sponge.

Linara stared into the swirling ribbon of flame in the gem. It curled and twisted with no rhythm, a dancer with no music. It was mesmerizing, like a flowing river. She felt the flow open from within, and another curl of red joined it, stemming from her palm. They met like lost lovers, entwining and becoming one, growing in size until it filled the entire quartz. It pressed out with some pressure, and Linara halted the flow.

Her heart thudded in her chest. It barely took any effort at all. Any amount of heat went straight into the quartz, not waiting for the point of combustion.

Nymin stared in awe at the quartz with the faintest hint of a smile. He stepped over and plucked it from her hands. "Quite a beautiful hue," he said, and spun it upon the surface of the desk, casting flickers of light across the room. "Perfection. The color of passion and freedom. The flowing of heat is like the flow of water. It goes where it wants, and does what it will."

He then pulled a similar sphere from a different pocket, glowing a deep shade of green. "The color of pine needles and structure. Orv's color. The unmoving, yet flexible. The flow of nature is like that of time. Slow, intentional. It goes only where it must, and does not waste time doing it."

The lump of natural energy was solid, and immobile. Sturdy as a tree trunk, imposing as a mountain. Now Linara understood Orv's thinking. To access his mark, he had to push through, like a knife through a brick wall. It surely required a honed concentration and a powerful will.

Nymin was right, though, about the heat. It was like a river, impossible to grasp, and to place. Staring into that flicker of power in the quartz, she understood her purpose with it. She was only a conduit, a guide. An extension of the flow that could go where she wished.

It was why that moment under the cart ended so dramatically. She shoved a stream with the full weight of her being. If it wasn't so slippery, it would've been far worse, but that initial fire was only the splash of a wave that slipped over the edge of a basin.

Nymin snatched the crimson sphere from the tabletop and pressed it back into her hands. "Now try to take it back."

Linara stared into the swirling quartz. A different flame now, this one a storm. A torrent, but calm and twisting. At its center was a beating heart, a flicker of life. She just as easily lost herself in that dance of energy as she did with the ribbon. Linara breathed in, and the power poured into her. The quartz sat empty once again, clear as ice and just as cold.

She could feel that storm within her now, pulsing in the depth of that massive well within her, slowly fading until it joined in harmony with the rest. It was a strange sensation, being able to recognize the power now. It had been there all along, always in the background.

"It reminds me of those panels in the hallways," Linara said absently, handing it back to Nymin. She'd touched them once before, and the light flickered, and felt cold. It was the first time she'd ever felt coldness before.

"Those panels are carved of quartz, and were one of the first discoveries," Orv explained. "They can be placed in sunlight for a day, and light a room for three."

"How do they do different things?" Linara asked.

"It's all about the cut," Nymin said. "A sphere is great at holding power. Sharp edges are better at expending it. It's all about finding a balance."

"Certainly sounds complicated," Linara said.

"Quite so," Nymin said. "More often than not, the different cuts are useless. But every once in a while we find a new use for an old discovery. Like just recently, we shipped off a new invention to Rivead, a mining town toward the mountains. Blastcores, we call them, kinetic quartz stuffed into clay shells and lit with a fuse will blow open stone as easily as toppling sand."

"Isn't that dangerous?" Linara asked.

"Yes," Nymin said, smiling weakly. "Thankfully nobody was hurt when we discovered it."

"Is there any progress on my little project?" Orv asked.

Nymin shifted a bit uncomfortably. "The latest batch has been . . . unsuccessful. Two cuts of quartz kept the lilies alive for a week longer than the rest, but…"

"Ahh," Orv said, face drooping. "We are close, though. I know it."

"We are," Nymin nodded.

Orv took a deep breath and turned to Linara, catching himself with a smile. "Now that you've seen what they can do, I'll have to take you down to their lab one of these days."

"It would be a pleasure to give Linara a tour," Nymin said.

"I am certain she would be interested in the progress of the airship designs," Orv said.

"Airship?" Linara asked. "Like that flying carriage?"

"Precisely. They've transitioned into more of a flying boat now."

"It's better on the landings," Nymin said, then frowned out the window as a griffin patrol passed by. "I apologize, Master Orvinth, but I think I must be going. Let us postpone. The same time next week." He smiled and bowed low to Linara. "Truly, it was a pleasure to meet you."

Before he reached the door, he spun back, reaching into his pocket and plucking out that first sphere of quartz, glowing red. He handed it to Linara. She tried to object, but Nymin closed her fingers around it. "Keep it; it could be useful." Despite the flames swirling within, she felt no semblance of heat. "Do not worry about it combusting in your pockets. It will only spark if you tap it with something hard." He pulled off his stone ring and placed it in her other hand. "Something like this."

Linara accepted it, wondering how useful it could be. She was certain her mark could fill that tiny quartz a thousand times over. It was a nice gift, though, and one she knew Nymin didn't give easily. She smiled and thanked the magister, slipping it into a pocket of her coat as he slid out the door.

Orv mumbled something about his forgetfulness and studied the bookshelf where Nymin had been. A book on Luman-Viri still sat open upon her desk, left from just before they flew to Blackrest. That felt like ages ago now. It had only been a day.

Linara stifled a yawn. It had been about that long since she slept as well. Hopefully, she would have a chance to head to bed sooner than later.

"Now then," Orv said, grunting as he lowered himself into the chair behind his desk. He pulled out a fresh pen and pot of ink. "Now that we've gotten the distractions and the uncomfortableness behind us, I want to hear about Blackrest. Tell me everything; spare no detail. We'll be here all day if we have to."

Cindavar, King of Aldebraan, slumped in his chair, Rhoam and Cire-na closing the door to the study behind them. He didn't feel much like a king. Neither did he feel like a father. Today he was some analogous mix, and it tore at him. One or the other was a manageable cause, but when forced together . . . The King of Aldebraan cursed and tugged at his beard. The antics of children could be excused, but this was far more than simple antics. And for his own daughter?

He plucked the medallion from his desk, rolling his fingers over the etched metal. It wasn't authentic. The lines were too rough, and too out-dated. Reginaan used a simpler emblem for their border guards now. How ironic, though, that the counterfeit would go through such lengths to match an outdated medal.

Neither of those was important, however. The medal was concerning, no matter how Cindavar spun it. Reginaan had denied all activity, as they always had. It proved nothing, for Cindavar had denied involvement as well. Involvement he himself had ordered. But perhaps there was truth to their claims . . .

"The ramblings of children" he called it, but the information given was reliable, no matter how reckless. It would be foolish to ignore. Cindavar thumped on his desk three times, and a runner appeared through a door in the bookcase.

"Send for Silas. I need a letter drafted to Reginaan."

CHAPTER TWENTY

In the early days, before there was a crown, before there were cities and capitals and border disputes, Aldebraan was little more than a collection of tribes and small nations. They warred, and they fought, but they were bound like blood, for they were still one people, collectively separated.

When a great threat would rise, someone would rise against it, to bring forth a banner to unite the people. Ushering in a new age and unified in victory, they would be named herald, and would lead until their death. Only then would the people fracture, and discord would reign once again.

It was a cycle so often seen, until Gaylin the Unifier, the last great herald, bound the tribes under one crown, and named it Aldebraan. He raised leaders of his own to govern beneath him, and he called them heralds, also, even if true heralds they were not.

Those traditions survived centuries, and when a great threat faced the kingdom, a Herald Summit was called. In recent years, those great threats were little more than trade disputes, or whispers of rebellions in the countryside.

Peace talks with Reginaan, though, were not something to be taken lightly, and required the show of a unified kingdom. Three weeks after Linara's return from Blackrest, the heralds were called, for a delegation from Reginaan had left their capital of Darhaba and crossed the border.

Evidently, the medal Linara brought back from Blackrest was not dismissed entirely out of hand. It was enough to start a conversation. Those were Orv's words, and he said them with great hesitancy. He was an optimistic man most of the time, but this was something he looked at with caution. Still, Linara was happy to have done *something* good.

The Spire had only a few weeks' notice to prepare, and the panic was palpable. Guards were busy tightening security, and the cooks were working around the clock. Raast was entirely preoccupied, and even Lorin was too busy to avoid any of her duties.

The morning the heralds arrived, the entry hall had been emptied—or as emptied as could be realistically achieved. A wide path led from the doors to the end of the throne room, but guards kept the pushing crowd from crossing those boundaries. The whole city packed close, from the base of the mountain to the peak, if just to catch a glimpse of a herald—or better yet, a Lord of Reginaan.

Even Cirena and Linara barely found places at the railing, overlooking from high above. That, she was certain, would have been impossible without Rhoam ensuring a sizable space was kept around the princess.

Linara had thought Cirena would've been a part of the meeting herself, but Cirena had a simple strategy to avoid it. No one thought to formally invite her, and any conversation with her father Cirena kept strictly away from Reginaan, lest he remember and think it a good idea for her to come. Then she'd have no choice.

Both her and Linara were content watching from afar. One by one, the heralds entered, and Cirena gave Linara the names of each. Of course, she remembered none of them. Except one.

Rendei, the Herald of Collis, was the last to enter. He arrived alone and made no show of it. He did not stop and shake hands, nor wave to the surrounding crowd. He strode through the room like he owned every brick. Unlike the others, he wore no opulent robes or jewelry of value. He came in little more than a simple shirt and trousers, faded gray and wrinkled along the edges.

A face of solid stone, the Herald of Collis. Leader of those who fought dragons, and won.

Hours passed before the delegation from Reginaan entered the Spire. Whispers spread from the city gates when they arrived, and the entry hall fell still. Unlike the heralds, no words were spoken when they stepped through the doors.

Four men walked in front, their skin dark as night, and heads shaved bald. Despite being a delegation for peace, they wore armor made of plates, layered like crimson scales. Their steps fell in unison, down to their long-bladed spears tapping against the stone.

Behind them trailed a dozen servants in dull robes, hoods drawn low over their eyes. Heads bowed, they stepped across the carpet in a strange gliding rhythm. Each carried elaborate wooden boxes and trays of food. All of them gifts, according to Cirena.

They entered the throne room, and the doors were shut tight behind them. All at once, the conversation returned, voices blending and echoing across the walls. Nobody moved or left—the crowd would wait for the meeting to be finished, to catch just one more glimpse. It would be hours before they were done. Maybe longer.

Cirena, Linara, and Rhoam, though, had seen enough. They slid out through the crowd, and their places were taken without a second thought.

The Herald Summit left a considerable gap in Linara's training, and it was noticeably strange how often she found herself in the library on her time off. The quiet within was palpable, specs of dust lingering in beams of sunlight, just waiting to fall. The whole Spire was suspended in that strange space of uncertainty. It had been a few hours already, and almost everyone was still congregated in the entry hall. It was clear there would be no quick resolution.

Not even the librarian bothered to stay at her station. It left some room for Linara and Cirena to spread out upon the main table, needing no private reading room to keep themselves focused.

The events of Blackrest may have put a stop to their pursuit of the troupers, but it created a certain paranoia. Linara expected the news of a dragon attack to break at any moment, and she searched for comfort in an increase of knowledge in the tomes of the library. Orv hadn't built up a collection on dragons, for he found no real reason to. Neither, apparently, did the generations of library scholars before him.

It was understandable now why Nerissa seemed so clueless about dragons. Most information came from the Collis Province, and came in the form of a collection of accolades for their accomplishments in fighting them.

Any other observations on dragons came at times of great tragedy, or from vast distance, and neither were very accurate. What Linara *could* gather was that it truly didn't make any sense for a dragon to be under Thatcher's control. They were an intelligent and ancient race, proud of their independence. That, of course, provided no real comfort at all.

Linara sighed and looked up from her book, an autobiography of one of the flight lancers in the Draco-Mountain War. "It says they made a pact with the dragons before. For space within the mountains for a city? Could something similar being worked out now?" Linara asked.

"That may be true, but it was hardly a negotiation," Rhoam said, not even offering a glance up from his own project. "There was a lot of bloodshed, on both sides."

"What even prompted the war to begin with?" Linara asked. "There's hardly a mention of why, as if they assumed we already know it."

"Well, it's a bit complicated," Cirena said. "The Collis people survived in those mountains for generations, before the unification. They pledged themselves to Gaylin's conquest, in exchange for help in their own battles. The dust was still settling from the unification before they turned their attention to the dragons, some say."

"In the end, they hardly needed Gaylin's help," Rhoam said. "They practically ended the war before reinforcements arrived."

"It's why those people scare me," Cirena said. "Always so cold, and humorless. Did you see their herald? He just walked in like he owned the place. It's good they're on our side at least."

"Rendei, right? He came alone. No servants, no staff." Linara shrugged. "I kind of like him. Compared to the others, at least."

"He didn't grow up in nobility, and he tries his best to remind everyone of it. He's been leading the charge on reforming trade deals, I guess. He's a bit of a grump, and doesn't like my father."

"He leads the only people who have history with dragons. He better be on his good side soon," Rhoam said absently.

"Lorin seemed confident in fighting the dragons," Linara said.

Cirena laughed. "I'd like to see her confidence once they're barreling down on her."

Linara leaned back in the chair, letting her finger glide across the old paper, rough and brown from age. She was glad Cirena and Rhoam were there to join her. These sort of history lessons must be common knowledge for people growing up in the city.

She had hoped more knowledge on the subject would lessen some of the lingering anxiety. So far, it wasn't working.

"What are you working on, Rhoam?" Linara asked, looking up from her book. He sat in careful contemplation, scribbling lines on a long sheet of paper. He was pretty adamant about leaving all talk of the troupers behind. In the end, he couldn't stop Linara, and hardly argued with Cirena over it before retreating to the end of the table.

Rhoam looked up at her, pen halting midstroke. "Poetry."

Linara laughed. "I didn't know you were a poet."

"I think poets have to know how to write poems to call themselves such," Cirena said casually.

"That's a little harsh," Linara said.

"No, I'm pretty bad," Rhoam agreed.

"He prefers to read it," Cirena said. "He writes a few poems in our downtime, but he usually just burns them after."

"Surely it's not *that* bad," Linara said, waving for the page.

Rhoam sighed and slid the page across the table.

Dust floating like dead soldiers
Rose of red book red of rose
Cover tough like dragon leather in the hallway
Secret words or history, only itself knows better
And the librarian, but she is quiet and mean
Boredom

"Yeah, that's pretty bad."

"Told you," Cirena and Rhoam said in unison.

"But you don't have to be good at something to enjoy it," Rhoam said.

Linara wished that were true. She never spent much time at anything she didn't have a talent for. It was why she was glad she took up flying as quickly as she did.

The door creaked open just then, a woman stepping in from the hallway. Her face was tired and haggard, eyeglasses hanging just a bit crooked. Thick curls bobbed as she glanced around the room, eyes narrowed in confusion.

"Nerissa?" Linara asked. "What are you doing here?"

"Not finding the king's study, apparently," she said. Her eyes drifted around at the bookshelves and then fell upon Linara. She brightened immediately. "Oh, hello, Linara. Hello, strangers."

Cirena laughed. "You're trying to meet with my father, today of all days?"

"Well, I don't know who your father is, but everyone is evidently quite busy. There's a Herald Summit today, have you heard?"

"You *have* been gone awhile," Linara said. "How was your trip? Did they take the dragon egg back?"

Cirena slammed her book closed, brows furrowed deep. "Dragon egg? Linara, why didn't you mention this before?"

"My trip was terrible, thank you for asking," Nerissa said, sliding into an open chair. "They took the egg, of course, but they didn't give me even a fraction of my offers for a favor in return."

"You returned a dragon egg, and they didn't kill you for it?" Rhoam asked.

"No, they were very understanding, all things considered," Nerissa said.

"How did you even find them?" Cirena asked. "I heard it's impossible to track dragons down."

"I have connections," Nerissa said. "There were rumors of dragons gathering in the Great Divide. I figured the Dragon Seat was meeting, so I rode west and followed the river through the mountains. I got far, to the base of a great waterfall, before a group of wyverns descended upon me. They did not immediately kill me, which was kind of them. One of them asked—err, no, he seemed more to yell . . . he yellingly asked why I trespassed, and I laid the egg upon the ground.

"He sniffed at it for a long while and then stared into me with a big gold eye. He yelled that I should be thankful it was still alive. At that point, I wished nothing more than to turn around and go home, but I left Avorren with a mission. I swallowed my gut and asked, rather boldly, I might add, to speak with the Dragon Seat."

Nerissa fell silent, her eyes going glassy, and she stared off into the distance.

Cirena leaned forward in her chair. "Well, what happened?"

"They laughed at me."

"Dragons can laugh?" Rhoam asked.

"It's like a handful of boulders being juggled by other much larger boulders," Nerissa said. "It was very grating. That's when I found out the Dragon of the West is missing."

"Missing?" Linara asked. "How does a dragon go missing?"

"They called a Dragon Seat, and he didn't appear, I would imagine," Nerissa said.

"Does that happen often?" Linara asked. Despite the few weeks of research, no books covered the topic of the Dragon Seat, or any of their hierarchy at all. It was good Nerissa returned when she did.

"I would think it doesn't happen at all," Cirena said.

"Quite right," Nerissa said. "Very unusual and quite perplexing for the dragons. One of their primary leaders and his entire brood up and vanishing? It's quite distressing, I think, which is why they nearly ate my legs despite my generously good deed of returning their egg."

"How do you lose an entire group of dragons?" Linara asked.

"The world is a big place, Linara Farrow," Nerissa said. "When somebody does not wish to be found, it can be difficult to find them, no matter how large they may be."

"The princess has experience with that," Rhoam said.

Cirena sniffed. "We hide in broom closets. It's quite different."

"It is worrying news, a brood of dragons missing," Nerissa said absently. "Will the Dragon Seat collapse under this news?"

"If it's that big of a deal, why don't they just replace him?" Linara asked.

"A dragon's title can only be passed to the dragon that kills it. It's very ceremonial," Nerissa said. "I'd imagine it's why they're so tense. If the Dragon of the West is *dead*, who is to lead? Does the foundation of their society collapse? Who are we to know?"

"Well, I'm glad you made it out alive," Linara said. "Did you leave after all that?"

"No, I asked a few more favors, which they ignored. They flew off with the egg without another word, and I waited a few hours to see if they'd change their mind. *Then* I left. The ride back home was quite lonely without the egg to talk to."

"That sounds more successful than you made it out to be," Linara said. "You met a dragon and lived to tell about it."

"Few people can say that," Nerissa admitted.

"We have," Cirena said.

Nerissa gasped and shot in closer. "A dragon? Here? While I was gone?"

"In Blackrest. It was with some troupers," Linara said.

"A dragon in a play? I didn't take them to be the expressive type . . ."

"No, the troupe was a cover. They smuggled feld fungus around Aldebraan."

"Very curious," Nerissa said. "Dragons would be terrible at smuggling . . ."

"Do you think the two are related?" Linara asked Cirena. "We may have only seen one, but could they have hundreds hidden away somewhere?"

"That many? I doubt it," Cirena said. "But I would've doubted the one a month ago."

"What kind of dragon was it?" Nerissa asked.

"Are they not all the same?" Linara asked.

Nerissa gasped. "Of course not! Drakes have four legs, wyverns have two, and wyrms don't have any legs at all. And no wings, for that matter."

"It was a wyvern, I guess," Linara said, chest tightening as she thought back. It was dark, but that much was clear. "It walked on claws at the end of its wings."

"Then perhaps it is so. The Dragon of the West is a wyvern, you know. How big was it?"

Linara looked around the room, gauging the size. Definitely smaller than the library as a whole, but larger than any other unit of measurement she could think of. "Maybe a bit bigger than this table?" Which was, by all accounts, the biggest table she'd ever seen.

"Oh yeah, that was just a wyvern, then. A cardinal dragon would be the size of the room, easily. Or more."

"You know more about dragons than you let on," Linara said, and lifted the book upon the table. "Certainly more than these authors."

Nerissa sniffed. "I make it my job to know."

"Has anybody ever made deals with dragons in the past?" Rhoam asked.

"There was a treaty made in Collis a while back," Nerissa said, after a moment.

"Something more peaceful than that," Linara said. "Thatcher, the head trouper, used feld fungus to keep his under control."

Nerissa perked up. "Feld fungus?"

"It calms them, apparently."

"Fascinating," Nerissa said. "And terrifying. With even one dragon under your control, they'd be among the strongest of forces in the kingdom."

The table fell silent, and Linara and Cirena exchanged glances. "Does your father know about the missing dragons?" Linara asked her.

"I doubt it," she said.

"It's why I wanted to meet with the king," Nerissa said. "I was going to camp out in his office until he returned."

"If it makes you feel any better, I haven't seen him in three days," Cirena said.

"You've been actively avoiding him, though," Rhoam said absently.

"That does make me feel better, thank you," Nerissa said. "But who are you?"

Cirena paused and glanced at Linara. "Cirena."

"Ahh. Nice to meet you," she said, before resting her chin in her hands. "Perhaps I'll just write him a letter, I doubt the guards will let me ambush him in the shadows, after all. But a missing brood the size of the West is a terrifying thing, no matter who they served. If they allied themselves with humans, who knows what they could do."

Linara and Cirena both looked at each other, a certain heaviness passing between them.

Nerissa yawned and stood, glancing around at the shelves and book, as if she was noticing the rest of the room for the first time. "I must be getting back. Ferin's been watching the shop this whole time I've been gone, and I suspect he hasn't made a single sale. Do any of you know the way out of here?"

"Two lefts out the door, and then straight on until the gate," Cirena said absently.

Nerissa slid out the door, dropping the library back to its usual silence. Linara slumped back in her chair, eying the open book on the table. She was no longer in the mood to read. Not that she ever truly was. With the Herald Summit going on, she was feeling at least a shred of hope. There were signs of peace, signs of progress. But there was a certain doubt lingering in the depths of her mind before that now took concrete form.

There were too many moving parts, and Linara didn't know what to make of it. Nerissa's news could be coincidence. It could be nothing at all. Or it could be everything. All she knew was that she couldn't quite shake the dread forming in her gut. Thatcher must still be out there, and with him was a dragon. Who knew how many he had under his thumb.

Cirena slammed her book shut and slid it into the center of the table. "Rhoam, if you couldn't have convinced me before, I'm convinced now. One dragon was daunting enough. I'm done."

"It's about time," he muttered, crumpling his poem and tossing it in the middle of the table. "Your courage to face one dragon is admirable."

"Don't mock me," Cirena said. "I just doubt even my father is prepared for this."

Linara let her own cover close, staring at the old, battered leather as she sunk into her chair. There was nothing more to be done. No information to be had that would help.

Cirena was right, this was bigger than any one of them. Bigger than a kingdom problem. No amount of time in the library would help now. Linara took some comfort in knowing that the issue was larger than she could prepare herself for.

What she did know was how much she hated that feeling underneath the cart. Helpless, and afraid. She couldn't let herself fall back into that place again. The only thing she could do now was get stronger.

Artoris the Historian entered the Last Free Menagerie with his nose pressed to a useless tome from the remnants of Treylon. An ancient little civilization. Worshiped dragons. Not as helpful as expected.

"A missing dragon and a Herald Summit. An exciting week," he said, slamming the book closed. Nerissa smelled of junipers and long travel. She'd been gone for far too long. Too long. That deserved a kiss. He leaned in close and placed it between her eyes.

"Dragons," Nerissa corrected, an emphasis on the plural.

"Mmm," Artoris said, sidling closer. "How was your meeting?"

"There wasn't one. I met with the girl, though, and the princess."

"Linara? Ahh, a pity I missed it."

"They met a wyvern in Blackrest. Linara was searching the library for answers."

Artoris laughed at that. Good luck to them. Orv never bothered himself with the activities of dragons. "Is it related, or was it a rogue dragon?" Artoris asked.

"Who's to say except the dragons?"

Artoris rubbed at his chin absently.

Nerissa turned and studied him. "You are worried?"

"Unknowns are troubling. Especially ones where there is no past to reflect upon."

"There is nothing in the histories?"

"A conflict of dragons leaves no trace. The heralds squabble over a war in the east. It will pale beneath the shadow of a war with dragons."

Chapter Twenty-One

The meeting with the delegates from Reginaan lasted a little over nine hours. There was no resolution toward any semblance of peace. They had agreed that there would be no further escalation of recent conflict, but the tension at the border would be the same as it had been for generations.

All things considered, everyone left happy.

Except Linara. She told Orv of the missing cardinal dragon, which he took with the same fascination as anything else. Of course, as Linara expected, there were far too many variables for any conclusion from him.

A few weeks passed, and Linara had no choice but to pour herself into her training. Ever since that moment in Orv's office with the magister Nymin, Linara's ability to absorb simple flames had grown. She could take candle flames without even thinking now, even going so far as to extinguish Orv's hearth a few times. They were progressing slowly, both of them wary after Blackrest.

Now, though, Orv wanted to do something more intense. More wild. More primal. A candle flame was tame, controlled. He wanted to see what she could do when nature itself burned.

They both stood in the golden grass fields outside the city walls, watching the sun ignite the clouds upon the horizon. She never thought it possible, but these days Linara didn't think much of the sun. A source of light and little else, easily forgotten as just another aspect of city life.

But then there were some days where the clouds were *just* right to light up the sky like a bonfire.

It was still early in the morning. The pond workers and local farmers hadn't even started their morning rounds. Only the city guard was awake, patrolling the wall, a few hundred strides beside them.

There was another small group a half mile behind, working with a collection of siege equipment. Since meeting Nymin, Linara began recognizing the green robes and vests of the other magisters in the city. There were three with the guards, supervising as they launched boulders far into the empty lands north of the city.

"I believe that concludes my preparations," Orv said, slowly pushing himself up from his knees. He left behind a circle of grass, nearly an arm's length across, growing up to Linara's calf and blowing gently in the breeze. He had hydrated a wide ring around it too, shortening the grass and turning it a deep green.

"I am going to light this on fire," Orv said simply. "It will be wild and chaotic, and I want you to rein it in. Not to absorb it or douse it, but to control it. Have the flames burn evenly, consistently small. Burn a hole in the center, a ring outside, whatever your imagination would like. Make the fire dance to your will."

"And if I light the whole field on fire?" Linara asked. The precautions seemed perfectly acceptable, but there was always that fear. She saw how quickly the trouper camp went up in flames, and she didn't want to repeat it anytime soon.

"I trust at this point you've identified the flows of power enough not to confuse them," Orv said. "And if a fire *does* get out of control, I am here to stop it." He stuck his cane into the dirt, and a patch of a grass a dozen strides away shriveled up and died.

He was right, of course. The more the days went by, the more Linara began to truly *feel* her mark. Every candle she absorbed was a gentle storm within her. Some days, though, it scared her. When she lay down to sleep, she would stare into the depths of her mark and feel it stirring. Like a sleeping dragon, waiting to be woken.

Orv had said his stores didn't feel nearly the same. Natural energy didn't wish to be touched. A tree was sturdy. It knew exactly what it wanted. And just the same, its power would not budge, until Orv pushed hard enough, and it gave in. It took him months to do just that, but once he had it, control came easy.

Linara, though, had a power that wished to be free more than anything. She had but to whisper to the flame, and it would move. It wanted to be anywhere it wasn't. When opened, the gate that let the flame loose could not be easily closed.

Orv stepped over to the patch of grass and pulled out a sphere of red quartz. "Now, begin!" He tapped a ring to the crystal, and a long spark ignited the grass.

The fire spread in a breath, engulfing the whole patch before Linara could make it over. She yelped and plunged her hand into the flame. It was fast and untamed, and controlling it was like putting a leash on a wild leatherboar.

The grass burned through in seconds, and before Linara could even grasp hold of the heat, the circle was left a pile of smoldering embers. She sighed and slid her hands into the chalky ash. There was still a faint pulse of life within, weak and fading. This was easy to take hold of.

Linara absorbed what remained of the fire and stepped back, allowing Orv to regrow the patch. They said no words to each other, both in silent agreement. She just needed another go.

In Orv's office, she could stare into the flame and lose herself within. Liza Burnfeather called it the "heart of the flame." Linara didn't know what it meant when she first read it, but now she could understand. Every flame was alive, it breathed, and it danced, and each had a beating heart.

It was easy to find on a candle. The flame was calm, tethered to a wick that would not let it go. The grass fire, though . . . it was too chaotic. She had spent all of her time finding her focus, but could not grasp it. She'd have to try something else.

Orv lit the flame, and Linara shoved her hand in. This time she focused elsewhere, turning within to the void, and her own swirling storm of power. There was always a flame present, if she looked hard enough.

Power engulfed her fingers, the heat from the fire trickling within. The storm clouds shifted, to turn in response to the flames roaring outside. There was a connection there, a latching point that Linara tugged upon.

She worked slowly, trying to bring the chaos under control. She imagined the grass to be like a thousand tiny wicks, burning low like candle wax. Instead, the flames instantly drew into her mark, puffing into smoke before her eyes.

She had to be close now. Linara turned to Orv and gave a firm nod. She knew what had gone wrong, she just didn't know how to fix it. She hoped it would come to her, as Orv lit the next patch of grass.

Linara stuck her hand in the fire and stared into the void. Like before, the flames in her fingers touched the well, and Linara felt the connection. But she didn't tug at it. If she did, it would all come within.

Instead, she just . . . emptied herself. She became the storm, became the well of flames. Every pulse of heat, every flash, she could feel and control. With little thought, Linara *breathed* into the flames. At least that was what it felt like. A breath from her mark, a surge of power like waves against the shore.

Linara opened her eyes and watched the flames flicker and grow, coming awake. The entire patch obeyed her command, burning low and steady. It breathed with her, like a furnace pumped with bellows. Even then, something felt different. She could still feel that connection within, a line from her palm to her mark. A certain glow, a feeling of control.

That was almost enough excitement for her to lose her grip, to quit right there and celebrate that victory, but she hardened herself and continued with what Orv had wanted. With a tight grip on the hold she had, she clamped the flow of energy, keeping it steady and pure. The flames held their height, burning steady and strong, only inches off the ground.

She could feel her mark begin to empty of power. The grass had long since burned through, leaving her own power to fuel the flames. It was still a drop in the bucket of the wealth she held, but even so, she felt like was losing something of herself.

Linara inhaled sharply, realizing she hadn't been breathing. The flames puffed away, burning themselves out once her concentration shattered.

Orv released a tense breath behind her. "Incredible. The control of plant life is far less mesmerizing."

Linara rubbed at her mark, staring at the pile of ash, growing cold. "It feels like I'm making progress on accident."

"Accidental progress is still progress once you remember how you did it," Orv said.

Linara stared down at her palm. "I think I can. It was like . . ." Linara tried to place it into words, but found she could not. "I don't know, I just . . . know how it feels."

Orv laughed, a thick belly-full laugh. "I think now you understand why I have found it so difficult to explain how it is done to begin with."

"It really is like explaining to a man with no eyes what it's like to read."

Orv stepped over and began regrowing the grass patch. "Maybe a little less dreary than that." He poured more into the grass than he usually did, growing the patch to the height of her head. With more to burn, she would have more time to bring it under control, and more fuel for the fire to burn before she had to supply it herself.

Orv lit the patch and stepped back. "Now see if you can replicate your progress."

Linara nodded and placed her hand in the flames, focusing again and trying to remember what it felt like to control the fire. It was like a gentle tug, a push, and pull from her core. A breath, a steady inhale and exhale, an ebb and flow. Linara latched on to that and began pushing out slowly into the flame.

There was a shout from behind her, a frantic call of alarm that pulled her focus away. Linara turned in time to see a catapulted boulder hurtling toward her. She was on her feet in an instant, scrambling out of the way, but it was on her in the blink of an eye. She tensed for the impact, but something flashed out and struck the boulder before it hit the ground, deflecting it away from Linara's path.

Thick vines cut through the air, suspended from Orv's cane. He was frozen in place, pain twisting across his face. She stopped forward to help him, but he waved her off in a grunt of agony, pointing frantically behind her.

The boulder had landed in the center of the flaming patch of grass, launching embers past the ring of wet grass to ignite the surrounding field. It had not rained in weeks and the grass was bone dry. Orange flames consumed each patch, spreading like lightning. Orv was hurt, and the nearest source of water was miles away.

Linara was the only one who could stop it. She leapt into motion.

The first fire she reached absorbed easily, puffing out a long section before her. Still, the boulder sent embers far, and many of the fires were not connected. She would have to get to every single one before they spread beyond her reach.

The next patch of flames she ran to singed her pant leg. The one after, her sleeves. If she wasn't careful, she would end this with her clothes burned entirely away. A thick clump of flaming weeds landed at her feet, and she quickly stomped it out. Embers were catching in the wind, being flung farther than Linara could reach.

White smoke billowed into the sky. Even if she had the endurance and the speed of a horse, it would be impossible. Nobody could do it, not alone. Even the city watch, with all the griffins in the city with all the buckets in the Spire, could not contain this without injury or damage.

But Linara had the power of fire at her fingertips. She would not see another death because she could not control what lay dormant inside her. She would find a way.

A griffin swooped down beside her, trying to land near Linara, but after a sharp cry and a swift flap of its wings, it flew off again, panicked by the smoke and the flames. Linara recognized Lorin's stag helmet as she guided Aria around for a second landing, this time a dozen long paces behind her.

Linara drew in the last bit of flames within her immediate vicinity as Lorin trotted up beside her. Without saying a word, Linara hopped in the saddle behind her, and they took to the air.

If Lorin could fly her between the fires, they might just get to them all. But Aria was not taking well to the smoke and fire. She flew in chaotic paths, Lorin barely able to keep her under control. Even Linara could barely find a clean breath.

Lorin hovered near the closest flames, indecisive, as she tried to balance Aria's flight. "I won't be able to get you close. I can take you to the next patch if it's too far, but—" Lorin said, voice choking for a moment. "My family is nearby." Lorin pointed to a nearby homestead, barely visible in the cloud of smoke.

Linara opened her mouth to respond, but a cloud of smoke blew in, and she coughed. "It's fine. Just get me down there."

Lorin nodded, struggling to bring her griffin down close to the flames where Linara could dismount. After three failed attempts, Linara pointed to a patch a hundred paces from the blaze and simply leapt from Aria's back before the griffin changed its mind about landing.

The impact shot through Linara's whole body, but she darted forward before her legs could protest. She could see the rest of the city watch now, flying in formation from the pond, dumping water in lines across the plains a far distance from the fires. They were leaving her to put them out while they focused on controlling the spread. That was fine.

But the wind was picking up too much of the stray grassy embers, flinging them farther away and starting fires all across the plains. Every patch she would stop, another two cropped up where she could not reach. She couldn't do it all, not now, not while they were so spread apart.

But if she joined them all herself . . .

Linara looked around at the field. If the fires joined into one gigantic, inescapable blaze, she could stop it all at once. Hopefully. Soon it would be ash, with or without her intervention.

Linara knelt to the dirt. The storm inside her was raging now. The new influx of power was upsetting the waves, and it *wanted* to be released. For once, Linara let it.

The flames exploded out, hot and bright. The grass accepted it easily, and the wall of flames spread out in every direction. She engulfed the field in her own fire, pushing out, farther and farther.

But it was growing too large, too out of control. There was too much heat, too many flames. Any farther and the connection would be severed. Her concentration was slipping, shattering into the void.

Fear rose up to meet the storm raging. It was like Blackrest all over again. She shouldn't have tried it. Nobody would've blamed her if she just let it burn out. Now though? She was causing so much damage.

Linara gritted her teeth and steeled herself, yanking back on the flames all at once. She felt a resistance, a momentum she herself had started, and now wanted reversed. The fires wanted freedom, and she had given it to them. But not anymore.

Tendrils of flames stretched from her hands, a dozen reins wrestling with the great beast of the inferno, burning for a mile in either direction. She pulled hard, and the flames finally obeyed, surging back through her hands into her mark where they belonged.

Power roared into her, like honey to her bones. A laugh escaped her lips, joy unbridled as the surge filled her body to the brim.

Then, as quickly as it came, it ended.

Linara inhaled deeply, tasting the smoky air. Her legs shook, and her mark was roaring for a release. Her legs collapsed and she let them. She had no energy to give anywhere else, all of her focus kept on keeping her mark contained.

The fire wasn't completely gone, patches still smoldered in the far distance. But the guards did good work. It was contained, and Linara stopped most of the blaze. The griffin teams could handle the rest, hopefully.

Smoke curled from Lorin's family farm. Griffins poured in, quenching the barn with buckets. Hopefully, Lorin evacuated them in time.

Linara tried to stand, to help, but her legs wouldn't budge. The thrum of power within was calming now, but she still felt the waves crashing against the sides. She ended up absorbing far more than she'd expelled, and she could feel her mark growing to fit the new power.

She collapsed onto her back in a bed of ash. White smoke poured into the sky, blotting out the sun like a thick cloud. The whole city would be blanketed by shadows today. There wasn't a soul alive that wouldn't be talking about it. They would blame her for it. Or worse, blame Orv.

Linara's eyes shot open wide, and she glanced all around, looking for where the fires started, where Orv was injured. She couldn't see him, or anyone, standing anywhere near. Maybe one of the griffins took him to safety. Yeah. That was probably what happened.

Linara settled back down, just as the loud crashing of the barn sounded across the plains. She glanced over at the pile of rubble, a cloud of smoke puffing out around the griffins now circling overhead. Linara didn't save Lorin's barn in time. Oh well. At least it wasn't the house itself.

Linara turned back to the sky and watched the smoke float up, up and away. Where would it all go? To the stars? Were they watching her now? She wondered if everyone made it out okay. She wondered if the grass would ever grow back. She wondered a lot of things before her eyes closed, and she wondered no more, as sleep took her.

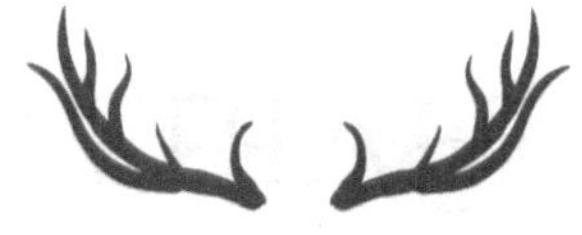

Lorin Kartridge, Stag Knight of Avorren, sat in her saddle, one hand on Aria's reins, the other on Linara's back. Linara was practically smoking only a few minutes prior, nearly burning Lorin's hands as she dragged her onto Aria's back. She couldn't leave her, however. Even as her fingers grew tender and blistered, she would never let go. She couldn't let Linara fall.

Linara had been almost mythical down there. Even while evacuating her family, she saw Linara standing among the flames with tendrils of fire flicking from her hands like she was taming the world. Red coat flicked back, hands outstretched, she had looked like something out of a dream.

A stark contrast to that day upon the wall all those weeks ago, after saving that recruit from falling to his death. She had been timid, then. In shock. Paranoid and small, like a mouse. Now she was like a dragon, straight backed and true.

One day soon she would realize that for herself. Now, however, she still couldn't quite stand on her own. Lorin looked back as Linara's unconscious form stirred, then fell still once more. She'd come a long way, that was for certain.

CHAPTER TWENTY-TWO

The acrid stench of burnt wood and leather hung thicker in the air than the densest mud. Lorin hardly seemed to notice, but Linara wanted to vomit and pass out all at once. She had been lightheaded even before stepping onto the property. She and Lorin were committed though, and the sight of the burned-out barn and scorched earth served as nothing but motivation for Linara to keep moving.

Since waking upon the wall of the city, Linara had found herself unable to sit still. The entire city was abuzz, griffins and city guards clotting the air from the Spire to the burnt fields around the northern wall. She still hadn't seen Orv, but had heard reports he was alright, just resting in the Spire.

Linara also overheard the rumors already filtering through the city. Stories were varied, but it was clear the fire was caused by a failed experiment from the magisters. They sent a boulder careening in the clear opposite direction as intended. All things considered, it could have been worse. It could have ended up over the walls, shattering somebody's home.

Nobody died, so instead of rage and anger, the city rumors took a turn for awe and wonder. They whispered of Linara the Inferno. Linara the Dragon. Linara the Savior. How, she wondered, could they think of her as such? A giant scar spread across the northern plains of Avorren, of blackened grass that wouldn't grow back so quickly.

Apparently, at the head of this charge of Linara's good name was a single man. Patrolman Elbert of the north-gate garrison of the Avorren city watch. The same guard recruit she saved on their first flight, all that time ago. She left quite the impact on him and his friends, enough to ensure that no slander was said against her.

At least the unwarranted praise was better than the alternative. She'd have to thank them eventually, but there were still many more loose ends to tie up. No injuries were reported from the fire, but a few farmsteads in the surrounding area didn't come through the other side unscathed.

One of which belonged to Lorin's family. After dropping Linara in the thick of the flames, Lorin had evacuated every member of her family while the fire licked at the edge of their property. Which, until earlier in the day, Linara wouldn't have realized was a difficult feat.

Forty-three people lived on this farm, all family, and all employees of their business. They made belts. Their barn was not full of livestock, but instead full of leather. More than enough to supply them for the next fifty years, apparently.

Fifty years of leather, for only belts. It was really a wonder why Lorin decided not to stay in the business.

She didn't even want to return, once the fire was put out. But there were compensations to be paid, and Linara felt responsible to at least ensure the safety of their barn. Such large structures, she was finding, could smolder for days.

Even now, a few tendrils of smoke curled from some of the blackened beams, sticking straight into the air. It was a wonder why they decided to build huge structures of flammable material. Blackness mounds were made of mud, and certainly couldn't burn. Even the moss that grew on top was never dry enough.

Though, despite the barn being leveled, the house was untouched. Quite big for a lonely little home, but how forty people lived within baffled Linara. It was a quaint little farmstead, not unlike a spot in Nelbren. Except the soft farmland out front carried only a thin layer of grass. Not even used for a garden.

No planting, no harvesting. Only belts. Such a waste.

And it wouldn't get any better. The contents of the barn that spilled into the dirt would surely blight the land for centuries. Linara had asked about the smell when they arrived, and Lorin revealed the family secret to curing their leather.

Urine. Their family gathered and stored their own urine for three generations, all packaged in barrels in the loft of that barn.

Linara stepped into the broken rubble, trying to ignore the wet mud squelching beneath her feet. If there was any salvageable material left in the barn, the family had stripped it clean.

Now that she stood among the wreckage, Linara knew she didn't really need to come at all. Every inch of wood was so saturated, it wouldn't hold a flame, even to dragon fire. The few sources of smoke, a few loose timbers hollowed out with embers, she quickly extinguished with a simple touch. Anything else she couldn't see or reach. If it made the family happy, she'd convince Lorin to do another flyover from the pond.

Lorin waited for her at the edge of the burned-out grass, shield strapped to one arm, stag helmet under the other, scowl pressed hard upon her face.

Once free from the barn itself, Linara gasped for a clean breath. It was amazing how much less the smell bothered her, now that she was even a few dozen steps from the source.

Lorin stepped up to the door and knocked. The curtains were drawn tight on the windows, but Linara could feel eyes upon her from within.

There was no answer, and Lorin knocked again. Her foot tapped impatiently, punctuating each passing second.

Then the door opened. The man who greeted them was half a head shorter than Lorin, gray hair lying thin across his scalp. His wrinkles were almost as deep as Orv's, but he was at least twenty years younger. His eyes fell to Lorin, and a deep grin crossed his face.

Then he looked to Linara, and it fell away.

"Who're you?" he asked, narrowing his eyes.

Lorin sighed and pushed through the door. "Her name's Linara, Pa. She's with me."

He grunted and let Lorin through, pausing a half moment to study Linara through the doorway before letting out a long breath and letting her through as well. "Buhna and Gehn didn't think you'd be back. You barely stayed a stamp's breath before darting out that door again."

Inside, tables were set up in neat rows, leaving space for the door to swing open, and little else. Strips of leather were stacked nearly to the rafters. Each table was occupied with some member of Lorin's family, ranging from a boy half their age to a woman just as old as Orv. The only ones to acknowledge her presence were a handful of children darting underneath the tables.

Lorin left her stag helmet on the stack of leather near the door and stepped through the clutter with more grace than Linara dared to muster. Her father stared at the helmet for a brief moment before shying away, like it was some sort of bad omen.

"The whole plain was on fire, Pa, I didn't really have time to loiter," Lorin said.

"There's always time for family. You made time to rush us all out of here without so much as a hello."

Lorin leveled a very simple glare, one of little patience. "Your barn was on fire."

"And I'd very much wish it never was."

"We all wish for things to be different," Lorin said. "I know the barn is not the first."

Her father fingered the rough strips of leather hanging off the table, staring half at Lorin, and half at the wall behind her.

Linara felt entirely out of place, standing awkwardly near the door. She would not take another step unless prompted to.

Despite their presence, those still at tables just kept working away, stamping and cutting leather as if their barn hadn't just burned down. On the stairs, though, a crowd was forming, most staring at Linara.

"Did you come to help us catch up?" her father asked softly. "We were behind even before we had to abandon the shop."

"You were gone for an hour. Are you that behind already?" Lorin asked.

"It's a big order."

"When isn't it?"

"This one is."

Lorin sighed and unhooked the pouch of tiles from her belt and tossed it over. Her father caught it and peeked inside with a satisfied grunt. "It won't be easy to put up another. We could use the extra pair of hands."

"There's enough in there to pay an entire crew to do it for you," Lorin said.

"That's not our way, you know that."

Lorin breathed in deep, but said nothing.

"There's a shipment going out to Elaan. Twelve hundred units. For their city watch. There's room for another hand. I figured I'd ask since it's for a similar cause and all that."

"Making belts for the city watch is not the same as being *in* the city watch, Pa."

"We won't be thanked, but I will know the work we did. No armor stays on without our work, and that makes all the difference."

"You make belts, Pa."

He slammed his hand upon the table sharply, then shrunk back, as if regretful for his outburst. "Yes. We make belts."

They both looked at each other in a painful stretch of silence, her father not even looking up from the carpet between her boots. No one on the stairs made a move, and the only noise was the stamping and the cutting and the measuring from the tables around the room. Even the children stopped their chasing, staring at the both of them in scared silence.

"Is that all you came for, then?" her father asked.

"Yes," Lorin said flatly, stepping toward the door. "If you have more problems with the barn, let me or someone from the Spire know. I'll make sure it gets done." She pushed past her father, who let her by with no objection.

"You're just going to let her leave like that?" someone asked from the stairs. A soft voice, a feminine voice. Lorin hesitated and turned as a woman descended,. a basket full of thin fabric hung under one arm. Her hair was tied roughly in a bun, her dress simple and worn, but without a speck of dirt upon it. She carried herself with poise and elegance, but in her eyes was a firmness not even the king could match. "Our own daughter steps foot in this house for barely a moment, and nobody thinks to fetch me? Not in my house."

"Technically, this is *my* house, mother," Lorin said.

"Technicalities are where the foolish make their perch."

"Technicalities is where the law does its work."

"Which is why I wonder every day what we did to drive you to that whorish system. A city watchman," she scoffed.

"It's Stag Knight now," Lorin said simply.

Her mother offered barely a glance to the stag helmet sitting near the door before gliding over to take the pouch of tiles, inspecting each in turn, with pursed lips. "Our barn burns to the ground and all you offer us is money? An apology won't replace what we lost."

"I haven't come to apologize," Lorin said.

"No? Then why have you brought her?" she said, leveling a cold glare at Linara. That glare numbed Linara's bones. Linara meant to apologize right there, to take the responsibility she felt she owed, but under that stare, no words came out.

"Linara came to ensure your barn was safe," Lorin said.

"Looked to me like she almost caught it afire again, if such a thing was possible. We don't need *her* to tell us what is safe."

"Tell that to the embers that were still burning," Lorin said.

"I'll tell that to my barn that's soaking in our heritage outside," she said.

"Grandpappy was in that barn!" a voice yelled out from the staircase. Lorin's mother snapped her head around, and the man who shouted sunk back against the banister. "Well . . . his urine, anyhow."

"It's *my* barn, mother, and without Linara, this house would've joined it."

"Without her, nothing would have been burning at all."

Even Linara knew there was some truth to that.

Lorin sighed and rubbed at the straps of her shield, still clung tight to her arm. "I don't even know why I came. I could've just sent a messenger, you know."

"You came because you're family. You'll always be drawn back here."

"No. I came because I had a responsibility. Now it is fulfilled." Lorin spun around and walked toward the door, jaw set.

"Your responsibility is here. It always has been. If you kept it that way, this never would've happened."

Her hand was upon the knob now, but she did not pull it open. "Yes, the plain burned down because I joined the city watch. Nothing good came because I left. Nothing at all."

"We wouldn't have lost what we did if we were still within the city walls."

Lorin's face darkened at that, and Linara grimaced.

Her mother continued. "We've built more orders in the last year than we have in generations, and we've had to do it without you. We'll have to rebuild without you. You abandon your family, and for what? To gallivant off on your adventures, wasting our taxed tiles on whorish griffins, all while you hang around with that . . . Odious witch!"

Lorin's shield slammed into the wall, and half the tools clattered to the floor. Every table stopped their cutting, stamping, and sewing, everyone now staring at Lorin.

Lorin, though, had eyes fixed solely on her mother. One of the children whimpered, but nobody moved to comfort them.

Lorin's mother sniffed and reframed her posture as she had moments before, as if nothing had happened. She opened her mouth to speak, and Lorin cut her off. She spoke calm and slow, like she was reining in what little patience remained.

"Mother, you may speak of me what you'd like. That is your right. My disappointments to this family are immeasurable, and that is fine. I do not care. I can take it. But if you *ever* speak in such a way of her again, all the fires of this world can come and tear your barns apart, and I will not be there to save you."

Lorin grabbed her helmet from the table and slammed it upon her head. Then she strode out the front door without another word, and Linara made sure not to linger.

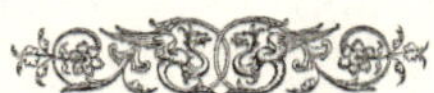

Lorin walked along the wall of the city, and Linara followed behind, silent as the grave. The blackened scar of the northern plain was their backdrop, stretching for a mile in all directions. Each of the main roads were clogged with travelers, gawking at the plains and watching the aftermath.

The stag helmet had been pressed tightly around Lorin's head since leaving the farmhouse, not a word being said between them. The anger that exploded in that place ended just as quickly, and they walked from house to city wall, leaving Aria behind to peck at the grass.

Linara knew not to press her. The outward anger might have been gone, but there was a lake of stewing, fuming rage still boiling underneath.

Not a few times did they pass a collection of city watchmen, or magisters, or some group of nobles with enough clearance to watch the ashen landscape from the outer wall. They would notice Linara and point, talking in excited whispers they thought she couldn't hear. Or they would shout after her, thanking her, calling her a hero. She didn't feel like much of a hero, but she thanked them and continued on, still watching Lorin march in silence.

Linara didn't know where they were headed. Would they loop the city endlessly until night came, and the city fell asleep? If that was the case, she resigned herself to that fate, to walk the wall for as long as it took.

Against the side of the wall, Lorin stopped at a straw dummy propped against the parapet. A metal bucket was set upon its head, like a helmet. It was probably used for some basic training, a practice target.

Lorin stepped over and rested her hand upon the leather shirt wrapped around the chest. It was torn and cracked, beaten and broken in more ways than one. A thick belt held together the straw, bursting out and littering the surrounding bricks.

She removed her stag helmet, letting her hair tumble free and drift in the soft breeze. She ran a hand through her sweat-dampened hair, staring out over the wall, toward an orange-soaked sky and blackened earth.

"You didn't have to follow me, you know."

"We're friends. It's what we do," Linara said.

"I'm sorry, by the way. For them."

"No," Linara said with a faint laugh. "I'm sorry."

"You're not to blame."

"That's not what I meant."

Lorin turned to face her then. A face hard as stone, and eyes soft as moss. Deeply sad and deathly afraid. She let her helmet clatter to the ground, bronze horns bouncing upon the stone before rolling to a stop farther down the wall. "I don't know what to do."

Linara frowned, and took a step forward, trying to think of anything to say, but finding no words would come. What would Orv do? He always had advice. Always.

But Lorin set her jaw and turned back to the dummy, grabbing a spear from her back and slamming it into its chest. "Everything I've done, I've done for them, you know," she said, staring at the wobbling spear. "I tried to lie to myself, claim that I won that tournament for my own sake. I didn't. I thought I did. I thought I trained every day because I didn't want to be another belt maker, but really, I did it so *they* wouldn't have to."

"And despite a new home, they still are," Linara said softly.

"I'm not mad at that. If they truly love making belts, good for them," Lorin said, pulling the spear free, and stabbing weakly again and again and again. "No. That's not why I'm mad. I hated myself because I thought what I had done wasn't good enough for them. And if *that* wasn't enough, what would be? It took them meeting you to realize what was wrong with me." Lorin was stabbing harder and harder now, working herself into a fury. "No. I know what to do. I've known for a very long time."

Linara shook her head and stepped forward, but hesitated. Just as nothing could stop a storm, Linara couldn't stop a raging stag.

"You saved their lives, and all they have for you is resentment. It's the same they give me every time I come home. And I could never see it." Lorin's spear cracked, and the tip flew off down the wall, but she hardly noticed, striking with all her might with the shaft that remained. "I break free from their prison, climb my way out of their *shithole*, work and work and work until I'm the best in this city, best in the *kingdom*. I beat every soldier, every knight, every man and woman before me until I kneel before the king himself. I *earned* that stag helmet, *earned* the right to wear it. I *earned* that land, convinced the commander and the king to move my family out of that slum before my service is finished. I triple their business in the first month just because of my name. I save them from ruin, I save them from despair, I save them from a sun-damned fire, *and what do I get?*"

Each word a roar to the heavens above. Linara took a step back, but stopped herself from moving any farther. She couldn't back away now, not after everything Lorin had stood with her through. The dummy was a mangled wreck of wood and straw now, barely recognizable as Lorin continued to wale down upon it, over and over and over again.

Lorin slammed what remained of her spear into the wreck and spun to face Linara, face set in the hardest of stone. "I won't let *anyone* tell me who I should be," she said, sweat dripping off her nose. "Not me. Not ever."

"Lorin," Linara said, stepping forward. She didn't know what to say. She brought only words to comfort her, but that no longer seemed appropriate.

"Do you remember that talk we had in the Spire a few months back? I said I set my bar low to avoid disappointment. Fuck that. Those statues in the entry hall? That'll be me. I won't settle for anything less."

Orvinth Vinhower III lay upon the hospital cot and wished for death. Well, perhaps not death. That would come soon for him, eventually. An escape. An escape from the pain lancing through his back, and from the massive cloud of smoke still hanging in the sky. A cloud of smoke and a field of ash that was his fault.

A cry of pain escaped his lips as the physician lifted him off the bed to inspect his spine. "It is just a sprain, young doctor. I promise it is nothing," he snapped.

The physician looked up at him with cold eyes. "I do not tell you how to grow your gardens. Now be still."

Orvinth grunted and returned to his brooding. Such an idiotic accident, in spite of his precautions. Never enough precautions. At least Linara was okay. At least the city was okay. He'd have to grow a new cane. That was always tricky. And the city would have to learn to trust them again. They'd blame him, of course. He shuddered at the thought. Or worse, they'd blame Linara. Even after she saved so many. His heart ached. Oh stars and sun above, let them blame him.

Chapter Twenty-Three

Linara roamed the servant halls, searching for Raast's room in a sea of doors. The curving hallway was endless, and the rooms identical. There was no one to ask for directions, of course. Every servant and cook in the Spire would be busy everywhere else in the Spire, not hanging around their rooms waiting to give directions to a wandering girl.

Which was why Linara was surprised Raast wasn't with them. She checked the kitchens three times that morning, and nobody had seen him. He hardly *ever* left the kitchen.

Nobody had heard from him since before the Herald Summit, and she had only heard rumors of how that went for him. He spent the whole week leading up it cooking, sleeping only an hour at a time in between the stirring of pots and checking on roasts in the oven.

It was his pride, a great test in his journey. He wished to cook for kings, and he finally had the opportunity to do even more than just that.

But after the week was done, and the Summit began, Master Dent didn't take a single step into Raast's kitchen. Nobody tasted his food except for the guards between their shifts. For that, the guards were very happy indeed, but Raast, surely, was not.

She probably should have searched for him sooner, but among recent events, news of a Luman-Viri cook spread slowly in comparison. Not to mention her lack of time.

Orv had been keeping her late practicing with flames up until the field fire, but now she had nothing but free time. Her lessons had been postponed while Orv was on bed rest. He insisted the injury was nothing unusual, a remnant of pain from his climbing days. But Linara knew he was just downplaying the role he played in saving her life. His reflexes were sharp, even if his body no longer was.

At the end of the curving hall, where the cobwebs grew a bit more frequently, and the walls were a bit more dusty, Linara found an open door. She peeked her head around into the tiny room, finding Raast's familiar blue hue sitting upon the bed. He stared at an open trunk open on the floor, entirely empty.

"Can I come in?" she asked.

Raast looked up, startled, then nodded solemnly. Linara sat on the bed beside him. The room was small, but still larger than her own bedchamber back in Nelbren. There was room to move about, if uncomfortably, but there was a bed, and a nicely sized dresser against the wall.

Raast kept his space tidy and neat. Neither dust, nor dirt, nor pillow out of place. The only irregularity was the collection of small objects on the dresser. A wooden spoon, a figurine of a wolf, even a crumpled up sheet of paper, among others.

"Nobody has seen you," Linara said. "Are you taking the day off?"

Raast turned and studied her. "Perhaps you have not heard? I have quit."

"Quit?" Linara gasped. News spread slowly about such matters, but she truly didn't expect *that* slow. "Here at the Spire, or cooking forever?"

"I have weighed the words of many men," Raast said. "The man who has trained me, whose abilities have formed the structure of my own, compared to the words of my closest friends. You have told me I am good, that I may cook for kings. My master told me different."

Raast exhaled a long breath, staring at his hands. "I have determined that a man can lie, but friends cannot. Even, I think, my own opinions can be lies. I thought I was not worthy, but I think that I am. I wanted to cook for kings, but that wasn't quite the truth. I wish to be the best in the kingdom. The best in the world. I can only learn from the best, and there is none here better than me. Therefore, I must leave."

Linara was silent for a moment. She had been telling him for months that he was better than the head chef. Cirena said the same thing. She just didn't think this was what it looked like when he believed them.

"I hope you weren't going to slip away during the night," Linara said, forcing a smile.

"Here, there is not much of a night to slip into."

"I suppose you're right."

Raast considered for a moment. "I would never leave without a good-bye," he said. "In fact, I am finding it difficult to leave at all. The core of my being is pulling me to travel, but I do not think I wish to."

"Then stay," Linara said. "You can always change your mind later, right?"

"It is not that simple," Raast said, searching for the words to explain. "Has Avorren become your home yet, I wonder? What would it be like for you, when your purpose pulls *you* elsewhere? Will you go? Will you listen? If I stay for my friends, what then? One day, you will die, and I will live on. When that day comes, will I still desire to be a great cook? Who will I be then? Who was I before this moment? I do not know those answers, but I *do* know who I am right now."

He hesitated again and scowled. "I have already decided what I must do. As a Luman-Viri, I am accustomed to forgetting people and experiences, yet I do not wish to forget you. Isn't that strange?"

"To me? No."

Raast nodded and stared up at the dresser. "I think it is strange. I cannot even bring myself to pack away my things just yet."

Linara stood and studied the objects littering the top of the dresser. She found a small glass vial, tinted red, but otherwise empty. She didn't have to uncork it know that it once held powdered feld fungus, a remnant from their time in the troupers' cart all those months ago. She had no idea Raast had kept it. There were dozens of little mementos.

"What are they?" she asked.

"I use them to remember events and people," Raast said, rising and standing beside her. "Some Luman-Viri keep journals, some write songs or poetry. I collect souvenirs."

"So you remember events after you otherwise wouldn't be able to," Linara said.

Raast reached for the wooden spoon. It was discolored and worn, dented in more than a few places. "This spoon was given to me. I don't know when, or by whom, but I know it is why I am a cook." He gently lowered it back to the dresser. "The vial I keep because it is the first day I met all of you. That book of poems I took from the troupers in Blackrest. It is an unpleasant memory, compared to the others, but one I wish to keep, I think."

Linara found a folded stack of papers at the edge, and she reached for them. They were a few of the encoded messages and notes from the trouper break-in. Raast had mentioned he had been working on them, but he probably abandoned it after Blackrest.

Something pulled at her, though. Maybe it was the unrest that had been forming, but Linara studied one of the images. It was a snake, drawn with one continuous line across the page. It twisted in strange, unnatural directions.

"Are you keeping this for a memory?" Linara asked.

"No. That is nothing. You can keep them if you'd like. I will not need them any longer."

Linara slid the page into her pocket as Raast studied his shelf. His eyes rested upon a small teapot at the end, and he frowned. "This, I no longer remember why I keep." He picked it up and placed it in a box by his door, filled with a few similar objects.

"What will you do with them?"

"I will look over them again, to see if they spark anything. Then I will throw them away."

"Just like that?" Linara asked, and he nodded. "You're not saddened by it?"

"Last week, when I remembered what it was, perhaps I would've been. But now, I do not know what disappeared. It's the turning of the Luman-Viri. We are used to it. Despite how sometimes I wish I was not."

"I don't think I would ever get used to it."

"You are human. Why would you want to get used to something that is not you?"

"I suppose you're right," Linara said. "I *will* miss you, though. We all will."

Raast smiled. "I will, too, Linara Farrow, at least until I forget who you are."

Somehow, that was comforting. At least she would know that wherever he went, he would latch on to these memories until they finally drifted away. But she didn't want to leave him just like that. He deserved a send-off, if at least just a trip with all of them, to say goodbye.

"Lorin, Cirena, and Rhoam are taking me to the hatchery to buy a griffin later today," Linara said. "Do you want to come? One last time?"

Raast stared at his dresser, eyes falling to each memento in turn. "I will go with you. Then I will leave this city behind."

Linara wrapped her arms around him and hugged him close. "Deal."

Contrary to Linara's assumptions, the Avorren Hatchery, the primary source of all breeding, raising, and training for the mounts of the city watch, was not within the walls of Avorren at all. Just as well, despite being labeled as birds, griffins didn't "hatch" anything at all. They were birthed like any other mammal.

This brought many questions, none of which Lorin would answer. They left the gates just after the midday bell. She pointed them northwest, into the endless grassy landscape. Lorin and Raast had the comfort of Aria, able to fly circles around them while Linara walked.

Cirena and Rhoam even had a horse to ride upon, trotting slowly alongside her. After only an hour, Linara envied them. It was tradition among the new recruits that any seeking a griffin must walk the entire distance from city to stables. Linara didn't complain initially until she realized just how far it was.

She had hoped to pass some of that time with Raast, but Aria could only walk for short stints. Griffins preferred to fly, after all, and couldn't walk so far without hurting their legs.

That led to more vocal complaints from Cirena about the animals. She had more than a few questions for Raast, ones that couldn't be answered if he was a hundred feet above them. The princess couldn't understand his desire to leave. Lorin did, same as Rhoam and Linara. They knew what it took to accomplish a dream.

Nobody *wanted* him to leave, but Cirena took the effort to try and bribe him to stay. She was certain she could get his meals in front of her father, to convince him to replace Dent as the head chef of the Spire. His goal would be complete then. But it wasn't that simple. His goal had changed.

Cirena asked him already where he'd go, trying to poke holes in whatever plan he may have come up with. But not even Raast knew where he was going next. He had no plan, and that was his way. It left the princess melancholy and quiet, a strange mood for her.

A bag of tiles clinked at Linara's belt with every step. It was more money than she'd seen in her life. More money than her father made in his lifetime. All this time she'd been in Avorren, she'd assumed she'd been living there for free. Her payment was just her life, spared in Nelbren so that she could serve.

When she told Cirena that, the princess laughed.

As it turned out, her room was not free, nor was her service. Being the kingdom Odious was a well paid position, as it turned out, and Orv had been handling the complicated exchange of funds since she arrived. The sizable sum sat untouched until a few hours ago, and Linara had no real idea how much it was all worth. Certainly enough to purchase a griffin of her own, as well as space in any city stable she wished.

Lorin swooped down on Aria, a flash of white feathers among the sky burning red and orange. Her eyes were more focused than usual, but her face was drawn low and tired. She wasn't herself, not since the field fire, but Linara suspected it was intentional. She had started sparring with Rhoam nearly every day, no longer avoiding patrols or minor assignments.

Raast smiled widely in the saddle behind Lorin, as if he were experiencing flight for the first time. From his perspective, he very well might be.

"One other thing," Lorin said, leaning down low on Aria's back. "You'll want to pick a griffin with a perfectly average wingspan. Too large, and you won't fit right. Too small, it'll be too slow. It might be best to sit in the saddle of a few to test out the fit. Oh, and check the beak. Make sure it's sharp and angled. A flat beak is a no-go."

As always, Linara listened and nodded along. She had already forgotten the other advice Lorin had given. Linara knew exactly what she was looking for. The conversation about buying a griffin began just after the fire. Lorin and Aria had been helpful while the fire raged, but not nearly as much as they could have been. Aria was afraid of the flames, and that was the only trait Linara had to avoid.

She wished she could just buy Dresborn. He had the spark she desired; fearless, bold, and patient. But too old. Griffins could live half a human lifetime or more, but she needed a partner that still had the majority of its life left in its wings.

"What is wrong with a flat beak?" Raast asked.

"Means it's more difficult for them to peck at food crawling around in the dirt. Seeds, worms, that kind of thing. Also, make sure their feather patterns don't have any stripes."

"Why's that?" Linara asked.

"Stripes are bad luck."

Linara rolled her eyes. "Right."

"You griffin folk and your superstitions," Cirena said. "No color patterns or wingspans to worry about with horses."

"Just bad temperament . . ." Linara mumbled, eyeing the stubborn beast. Even now, it glared at Linara, puffing hot breaths from its nose. The royal family sure had a knack for picking out stubborn mounts.

A moment later, Linara nearly walked straight into a massive ravine. It opened up like a gash upon the earth, grass growing to the very edge. She tried to move to the side and walk around it, but Lorin blocked her path. She gestured over the edge of the chasm, Raast craning his neck from behind her to catch a glimpse. Linara hesitated, and eyed Lorin wearily. Guard traditions could get strange, she knew, but all fear dropped away as Linara saw the bottom of the pit.

The landscape around Avorren was pocked with caverns and ravines, but none were so large and so deep as this. The ground cut away to a sharp drop a half mile down or more, like a great knife had plunged into the ground, leaving a scar of rock a mile across.

But what caught Linara's attention the most was the sea of griffins, flying in endless swirling patterns. Hundreds, maybe thousands. Linara stopped counting quickly.

"The stables are underground," Linara breathed.

"A bit of a well-kept secret," Lorin said.

"But why?" Linara asked.

"It's large enough, and not easy to spot. There's a certain advantage in keeping our numbers hidden."

"Not that hidden if you're above it, I'd imagine." Linara glanced up, but noticed there weren't any griffins flying overhead. No patrols, no messengers, not even a lone traveler.

"If anybody gets close enough, sure, but you can't even see it from the Spire," Lorin said, kicking Aria forward. "Now, come on, the path down won't walk itself."

Linara glanced around, trying to find the way down. Rhoam and Cirena were already moving toward it, starting down a ramp overgrown with grass. It blended in well. She probably wouldn't have noticed anything strange about the ravine at all if Lorin hadn't stopped her.

Twice Linara almost fell off the side as she watched the griffins around her. Most had no riders, not even a saddle. None strayed too high, keeping to the walls of the cavern. That surprised her. She knew griffins loved the sky, and the wind. The air was clear here, sure, and the sky still shone bright overhead, but it must've taken a great deal of training to make sure they didn't stray from the pack. They all looked happy enough, and Linara liked to think she could tell.

They neared the floor of the ravine, revealing flat ground covered in moss and sparse grass. Tall fences sectioned off areas into pens, which probably served little purpose for winged animals. But even so, hundreds more griffins hung around within, grazing or sleeping in the shadows of the cavern walls.

At the back was a long wooden building. Arches and pillars filled the exterior, set in more detail than Linara would have expected of a hidden cavern stable. It was enormous, but Linara wasn't sure it could hold all the griffins inside. Perhaps they really didn't have to. Stable hands filtered in and out with buckets of feed or water, all wearing simple yellow vests.

They stepped through a wide wooden arch at the bottom of the ramp, carved with images of griffins and riders. Toward the top, they battled with dragons, holding lances and spears, ready to attack. At the bottom were the messenger birds, flying poised with honor toward distant cities.

Lorin and Rhoam left their mounts at the arch as they continued inside. Raast, though, stayed behind to study the posts. He knew what he wished to remember the most. Maybe he would even find a souvenir to remember this day.

Lorin led the way through the stable yard toward a man in a long yellow coat. Odrin, the stable master, if Lorin's descriptions were accurate. His arms bulged against the fabric of his sleeves, and a scowl was pressed hard upon his face.

A boy stood before him, barely younger than Linara, wearing a plain shirt with a yellow sash tied around his belt. He stood a full span shorter than Odrin and stammered over half his words as he spoke. In training, most definitely. His words halted entirely as he noticed them approach.

Odrin followed the boy's gaze, his frown deepening at Lorin. "Taking the Tenderfoot Trot again, young Stag Knight?" He grumbled.

"I haven't fallen *that* far," Lorin said, but gestured to Linara. "But I brought one who has."

Odrin turned and stared her up and down. "You're no recruit."

Linara opened her mouth to respond, but she had no idea what to say to that. Odrin reminded her a great deal of her father, if much larger. Kindness came easily, but when it came to work, there was no room for nonsense.

Instead, the boy beside Odrin gasped, eyes growing wide. "Linara Farrow," he breathed, sticking out his hand. Linara shook it apprehensively. "I saw everything you did. It was . . . amazing! I was on a training flight, you see, with the hatchlings . . . they needed exercise, and anyway, the field was on fire, and then you tamed the fire like a dragon!"

"Uhh—" Linara said, smiling awkwardly. "Thank you?"

The boy blushed and stammered over his next words. Why was *he* so embarrassed? He still held Linara's hand, and it was growing sweaty.

"This must be your first time here. It's amazing, isn't it?" he said, noticing the dampness and releasing his grip. "We breed and hatch our own griffins, you know. We're rivaling most stables in the Collis Province now." The boy glanced between the landscape behind her and some place on her head. "You know . . . I didn't expect your hair to be beautiful."

Linara choked on her next breath. This kid *had to* be like four years younger, right? She was always terrible at judging those things. The silence spread between them far longer than she would've liked.

The words caught in Linara's throat, but she could already feel herself taking a step back. All she could manage was a weak, "Uhh . . ." which was not what either of them were hoping for.

Odrin stepped in front and waved the young stableboy back to the building. "Get out of here, Simon. You're scaring the poor girl."

The boy flushed a deep shade of crimson and turned to run off. Linara tried to call out in thanks, but he was too far gone to hear. Oh, stars above...

"With that personal show of embarrassment over," Odrin said, looking her up and down again, "what are you here for? Pleasure flight, patrol bird? Messenger? We don't usually sell to the public."

"Probably more guard stock than anything else," Lorin said, considering.

"You're neither in the military, nor a noble."

"She's the kingdom's new Odious," Lorin said. "She just saved the whole city from a fire."

"The best I can do is C grade."

Lorin folded her arms. "Top stock, or we import from Collis."

Odrin scowled at the threat. "She's not in any hierarchy and can't just override the system. She'll need a letter of approval for that, and good luck getting one from Nilya."

"You owe me a favor, Odrin," Lorin said, locking her gaze to his. They stared at each other for a long moment before the stable master growled and turned away.

"Never should have made that bet . . ." he mumbled, leading them farther into the stable yard. They passed pens full of griffins, all of them watching as they walked by. It was like they knew why she was there, all of them curious and waiting.

Odrin stopped near the stable itself and gestured to a group of griffins standing in the moss. "This lot here is fair game. There's some that might prove useful, some not so much. Take your time, choose wisely, and all that," he said, waving apathetically over the fence.

A dozen griffins walked proudly in the field. Linara watched each of them carefully. They all looked a little too . . . snooty for her taste. Like they knew what they were all about, but not in a good way. Lorin pointed out talon lengths and color patterns, which Linara ignored.

She instead squeezed underneath the fence and grabbed a fistful of moss. Rolling it into a tight ball like in Blackrest, she sparked a flame into the center, keeping it burning low and steady in her palm. Every griffin around her was watching now. Most backed up, but some stepped closer, surrounding her with curious eyes.

It wasn't enough, though. She had to be *sure.*

Linara knelt and slammed the flame into the ground, igniting the moss at her feet. Every griffin around her cried out at once, fleeing into the sky away from the fire. Odrin and Lorin both yelled out to her, but Linara ignored them. It was the only way to test them, and she would keep the fire under control.

The fire trickled and spread, the moss hydrated and healthy. It wouldn't spread wildly like the fields above, but she still kept her fingers ready to snatch it back at a moment's notice.

Her eyes scanned the yard, watching the griffins that remained. Many were watching nervously, others looking on with a curious caution. One griffin, though, caught her eye. Its feathers were dark black, wings outstretched and beating furiously. It didn't take to the air as she expected, but leapt over the tall fence between them. It landed in a cloud of dirt and sprinted over, stomping at the fire with furious talons until it was out.

Then it looked at Linara and cocked its head, searching for approval. Its eyes burned with fire, its gaze curious. Linara smiled and slid a hand beneath the feathers on its neck. "I'll take this one," she said to Odrin.

The stable master scowled and grabbed the bridle. "Too bad. He's not for sale."

"Oh," Linara said, shoulders slumping. "Why not?"

"I told you to pick from the pen, and not anywhere else."

"There are no others in this pen," Raast noted.

"Yeah, she scared half the flock and burned a hole in the moss," Odrin said. "Not to mention he's not. For. Sale."

"There aren't any others. They're all afraid of her," Lorin said. "You can't argue with that."

"I don't care," Odrin said. "You just can't take this one. Find another."

"It's more than just fear," Linara said. "He came over from across the yard to stomp it out. He's different."

The griffin clicked its beak and turned its head to look at her, finally nuzzling down and touching its head to hers.

"Even you can't deny it," Lorin said. "The connection has been made. He made his choice."

Odrin laughed. "I see nothing. Bonds and connections are superstitions, and this griffin *does not belong to you*." Even Linara was skeptical about that. She had only just met this griffin, and they hadn't even flown together. But she didn't argue.

Lorin and Cirena shared a glance, then stepped forward together. "Then we're both invoking our authority in outranking you," Lorin said.

Odrin crossed his arms. "Don't think for a second that will work on me. I'm not budging on this. If you want to grab the king, or Nilya, so be it. I'll be here."

Lorin hesitated, probably knowing they would both side with the stable master in this.

Linara glanced at her belt, at the pouch of tiles. "I have money," Linara said, stepping between them. She opened the pouch and offered it over.

Odrin's scowl lightened as he stared inside. He glanced at Linara, at the black griffin, still nuzzling Linara's shift, and the pouch of gold tiles. He plucked the pouch from her hand and tucked it inside his coat. "Fine. Take him and get out of my sight."

Linara released a long breath and grabbed the griffin's bridle before the stable master could change his mind. Odrin was already stomping off toward the stable, though, one finger digging through the pouch of tiles.

"I can't believe you let him take all of that," Cirena said, shaking her head.

"Was it too much?" Linara asked, daring a glance back as they passed through the wooden arch leading back to the upward slope.

"Most definitely," Lorin said with a laugh. "That was for the stable costs too. But if this griffin was worth it, who cares. He's a very interesting color."

"Unlucky?" Linara asked.

"No, just strange."

"The color of ash and smoke," Raast said.

"Quite suiting," Rhoam agreed.

"Have you decided on a name?" Lorin asked.

"A name? He doesn't already have one?" Linara said.

"Probably not. Most hatcheries like that one wait for their owners to name them," Lorin said. "Think on it, but don't wait too long. You can't very well walk around with a nameless griffin."

"What kind of name?" Linara asked. She'd never named anything before, not even the chickens back home.

"Something that encompasses everything about him. His character, his talents and abilities. Everything that makes up his personality, compressed into a single name that cuts through all understanding and tells everyone who hears it exactly *who* your griffin is."

Linara thought about it for a long moment. "That seems complicated. What about Ash?" She looked up at her griffin, who lazily arched his head to stare into her eyes. He ruffled his feathers, pecked at a spot on his leg, and continued on.

"Remarkably neutral about it," Cirena said.

Lorin shrugged. "Yeah, well, he is a bird. What did you expect?"

Linara held Ash tight as they started the long trek back up the slope of the pit. Something palpably and undeniably *hers*. It was a strange feeling. Like a sense of belonging, one she hadn't truly felt since leaving Nelbren.

Ash watched the sky now, staring at the flying griffins in their endless pattern. That was a look Linara recognized. The same longing that Dresborn had. She knew why the recruits had to walk to the stables. It wasn't just about tradition, or sense of hazing. More than anything, she knew that everyone who left with a griffin would want to fly them back before anything else.

Thankfully, Ash was already saddled. She passed a glance to Lorin, and she nodded in perfect understanding. "I'll meet you back in the city," Linara said, climbing on Ash's back. She had no chance to hear their reply, for Ash was already dashing up the slope.

He wasn't gaining enough speed to catch the wind, but he certainly didn't need to. Once they were high enough, Ash leapt off the side and caught the air with black feathered wings.

Wind rushed through Linara's hair, and she let her eyes clamp shut. She felt the wind, felt the sky and the air. Ash rode alongside the wall, and Linara held on with all her might, still adjusting in the saddle. They passed nooks and alcoves where griffins rested upon the stone before joining the thick parade of griffins in the center.

She could tell now why they didn't stray too far to the surface. It was routine for them, a comfort. Like Dresborn falling into his old patrol routes. But Ash was far too impatient for such simple pleasures. He darted forward, weaving between the riderless griffins.

He flew like a debonair. Every maneuver, no matter how simple, aimed to impress. Dresborn may have had the wisdom and age, but Ash had the recklessness and arrogance Linara would need. They were a perfect fit, and he knew it, too.

Ash banked toward the wall, heading straight toward a cavernous hole, shadowed and dark. Linara's heart thudded in her ears, but somehow, she trusted Ash with her life. They crossed beneath the stone, flying in near darkness. Spikes of rock jutted out from the floor and ceiling, and Ash flew between them with practiced ease.

Orv had mentioned the caverns around Avorren and how they were often interconnected. He spent much of his youth exploring the caves, disappearing for days within. Who could tell how far they went, but wherever Ash was leading her, he had been there before. That much was clear.

A shaft of light appeared ahead of them, growing brighter by the second. Ash shot up toward the ceiling, breaching through the final stretch into a hole leading straight to the surface. Sunlight beamed from above, and Linara held on to the saddle, feeling her eyes burning with the sharp change of light.

Ash emerged with outstretched wings, catching the gusts of wind blowing through the plains. He rode them high up toward the clouds. He slowed only when they could touch the heavens themselves. Only the Spire stood higher than them.

Linara could see ravines and rock outcroppings clearly. The hatchery cavern was visible, but even now she couldn't tell the stables laid within. It was strange, seeing the patterns of the rocks laid out below her. Almost like points of stars along the Blackness sky. If she tried hard enough, she could even form shapes and constellations. Certain edges of rocks and cavernous holes wound their way along the countryside like the path of a hunting mosskimmer, or the outline of a . . . serpent.

Linara's eyes grew wide, and she searched desperately in her coat for the drawing she'd grabbed from Raast's chambers. Ash tried to pull away, eager to be off to something new, but Linara urged him to stay. She opened the folded paper, guiding Ash to circle the formation of rocks until it lined up just right.

There. It was a perfect match. She could trace the lines between each formation, like a snake twisting in unnatural directions. The patterns on its skin were holes in the very ground, the edges of places where stone jutted clear through the grass.

And centered on the eye, circled with importance, was a formation of stone unlike any other. It rose up like a monolith. It was the central point of a complicated map, just as Cirena theorized.

That was it, that was the trouper's secret. They couldn't find answers on the map of Avorren because it *wasn't* a map of Avorren.

Linara pulled Ash back toward the ravine, toward the hatchery and the faint outline of a horse breaching the rise. They had one final stop before returning to the city. She just hoped she could convince Rhoam to go through with it.

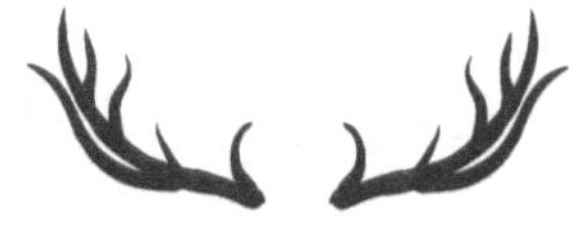

My dearest Linara,

I'm afraid I was vague and mysterious far before Nela kicked me in the head. In fact, that was what your mother loved most when she met me. I believe it was what she disliked most in the end, but I think you'll find that's just how it goes.

I picked up a crate of Crisyll Root and have been thinking of you. I thought about keeping a handful for myself, for the long roads, but I must remind myself how much I detest the stuff. That was a rare food you and your mom shared. I will stick with dried moss.

These roads can be long. Sometimes I even miss Nelbren, but I believe I just miss your company. The long nights are lonely, but they'd be lonely in that mound just the same. I'm glad to be back on the road. It seems to fit me like an old pair of boots. I'll have to swing my way toward Avorren before long, but before then, I have a route to take. I am headed to Edenus, to a few rural villages on the southern edge. Direct your letters to Elaan. I'm sure they will end up in my hands before long.

Peace below the stars,

Frennik Farrow

Also, tell Raast he will always be my favorite, because he keeps you well fed.

Chapter Twenty-Four

Cirena and Rhoam were already a half mile toward the city by the time Linara caught up. Words came slow to her, despite her mind racing. It took a bit to explain the map, and the things she saw from above, but Cirena was quick to jump on board. The troupers never truly left her mind, even less than Linara.

Rhoam, though, was hesitant at best. After spending the better part of an hour in front of the king with him, Linara didn't blame him. The same curiosity gnawed at him, and Linara knew it, but he had the strength to resist it.

It was Lorin, though, who ended up convincing him in the end, circling back on Aria a few moments later. The place was marked with intent, but what other purpose would they need from it so far from the city, if not a storage cache? Lorin doubted it would be any more than a small crawl space, packed with old crates and surplus supply. Especially after their caravan burned down, Rhoam could admit they likely hadn't even touched it in months.

Before he could change his mind, Linara took Ash back into the sky and led the way to the rock. Lorin and Raast were keeping pace on Aria, but the horse was little more than a spot of black upon the landscape. Linara pitied them. There was no true freedom on the ground. You could feel the wind on a horse, sure, but it was counterfeit.

Linara was amazed by how quickly she lost the boulder that marked their destination. Without the map, every rock was just a rock. It took two passes to find the serpent's eye, and by the time they landed, Cirena and Rhoam had nearly caught up. The boulder stood almost twice her height, overgrown with grass and covered in a thin layer of moss. It wasn't anything remarkable up close, but Linara wasn't sure what she expected.

Lorin moved slowly around the rock, rubbing her hand along its surface in search of any hidden openings. Nobody truly knew what to look for, but Lorin, at the very least, had *some* measure of experience.

"Do you think it is a coincidence that this boulder is shaped like Deydalus?" Raast asked.

Lorin frowned and stared up at it. "It's not Deydalus."

"You're not looking at it correctly," Raast said.

"I don't see it, either," Linara said, moving beside him. Though, she hadn't studied maps that often. Those Orv put in front of her were mostly of Aldebraan.

"See," Raast said. "It's flat on the western side. And there's a crack where Arkya used to be."

If Linara squinted her eyes enough, she could see it resembled *something*. She just wasn't the right person to ask.

"Do you think it is a coincidence?" Raast asked again.

Lorin didn't bother looking up. "If I believe it *was* in the shape of Deydalus, then yes, I would think it was a coincidence."

"What if the map is left by a conspiracy?"

"It *is* a conspiracy, Raast," Linara said.

Raast frowned. "I seem to be missing memories."

"It is far more likely they picked this rock because it's far from the walls, not because of its shape," Lorin said. "Now, are you two going to stand there all day, or are you going to help me?"

Linara waved for Raast, and they stepped to the boulder, walking alongside as if they knew what they were doing. Cirena and Rhoam rode up then, reining in their horse. "Why is it shaped like Deydalus?" Cirena asked. Nobody bothered to answer. "Well, did you find anything yet?"

Linara grunted, hands deep in moss. "The drawing wasn't exactly labeled."

For a hidden rock in the middle of the countryside, they did a good job hiding whatever secret it held. Lorin, at one point, tried to climb to the top. It was far too steep, and the moss peeled away with too much ease. Linara almost conceded that the drawing was just a drawing, and a map to a cool rock. Nothing more.

But it wasn't a simple rock. Raast found the secret first: a hole at the base of the boulder just below the section he thought looked like Arkya. A portion of stone had broken free to cover the gap, and it took the four of them to move it.

The opening it revealed was barely large enough to fit a grown man, and was overgrown by grass and clumps of dirt. Above it, after pulling away the moss, was a small carving of a snake, almost imperceptible. That was confirmation enough that the drawing was not simply a co-incidence.

They gathered around it, none willing to venture inside. It was clear it led far, and was not a simple cache for hiding a few sacks of feld. Even Cirena was quiet. A dark hole was far more excitement than they were looking for.

Rhoam had his arms crossed, frowning. "I don't like it."

Lorin knelt to brush away some of the overgrowth, but flinched back as a mouse scurried from the weeds. "It hasn't been touched in years."

"This entrance, sure," Rhoam said. "Who knows where it leads."

Lorin sighed and brushed off her hands. "I understand if you want me to check it out first."

Rhoam shrugged. "Only if you're comfortable."

"So be it. I can fend off a few mice," Lorin said, pulling her stag helmet from Aria's saddle. She grabbed a pair of spears beside it, pressing one upon her back, and keeping the other in her hand. Rhoam at least took the effort to dig in his pack for a small milky white sphere of quartz to light her path before she disappeared into the hole.

Then they waited. Rhoam watched the entrance, unmoving. He rested one hand upon the hilt of his sword. Cirena was staring in disgust as Raast balanced a long centipede upon his finger. He watched with delight as it twisted and curled within his hand.

Linara sighed and kicked at the grass. This rock harbored a lot of life, like an anchor in an otherwise unremarkable landscape. If Linara weren't so anxious to see what Lorin discovered, she might've been just as interested in the bugs as Raast.

Instead, her thoughts dwelled upon the troupers. What was special about this place? It was a far way from both the road and the city. Five miles or more, at least. Linara could barely spot the dots of flying shapes circling Avorren. Even from so high, they wouldn't be able to see much so far out here. A caravan wouldn't go unnoticed, but a few lone people could sneak out here with ease.

Maybe that was why it was so overgrown. Had it even been used? Or was it simply a backup if they were out of all other options? How far did it go? Was it just a place to store goods, or something far more sinister?

The centipede on Raast's fingers plopped to the grass and scurried off. Cirena shuddered and backed away, but Raast was already searching in the grass for more.

"Do you remember much of your home, Raast?" Linara asked absently.

Raast brushed his hands across his pants. "I do not. But there is an impression no memory can give. A knowing and a longing that I cannot explain. A feeling no other memory gives. Probably not even Avorren will, in the end."

"Have you decided where you'll go?" Cirena asked.

"Not to Reginaan, I think," he said, with a smile. "Perhaps I will stay in Aldebraan. To Elaan, perhaps."

"The herald there will have her own chef, as well," Cirena said. "I'll see if I can connect you. Though I doubt you'll need my help."

"I read recently they cook mushrooms there," Raast said. "I would very much like to know how that is done."

"Just don't eat luma," Linara said. From her experience, no mushroom tasted especially good, but Raast made moss taste heavenly. Luma, though, was a certain kind of bitter that didn't wash off the tongue.

The grass rustled from the rock, and a pair of stag horns poked out a moment later. "It's clear," Lorin said. "Nothing living except the spiders." Then she was gone again. They all looked to Rhoam for confirmation, and he nodded hesitantly before leading the way through the hole.

Cirena followed close, with Raast and Linara behind. The fit was tight, but once they were inside, the tunnel was surprisingly spacious. The path dipped down, supported by beams of wood like an old mining tunnel, ending fifty paces in at a large, round chamber. A natural cavern, like many surrounding Avorren. The ceiling rose a dozen strides above them. Thin pallet beds lined the walls, some sodden with the water dripping from stalactites.Crates were stacked in piles, but most were rotted and empty.

Their steps stirred up old dust, filtering through the air in the light cast from Lorin's quartz. She was inspecting a map hung upon the wall, the paper worn and faded. Raast pushed past to a crate of dried rations near the entrance. He even dared to taste a chunk of old bread, scribbling in his notepad as he did so.

Linara, though, couldn't tear herself from the doorway. There were no shadows to hide in, no places for troupers to leap out in surprise. Yet, she could not relax. The room smelled of age and dampness, but beneath it was unmistakably the stench of feld fungus. No matter how old this hideout may have been, it stunk of Thatcher.

After a long, deep breath, she stepped inside. Each step she took slowly, not daring to disturb the dust. The walls of the cavern were jagged, but unblemished. Save for a long crack in the stone on the opposite wall. The light danced upon the edges, casting a deep shadow on the opening. It was taller than a man, and certainly wide enough to squeeze through.

Beside it were more crates, but these seemed newer. No dust, no age, unrotted. Stamped upon the side was a symbol in black ink. A *W* in elaborate script, circled twice. Linara shuffled closer, studying the mark. It wasn't anything she immediately recognized, but something about it was familiar. She looked up into the crack, turning her ear to the silence beyond.

A loud shuffling of feet from behind her broke Linara from her thoughts. Voices echoed from the entrance, with the clanging of metal and stone. Had the troupers returned? Surely this couldn't be another trap, right? She shot her eyes to Rhoam and Lorin, but they already had weapons drawn.

Raast was still scribbling in his notebook in the corner, and Linara grabbed his arm and pulled him to safety. They gathered beside the entrance, Cirena, Linara, and Raast huddled together.

A light pooled in the opening, a soft glow like firelight. A moment later, a man burst forth in a simple metal helmet, holding a torch in one hand and a short spear in the other. His eyes scanned the room before finally landing upon them. His face curled into a snarl, ready to stab out with his spear, but he hesitated, his face softening into confusion. "Stag Knight?"

"Dram?" Lorin said, hesitantly.

The soldier lowered his spear, looking to Rhoam, and the group huddled behind him. "What are you doing here?"

"I would ask you the same thing," Lorin said, keeping her spear leveled. Linara could see now he wore the black coat of an Ebon Wing soldier. One of Lorin's own men.

A golden griffin helmet appeared from the tunnel next, and Lorin relaxed as Commander Nilya entered the room. She studied the soldier, standing puzzled in the doorway, then turned to Lorin. "What's going on here?"

A dozen soldiers poured in behind her, all in the black coats of the Ebon Wings. They pooled through the room, checking every wall with detail. Nobody said a word. Rhoam still held his sword at the ready, eyes darting between every soldier.

"Kartridge," Nilya warned. "I won't ask again."

"I . . . don't know. I'm just as confused as you are."

"You don't know how you got here?" the commander asked flatly.

"No, I don't know how *you* got here," Lorin said.

Even beneath the helmet, Nilya leveled a glare that prickled the back of Linara's neck. "I was under the impression you would be seeing Odrin today." Her words were thick with anger now, an impatience that even Rhoam flinched at. It was clear why Lorin was never favored among the Knights. Old habits died hard.

"We did," Lorin said. "We were riding back when we saw this rock."

"This cavern is a far ride from the stables."

The soldiers began ripping apart the room, tearing Linara's attention away. They dug through the old crates piled high with dust, finding only dirt and empty air. One pulled at a stack of maps, inspecting each briefly before discarding them with little thought. Two other soldiers slid into the wide crack, disappearing into the darkness.

"Why have *you* come? It's a far ride from the city, as well," Rhoam said. His voice was firm, matching Nilya. He stood with one hand on Cirena's shoulder, but it was clear she was just as concerned and wasn't going anywhere. "What do I need to know that you've brought a dozen Ebon Wings here, of all places?"

Nilya sighed and leaned on her spear, watching her men search the cavern. "We've received reports of movement in the countryside. Of dark shapes moving among the grass, only to disappear. What a surprise when we investigate and find griffins standing beside a lone rock, one black as night, and my Stag Knight creeping about in an old smuggler's tunnel."

A dark-haired soldier shuffled over, slamming a crate upon the table. It was one of boxes that had been stacked near the crack in the wall. The guard pulled a long knife from his belt and wiggled it into the lid, trying to pry it open.

"What else have you found?" Rhoam asked.

"Nothing else. Just rocks and grass, and you five. The woman who spoke to us in the city was convinced she saw dragons, but dragons do not crawl upon the dirt. It was probably nothing more than the shadow of a cloud."

"She probably saw us," Lorin said.

"Two hours ago?" Nilya asked.

Lorin shrugged. "Maybe not, then. But there's nothing of note here, just an old cache, nothing more."

"Truth or not, those rumors alone worry me," Rhoam said, sliding his sword back into his scabbard. "Coincidences can be decided long after the fact. For now, we should be leaving. We never should have come at all."

The lid popped off the crate with a great crack. The soldier riffled through the packed hay within, pulling out a small clay ball. He chuckled and tossed it to Nilya, who barely caught it.

She glared at him. "What is this?"

The soldier shrugged. "Thought you'd know."

They were familiar to Linara, but she knew not from where. Her heart thudded wildly in her chest, an unease that had been growing since they entered. Something was very wrong.

Nilya gestured for one of the torches and held the little clay ball closer to the light. Linara stepped up to the crate, studying the symbol again. She turned her head just slightly and gasped. The crate was upside down. It was no *W* but an *M*. Memories flooded all at once of Nymin the magister in Orv's office. He mentioned an invention shipped to a mining town north of Avorren. Blastcores, he called them.

Linara shot forward and grabbed Nilya's hand before it got too close to the fire. "I wouldn't do that," she breathed. "This is magister work."

Nilya flinched, remembering all too well the boulder incident that caused the field fire. The room fell still, all eyes upon them now. Even the guard did not move. One hand plunged into the crate.

"What do you know of this?" Nilya asked, slowly. Calmly.

"Nothing, really," Linara said, stammering over her words. "Just that they're dangerous. They sent these to Rivead to help in their mines."

"It will break rock?"

"In confined spaces."

"Like this cavern?"

Linara nodded.

"Who knows of this? How many have access to this technology?" she asked.

"I—" Linara stammered out. "I wouldn't know."

Nilya released a long breath, still holding the blastcore at her side. She stared around the room, at the maps, the tables and crates. "There is something here that we are missing, but why do I feel as if we were too late—"

A guard burst through the crack in the wall, panting heavily as he squeezed through. "Commander," he shouted, barely able to catch his breath. "We found a chamber. Full of men. And dragons."

Droooooom . . .

The earth shook like a roll of thunder, the echoing roar suffocating all senses. Rhoam tackled Cirena to the floor at Linara's feet, and they huddled together, waiting for the walls to collapse upon them.

The waves of sound faded to silence. Linara cracked open her eyes. Dust filtered through the air, but nothing had collapsed. At least not yet. Nilya and Lorin were back on their feet, eyes scanning every wall, prepared for whatever came next.

A second guard pushed through the crack, face and uniform layered in black dust. His breathing came hoarse and shaken. "They blew out the cavern," he said, wide eyed. "The ceiling was gone."

"They're fleeing?" a soldier said.

"No," Lorin breathed, already moving toward the tunnel exit.

"We were too late," Nilya shouted, following close behind. "Back to your mounts, back to the city! We're under attack!"

A silence passed, an endless second of calm understanding, before the room erupted in motion. Linara glanced briefly at the store of bombs lying on the table, then at the empty crates littered around the chamber. If such a thing could blow open a cavern, what could they do to a city?

"To your posts!" Nilya said, shoving her men through the tunnel. "Protect the city! Protect the king!"

Orvinth Vinhower III sat in his office, staring out the window at the stretch of city and the plains beyond. He didn't often leave space between his bookshelves to see out, and now he remembered why. It was certainly difficult to concentrate, knowing there was a whole world out there. He blew out a breath and focused on the journal before him. He was supposed to be on bed rest. But he was finding his entire life was being defined by not doing what he was supposed to.

Drooom . . .

The tower shook with violence. One, then another, and another. Orvinth clutched at the armrests, watching the walls and the ceiling, waiting for them to cave in. A shadow passed the window. Orvinth stood and crept closer, the pain in his back throbbing at the movement still. He peered out the crack between the bookshelves. Plumes of dust curled out from the streets where buildings had collapsed.

Another shadow darted by, and Orvinth stumbled back. Was that . . . a dragon? The tower shook again, but Orvinth was already through the door. Where was Linara? She was out on her flight. Oh, sun above. Where was the king?

He was too old for this. He started up the slope toward the study. Fingers dug into his pockets, feeling the seeds lying dormant within. He only hoped he had enough.

Chapter Twenty-Five

Chaos.

The soldiers flooded out of the cavern, one by one. Linara looked to Cirena. Cirena looked to Rhoam. Rhoam looked nowhere. Dragons above, caverns below? Where would they flee to? Neither obstacle they could fight. Dust choked them all. No breaths to take. The city was under attack. The capital. Those people. The Spire. The king . . . and Orv.

Linara snapped up, looking for the exit. The last two soldiers slipped through and disappeared. The cavern shook again. Another blast? Or the ground settling after the first one? Rhoam clutched the hilt of his sword, keeping Cirena low. A blue hand entered her vision, faded with dirt. Linara grabbed it.

Raast stood tall. He smiled warmly and touched Rhoam upon the shoulder. "Let us go."

Rhoam stared at the hand, his own shaking upon the hilt of his sword. Then he took it, standing up with renewed strength. He helped up Cirena's huddled form and led her toward the exit. Better to face what lay above than to die by falling rock.

The faint light of the sun guided their path through the cramped hallway. Linara almost tripped on her own shoes in the panic. Had she been so used to the light she couldn't run in the darkness any longer?

They pulled themselves through the tiny opening, back into open air. The dozen griffins were scattered around the plain, startled by the blast. Soldiers scrambled to secure them. In the distance, the city smoked, swarmed with dark figures. Flashes of fire arced through the air from the spined outlines of dragons.

"We have to get to the Spire," Lorin breathed, stepping off toward Aria. Rhoam's hand shot out and grabbed her arm before she could take another step. His other fist clung tightly to Cirena's shoulder.

"You are the nearest soldier to our princess. Your job is to protect her now," he said, voice firm.

"I can protect myself, Rhoam," Cirena yelled, trying to yank free. "The *city* is in danger, not me!"

"Cirena's right," Lorin said, struggling against Rhoam's iron grip. "The Ebon Wings are the best trained for this, and we're five miles from the city. We have to leave *now.*"

"No!" Rhoam yelled, and they all fell still. "Before, it was different. Now, this is war. I cannot protect the princess alone."

"The knight protectorate is correct," Commander Nilya said, turning away from the city. "I do not care who is attacking, or with what. They surely have four targets. The king and Orvinth are secure in the Spire. But you, Princess, and Linara, couldn't be further from safety. If the king falls, you must survive. If you fall, and the king survives, I fear the result might just be the same."

Cirena thrashed at Rhoam's grip. "My father can't die, not yet!"

"Not even *we* can help him now," Nilya said softly. "Once they discover you are here, nothing will stop them from getting to you. Your only path is to slip away undiscovered."

"We won't make it far alone," Rhoam said.

"You'll get Kartridge," Nilya said. "Any more will draw too much attention."

"No, I'm coming with you," Lorin said, pointing to the city.

"I cannot send more than one," Nilya said, voice almost pleading now. "And you, Lorin, are worth three. Do this. Protect them. Then you'll have proven yourself truly worthy of that helmet."

Lorin fell still at that, and nodded silently.

One of the soldiers returned, leading the bridle of Cirena's horse. Rhoam helped Cirena into the saddle before hopping up behind her. "I'm taking Linara and Raast with me. I trust him more than he probably wishes."

Raast shifted uncomfortably. None of them had forgotten Raast's demonstration in the training hall, but what use would any of them be against dragons? Linara stared off at the Spire, wishing she could be there with Orv. Rhoam was right, though. Cirena was more important, and they needed to stick together.

Nilya hoisted a long spike of metal from the saddle of her griffin and fit it atop Aria. The great lances of the aerial guard were wicked things, twice the length of their mount and narrowed to a sharp point. Without such a thing, Nilya would be defenseless.

"Our lances were made for dragon flesh. Use it well," Nilya said, as Lorin mounted. "Listen to the knight protectorate. I don't need to remind you he outranks us both."

Then the commander swung into her saddle and took to the air. The rest of the Ebon Wings followed, a flurry of griffins and black coats flying off to the city under siege. Their lances glinted in the sunlight, a warning and a welcome that help would come.

For Linara and the others, though, it was a reminder that they were now truly alone. Linara's heart thudded wildly, a pulse of heat and fire flickering from her mark. A panicked flame, building to escape, but Linara breathed deep and shoved it down.

Lorin turned toward them, determination burning in her eyes. "I will take Aria and scout ahead. Linara, take Raast and follow Rhoam north toward the mountains. If they spot me and pursue, I'll draw them away."

"You can't just fly off like that," Linara said. "You're the only one here who can actually defend us. We'll be safer together—"

"*You're* not expendable," Lorin said. "I am. You're Odious. You can protect Cirena far better than I can."

Linara's gut twisted. Rhoam was already saddled, Cirena pressed close to his chest. He held Ash's reins out to her. They had no choice, really. Ride back toward a flaming capital city, or away from danger. Somehow, though, that didn't seem like it would be any safer.

Rhoam and Cirena took off before Linara pulled Raast into the saddle behind her. Even Lorin scrambled to take flight to catch up. Linara could tell Ash was skittish, frightened by the explosions in the distance, but once they were in the air, they both seemed to calm.

Rhoam was pushing their horse at full pace, putting as much distance as possible between them and the city before the attack was over. Linara kept low to the ground, hovering a dozen strides from the grass. Lorin flew far ahead, signaling ahead for any ravine Rhoam had to ride around, but each ate up time and slowed their speed.

Linara dared a glance back only once, enough to see the city as little more than a rise upon the horizon. It was clear they had no pursuers, but that still didn't ease any fear.

Aria suddenly jolted up into the air ahead of them, her cry barely audible over the wind. Four great masses rose from the ground, leathery and gray. Dark sinewy wings unfurled and caught the sky like terrible serpents. Wyverns, just like the one in Blackrest.

A scream formed in Linara's throat, but it never came. Instead, she tightened her grip on the reins and tugged them over, pulling Ash off their path as Rhoam did the same. Were they hidden in a cavern? How did they find them?

One peeled off after Cirena and Rhoam, weaving between the hills. Another went for Lorin, circling in the air far above them. The other two came straight for Linara. Raast clung tightly to her waist, and Linara held on just as tight to Ash, who knew they were in danger before any of them could act.

Ash pulled at the air with each flap of his wings, rising high into the sky. Linara barely remembered to guide him. He was moving off instinct alone. She tried to turn to catch a glimpse behind her, but saw nothing.

She heard the piercing cry of a wyvern from the side, a terrible mass of scales and teeth, jaw open wide for the kill. Linara jerked the reins again, but Ash was already trying to dodge out of the path.

A flurry of white feathers appeared from above as Aria dove into the wyvern, the both of them tumbling into a free fall until they landed in a cloud of dirt and dust. Lorin pulled her lance from the dead wyvern and took Aria back to the sky, barreling to the side as a second wyvern crashed through where she had been not a moment earlier.

Linara gasped, wondering how Lorin was alive, processing every event several moments after they happened. Despite all the skill Linara thought she had in flying, she had no right to compare.

Heat rose upon her skin with each ragged breath. There *was* something Linara had that Lorin did not. And she wasn't even prepared to use it.

A storm waged within her mark, unprompted. She just had to let it go, direct it away from Ash and Raast. She promised herself she wouldn't hurt another soul with her mark again, but dragons weren't people, right? They were flying lizards, sent on a mission to rip them apart.

Linara kept her gaze on her own path and flight. One wyvern may be dead, but there were three others still in pursuit. Lorin was dancing between claws and dragon fire overhead, and Linara could see the other still pursuing Rhoam and the horse.

A deafening cry shattered the air above them, and a mass of flailing limbs tumbled through the sky. Wings clipped, the wyvern crashed into the ground with a cloud of dust, its roar falling silent. Two left, then. But where was the other?

Raast cried out and pulled on her shoulder. She turned to see the missing wyvern gliding just above the grass. Teeth bared between twin horns curling around its jaw, it flew to intercept their course. Lorin was too far away now to save them. It was up to Linara.

Linara pulling upon the fire, feeling the memory of Vahn and his hands upon her throat. This time she wouldn't let it go so freely, so chaotically. The flames pooled into her fingertips, directed now, but ready to be free. A jet of fire erupted into the air, bright as the sun. Her mark wavered and emptied of more power than she intended, like a hollow cavern forming in her chest.

The wyvern curled in its wings and hit the wall of flames in a gush of wind. Then it came out the other side, completely unaffected, hind claws outstretched. Linara gasped and yanked back on Ash's reins.

He cried out in surprise as he reared up and flapped hard to stop his flight. Linara barely held on, but she felt Raast slip off. They weren't far up, maybe a dozen feet or more, but he hit the ground and lay motionless as the wyvern spiraled through the space Ash would've been a moment later.

They had to get to Raast. Linara turned Ash around, but the second wyvern appeared then, barreling through the sky like a bolt of lightning. Ash banked out of the snap of open jaws and took off, wings beating furiously to escape the terror.

The dragons didn't pursue. They both flew above Raast's form, circling like vultures. Lorin and Aria kept their distance, waiting for an opening. Raast stirred on the ground below. He wasn't dead, but the wyverns were lying in wait, knowing they wouldn't leave without him.

That was fine. Rhoam and Cirena were a distant blotch on the horizon now, and that was all that truly mattered. If Lorin and Linara fell here, it wouldn't be hard for the dragons to catch up, but any further time they could buy would be a benefit.

Only Lorin, though, had the skills to defend them. Linara's fire was useless, the dragon's leather too hardened for simple flames.

Lorin must've realized this as well. She didn't wait to regroup, instead diving forward with Aria, body pressed low and lance outstretched. Both wyverns lunged toward her. Meeting her attack with their own.

But that left an opening to get to Raast. That must have been her plan all along. Linara spurred Ash straight toward him, urging every drop of speed left in his wings. They touched the ground just as Lorin met the first of her attackers, spiraling out of a plume of dragon fire.

Raast groaned and tried to sit up. He seemed in one piece, but his skin was noticeably paler. His eyes scanned around, finally setting on the battle waging above them.

"Raast, can you hear me?" Linara shouted over the roars splitting the sky.

He nodded, trying to lift his arm. "I believe I am alright. This has been quite exciting."

Linara dropped low to the ground as a wyvern tumbled overhead, wing pinned by Lorin's lance. The lance held firm, and Aria was stuck. The dragon's flailing form struck the ground in a cloud of dirt and dust. Lorin and Aria whipped down with it. Linara gasped and ran toward them.

But the wyvern was still alive somehow. It screeched and thrashed, trying to work broken limbs. Lorin rose from the grass outside its reach. She held her side weakly but pulled a spear from her back. Aria scrambled out of a cloud of dust, wings broken and bloodied. It cried out for Lorin.

Then the wyvern's tail came down, crushing the griffin into the dirt.

Lorin paused slightly in her step. But she wouldn't let that grief overwhelm her. Not yet, at least. She rushed forward, spear in hand. Linara followed close behind. She wouldn't be able to harm the wyvern directly, but she could still help.

The wyvern rose to its feet before collapsing again on a twisted leg. It turned its head toward Lorin, ready to make its stand. Before she closed the distance, Linara slammed her palms against the dry grass and unleashed a jet of fire along the ground. She controlled its spread, snaking a line of embers through the grass until it smoldered just beneath the wyvern's neck.

Then she shoved hard with all her power, sending a billowing pillar of flames underneath its jaw and into its eyes. Dragon scales may be impervious to all but the hottest of flames, but there were still some places that were not covered.

The cry of pain split the air and sent Linara to her knees, but Lorin never stopped. In a flourish of motion, she slid underneath the dragon's mouth and stabbed her spear through its jaw until it broke at the handle. In a moment, its cry was over, and silence filled the air once again.

Linara rose, panted breaths finally coming clear again. She scanned the sky and found the fourth wyvern, a distant shape flying back toward the city.

"Are you alright?" Lorin asked, limping up beside her. Her face was battered and exhausted as she leaned on her last spear.

"I should be asking you that," Linara said, staring off at the corpse of the dragon. "I can't speak for Raast, though. And Aria—"

"She's gone," Lorin said, flatly. "There will be time to grieve later."

Raast met them a moment later, cradling his arm next to Ash. "I believe my arm is broken in half," he said matter-of-factly.

Lorin swung herself into Ash's saddle. "Linara, you'll have to help him ride. Cirena and Rhoam can't have gotten far. Thankfully, they didn't think them of much importance, or they'd surely be dead by now."

"What about the other wyvern?" Linara asked, watching the fourth dragon become a distant dot on the horizon.

"My lance is broken. Best we can do is run fast and hide well. Ash will have to carry all three of us."

"Where do we go? We can't run from them," Linara said.

Lorin's face was impassive. Dirt smudged her face and her clothes, and blood pooled at her side. "No. We can't. But I can name a few places I'd rather be than right here."

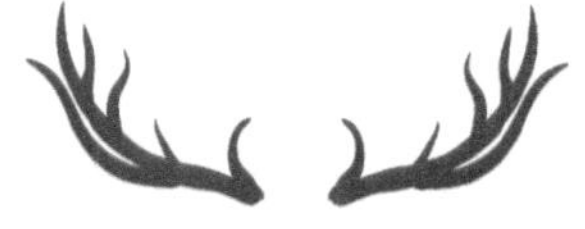

Orvinth Vinhower III cursed softly under his breath, removing his hand from the corpse at his feet. A gold bear helmet lay just beside, ripped from the man's head by the blast that had torn open the wall itself.

At least now there was some quiet. Peace for the dead, and peace for the living. The final silence before the last push. Young Linara and the princess were missing, but Orv had not the strength to think of such things. There was nothing he could do to save them now. Maybe if he was younger. But he was not.

The king stood at his desk, stoic and unafraid, sword point pressed between his feet, ready for the attack. If only Orv felt the same way. Dragons circling the city, soldiers in the palace. From Reginaan, perhaps, but why did it matter? There would be many dead to bury this day.

A great blast burst open the wall, knocking Orvinth to the floor. Soldiers flooded in and were upon the king in a flash. Orvinth couldn't even stand. Curse his age. Curse their attackers. He fumbled in his pockets, feeling only the lumps of a few lowly tree seeds. His mark still thrummed with power, barely dented from the attack. Curse his preparation, stockpiling so much, and for what?

But an idea sprouted from there. One final final plan. It would be quite the way to go. Yes. Stories would speak highly of that.

There was no time to think. The king lashed out with his sword, deflecting a blow, but taking a cut across his arm. Orvinth opened fully to the power, removing all reservations, and all safeguards, letting it flow. It was honey to his bones, pleasure on his skin. The trees grew and molded, *lashing out like extensions of his own limbs. Orvinth drank it in and let it go, laughing all the while.*

Chapter Twenty-Six

They fled west, riding for half a day or more before collapsing at the site of an overturned wagon, the only blemish on an otherwise empty landscape. No dragons pursued them, at least not yet. Rhoam was clear that they would not turn back until allies found them.

The sun dipped below the horizon now, dropping the world into a strange twilight. They traveled far enough to no longer be under its light, but not far enough to be under the stars. The place between Illumination and Blackness, where the world couldn't decide what it wanted to be.

Ash collapsed as soon as Lorin removed his saddle. He wasn't built to carry three, but he did well. He deserved the rest. They all did, though she wasn't certain sleep would come easy.

Linara was sore. The awkward seating brought a new definition to *saddle sore*. Raast had to have been in worse shape, enduring a fall as well as a broken arm. He didn't show any pain, though, even when Lorin wrapped his arm in a makeshift splint. He paced around the cart now, inspecting the wreckage with curious eyes.

Linara had slumped against the flat of the carriage shortly after they arrived. It looked like it was a recent wreck, maybe a few months or more. The wood wasn't rotted, but any wheel marks had long overgrown with moss. What caused it to venture so far from the road? Who cared?

Linara was drained. From both spirit and her mark. Like a basin after patching a leak, she knew that a void was left. She lifted her shirt to catch glimpses of the webbing pattern. It was smaller, no doubt about that. The veins and edges weren't climbing up her neck any longer. She knew she hadn't even used all the flames she gathered at the field fire. Why then did she feel so . . . empty?

The rest of the camp was quiet. Rhoam sat upon the overturned wheel, half embedded into the mossy dirt, sword draped across his knees on vigilant watch. Cirena sat beside him, legs curled up against her chest, silent and brooding.

Linara ran her fingers across the ground, through the dense moss growing against the cart. No tanglegum trees grew out in these plains. No bushes, no plants. No luma or mushrooms, either. The world was pretty uninspiring away from both worlds. Light and dark, vibrant in their own ways. But in between, nothing at all.

She took a fistful of moss. Rough, dry. No movement. No worms or tiny bugs. No signs of life. A few tiny spores clung to the fibers, dormant and waiting for rain, or a particularly dark day. Orv could bring life to the fungi here. It would be easy, just a touch, and the field would be a canvas of stars.

A shudder passed through her. Was Orv still alive? The king safe? Did Nerissa and Artoris make it out with Ferin? Her worries swirled endlessly by the time Lorin returned. Her face hung low, eyes damp and full of grief. She slumped down next to Linara, hard enough to sound painful, but her face only showed a clear sense of relief.

"We should be alright for a few hours," Lorin said, unbuckling her spear and laying it beside her. "We should get some rest while we can."

Linara nodded, but knew she wouldn't sleep. "Do you think every-one's alright?" she asked, looking off toward the distant glow on the horizon, where Avorren lay some miles away now.

"Maybe. The city will be fine. That was no invasion force," Lorin said. "They were after a big target, like Nilya said. If they took out the king, Orvinth, or the princess—or even you—it would make an easy war for them."

"Is that why they planted a trap for us?"

"I'm not so sure that was a trap. If they knew for sure either of you would be there, they would've sent more. But it still almost worked. They must've seen us coming, planted a few scouts behind."

"Thanks to you, it didn't."

Lorin grunted and closed her eyes to the pain. "Thank Aria."

"I'm sorry."

"Don't be. She died well." Lorin sighed and punched the dirt lightly. "Won't say I won't miss her, though. You should thank Ash, too. He saved your skin more than a few times. And pulled more than his own weight in just getting us here."

"Will he be okay?" she asked, watching her slumbering griffin.

"Yeah, he'll be fine. A night's sleep and he can carry us another day or more. He'll just need to catch up on rest after all of this. We all will," she said, looking over and studying her. "You know, I'm surprised that fire didn't work back there."

Linara shrugged. "I heard before that only dragon fire can melt their scales. I can't create that heat even if I wanted to."

Lorin shrugged. "Still, it was a good try."

Raast hobbled over from around the corner, dragging a large crate along the grass with his good arm. He stopped in front of them, dropping it to the dirt with a soft thump, saying nothing as he sat with them.

"What is it?" Lorin asked.

"It is a box," Raast said.

Lorin didn't have the energy to respond. Even Linara found herself not even the least bit curious. Rhoam, though, stood from his post and walked over, pulling out his knife and shoving it into the top. With a twist, the lid cracked off and fell to the ground. Rhoam pulled out a clay blastcore, and Lorin and Raast both scooted a few strides away.

"At least we know whose cart this was," Rhoam said, tossing the bomb to Linara, who barely caught it.

Lorin pulled herself to peer inside. "Probably on its way to Rivead."

Linara turned the bomb over in her hands, inspecting it for the first time up close. The clay seemed smooth and seamless, except for a small rope wick poking out of one end. These were made to be set off at a distance.

The dragons have protection against heat, sure, but what about other types of power? How much force could this expel, if it could crack rocks as easily as Nymin claimed? They could be useful, if she could take a few safely.

Linara heaved herself up. She pulled out a handful of straw, rubbing it between her fingers. It was dry, for sure, and offered ample padding, but other than that, she couldn't figure out anything else special about it.

Linara gathered another handful and packed it around the bomb, covering the clay completely before sliding it in one of her deep coat pockets. It hit another thick object within and Linara flinched back. She fished inside and pulled out a glowing ruby sphere of quartz. The gift from Nymin in the lab. She'd forgotten all about it.

Linara slid it into a separate pocket, far from the bomb. She twisted and walked a few steps, feeling the weight within, and decided it wasn't too inconvenient. Five more fit in a few other pockets, all with room to spare for the clasps to be fashioned.

Linara turned back to the cart to see Lorin's pale face. "You're taking some with us?"

"Why not?" Linara asked.

"I can name a few reasons."

Linara shrugged and sat beside her. "It'll be the best defense we have against another wyvern."

"Yeah, but—" Lorin cut herself off. "I mean . . . it's still . . . unnerving."

"And *I'm* not? I could explode with fire whenever I want to," Linara said.

"*You* won't explode if we drop you the wrong way," Lorin said.

"To be fair, we've never found that out," Linara said.

Lorin shuddered and leaned back. "Do whatever you want . . ." she mumbled.

Linara lay out on the moss and closed her eyes. Her mind raced, despite the fatigue resting firmly on her bones. How could she sleep in such a place, so far from home, so far from everything? She wished everything to be back the way it was.

Except, how far back would that be? Before the attack? Before the troupers? Before Avorren, and Vahn, and Nelbren?

A distant roar split the sky and echoed across the plains, fading back into silence as the camp grew painfully still. It sounded far deeper than the cries of the wyverns, and too distant to be any danger to them now, but it still came from something far more massive than they'd seen so far.

Linara met Rhoam's eyes, and he stood, circling the camp before returning with no news. "What was that?" Linara asked, but nobody answered. It really didn't need to be answered, for she knew it did not come from a griffin, or even a simple wyvern. At least it didn't come from the direction of the city, but now they were riding straight into it, toward the mountains and whatever dragon was calling its family home. A friendly reminder that they weren't yet out of danger.

Thatcher stood amid a field of feasting dragons, gripping the report in a tight fist. A void was forming within him. Deep. Endless. He missed Kurtrus. What had all this turned into? The stench of feld and sulfur hung on his tongue like a bed of moss.

Five weeks crawling through the underground, finding paths that could fit dragons. Even with feld, dragons didn't do well without the sky. It almost ended in disaster. And after all of that, did it end much better? So many dead.

He missed the old days. He missed the simplicity. He missed the troupe.

Thatcher forced himself away from such droll thoughts as a wyvern shrieked past. Regret was just weakness, and he needed to be indomitable. Not just a front for the dragons, but for what men he had left.

The attack on Avorren hadn't been enough of a guarantee. To start a war, they'd need the princess, or that Odious girl. Either would be a success, and both would bring a sizable raise. Enough for him to finally cut his course and leave Aldebraan behind. Except he said that the last payout. And the one before that.

This was just another performance, another script to follow. All journeys had twists and turns. Thatcher just had to be patient. Twice now they escaped his grasp, but not a third. They could run for now, but not forever.

CHAPTER TWENTY-SEVEN

Linara awoke with a start, her eyes heavy, but still searching for danger. The camp was calm, Ash slowly rising to a stand beside Lorin as she tied the straps of his saddle. Rhoam was doing the same to his horse, and Raast slowly paced through the camp, expressionless. Cirena crouched over her, ready to shove her awake again.

"Are we leaving?" Linara asked, words slurred and groggy.

"Soon. We need to get to Rivead."

Linara yawned and stretched her stiff limbs. Now even her neck was sore, pressed up against the cart for so long. However long they'd been there, it certainly wasn't long enough. Even Ash and the horse seemed exhausted to even be awake, let alone be moving out so soon.

"I'm surprised you slept," Cirena said, helping her up.

"Me too. It took me three weeks to sleep through the night in the Spire." Linara checked the sky. There was no moon out, but she wasn't sure what time they even got to the camp.

Cirena seemed to know what she was thinking. "It's been a few hours."

Linara sighed but forced out a laugh. "We'll sleep when this is over, right?"

"I really wish that wasn't exactly what Rhoam told me a few minutes ago," Cirena said. She sighed and shook her head. "He's a real ass when he's like this, but I suppose that's why I'm alive."

Linara laughed. "I'm starting to think that's why we're *all* alive."

"Maybe true," she said, averting her gaze. "I wanted to apologize, by the way. I hate when Rhoam's right, but I shouldn't have put you all in danger."

"You don't need—" Linara tried to say.

"No. If I let Rhoam do his job and keep me out of that hideout, Lorin's griffin wouldn't be dead, Raast's arm wouldn't be broken, and we wouldn't be camped out in the wilderness."

"It was my idea, as well," Linara said. Memories flooded in, of the smoldering city, the broken Spire and the swarm of dragons spouting fire all across the city streets. "Maybe we were lucky, in the end. Maybe being out here really *was* the safer place to be." Cirena's eyes went unfocused and dark. She wasn't the only one with somebody to lose back home. "I'm sure he's fine," Linara said, swallowing the pit in her own throat. "I'm sure they both are."

Cirena was silent for a long time. "I thought I had another twenty years to stop fooling around. It wasn't supposed to happen this quickly. I'm not ready yet."

"I'm sure he's fine," Linara said, more firmly.

Cirena sucked in a ragged breath. "If I'm reckless and stupid with the people I'm closest to, how much more will I be for the people in this kingdom? It all falls to me, and I'm not a character in a fairy tale."

Linara wanted to object, but she didn't know what to say. Who was she to know what it was like? So she let Cirena stand and walk back toward Rhoam, regretting saying nothing but knowing she couldn't change her mind either way.

Raast appeared around the corner of the cart, straight backed and far more awake than he had any right to be.

"How are you not dead tired like the rest of us?" Linara finally asked, rubbing at her eyes. "It's almost annoying."

"Luman-Viri do not feel tiredness," he said. "We will begin to work slower until our bodies shut themselves off and we collapse."

"Oh," she said, wishing she never asked. "Good to know."

"I have seen shapes on the horizon," Raast said, looking out over the cart. "Do you think it is the commander, or the return of those dragons?"

Linara scrambled to her feet and tried to follow his gaze. If she focused hard enough, she could spot the small blotches just over the clouds. She would never have noticed. If they were griffins or dragons or whatever new unsightly creatures may be on their tail, she hoped Raast wasn't the first to notice.

She hurried over to Lorin, inspecting Ash and the saddle one final time. "Rhoam spotted them a little while back," Lorin said, glancing at the horizon before pulling the last strap tight. "We're not taking any chances. I'd rather be in Rivead before we find out who they are."

Linara nodded and busied herself with the preparations, which admittedly wasn't much. They had no camp to pack up, and no possessions to secure. Once Lorin was up in Ash's saddle, Linara helped Raast into the seat in front of her, then scrambled up herself. She'd never been so consciously aware of her discomfort. The saddle wasn't made for three people, and her legs stretched in the same unimaginable way as yesterday.

Rhoam had made sure everything was ready like clockwork, everyone ready to head out within minutes of waking. They started off from the overturned cart with speed, Rhoam breaking into a full gallop as soon as his horse was able. Ash surprisingly made no complaint. He seemed happy just to be on the move again.

Despite the anxiety looming behind them, and the fresh wind whipping across her cheeks, Linara could barely keep her eyes open. Even sitting nearly off the back of the saddle was barely uncomfortable enough to not drift off. They weren't *that* high up, and Raast survived *his* tumble to the ground, right? Surely it wouldn't be that much more unpleasant than staying awake the next several hours, right?

Linara let her eyes flicker shut and drifted off, just long enough to feel herself nearly slip from the saddle. She scrambled back into her seat, pulling on Raast's good arm to steady herself. She thanked him and rubbed the tiredness from her eyes.

The hours passed slowly, and nobody talked. The distant mountain range grew larger on the horizon, a great sheet of rock that blocked their path. If the mining town was truly at the base of the mountains, they weren't too far at all.

But neither were their pursuers. The distant spots behind them grew quickly, forming the shapes of griffins in full flight directly toward them. Linara couldn't tell who rode atop them, but Lorin seemed convinced that it wasn't anybody friendly. So they rode on, pushing every ounce of speed out of their exhausted animals, a careful balance of haste and endurance.

On a good day, a griffin could outrun a horse twice over, but Linara could tell Ash was too tired to outrun a field hare, even without three passengers. By the time the mining town came into view, a small collection of buildings on the otherwise flat plains, Linara could see the feathers on the griffins pursuing them. The helmets of their riders didn't *look* like the Avorren guard, and when Linara asked Lorin about it, she said nothing at all. That was clear enough of an answer.

"Will we make it?" Linara asked over the rush of wind.

"I doubt it," Lorin said, after a long pause.

Linara glanced back, the nearest griffin barely a half mile away now, the smallest of details too visible for Linara's comfort. "Isn't there something we can do?"

"I have no lance, Ash is exhausted, and I can't outmaneuver anything with three people on his back," Lorin yelled back. "You could hurl fire at them, but I know you said you didn't have much left."

Linara definitely had more than she let on, but those griffins had riders. Was she willing to face the idea of killing another person, again? Was it worse than the death of of all of them? Probably not. She wouldn't be able to do anything from this distance anyway, without emptying her mark of everything within.

Linara felt at the blastcores, nestled firmly inside her pockets. Perhaps there was a way to help. "I have an idea," she said, carefully pulling out the first clay sphere and brushing away the straw. Lorin visibly stiffened, but kept her gaze ever forward.

"I can light these, but I can't throw them . . . I'm not strong enough." That wasn't a complete lie, but if she didn't throw them, their deaths were not from her hands. Not directly. She could live with that.

"I'm a little occupied," Lorin said back.

Linara glanced around. Raast was barely holding on with one good arm. Cirena was pressed into the saddle too tight to turn around. "Rhoam, you'll have to."

He looked up, and then back at the griffins, nodding firmly as he handed the reins to Cirena.

"Wait until the wick burns low enough," Linara said. "Otherwise it will just hit the ground behind them."

"Easy for you to say," he shouted back. "You won't be the one holding a bomb!"

Linara didn't respond. If they tried too soon, the bombs wouldn't reach them; too late, and they'd be caught in the same blast. She watched her pursuers closely until they were nearly upon them. Linara inhaled a deep breath and lit the first wick, tossing it to Rhoam, who caught it gingerly in both hands.

Seconds passed like an eternity, and only Cirena and Lorin kept their glances on from the road long enough to keep their paths straight. Rhoam gritted his teeth and tossed the bomb behind him in a final grunt that sent it flying fast toward the griffins, still gaining from behind.

It blew halfway through the distance, bursting open with a sharp crack that split the very air around her ears. There was no flash of light, no other sign that anything happened at all, but one of the griffins chasing them cried out in pain, blood spurting out from its wings as it lost control and tumbled to the ground in a cloud of dirt. The force of the blast itself could probably kill any of them, but the shards of clay seemed to be the true danger.

Linara's heart fell and her stomach turned sick as she grabbed another bomb. It couldn't be helped, she told herself, over and over and over again as she lit the next wick and tossed it over to Rhoam. He threw them; the magisters invented them. She just lit the rope. Not her hands doing the job.

The other griffins peeled off and separated, flying as high and as far to the side as they dared without losing their prey. They wouldn't make the mistake of flying into the bombs again, but maybe it would be enough to delay them before they made it to the town. There they could hide and bunker down, fight on even ground.

Rhoam threw the next one, but overshot, the core bursting apart far after the griffins flew past. Linara didn't hesitate to light the next one, and each one after. They fell into a steady, careful rhythm. The griffins dodged around Rhoam's throws, but the bombs were so small they were impossible to see once they left his hand. His timing grew more precise, each blast growing closer and closer with every throw.

But it did no further good. The first bomb gave them valuable time, enough to nearly make it into the town, but the griffins were close enough to see the faces on the riders. Linara did not look at them, did not look into the eyes of their pursuers as she lit another bomb, the last they would throw. It would hardly matter. It was up to Ash's speed and Cirena's riding now.

Rhoam fingered the blastcore, teeth clenching. He glanced at the nearest griffin, only a few dozen paces behind them, and closing. He tossed the bomb straight into the air; the sphere flashing out of sight as they rode on. The timing was irrelevant, as the bomb struck the rider straight in the helmet and exploded by sheer impact.

The man's head hit the ground before the rest of his body, and Linara forced herself to look away, clinging to Raast's waist.

The flat landscape turned to moss mounds and stone buildings. The road, though, was empty, and they passed each building in a blur, barely slowing.

Lorin glanced back. "That seemed too easy."

"Don't question, just react," Rhoam said. "Where do we go?"

"Where are all the people?" Linara asked, trying to look into the houses as they rode by. No light shone through the dark streets from any windows or chimneys. It looked empty and abandoned.

"I do not think this place is safe," Raast said.

"No," Lorin agreed. "Maybe we can hole up in one of these houses until reinforcements arrive."

"Wherever we go, they'll bring an army," Rhoam said.

"We don't have many options," Lorin said, starting off toward the nearest building.

A gigantic mass flew up above the mountains, casting the world into a deeper shadow. A great wyvern, dark as the Blackness sky, unfurled two massive wings and beat against the sky. Spines crossed its back, each the size of a griffin, and sharper than any lance. No spikes ornamented its jaw, but it did not need any. Its teeth were bared, and snarling, glowing with the inner deep of liquid flames. It hovered there above the mountains, a terrifying silhouette of their doom, watching. Waiting.

"That can't be a dragon," Linara breathed.

"A cardinal dragon," Lorin said.

"The missing Dragon of the West," Linara said, putting the pieces together.

"Then we're out of options," Rhoam said.

"Not completely," Lorin said, yanking Ash around and heading straight toward the hovering wyvern and the mountains behind it. "Into the mines!"

Don't question, just react. The mine entrance lay at the end of the road, a hole in the rock twice the size of any griffin. They would fit, they'd have to.

The Dragon of the West unleashed a heaven-crushing roar. It curled in its wings and dove down the mountainside, knowing where they rode and knowing it could catch up. It opened its jaws and roared out a mighty jet of flame. White, liquid, dragon fire. Even Linara could feel the heat of the flames as it fell.

Linara prepared to absorb it. Would she even be able to? She didn't have to find out. Ash pulled out a final burst of speed and flew just under the torrent as it exploded into the streets. The dragon landed with a quake of the earth behind them, already rearing up for another jet of fire.

They passed through the mine entrance before it had a chance. Ash touched down in a staggered landing, nearly throwing Linara and Raast from the saddle entirely. He collapsed onto the rock, too tired to continue any farther, and Rhoam's horse was in no better shape.

Lorin leapt from the saddle, stumbling as she caught her footing. With one fluid motion, she pulled her spear from her back and readied her shield, Rhoam already beside her with sword at the ready.

"It's too big to fight," Linara protested, scrambling off Ash's back.

"We don't have a choice," Rhoam said simply.

"There's always some kind of choice," Linara said, reaching in her pocket for the last of the blastcores. "I can collapse the tunnels."

Rhoam looked at Lorin, then at Cirena, and nodded firmly. "Then do it."

"But—" Cirena said, stumbling to her feet.

"Don't argue, just do it!"

Linara was already running, lighting the wick before she even made it to the entrance. Massive wooden supports ran from the floor and across the ceiling. Linara shoved the bomb behind one of the beams and sprinted back as fast as her legs could carry her. The first pursuing griffin landed outside the tunnel and started inside when the bomb burst apart. The thunder crack blew Linara off her feet, an avalanche of rock and stone cascading around her.

Linara curled upon herself in the darkness, listening to the fall of boulders slow to a trickle, the echoes fading to silence. She worked herself to her feet, and tried to call out for the others, but a cloud of dust sent her coughing and struggling for breath. Her ears were still ringing, but she could hear a voice call her name from down the tunnel.

One hand pressed to the wall, Linara moved slowly, careful about what she would find in the darkness. She collided with a wall of feathers. Ash still lay curled against the ground, exhaustion proving stronger than his fear of the cave-in. His breathing was slow, but deep. She sighed and buried her face in his coat, half-crying, half-laughing in some mix of relief and panic.

A soft light illuminated the cave, the cloud of dust like a blanket of fog around them. Rhoam held another sphere of quartz, this one larger than his hand, glowing a bright white. Cirena knelt beside him, tears flowing freely, clumping dirt and dust across her cheeks. Linara didn't feel much better. Lorin was already checking the nearby walls for exits.

Ash was alright, still barely awake, but unscathed. The horse, though, was dead. Crushed by an unlucky boulder. The tunnel entrance was truly closed off, small rocks still tumbling down the landslide as everything settled. Nobody would be getting through there for a long while, but Linara just hoped it wasn't the only entrance.

Linara covered her mouth with her coat and forced herself to breathe deep. Even in the darkness, at least they were safe. Safe from a cardinal dragon, trapped under a mountain leading stars knew where.

"You've let my prey escape."

It was the sound of boulders. The sound of Irea itself grinding beneath the mountain. It was the sound of Kraktaal, the Dragon of the West, speaking the words of men. Most of his men were afraid of the dragons. Thatcher, though, knew them to be beasts of oaths and honor. As long as the deal still held with Herald Rendei, they were safe. Still, Kraktaal was a wild variable. No amount of feld could calm him.

"If their bodies are not intact, the pact becomes broken," Thatcher said, rubbing the bronze tile between his fingers. "I will remind you of that after you nearly incinerated them."

The dragon grumbled, a deep sound that shook Thatcher's chest like a taut drum.

"Find them, little Graakling, or I will break the mountain apart."

Then the Dragon of the West leapt off with a flap of wings that blew apart the ruined buildings. Thatcher breathed in deep, remembering the smell of sulfur and feld. Remembering what it meant to fail. Kraktaal tearing apart the mountain would be the death of all of them, if Thatcher did not find the princess first.

Chapter Twenty-Eight

Beneath the smothering darkness, under rock and stone, there was no time. No movement of air, no feeling of life. Seconds passed like thick mud, hours felt like days. There was no moon, no sun, no stars to guide the passing minutes. Only the faint, unnatural glow of quartz. Who knew how long it would last. No one wished to ask.

Rhoam studied a worn map under that light now, nailed to a wooden frame against the stone of the tunnel wall. They had walked some miles since the entrance. Ash had fallen asleep again, collapsing as soon as they stopped to rest. That was only a few minutes ago now. Probably. Or maybe hours.

They had moved down the main mining path, hoping to find an exit somewhere along the way. They passed several other paths, tunneling further into the mountain, but where they truly led, only the map would tell. The longer Rhoam studied it, though, the more hope faded.

The mine itself seemed abandoned. Rivead wasn't supposed to be empty. It was a thriving town a few months back. At least, it was enough to justify sending experimental magister tech. Were they just another causality of this engagement? Another list of the dead in this impending war? Dragons ate many things, Nerissa had told her once. And that list never excluded people. Linara shuddered and tried to think of other things.

Rhoam's eyes were heavy, weighed down by a sleepless night. Cirena wasn't faring much better. She held the quartz torch over Rhoam's shoulder, casting white light upon dark, puffy eyes. Cirena never hid things well. Linara could see the anger, the regret, and the guilt.

"It looks like there's a path to the other side," Rhoam said, finally stirring.

"Finally," Lorin mumbled with a heavy sigh.

"It starts here," he said, dragging his finger along one of the dark-colored lines, "then runs down through the first four main shafts cutting across much of the mountain before climbing back up to an exit."

"That's a long way," Lorin said, studying the map beside him. "We'd be in the middle of the mountains. Does anyone even know where? This main shaft is an old underground river, it doesn't look like they bothered exploring that deep."

"Unless you want to try your luck down this ore elevator, it's really our only option," Rhoam said, gesturing to the wide hole burrowed deep into the earth, a single chain descending to its depths, attached with pulleys to a room across the way.

"There's no mule pulling the rope. We'd be climbing down by hand," Lorin said, kicking a stone over the edge. It took far too long for the echo to return.

"It was a joke," Rhoam said softly

"It looks like there are other entrances this side of the mountain. I'm sure some of those griffin riders found one of them by now," Lorin said.

"Then we should leave quickly," Rhoam said, shouldering his pack.

Linara sighed and hesitated to stand. A few minutes of rest, just to walk another day or more. And what waited for them then?

"If we make it to the other side, where would we go?" she asked, almost to herself. She looked to Rhoam, to Lorin, Cirena, and Raast, to anyone who might have the answer. But nobody did.

"She's right, Rhoam," Cirena said. "What *does* come next?"

"It doesn't matter," Rhoam said. "What matters is that we survive long enough for help to come."

"*Will* help come?" Linara asked.

"We can't stay here," Rhoam said. "It's no longer safe."

"It's not safe *anywhere*, Rhoam," Cirena said.

"And what would you have me do?" Rhoam yelled. "Give up? Stop fighting?"

"I'd have you be realistic," Cirena said, softly. She had no strength to fight. None of them did.

"My last breath will be to protect you, Princess," Rhoam said, looming over her. "If I fail, it will be because I have none left. So we keep going."

A painful silence fell as his words softly echoed across the stone wall. Cirena stared back with quivering defiance, but Linara wasn't sure how long she could keep it up.

"Even I'll admit," Lorin said, the only one bold enough to speak. "None of *us* have much life left. We've given it a good run."

Rhoam wiggled the flat of his knife under the frame of the map, trying to wiggle it free. "My duty is to protect the princess. Stay if you wish, but we will be going."

Lorin sighed and reached out to stop him. "Fine, but we have a better chance of surviving if we take the time to think about where we're moving first. We're better off hiding than running."

"We can't hide here," Rhoam said. "No one would ever find us, even our own allies."

"Then we don't hide in the mine," she said. "They'll expect us to go through it, but what if we turn around and come out of it first?"

"Back toward the dragon?" he asked.

"Back toward the last place they'd look," Lorin said.

"Into Rivead?" Linara asked.

"No, too far now that the main entrance is sealed," Rhoam said, carefully considering. "But that doesn't mean Lorin's wrong."

"This mountain is pocked like a honeycomb," Lorin said, "There are caves and tunnels jutting out everywhere. Some link up to this mine, but most do not."

Rhoam actually considered this idea. It was the first he'd considered any idea since the attack began.

"We have a better chance on this side of the mountain," Lorin continued. "The minute we step out the other side, we'll be swarmed by a dozen wyverns."

"Yes, you're right," Rhoam finally said.

"That's a first," Cirena mumbled.

Rhoam whirled on her, and Cirena leapt up in surprise. "Princess, I consider it a blessing that I can be your friend, but remember that I treat that as a second priority. If I've done something to offend you, I ask that you learn to forgive me, for I will not apologize."

Rhoam turned and finished prying the map off the wall, the same painful silence hanging heavy in the air. Linara found no difficulty in standing now, and quickly prodded Ash awake, plunging a hand beneath his feathered coat. This was quite the first day for the griffin. Was he expecting such a life when he stamped out that fire? Hopefully, he wouldn't live to regret his choice.

She scratched at a spot behind his neck, causing a long, pleasing shudder to pass through his body. That got him awake, and he stood quickly, nudging her over with his head before shaking out the rest of his feathers. No, perhaps that was not much of a worry. She could tell he did not enjoy the monotonous life in the hatchery.

Rhoam slid the map into this pack and pulled a long knife from his belt. It cast a glow upon the walls where the metal glinted against the quartz light. He stepped to Raast, but the Luman-Viri backed away, knowing the intent before Rhoam said a word.

"Please, Raast. I know you said you will not, but please stay near Cirena. For me. If anything happens. Please."

Raast stared at the blade, as if he were being handed a viper. Then he looked to Rhoam, and his face softened at once. "I will do this thing. Just this once. For you."

"I should have gotten you a proper blade," Rhoam said. "But that is the best I can offer."

Raast held the knife at arm's length, staring at his reflection in the flat of the blade. "I am glad that you did not."

Rhoam ushered Cirena forward, and they started up a sloping path. Linara glanced at the tunnel, a lower ceiling than the one they traveled now. Ash ruffled his wings and pecked at a stone, curious and a bit anxious. "Will Ash fit?"

"These tunnels are made for carts big enough to haul ore and stone," Rhoam said from ahead. "He'll be fine."

Fine? Probably not the right word. Ash was happy to be moving, and maybe content being away from the hatchery, but the underground was no place for a griffin. Even Linara felt uncomfortable without open sky. The walls were too close. There was nowhere to move except forward and backward.

At least Lorin had some sympathy. She smiled weakly and guided Linara up the path, taking the rear with her last spear at the ready. Always moving, never stopping. At least now their destination led them to some rest. Maybe there they could finally sleep. How long would they hide? Until every cavern of this mountain was searched and until their legs gave out and the dragon caught up? Linara kept hold of Ash's bridle, if anything just to keep her own footing.

Their path twisted up into the mountain. She knew they'd have to venture deeper to get out, but that thought seemed terrifying. The walls were solid rock. No wonder the blastcores were so useful here. Rhoam was right, though. The tunnel did not shrink in the slightest, and Ash fit comfortably. More thought was put into these tunnels than Linara thought, each curve and turn carved with intention. Maybe the map could be trusted, after all.

The walls glistened with water, dripping into small puddles forming in the indents in the rock. Those tiny noises, the heavy footfalls, the pebbles kicked along the stone were the only sounds that broke the silence.

Hours passed, Linara's thoughts dragging themselves in circles, from despair to hope and back again. Nothing about the tunnels changed, and they climbed forever. Up and up, and deeper and deeper until the maw of the mountain would eat them whole. She was tired. Tired and horrendously afraid.

The crack of wood and the echo of voices broke Linara from her thoughts. Rhoam had stopped ahead of them, daring not a single step further. They were no longer alone.

An orange glow appeared down a branching tunnel ahead, faint hints of a flickering flame cutting through the darkness. Underground like they were, such light could spread far. There was no telling just how close they were. But whoever held the firelight could see Rhoam's quartz light just the same.

He clamped his hands over the crystal, trying to smother the light, but tiny beams crept through his fingers. The voices were growing louder now, faint echoes of sounds drifting across the rocks. They came from nowhere, and everywhere.

A voice called out from ahead, loud and deep, asking for an update on the search. Rhoam looked at them, searching for an answer, but nobody had one. The voice called up again, more hurried and angry.

"Nothing up here," Rhoam yelled back, wincing. "Just a lot of . . . rocks."

"Hah, ain't that the truth?" the voice called back. "Stay there. We'll link back up with you."

"Negative," Rhoam called back, frantically waving everyone forward. "We're going to loop back around, see if they slipped past."

They moved quietly, slowly, trying to move past the branching tunnel. A long pause came as a response. "Loop back . . .?" The voice mumbled, before yelling. "Who are you?"

"Run," Rhoam whispered back to them, breaking into a sprint up the long stretch of tunnel. It took a few short, agonizing moments for them to respond, but they all followed, pushing their legs as hard as they could through the rocky terrain.

"Oh, shit," the voice yelled. "Gen, get up there, you're closer!"

They passed the tunnel entrance, quartz-light bobbing frantically down the path, but Linara kept her eyes on the floor below her. Rocks jutted out in odd patterns, and every footfall could very well be her last if she caught it the wrong way. Rhoam was moving too quickly, sending beams of quartz-light in all directions with every heavy footfall.

A soldier burst out of the tunnel path ahead, sword at the ready. Linara barely had time to react, flinching back and under just as the sword passed above her head. Her foot caught on a rock a second later, sending her sprawling to the tunnel floor. She scrambled forward, daring a glance back as the soldier brought the sword down toward her head.

Ash cried out, trying to scramble back, but the tunnel was too small for him to move swiftly. Linara winced, eyes clamping shut to prepare for the blow. But it never fell.

Lorin's shield slammed out against the blade as she leapt over. The spear pulled smoothly from her back, and Lorin thrust forward. Once. Twice. Three times. The soldier pedaled back, defending each blow until his back hit the wall. Lorin jabbed her spear into the man's gut with a spurt of dark blood. His body slumped lifeless, leaving a dark stain against the stone. Dead. Just like that.

Linara couldn't tear her eyes away. Another soldier darted out from the adjoining tunnel, but Lorin was too slow to react. She couldn't get her shield up in time as the soldier charged, sword pointed straight for her heart.

A blue form darted in, and Raast grabbed the soldier's arm, yanking him back. His screams died upon his lips, as Raast spun around his back, jabbing his knife between the plates of his armor, one in the armpit, two in the side, and then a dread line across his throat.

The guard slumped, lifeless before he hit the stone.

Linara scrambled away from the corpse, eyes finding Raast, slack-jawed and shaking. His eyes were locked with the knife thick with blood. It clattered to the floor, and he shuddered into silence, arms folded around himself

Lorin caught her bearings first. She grabbed both their arms and dragged them down the tunnel before anyone could process a word. Ash stuck close this time, his bridle clamped in his own beak. More soldiers flooded into the tunnel behind them, but they did not slow for their fallen comrades.

Rhoam and Cirena hadn't slowed, either. He had warned them, after all, all those months ago. He would not hesitate to choose between them and the princess. His quartz light was barely visible, providing barely enough light to see where they stepped.

The tunnel straightened, and Lorin broke into a sprint, dragging the others with her. Light burst out ahead of Rhoam as another group of soldiers cut off their route. They all skid to a stop, huddled together with panting breaths.

Cirena was shoved back against the wall, Rhoam and Lorin setting themselves as the final defense on either side. Raast, now weaponless, didn't look in any shape to help. A dozen men surrounded them on either side. Against so many, they wouldn't stand a chance.

The soldiers didn't hesitate to attack. Rhoam and Lorin both fell into their own dances, fending them off. It was clear they were outmatched, not in skill but in numbers. The tunnel was only so wide, but neither of them escaped each wave of attack without lost ground or some wound. Even courageous Ash stood his ground, lashing out with wing and beak at any who came close, but the walls were too confined for him to help, and he knew it.

"Linara," Lorin shouted over the crash of steel. "Do something!"

What did she want her to do? Fill the whole cave with fire? Did she even have the control for that? It would burn Lorin and Rhoam just as much as the others. Rhoam stumbled and cried out as a spear clipped his leg. Lorin grunted as a sword cut across her shoulder.

"Linara," Cirena said, shoving her forward. "They need you."

She was right; they did. If she did nothing, they would die. But if she acted . . .

Even in the battle's chaos, Linara could see the faces of their attackers. Men, with lives just the same as their own. How many had families? Who were they, and whose orders did they follow? Linara had been in this place before. She took the path that ended Vahn's life, but at the cost of Trel and Pen. Would she do it again?

Yes. Because she was not alone. It was not just her life, but the lives of those around her. Those she cared about.

A spear cracked down against Lorin's helmet, and she crumpled to the ground, unmoving. "Linara!" Cirena shouted, as soldiers moved over her toward them at once. Rhoam tried to close the gap, but he took a sword across his arm and dropped to his knees, crying out in pain as blood poured across the stone.

Soldiers closed in and Linara acted. Curse her indecision. Creating flames from nothing used far more of her source than she was willing to part with, but she still had one last trick in her pockets. Linara clasped her hands around Nymin's quartz and, without hesitation, threw it up against the ceiling.

It shattered instantly, flames pouring out like dragon fire. Linara was ready for it. The flames hit her hands first, and she took control, shoving them out. Away from Ash and her friends.

The firelight blinded her, engulfing the tunnel walls, pouring like water. It slammed into the guards, searing armor and flesh. No distinction between. Chilling screams split the air, sharper than the roar of the flames, and Linara could not close off her ears to the noise.

The flames died and extinguished to nothing. She gasped and fell to her knees. Smoke filled her nose, the stench of burning flesh and metal. Bodies lay smoldering around her, where living men once stood. Linara retched dry air onto the stone, nothing to come up with it.

Someone was calling for her, distant and muffled. They took her arm, pulling her up and away. She couldn't help but look down, stepping over the blackened bodies at her feet. That was a mistake. Linara nearly stumbled as her stomach lurched again, but a hand caught her mid stride. It was Cirena, face ashen and pale.

Linara allowed herself to be pulled along until the air was clear enough to breathe. Ash followed close behind, oblivious, feathers singed, but unharmed. Rhoam carried Lorin's weakened body in his arms, struggling up the path toward the faint daylight streaming through ahead. Blood poured from his arm, and Lorin struggled to remove the bronze stag helmet from her head. Linara caused that. Hesitancy caused injury, and if she'd waited even longer, they both would've surely died.

Linara's gut clenched, and she tried to forget the fight and the smell and everything that went with it. She wanted to stop, to crawl into a ball in the darkness and never be seen again, but she kept running, knowing that she owed them something now, a debt to be paid for her negligence.

"Everything's spinning," Lorin said, clamping her eyes shut.

"You took that blow pretty hard," Rhoam said through his panting breaths. "Linara took out the rest."

Linara's heart thudded loud, and she choked back a sob. Pushing through the sorrow and the guilt, she could see what responsibility the mark gave her. They could've done better if she just acted sooner. Linara pulled it in, steeling herself against the pain and the sorrow. Those men were dead by her hand, but now her friends were alive. She broke one promise and made another. No man or woman would die by her hand, unless it was to save another.

Linara steeled herself to make that decision again. Their enemies were catching up. She'd have to kill more. She wasn't sure she would be ready, but there was no choice. At least they'd be free of the confining tunnels soon. But what would they be walking into?

The faint twilight of the outside world expanded until they cleared the final rocky walls of the mine shafts and stepped back onto the mountainside. A much lower-to-the-ground mountainside than they expected, with only a few short strides to the flat mossy plains. They stood at the end of a small valley, a ravine between the mountains where the grassy plains snuck in to take hold. Rhoam craned his neck up to check above them, but the wall was sharp and impossible to climb in any direction.

Dark, deep clouds rolled overhead, bathing the world in shadow. The world wasn't much brighter than the tunnels, but at least fresh air and open skies were available to them now.

There were no signs of dragons. No wyverns or griffins or enemy soldiers patrolled the air, and no torchlight searched upon the mountainside. Lorin was right, the soldiers were all expecting them on the other side, but how soon would that change? Just one griffin or wyvern could spot them from a thousand paces from where they stood, and there weren't many better options.

"The walls aren't twisting as much as they were. Put me down," Lorin said, forcing her way out of Rhoam's arms. She hit the ground and wobbled before catching her footing and standing mostly tall. "I'll just have to vomit a few times on the way, but I'll be alright."

"What now?" Cirena asked.

Rhoam ignored both of them, staring off at the plains with a stare that stretched for miles. "I do not know."

Lorin staggered and caught herself on Linara's arm. "Nothing too uphill, I hope . . ."

"No. We move forward across the plains," Rhoam said.

"That's suicide," Cirena said.

Rhoam's quartz flickered twice before the light went out entirely. "If we go back in, we lose ourselves in the darkness. We're not much of a fighting force here anymore, unless Linara has more tricks to pull from her coat pockets, but I doubt you have much fire left in you to last."

Linara was efficient that last time around, but she didn't interrupt to correct him. Cirena gasped as torchlight appeared around the corner of the tunnel behind them, faint, but growing with each passing moment. Even if they wanted to turn back, that option was now closed.

"Let's go," Rhoam said, ushering Cirena ahead of him before sliding down the gravel slope. Linara followed, helping Raast down before trying to catch up. Linara's legs already burned from their flight through the tunnels. Ash wasn't faring much better. He desired to be in the air, but he couldn't carry them all. How far was Rivead? Could they even run there in time?

The entire earth shook as the Dragon of the West landed upon the mountain peak behind them. Loose rock rained down the mountainside, and the wyvern split open the sky with a thunderous roar. The rest of the brood poured in from above, filling the valley with a hundred wings and snapping jaws.

They were cut off now, nowhere to hide and too slow to run. Nobody dared to stop, though.

The massive wyvern leapt from its perch and dove down the mountainside. It passed overhead, massive, sinewy wings sending a dust of wind that brought them all down to their knees. Linara caught her footing and kept on, barely affording a glance around to see if the others followed.

Then the Dragon of the West plummeted from the sky like a meteor, landing in a burst of dirt and moss that sent Linara tumbling head over heels in a blur of darkness.

Her vision flickered black. Enough to tell she was no longer standing. The dragon was gone, flying back into the air, but leaving the crater of its impact behind. Linara searched for her friends. Cirena lay still. Her chest was rising with shallow breaths. Rhoam struggled to his feet, sword held out to support his weight, and he searched the skies.

Lorin cried out from beside her, clutching her ribs as she tried to sit up. Nobody was in shape to fight. Even if they could face a dragon. Linara looked for Ash, and found him limping from the impact, wings muddy and weak. They truly had no way out.

Wyverns surrounded them, black stars on a backdrop of shadowed skies. The beasts waited and watched, making no move to attack. Same with the soldiers, a dozen men surrounding them on the ground, and more still pouring from the tunnels. They kept their distance, though, only there to cut off their escape

The Dragon of the West's wings beat like claps of thunder. It soared overhead, unleashing jets of flames carelessly into the air, lighting the valley in a ghostly red light. The flames dissolved on descent, fizzling to nothing before they even touched the ground. The wyvern could've ended them long ago. It was toying with them. Its final entertainment before annihilation.

One soldier was walking closer now. A man Linara would recognize even in the darkness. A scar cut across his caramel skin. Thatcher. He looked at each of them in turn. To Lorin and her crumpled form, to Rhoam and Cirena, huddled together. Then to Linara, a glimmer of amusement crossing his eyes.

"Linara Farrow," he said simply. "We did not get the chance to meet. I presume it was your doing that set my carts on fire?"

She swallowed weakly. "And if it was?"

Thatcher scratched at his scar. "Then I will admit when I am wrong. You've proved to be a bit more than mice, but equally as annoying."

"We still have a few tricks up our sleeves," Linara said.

"I doubt it," Thatcher said. "I underestimated you all that day. I was arrogant. My mistake cost me everything. But in the end, the money we made in feld fungus was just a drop in the sea of the gold Herald Rendei is paying us. Collis is feeding us well this night. So thank you for burning down my carriages, for now I'm ordering around a cardinal dragon, hungry for violence."

"Is that all that matters to you? Gold?"

"Of course."

"And for what? Just to kill us here?"

"No, not just to kill you." Thatcher smiled wide, unresistant to a show of performance. He really was a trouper at heart. "We're here to start a war. It's all just an elaborate performance, old uniforms and all. You weren't always at the center of all this, but when you forced yourself into the light, it all just made sense to shift directions. Now I must ask you to come with me. Herald Rendei would prefer you alive."

"That's not an option," Rhoam said. Cirena still lay unmoving behind him.

Thatcher shrugged and gestured to the great dragon still flying behind him. "I can perform my task just as well with a charred corpse."

"Do your worst," Linara said, spitting upon the moss. Her words of obstinance were empty. She certainly didn't feel it.

"So be it." Thatcher stepped away, waving to the dragon above. Linara clenched her teeth and stood her ground. She did what she thought Lorin would do, or Rhoam. Better to be dead than used for their own devices.

Linara stumbled forward, toward the Dragon of the West hovering before them. It studied them each under massive yellow eyes, sending bursts of wind upon the plains with every flap of its wings. A low rumble from its chest greeted her at her approach, almost like a deep, mocking laugh.

She glanced behind her, at Lorin, on a knee, defiant. At Raast, emotionless and stoic. And then at Rhoam, who held the unconscious Cirena gingerly in his arms, helpless. She failed them once, but not again. If the dragon didn't destroy them, who else then would it go for? Avorren? If she could stop it now, she would.

The dragon straightened and opened its jaws for a final roar, the glow of hot fire joining the primal rage. A glowing mass of liquid fire, inescapable and unstoppable. Linara planted her feet before it. It would have to kill them with claw or teeth, for flames would not work upon her. Linara stepped forward and thrust her hands into the wall of fire. It split at her command, swirling around them in a dome, hot as hell itself.

A yell escaped her lips, of both pain and defiance. Dragon fire burned hotter than anything she'd ever felt before. Hotter than she could absorb so quickly. But facing the end, she would not let go. She wanted to drop the focus, to yell and flee, but it took all of herself to stand her ground. What would she do with it?

Like a phantom from her mind, words echoed. Only a dragon's own fire can melt their scales. She couldn't form a flame that hot on her own, but she *could* shape what was already there.

Her heart of the flame, the flickering candle of focus, wavered. There were too many counting on her. Cirena and Rhoam. Raast and Lorin. If all of them could fight this far, she could, too. She snapped her mind back into focus, digging deeper through the pain into the flames themselves.

Dragon fire was different from other sources of heat. Candle flames were a simple thing, but this was something solid, a thick fire that writhed like oil. So deep and so dense that Linara could shape it at a thought.

She mustered the strength and stepped forward against the weight of the world, flinging the fire out from her, out from her friends.

The flames curled out into the purple dusk sky, arcing into a lance of pure, molten fire. The Dragon of the West hadn't moved since his attack, a fatal, arrogant mistake. It tried to flee, wings thrashing in panic and terror, but Linara released the flames with the speed and force of a thunderbolt. The pillar of fire slammed into scales and flesh, piercing hide like a lance, burning the wound it left behind.

The dragon uttered no cry of pain as it fell from the sky. It slammed into the ground, throwing Linara off her feet. She had no strength to resist, no strength to return to her feet. Her fingers thrummed with pain, but Linara held back tears. Her eyes fell upon the corpse of the cardinal dragon, burning like a beacon.

She collapsed and fell back into the moss. Wyverns cried overhead, angered and mourning. They dove at once, like tiny black raindrops on a sky of gray. Linara's actions would not go unpunished. *Now* they would die, but at least Linara did *something*. The Dragon of the West was dead. That was enough. Now it was time to rest. Yes. Rest now.

Rhoam Litighast, Knight Protectorate for Princess Cirena Dorine Lavindus Romaana III, cradled her highness in his arms, eyes nearly blinded. That flash of light, the sunlight of Linara's power, burning endlessly upon the charred and withered corpse of the great dragon. If such power truly existed in the form of men, Rhoam would never be able to truly protect Cirena. He was a man among dragons and gods.

At least he could form some comfort knowing Linara did his task for him.

Now, the wyverns that circled them like vultures would soon descend, a last revenge for the fallen. The final failure of Rhoam Litighast. What could a sword truly do against the battle from the heavens?

The first dragon dove, and he closed his eyes, bathed in that reality, waiting for death to come. Screams rang out among the roar of dragons and steel, but no death greeted him. Only the lancing fire in his leg let him know he was still very alive.

Rhoam opened his eyes, watching the dragons tear apart the enemy soldiers around them. Men ran, griffins fled. But all were hunted like rabbits. He swung his eyes back to Linara's crumpled form, untouched and still alive. One man ran toward her now. Thatcher, the bastard leader, unphased by the madness around him. Someone had to save Linara. Would he leave that to the dragons?

Rhoam looked down at Cirena, still unconscious from the fall, but breathing steadily. To leave her side, even for a moment, meant death for him. His heart ached, but Rhoam Litighast, Knight Protectorate for her highness the princess, rose from his place and stepped away from his duty for the first time in his life.

He met Thatcher with the strength of a lion. His sword rang as it clashed against steel, and sang as it bit into flesh.

Chapter Twenty-Nine

Linara dreamed of wind and of flying. She soared high over Irea, above the clouds, above the heavens. She touched the stars with wings of feathers, with no reason to land ever again. She dreamed she could fly forever, to chase the sun wherever it truly lay.

She dreamed for so long, the only sign that she awoke was the pain.

Tufts of feathers and the passing ground rushed by like fleeting smoke. The wind in her ears nearly deafened the sound of the griffin's wings, but the color was familiar. Ash was carrying her somewhere, and fast, and by the pressure on her back, somebody was guiding him. She pushed up on Ash's neck, but pain erupted from her palms, and she cried out, dropping back into his neck.

A hand wrapped around her shoulder and gently pulled her up. She turned slightly to see Rhoam in the saddle, balancing between guiding Ash and holding her in place. Her hands pulsed with the burning pain, shooting through her fingers and up her arm. An unfamiliar pain, one that she didn't think she'd ever have to face. She lifted her palms to reveal oozing and bubbling skin pressing out of the thin cloth hastily tied around her hands. Her vision was hazy, unfocused, and the sight just made the spinning worse.

"We didn't have a chance to treat it. Raast knows burns, but we had nothing to truly help," Rhoam yelled over the roar of wind.

Linara hazily remembered the pain of the dragon fire, too hot to fully absorb before it burned her skin. A flame so hot that Linara could *feel* it. Anybody else wouldn't have hands left at all. Her mind was swimming, trying to grasp at memories as they rushed by. She had enough strength, though, to lean forward and vomit off the side of Ash.

"What happened?" she asked, wiping the bile from her chin with the back of her sleeve.

Rhoam was silent, considering how to answer, as he usually did. "You killed the Dragon of the West," he said simply.

"That I remember," Linara mumbled. "I thought we were dead."

Rhoam took a moment to gather his thoughts. "The dragons turned on their allies. Thatcher is dead."

"What about Cirena?" she asked, assuming the worst.

Rhoam didn't answer at first, and that only made it worse. "My vows were in conflict, between never leaving the princess's side, and protecting what is best for the kingdom. She is safe, as well as the others. They are following close behind. Reinforcements came from the city, but for the first time in my life, I have abandoned my direct duty for something I deemed far more important."

"Where are the dragons now?" Linara asked weakly, feeling her strength wane.

"You should rest. We're safe now."

That was good. Everyone was fine. The edges of her vision darkened again, and her eyes fluttered closed. "I appreciate . . . you . . . Rhoam." She felt herself mumbling as she collapsed back into a neck of feathers.

Linara awoke again in a room darker than she was used to. Which was strange, because in Nelbren, the darkness was familiar, and now it was not. She was in her bed, or one equally large and comfortable. Which was also strange, since she remembered when it wasn't comfortable at all. Someone sat with her, a faint, raspy breathing cutting through the silence.

"Are you awake, young one?" Orv said in a faint whisper.

Linara answered weakly, a faint grunt that caught in her throat. She coughed and rubbed her eyes. "It's dark."

"I thought it would be comfortable. Shall I open the curtains?"

Orv was at the window before she could answer, bathing the room in soft sunlight. He watched outside the window for a few moments before returning to the chair beside her bed. He looked uninjured, for the most part, which was good. Linara tried to lift her hands but found them wrapped thickly in cloth.

"How long was I asleep?" she asked weakly.

"Through the night and half the day," Orv said. "To be expected for how much of your source you used."

She reached inside, toward the flame in her mark, but found nothing at all. She gasped and felt the skin where the mark had lain. "It's gone."

"Well, not *gone*, gone," Orv said. "I suspect you used most of it during that final confrontation."

"It didn't feel like I did," she whispered.

"I'm sure you felt much stronger sensations. Quite amazing, though. Dragon fire can melt stone, and yet your hands are only burned on the surface."

Linara lifted her cloth-wrapped hands to study them. So that was what a burn felt like. Ironic, after all this started with Jon's and Fenton's burned and blistered hands. They certainly didn't hurt as much as they did on the griffin, but she was scared to touch them. She wondered how Raast's arm was faring, when the realization hit quite suddenly. "The others—" she tried to say, nearly leaping out of bed.

Orv gently pushed her back down. "Are safe. They arrived only a few hours after you did. Their injuries are no worse than yours, and I think it would be best if they shared their travels with you directly. Have patience."

Linara forced herself to sit back and relax her thoughts. The last few days had been a constant sprint, and her mind still raced through the memories. How much of it was real, and how much was a dream? It all felt like a blur, an unreal story with no pause for rest until now. "That dragon. It was the Dragon of the West," Linara said, slowly. "It's been missing, and I killed it."

"Yes, you did," Orv said. "That's something I meant to wait to address, but I think it's good that you know. Dragon Law is scarcely known, but there are some pieces we know of. Whoever defeats and kills one of the cardinal dragons takes their title and position. Which I believe makes you, Linara Farrow, the new Dragon of the West."

Linara laughed. "But I'm not a dragon."

"According to the brood of wyverns at our doorstep, they don't care."

Linara had no words to answer. Was he joking?

"Once you returned from the mines, the brood of wyverns came after you, setting up outside the south gate to wait for you to recover. They won't respond to any orders, except from their leader. Who, by their own customs, is you."

"What?" Linara asked firmly.

"You're now the brood leader of a hundred wyverns."

"This can't be happening," Linara said, pressing her thickly wound hands into her face to mild discomfort.

"Unfortunately, there is no way to cede your power unless you desire to be eaten by one of your dragons. I've already asked on your behalf."

"Well, what do I have to do?" Linara asked.

Orv grimaced and shrugged. "Nobody rightly knows, and I think it's important to find out. It might be a wise idea to speak with them before the day is out."

"Speak to them?" she asked. "They were trying to kill me a few hours ago!"

"Cindavar has the same sentiments about sending you out there, but I believe it will be safe. I have learned much from talking with them, and they seem to be creatures of great resolve and honor. I trust what they say, and I believe in their company you are the safest you will ever be."

The cascading avalanche of thoughts sent her head spinning. There was just too much to process. Too many implications. Her life was upended again. She needed something else to think about.

"What happened here? During the attack?" Linara asked weakly.

"Ahh, *that* I'll have to explain at a later date," he said, reserved. "You need more rest."

"I've rested enough, and I need a distraction."

"Alright, fine," he said, growing excited as he stepped over and helped her up. He certainly wasn't making a great fuss over it. "It will be easier to show you before I begin to explain." Her feet were shakier than she expected, and now even Orv was trying to move faster than her. Eventually, they made it to the door, and he paused, turning around with a slight grimace.

"I will apologize in advance about the state of your rooms." He swung open the curtain, revealing walls broken apart by tree roots thick as wagons, twisting and flowing through the ceiling and the floor. Small trunks and branches spread from the wood, growing thick with leaves.

Linara stood slack-jawed, taking only tiny steps toward the table, the bath, the massive window shattered by wood and rock, before settling back and taking it all in from a healthy distance.

Orv laughed, a deep and childlike laugh that permeated the room. "Like I said, I *can* be of great use in a battle."

Birds fluttered among the branches, gathering fallen twigs, cloth, and other debris along her floor, flying through the open window. Was this the product of an attack from Orv, or just his way of holding the building together after the bombs ripped it apart? She could see scorch marks and ash, and the walls seemed to be in worse shape than before, but Orv was already leading the way out of the room before she could ask.

A few bricks and other larger pieces of rubble lay scattered along the path of the hallway outside, smaller branches and trunks weaving through the stone. Other than that, everything seemed alright. The attacking force may have damaged the outside, but there was little sign of battle within the halls.

"Linara!" Cirena's voice called out from behind them.

Linara turned and nearly tumbled over as Cirena collided into her with a tight embrace. She pulled back and gasped, gingerly lifting her thickly padded arms.

"Your hands!"

"They'll be fine," Orv interjected, carefully removing Cirena's grip from the bandages. "Scarred, maybe, but the physicians say they'll be fine in a few weeks."

"Oh, thank the heavens," Cirena said, forcing a smile. Her face still hung low, dragged down by the deep sorrow Linara saw in the mines. They were all safe, but that wouldn't leave so easily. Perhaps it wouldn't for all of them.

Rhoam stepped up from around the corner, walking with a small limp, his leg bandaged, but otherwise fine. Linara wasn't certain any wound would keep him from Cirena's side. He bowed in respect, hands clasped before him. "Dragon Slayer."

Linara paled. "Are people calling me that?"

"Not really," Cirena said, laughing. "Nobody has enough courage with those wyverns outside our gates."

Linara grimaced. "You heard about that?"

"It's all anybody can talk about," Cirena said. "Unnerving, really. They were terrorizing the city just a day ago, and now they're loyal to us just because you live here. You haven't been out for long, but a lot has happened."

"We'll see it for ourselves once we're outside," Orv said, waving them along.

"How are the others?" Linara asked, falling in beside Cirena.

"We're all fine. Raast is in the kitchens again," Cirena said, rolling her eyes. "He's trying to do what he can with his arm, staying in Avorren for the time being to cook for the displaced families in the city. I don't blame him, really. I think he's trying to forget what happened in the tunnels. Lorin says he saved you both."

Linara nodded at that, remembering his display with the knife. The precision of his movements, and the gurgling blood. With how distressed he was with just disarming Rhoam in the sparring hall, that memory must be imprinted deeply upon his mind. More questions were added to the pile, but Linara couldn't tackle them all.

"Lorin's still on bed rest," Cirena continued, "She broke a few ribs at some point. I'm the only one who came out relatively unscathed."

"As it should be," Rhoam added.

"And you?" Cirena asked.

"I've been better," Linara said, shrugging. "But I've also been worse."

"Yeah, there's a lot of that going around," Cirena said, and she sighed deeply. A long silence spread between them. "Oh," the princess said, forcing another smile. "Lorin got a promotion. Her helmet is silver now."

"How much does that change?"

"It brings a certain amount of respect, that's for sure. She was the youngest knight, *and* now she's the youngest to hold a silver helmet."

"I suppose that's exactly what she wanted," Linara said. "Once she actually put effort into it."

"Have you seen the rest of the city yet?" Cirena asked.

But Linara didn't have a chance to answer. They passed into the great hall, roots curving in and around the open space like a spiderweb of wood. A few statues were toppled and broken, but most were unscathed by the intruding branches.

Then they passed through the spire gates. It took a moment for her eyes to adjust, but once Linara could see, her breath caught.

"What did you *do*?" she breathed, stepping outside. The tree branches inside were all part of a larger source, the limbs of a gigantic tree enveloping the Spire itself. Massive roots, reaching to the second floor, and wider than a dozen horses, snaked from out the gate through the path ahead of them and up the walls of the Spire. A hundred limbs jutted into the sky, forming a canopy of deep-green leaves that stretched a mile in every direction, bathing the city in a deep, earthy shadow.

"I spent a lot of my youth at the World Tree," Orv said. "Turns out, I had enough power to make another!"

Linara gaped. "So we're both . . ."

"Completely spent of power, yes."

"The Spire is covered in a tree," Linara said, still not taking in the sight.

"The entire city, actually," Orv said, grimacing. "The king was in danger. Soldiers were crawling through the halls, so I helped in the only way I knew how. I saved the king's life, but tore apart most of the city to do it. Few people are thrilled about it, but my friend is alive. Not to mention I trapped a few soldiers to interrogate."

"Thatcher and the troupers were behind the attack," Linara said. "He said Rendei hired him."

Rhoam nodded. "The wyverns confirmed the report we brought back."

"The Herald of Collis," Orv said grimly. "To think we've been betrayed by our own countrymen . . ."

"We may have stopped a war with Reginaan, but now there's one brewing in our own borders," Rhoam said.

After everything, Linara ended up planted in the center of a war she could not escape. And now there were dragons involved. She remembered Rendei from the Herald Summit. He'd walked in alone, with no servants, and no weakness.

"Shadows loom overhead, just as always," Orv said, stepping toward the staircase that climbed the Spire garden wall. "Best to focus on what's in front."

The view even from so high couldn't put the damage in full perspective. Starting from the Spire, roots dug their way through the city itself, burying buildings, streets and city walls. She could see crews forming paths through and around the rubble and debris, but the city had stopped for once, brought to a standstill by nature itself.

Out the south gate, Linara could see a patch of brown and gray, shifting and moving in the glinting sunlight. Dragons. More than she could count from so far. Even the skies were flooded with griffins and guards, twice as many as she was used to. Everyone was on high alert, prepared for an attack that might not even come.

"Did I make the right decision?" Linara asked after a few long moments. She wondered which decision she meant. The last few days were filled with them, and each one Linara second-guessed.

"It sounded like there really wasn't much of a choice," Orv said. "Kill the dragon, save thousands. None of our actions are so black and white. We're remarkably gray creatures, young one, we try to do good and destroy a home. We protect someone we love and hurt perfect strangers. It's all a matter of which side of the glass you're standing on. You've made your choice. Now it's time to stand by it with confidence."

"Do you think *you* did good?" Linara asked.

"Good? Hah, what is good? What I know is that I sure like nature, and this tree is pretty cool." Orv stepped around the rubble to climb a gnarled root beside him, laughing like a joyous child.

Linara smiled weakly and stared off toward the brood again. Her brood? A shadow caught her eye from above, and she noticed a dark shape descending toward them. As it grew closer, Linara realized it was no griffin or patrolling guard, but a gray-scaled wyvern.

She backed up until she was up against the stone edge of the wall. Orv and Cirena, though, were rather unaffected by it, though they seemed visibly tense.

"Ahh, he's noticed you've awoken," Orv said, squinting up at the wyvern. "Don't be afraid, he's rather friendly from the brief words we've exchanged."

Questions flooded her mind, but the wyvern landed before she could ask them. Her heart thudded in her chest as Cirena and Rhoam walked farther down along the wall. Only Orv stayed by her side, and that was her only comfort. The wyvern stood a full length taller than Linara, and twice as wide, pressed almost flat, supported by the bony edges of its sinewy wings. The wyvern moved awkwardly, the wall barely able to fit his girth.

His head bobbed back and forth, studying her with each of his dark, yellow eyes. There was an age behind them, a history that flowed deep. The scales upon his head were smooth, like leather. No horns adorned his head, and he did not bare teeth. Instead, the wyvern bowed low, touching snout to the stone.

"Hraandieve," the wyvern said, a deep grumbling voice that shook her chest. The word was foreign to her and sounded like rocks scraping against the ground. "We live to serve."

Linara shifted her weight uncomfortably. A few hours ago, these wyverns were trying to kill her. The dragon lifted its head and stared at Orv, who still hung around a few paces back. "We must speak alone, Nuutruul," it said.

"Ahh," Orv said, bowing low. "Of course."

Orv began to leave, and Linara struggled to form the words that would get him to stay. But she could think of nothing and instead stuffed her fears in a box. When Orv was appropriately out of earshot, the wyvern turned back to her, Linara feeling quite small.

"What is your name?" she asked, hoping the shakiness didn't show in her voice.

He studied her. "I am called Ulruus. I speak for the brood."

Linara let the name sit on her tongue, processing the strange syllables that came from the dragon's throat. She resisted the urge to reach out her hand. "I am Linara Farrow."

The wyvern grumbled in disapproval. "You are Hraandieve."

"Oh," Linara said, unwilling to question him on that. "What does it mean?"

"Hraandieve," Ulruus said, moving his jaw back and forth in consideration. "It means in your tongue, One Who Burns Hotter Than Fire."

"Uh-huh . . ." Linara said, hoping the title didn't catch on. "Then I'm your leader now?"

Ulruus dipped his head in respect. "I have come to offer our oaths from the brood. Most gave the fire pledge, but some did not and were destroyed. We all live to serve."

"And if I do not accept them?" Linara asked.

Ulruus looked up, his eyes searching her own, confused. "None have done so. But the law is sacred. You would need to be destroyed. We do not wish to."

"Why not?" Linara asked.

"You are our liberator. You have burned to ash our strongest. You are strong, and we follow. It is our law, and our law is sacred. Those who do not obey are cut off from the law and are destroyed."

Linara's chest sunk deeply. If they followed her because she could kill a dragon, she was terrified of what they would do if they found her power to be nearly gone. She'd have to refill her source, and quickly.

"And you are okay with this?" she asked.

"It does not matter. The law is clear," Ulruus said. "But yes, I approve. Kraktaal was brutal and cruel. Many contested his ways, but none could stand against him. All who grew strong enough to try, he destroyed. Loyalty meant nothing, only strength."

That was good, at least. If some followed her simply because she was less than a tyrant, that might help. "Is that why you served Thatcher?"

The wyvern made a deep grumbling sound in his throat. "The barbarian served the mountain humans. Our oaths were made as part of a blood oath, given to the leader of men."

"Are you not bound by this oath still?" Linara asked.

"The cursed vow made by Kraktaal was broken by fire when you burned his body."

"I see," Linara said, not knowing what else to add. Their customs were surely quite strange. "What do I do now? I'm not sure what you want from me."

"You must lead us," he said. "Take us to fresh skies, where the wind blows clean. Clean winds are where our kin multiply."

"I don't think I can leave," Linara said, staring out over the city. If war was coming, the king would not let her stray far.

"Then we shall stay. The winds blow here. Not clean, but not foul, either. The humans cause tension among us, but we shall stay where Hraandieve stays. Always."

Linara nodded and allowed a stretch of silence to pass between them. The wyvern shifted and straightened its posture, staring into her eyes. "Are you ready to accept our oaths, Hraandieve?"

What other choice did she have? The alternative was death, after all. "I am."

"Then please climb upon my spine."

Linara stepped back. "Your . . . back?"

"We must join the brood."

"Can't I take a griffin?" Linara asked.

"I do not offer this lightly, Hraandieve."

Linara glanced back at Orv, trying to find another excuse.

"Is it the wind that you fear?" Ulruus asked, bringing its head back up to look at her.

"No," Linara said, forcing herself to look into his eye. "It is you I fear."

"It is good for a human to fear a dragon," Ulruus rumbled. "But *you* are a dragon now."

Linara cleared her throat. If they could read her fear, how quickly would they turn against her? "Fine, let's go."

Ulruus lowered himself again, folding one wing to the bricks. She scanned the scaly surface, trying to find handholds that did not seem to exist. She stepped up on the edge of his wing, and the wyvern grunted softly. Eventually, even with hands wrapped in cloth, she heaved herself over and nestled between two of his long spines.

Ulruus shifted his weight, clearly uncomfortable, but he did not object. With all the strength of a dozen griffins, he leapt up over the edge and caught the wind with an enormous flap of his wings. Such strength, to fly from a standing position.

Linara wrapped her arms around the rigid spine, eyes clamped shut. This type of flight was not entirely enjoyable, each scale shifting and tightening with each flap of wings, pinching skin and fabric alike. Nerissa, though, would be delighted to hear of it.

Ulruus approached the brood, and Linara forced herself upright. She could show no fear. If respect kept her alive, then she would need to show strength. Linara took a deep breath and opened her eyes.

And saw the dragons. Rows and rows of wyverns, sleeping, feasting, watching. One by one, every scaled head turned to the sky to watch Hraandieve descend. Her heart thundered in her chest, louder than even the wind, but she watched them back, not letting the fear reach her eyes.

Ulruus reared up and landed with a thump, sending a plume of dust and dirt piling up around them. He lowered one wing, and Linara quickly scrambled off the back, still entirely unsure where to place her feet. A hundred dragons watched her fumble her way to the ground. If she fell, would they eat her? Linara wasn't entirely convinced they weren't about to, regardless.

The air smelled of ash and sulfur, but if it was warm, Linara could not feel it. Stacks of raw carcasses were piled around, of cattle, heffen, and sheep. The grass was unsinged by fire. A curious thing, as the burnt patch of field on the north side of the city would've made better resting grounds. It seemed they preferred healthy land.

Linara finally summoned the courage to turn and face the brood, still watching, still waiting. Every eye was trained on her. Deep, dark, bottomless eyes. Their scales were varied, colored from browns to grays, to even dark greens. Their horns were sharp, curved and patterned at random. They reminded her of a herd of griffins, multicolored and beautiful, except now she felt only dread.

Humans had been able to fight back for centuries, but only rarely, and with every tool they could muster. Linara, though, stood among them, entirely defenseless. None of them came to the height of the old Dragon of the West, but any of them could tower over any mounted knight in Avorren without even trying. How had she *killed* one of them? The *greatest* of them?

Ulruus spoke to the brood in the language of dragons. A deep and powerful thing, full of rumblings that sent vibrations into Linara's bones. "Hraandieve, Hraaktine!" Ulruus shouted, and the brood echoed. The voices carried far, then fell into silence. "The West has been reformed. Let it not be torn asunder!"

Ulruus was the first to bow, tucking his head and touching it to the flat of the ground. The others followed in waves, dropping to the grass row by row. Linara didn't know what to do, what to say. She stared across the bowed heads of a hundred dragons. *Her* dragons.

How did she get here? A week ago, she'd barely stopped the entire field from burning to the ground. But now a war was coming. What was her part to play? How would these dragons turn the tide? A thousand questions burrowed in Linara's mind, all fighting for her attention.

Only one stuck. It tugged at her mind like a thorn upon a creeping vine.

At once, the dragons rose, their roars erupted from every jaw, ripping open the sky above. The ground itself shook beneath her feet, her chest thundering. They came here for *her*. Linara Farrow, luma farmer from Nelbren. Now she was the Dragon of the West, and she had no idea what to do.

ACKNOWLEDGEMENTS

Writing a novel is a journey that stretches beyond the solitary act of putting words to paper. It is—no matter how much we'd like it to be otherwise—a collaborative effort. The support, encouragement, and inspiration of the people and works around us make up the foundation in which our creative energy can stand.

This project alone has taken me several long years to produce, and I can't rightfully say that the journey did not begin long before the idea for the story was conceived. Behind many novels are a graveyard of failed pieces, and Roar of the West is no different.

So first and foremost, I would like to thank the individuals who spurred me ever onward. Mainly, my wife, whose constant encouragement and infectious determination was a currency that never ran dry. And to the rest of my family, who have waited with bated breath for the release of a novel of mine, ever since I announced my plans in high-school.

To my many beta readers, your feedback has been crucial to shaping the narrative and characters into what they are today. Especially so for that particular pair of you, whose late-night debate about the realism of blunt force trauma by a milk laden bucket, caused the biggest change in structure to a piece of my work to date.

I would also like to thank you, dear reader, for taking the time to read my work. Your presence is the final brushstroke that completes this canvas. Your curiosity and engagement for new worlds is a contagious entity, constantly driving the motivation of authors everywhere to create.

But above all, I thank the Lord of the Heavens and the Earth for his perfect love and mercy upon me. Every word upon these pages is His work in me, for I am nothing without Him.

This novel is a testament of perseverance, that even the slowest of writers can finish something if they work at it long enough. I hope you enjoy reading this novel as much as I enjoyed working on it. Now, to delve into the sequel, in hopes that it can be released in a fraction of the time.

With heartfelt thanks and maranatha,

Robert H. Lange

ABOUT THE AUTHOR

Robert H. Lange is the author of Roar of the West. He's been writing since high school, after one creative writing project set him on the path to engage in his love of magic, adventure, and dragons. Currently, he lives in Ohio with his wife—a fellow author—and when he isn't writing, he's procrastinating.

TikTok: @robertlange_author
Facebook: @AuthorRobertLange
Instagram: @robertlange_author

9 798985 765687